THE FAE CHRONICLES

Taunting Destiny

AMELIA HUTCHINS

Taunting Destiny. Copyright © 2013 by Amelia Hutchins

ISBN-13: 978-0991190959
ISBN-10: 0991190955

Amelia Hutchins

P.O. Box 11212

Spokane Valley, WA 99211

Amelia-Hutchins.com

Ordering Information: https:www.createspace.com

Quantity sales. Special discounts are available on quantity purchases by corporations, associations, and others. For details, contact the publisher at the address above.

Orders by U.S. trade bookstores and wholesalers. Please contact Amelia utchins ameliahutchins@ amelia-hutchins.com

Printed in the United States of America.

Dedication

To my family for understanding mommy was
busy writing.

~~*~*~*

To my fans, without you there would be no
Chronicles.

~~*~*~*

To Gina, and all the countless hours of helping me.

I can never tell you how much you mean to me!

And to the boys, who helped so much with the
fighting scenes.

~~*~*~*

Dina and Genevieve for the hours of editing and
help, thanks!

~~*~*~*

The Beta groups, and once again the fans for
waiting countless hours while I got this right.

Thank you so much! Hope it is worth the wait.

Books also by Amelia Hutchins

Fighting Destiny Book *1*

www.amazon.com/dp/B00D5M4PTM/

Book 3

Escaping Destiny

Out now

Book 4

Seducing Destiny

Fall 2014

WARNING

This book contains sexually explicit scenes and adult language, and may be considered offensive to some readers. It is intended for sale to adults ONLY, as defined by the laws of the country in which you made your purchase. Please store your files wisely, where they cannot be accessed by under-aged readers.

This book is not intended for anyone under the age of 18, or anyone who doesn't like lip biting, throw your ass on the bed, tear your clothes off and leave you panting dominant alpha male characters. It's dark, dangerous, intense, gritty and raw book. Scenes are dark, disturbing and scorching HOT. This read is soul crushing, tear jerking, leave you hanging on the edge of your seat, fast paced read.   Side Effects may include, but are not limited to: Drooling, lip biting, wet panties, crying and screaming at the author. If any of these things happen, do not seek medical attention— get the next book in the series and enjoy the ride!

The
Fae
Chronicles

Chapter ONE

I turned away from the window and ran like my life depended upon it. Because, right then, I thought it did. Instinctively, I knew I wasn't supposed to see what I had. Ryder had been torturing Guild Warlocks along with some other men that I thought were Fae. I wasn't sure what they were—they could just as easily have been human. I knew better than to try and be some kind of army of one just so I could figure it out. I sped up, narrowly avoiding the manicured shrubbery on his extensive lawn, dodging trees as I refused to look back. I wasn't dumb enough to turn around and peek over my shoulder. I was the type who yelled at the girls in scary movies who did so.

I didn't stop running. Not even when I heard the hounds let loose a series of horrible sounding howls. They were far enough away that if I made it to the highway, I might be able to live long enough to get away from them. As far as I could tell, none of the Fae inside the house had sifted out, and I was still unable to sift myself.

A horn blared as I hit the pavement, and I barely avoided becoming a pancake. I jumped backwards to avoid an eighteen wheeler loaded down with logs. The old green Buick behind it screeched on its brakes and came to a stop about a quarter mile up the road.

I exhaled a deep, shaky breath and looked down the highway. No cars were around, besides the one that had stopped. I looked back up as reverse lights came on and the car started backing up. I turned and looked back at the mansion. I could just make out its lights in the distance.

I caught a glimpse of a pair of green, glowing eyes from the bushes that were surrounding the protective fence that encompassed the property. A sharp snuffling noise was all the additional incentive I needed to book it toward the car that was still backing up. When I reached the pale green Buick, I slowed again. The older female driver reached across and rolled down the window. She had graying hair and a pair of thick glasses perched on her nose. Her misting, gray eyes were sharp though.

"Are you crazy?" she shouted as she bobbed her head to get a better look at me.

I was dressed in jeans, wearing flip-flops, and hanging on to my purse for dear life. I tried to speak, but my words were jumbled up in my head after what I'd seen.

"You look half-scared to death. Get in. What are you doing out here?" she asked as I quickly opened the car door and took my seat beside her.

"I need to go to the Spokane Guild. I need to get there as fast as this old car can go, lady," I said, already grabbing the seatbelt and clicking it.

"Are you one of those Fae?" she queried, eyeing me carefully.

"No. I'm an Enforcer for the Guild, and this is an emergency!" I shouted and felt bad for all of one second. I had slightly lied. I wasn't technically an Enforcer, anymore and I hadn't fully Transitioned to Fae yet—see, only a little white lie, really. She hit the gas, and the car's ass-end fishtailed back onto the highway.

"Well, why didn't you say so?" she raised her voice to be heard over the old engine.

We pulled up to the Guild about twenty minutes later. I thanked her for the ride and ran up the steps. I was met and surrounded by the Guild's guards. Ten built Enforcers stood around me, forming a circle to keep me contained. I was getting dirty looks, and most of these guards had been in my class. "Micah, this is serious!" I said to the squad leader. Micah smiled coldly, his hazel eyes showing excitement that made a chill sweep down my spine. "Either tell Alden to get down here, or let me go up!" I shouted, not caring that they had weapons trained on me. I was not the enemy, and I was a hell of a lot faster than they were. I tapped my foot and glared at them.

"*Your* kind is not welcome here, Synthia," he smiled coldly.

"*My kind!?* You mean the kind that saved your stupid ass on countless trial assignments? My kind that saved you from being kicked out? That kind, Micah?" I seethed. *My kind* my ass!

"You're not even one of us! The only reason no one has placed a fucking mark on your pretty little head, is because your 'uncle' is refusing to issue—"

"Enough! Micah, go inside. Now," Alden said coming down the concrete stairs swiftly. His eyes scanned me briefly, before he nodded to Tate who gave me an apologetic look before patting me down.

"She's clean," he said after stepping back.

"I'd like to speak to you alone, Alden," I growled narrowing my eyes.

"That won't happen ever again, Synthia. The Guild does not associate with the Fae. Not unless you have a job that you need us to take."

Does not associate with the Fae?

"You might change your mind when you hear what I tell you," I snapped.

"Go home," Alden replied.

"No! I won't go home. You need to hear what I have to say. I just—"

"I said go *home*," Alden snarled and glared at me.

The Enforcers behind him snickered and laughed at me. I fought the urge to give them a solid jolt of my magic, but, with my luck, I'd end up in chains for it. That is, if I could still tap into it. I hadn't been able to tap my magic since Larissa had died. "Alden," I replied coldly. "I need to talk to you."

"Go home, Synthia, I'll call you later."

Something in his eyes made me hesitate; something was off here. I could feel the hostility from the Enforcers, but I could also feel the urgency in Alden's voice, and something else I couldn't place yet. "Fine, but you need to hear what I have to tell you."

"The Guild is no longer helping the Fae. If it pertains to that, you can forget it. You are no longer welcome here Synthia, nor is Adam. You have been warned," Alden said as something passed in his eyes.

He turned and left me standing there gawking at his retreating back.

I turned the other way and started down the stairs as the Enforcers closed in and escorted me from the building. I'd come here to report to Alden that people were being hurt—Guild members were being hurt! What the hell had happened in the week that I'd taken off to mourn my best friend? Had the entire world gone crazy?

I had expected to get the cold shoulder from the Guild, but not from Alden. Something was up, and it seemed like he just wanted me away from the Guild. Mix that with what had been going down with Ryder and his men, and you had a shit soup being stirred. It wouldn't be served cold, either.

I'd walked home, oblivious to anything around me. I was so lost in thought that I almost missed my house. I shook off the dark images of what I'd witnessed at Ryder's hands, and walked up the sidewalk that made a path over the dead grass in my yard.

I'd gotten my key into the lock and was pushing the door open when I felt his presence. That tingly electrical feeling like there was a downed power line nearby. I pushed the door all the way open and stepped over the threshold, hoping the wards would prevent him from entering. "Ryder," I whispered as the memory of him worshiping my body flashed through my mind.

"You ran from me again, Pet," he growled as he stepped out from behind a large rose bush. He was still wearing his cloak. His eyes flashed golden fire as they raked down the length of my body.

"Yeah, I saw what you were doing and wasn't sure if I'd be next. The Guild gets a bit upset when their own are abused, so, unless you want to tell me why you were torturing a room full of Guild Warlocks and those other guys, go away." Sometimes I really needed a filter for my mouth.

"What I was doing inside my property isn't any of your concern. You've been through enough lately."

"Give me one good reason why I shouldn't call the Guild and report this, hmm?" I bluffed, crossing my arms and meeting him head-on without showing a lick of fear.

He strode forward and stopped inches from the door frame. I backed up, far enough that I was pretty sure he couldn't touch me or force me from the house. I smiled and cocked my head at him.

"I could make you come outside," he grinned, and tilted his head to mimic mine, which caused his inky black hair to fall gently over his face. He was distracting me, and I wanted to know what he'd been doing in his mansion.

"Try," I growled.

"I think you like it when I force your decisions."

"Think again," I snapped and narrowed my eyes on him.

"How does it feel to have my brand on you, Pet?" I was going to get whiplash one day from his topic changes. His smile was cold, but somehow still managed to be beautiful. He gave me a smug little look as he folded his arms in front of his chest and leaned his shoulder against the door frame. "I know that's why you came to the mansion. I could feel it as it was etching itself into your beautiful flesh."

"I told you I couldn't be owned. You had no right

to put it on me in the first place," I replied coldly.

"You *are* mine, Syn. Make no mistake of thinking otherwise. I own you until after your Transition." His lips kicked up into a wicked grin and his eyes slid down my body slowly. His voice was soft, tempting, and beguiling.

"I agreed to it, yes, but not a single moment after it."

He snorted, and shook his head. "Who says I want more?"

Ouch. I actually flinched at his words. "Is there an actual reason you're here, Ryder? Or, did you just come to gloat, because you branded your fucking *pet*?"

"I came to tell you that you have two days. I want you close to me when your time comes. I want to be the one that sees you through Transition. You didn't argue it in the contract you signed. I'm holding up my end and taking care of Adam while he Transitions. Yours is coming very soon, Syn. I can smell it on you. Soon, every fucking Fae in Spokane will as well. Hence the reason for the brands. It was designed to show at the first hint of your Transition. I won't share you with them. Two days, Pet, and then I plan to bury my cock inside of you. Repeatedly."

"Contract or no, you have no right to order me around, and I plan on getting this damn thing taken off. Do I need to spell it out for you?" I shouted, retreating as he moved forward.

His lips pulled up in the corners as his eyes flashed with anger. "It can't be removed by anyone but *me*, Pet." His eyes scanned the walls and his smile grew darker. "You can't hide inside this house forever."

I smiled back at him. "What's the matter, Ryder; afraid to get knocked on your ass again?"

He shook his head. "You never learn, do you? There is nowhere in this fucking world where you can hide from me now. Anywhere you go, I'll find you. I'm faster, smarter, and you are *mine*."

"But you can't come inside my house." I smiled in victory. It was childish, but it felt good.

"You think I wouldn't come inside to get you?" he challenged.

I swallowed and shook my head. The wards my parents had placed on the walls inside the house had already taken Ryder down once; it was the only time I'd ever seen anything affect him. "No, actually—" Before I could finish my sentence, I was yanked from the house by invisible hands and pressed against the exterior of the house by Ryder's massive body.

"Like I said, you can't hide from me. Ever." His eyes heated with liquid gold. Heat seared between us, instantly. "If you try to hide from me, Pet, I will tie you to my bed and fuck you until you not only acknowledge my ownership, but *beg* me for it."

I licked my lips to reply to his taunt, but his mouth lowered and claimed mine. His kiss was more than just a kiss though—he was claiming ownership. I brought my hands up against his chest to push him away, but the moment they landed on him, I forgot everything else but Ryder. Once again my mind was his, instantly becoming a tool of my own seduction and caving to his need. It was as if he took control of my mind and my body, with the slightest effort. I moaned against him, feeling his erection press against my stomach as his hands landed against the clapboard siding of the house, trapping me between them.

My body flamed with need. Liquid fire began to race through my veins. He deepened the kiss and groaned as his hands went down to pick me up. I wrapped my legs around his waist as my arms went around his neck. My hands fisted his hair, holding him against my mouth. When he finally managed to pull away from me, I was shaking with need. I hated that I still responded to him, even after seeing what he had done. My body wept for his touch, demanded it, even.

He chuckled, his eyes searching my face as I leaned back against the house. "You're closer than I thought you were." His lips drifted down my neck and stopped on my carotid, his tongue flicking out to taste my heartbeat. "You smell good, Pet, so fucking sweet. You're already wet for me."

"Tell me why you were hurting those Warlocks," I whispered as I ground my body against the erection I could feel through his cloak. Something about Ryder left me helpless to refuse him. It left me confused and upset, which was an unstable combination.

"It's none of your concern, Syn," he growled.

I shook my head with that wake-up call and pushed him away, dropping back to the ground and righting myself on my feet. "Not my concern? I was part of that Guild until last week."

"You're not anymore, remember? Right now, you need to keep out of this, because you won't like what you find." His voice turned hard and intense as he drove the meaning home.

"Go away, Ryder, now."

His lips pulled up into a dangerous smile. It was one I'd seen many times before. I quickly stepped backwards as he stepped towards me. I glared at him.

"Soon; very fucking soon, Syn," he said softly.

"Only for Transition, then we are *done,* Ryder. You're too much—this is all too much. The contract only stated that I was yours until a time of mutual choosing. I'm choosing now; the minute I'm done with Transition, we are done."

Chapter
TWO

It took me at least twenty minutes in the shower to get the feel of Ryder off my skin, and it still wasn't one hundred percent gone. I had managed to once again rub my skin to a bright shade of red over that man. The last thing I needed to do was get any closer to that egocentric tyrant. I wasn't built for hanging around like a good little doggie until he wanted me. His words, *"who says I wanted more,"* flashed through my mind again, like a splinter I couldn't get out. Frustrating Fae, and his stupid secrets. I tried to find a bit of distraction for my running mind by puttering around the kitchen and living room at first. Then I watched a little TV, walked on the treadmill, then gave up, and jogged, which only managed to kill about an hour.

I was so used to having my coven around that without them, I was lost. I missed Larissa, but I was a mess without Adam. I didn't have a chance to ask Ryder what his being my Familiar meant. Ryder had that effect on my brain. I sat staring at the TV for a while, before I broke down and stretched out on the couch. It wasn't long until my cell phone rang. I didn't recognize the number.

"Hello?" I answered cautiously.

"Synthia?" Alden asked back. I relaxed a bit.

"Is it secure?" I asked calmly, wanting to talk to him about what had gone down at Ryder's without an audience.

"It's secure. Is everything okay?" Alden asked carefully.

"Know why Ryder would have Guild members at his mansion? And what the hell was that on the Guild steps?" I asked, listening for his tone to change.

"Syn, stay out of it."

There it was. I groaned. "He will kill them, you know that, right?"

"And for a very good reason. You're smarter than that. I gave him those Warlocks. That's all you need to know for now."

"Seriously, have you been taking lessons from Ryder on how to deflect?" I snapped, completely pissed that I was being kept in the dark about what was going on by both men.

"I have a job for you. If you're interested that is," he countered.

"I'm alone. Adam went into Transition."

"I'm aware. It's not a mark, it's a tactical one, but you'd have a team standing by ready for your call." Mark was what the Guild referred to as marked for death; within sanction law we could kill anyone who had been marked.

"Job? I thought since I was Fae, I was no longer welcome?"

"The Guild will still subcontract out to Otherworld

creatures, if the job requires it. I want you to get over it, Syn; there's more going on here than you know. I need you to take this job, for me. There's a new vampire in town. He's been seen frequenting Vlad's bar. We can't get inside, but you probably can."

"You know that Vlad *is* Dracula right?" I asked carefully.

"Yes, of course I know who he is, Synthia. What is happening takes precedence over who he is, though. We found four bodies drained. One of them was a thirteen year old runaway. Seattle Guild is calling for blood, as this went down in their jurisdiction, and they feel he is targeting those that typically wouldn't be missed. They think this Marcus might be here in Spokane now. I need you to find out if he's here, and tail him."

"I have no magic, Alden," I reminded him.

"Syn, you're good, even without your magic. I trained you myself."

"If he is here, and I find him, what are my instructions?"

"You call in. Don't try to take him down. Call me and I'll call in a strike team. If he leaves before we get there, tail him."

I hung up after getting a description and a rough time of when they thought he would be there. I only had fifteen or so hours to kill. I eyed the wards and then the door. Letting out a huff, I got up and headed for bed. It took a bit of time to clean up the mess from Adam's destruction of my room and bed earlier. When I was finished cleaning, I had most of my bed left, minus the shattered headboard that I hadn't been able to save.

I tossed and turned in my bed. Golden eyes flashed at me every time I closed mine. I must have lain in bed for hours, before I finally succumbed to sleep—where he was waiting for me.

He was there the minute I closed my eyes, waiting for me in my dream. I looked around the room we were in. It was completely white, with the exception of the male standing there. His dark black button up shirt was unbuttoned to mid-chest, and his jeans clung low and seductive against his tapered hips. Sex incarnate was staring at me. He smiled slowly, his eyes consuming me from where he stood. "Can't I get a break? You're even in my fucking dreams!" I growled, thinking how crazy it was that he was here.

He didn't answer. Instead, he moved closer and tilted his head as his hands pulled me to himself, melding our bodies together until I could feel his erection. Oh, what the hell, it was a dream anyway, right?

"Tall, dark, and silent, hmm? I think I like you better in my dreams," I said, looking up at his beautiful face. Sharp angular lines defined every inch of his face. He had a harsh masculine beauty that most men couldn't manage. Ryder, on the other hand, managed it beautifully.

"I'm going to fuck you, Pet."

"Oh, you *do* talk. Damn."

He chuckled and pushed me away from himself gently. "Take your clothes off, or I'll do it for you."

"This is my dream, you take off *your* clothes," I growled low, letting my eyes slide down the hard length of his chiseled body. He was sex personified, and deadly.

"I said take your fucking clothes off, now." He smiled wickedly as the words slid over his tongue like silk.

I smiled, and figured I'd play along. I mean what was the harm in it? I reached up, removing one of the thin straps of the black lace nightgown from one shoulder, and then the other one. I slowly let the nightgown slide to the floor, before stepping out of it. I enjoyed the sharp hiss that forced through his teeth when he feasted his eyes on my naked flesh.

"Any other demands, big boy?" I asked playfully.

"Come here," he answered in a husky tone.

I did and, when I stood directly in front of him, I paused as a shiver of fear and anticipation ran through me. "This is a dream right?"

"You dream about me, Pet? Do you dream of me fucking your tight body until it trembles from my touch?" he asked as heat swirled in his eyes. His fingers came up and pinched my nipples. It felt real, except for the fact that I knew it wasn't. I was asleep, in my bed, safe from him.

"I have to be dreaming of you. I'm asleep in my bed, at my house. You can't get inside." I admitted it out loud, since he'd never remember it from my dream. I felt a tingle and pulse of magic swirling inside the room.

"Lie down on the bed," he growled, nodding towards a wicked looking four poster bed that had silver manacles attached to chains resting on the coverlet. The wood of the headboard and posts were so dark, they were almost black. The posts rose well over seven feet and were shaped like thin spires. Bright crimson silk covered it invitingly.

I snorted. "As if."

"*Do it, now Pet*. I want to taste your pussy." His voice was half growl, half need, and all sexy.

Okay! I smiled, tilted my head and took him in. Dream Ryder looked hungry and hot. I turned and looked at the bed again, carefully. Even in my dreams, the beds associated with Ryder could host several people comfortably and still have room to spare. *Oh, what the hell.* I turned the rest of the way and walked to the bed, slowly. My hand lowered to trace over it. I tested the length of chain in my hand and grinned.

"Are you planning on chaining me up?" I asked quietly. I felt him at my back, even though I hadn't heard him walk across the tiles on the floor.

"Be a good girl, Syn, and get on the bed," he whispered, making the hair on my nape stand up as his hot breath touched along my neck.

I moved the rest of the way onto the bed and crawled high enough on it that I could lay my head on one of the many soft pillows. I met his eyes and held them. "Give me your hand," he said, locking his eyes with mine.

I did what he asked and flinched when I felt the silver cuff click into place around my wrist. I swallowed as he leaned over me. His shirt was soft against my naked skin. He did the same with my feet, locking them into place, before he smiled wickedly. His fingers once again tugged on my nipples. I moaned and shivered at the delicious tremble that erupted over my skin.

His head bent low as his mouth suckled one nipple, and then the other. His hand moved down my body slowly, leisurely, as he explored it. He watched me as his fingers stroked over the sensitive flesh of my slick heat. I growled in response, my hips moving off the bed to follow his hand as he removed it. "You're wet already. Do you miss my cock?"

I whimpered as he backed away from the bed. I wanted him—in this place and time I could allow my weakness for him to show. Because this wasn't reality.

"I thought you were going to fuck me."

"Oh, I plan to, Pet. First, I plan to make you beg for it." He smiled, and I felt magic pulsing again in my dream room as a table appeared next to him. His lips kicked up into a wicked grin as more magic whirled inside the room. A silky looking material which looked like a black blindfold was now draped over his arm. "Lift your head," he commanded, and I swallowed the frightened groan that threatened to escape my throat.

It's a dream, nothing is real. Relax, Syn, just relax.

I held his eyes for a moment before lifting my head to allow him to place the blindfold over my eyes. I listened, now that I couldn't see anything. Only my breathing could be heard inside the room. "Ryder?" I asked, moving my head to listen for noises. Nothing. Okay, so maybe it wasn't a sexy dream, maybe it was a nightmare. *He'd tied me up and left me.*

I yelped as pressure was applied to my nipple, and then, a moment later, the other one, as well. His mouth touched it, but magic must have kept the pressure applied to both his hands just couldn't feel like they were everywhere at once otherwise. I moaned against the pressure, and it got louder as his tongue licked around the pink tips and his fingers entered my slick heat. The combination was heady and intense.

"Your pussy knows who owns it, Pet. You're so fucking wet, and it's because of me. Because it knows I'm going to fuck this silky flesh until it is sore."

I whimpered and lifted my hips, needing more, which he gladly gave. Another finger joined the other as his thumb played against my pleasure button. I rocked against his fingers, crying out when they left my body abruptly. I could hear him licking them, and it drove me wild, knowing he was tasting me. I growled with need and whined when all it got from him was a husky chuckle.

His mouth crushed against mine, and I reveled in the taste of myself on his lips, in his mouth. When he pulled away, the room went silent again. I waited in anticipation for him to enter me, but he didn't. Instead, I felt something else down there, something hard and yet soft as it slowly entered my body. I moaned and dropped my legs to the sides, giving him better access.

It went in and out until my core was slippery with the need he was creating. I felt the orgasm building inside. His breath was hot against my clit as his mouth came closer, and then his tongue was licking it, suckling at it, while he fucked me with whatever he was using, and yet, I felt both his hands on my flesh. I lifted my hips and fought the restraints with the need to hold his head there.

"Ryder," I shouted, needing to come. The moment I thought my body would shudder with release; he pulled it out, and removed his mouth.

"I didn't say you could come yet, Pet," he growled.

"I need it, I need to come, Ryder," I pleaded, still rocking my hips in a silent appeal for him to continue.

When the feeling had passed, he let his fingers

trail over my core. He allowed himself to sink one, and then another inside of me. He then pulled them out, and repeated the action several times. "Who owns this?" he asked, licking my clit slowly, surely, as his fingers pleasured my core.

I moaned loudly. "Ryder." I lifted my hips hungrily to take more of him inside of me. He smiled and removed his fingers—instantly I was filled. He was using his magic to pleasure my body. I was full, and when it started moving inside of me, he moaned. It was the sexiest fucking thing I had ever heard in my life. As if his magic was touching him while it was inside of me, and he could feel it.

"Tell me who owns you, and I'll let you come."

"No one owns me," I growled hungrily, and then cried out when the fullness was suddenly gone.

"That's the wrong answer, Pet. *I* fucking own you. This pussy wants me, *you* want me. And I want to fuck this sweet tight pussy, but I can't unless you tell me who owns it. Tell me," he demanded huskily.

"Ryder, I hurt."

Silence filled the room. I struggled against the chains and then cried out as his hands went around my neck, and his mouth crushed against mine hungrily. One hand snaked around to grab my hair as the other kept my face upright for his mouth.

The feeling of being at his mercy was erotic and terrifying. The combination together was overwhelming. I reminded myself that it was only a dream, and he couldn't hurt me. I flinched as I felt his legs spreading mine even farther until the chain would allow them to go no more. I felt him then; he was there, teasing me with his hardness. The bulbous head pushed at my entrance, sliding over the wet heat.

"Oh God, I need it now, Ryder," I cried, trying to push him in deeper, but failing.

"Who owns you?" he purred above me.

"No one does," I whispered as I moved my hips.

He shoved himself fully inside of me until I gasped and cried out. It was too much, and I felt him pushing against my womb, stretching me until I could take no more. Once again, he pulled out just as quickly as he had entered. "Who owns you, Syn?" he growled, before his lips crushed against mine. He pushed fully inside of me again, the combination almost sending me over the edge of the precipice.

I whimpered, savoring the feel of him inside of me. My muscles tightened around him, sucking him further into the slick wetness he had created until he pulled out again. "Who owns you, Pet?"

"No—" he cut my reply off as his mouth crushed against mine, his cock filling me completely.

He did this several more times, and each time I replied with the same answer. I felt his anger rising. He growled low, the sound rattling inside his chest. I was soaking wet; sweat covered my body while liquid pooled between my legs. "I can do this all fucking night, Syn, now tell me, who owns this pretty pink pussy?"

"I do," I rocked my hips, waiting for him to enter as he had done before. "Ryder?"

"You want this cock?" he growled fiercely, and shoved himself home inside of me and quickly pulled back.

"Beg me for it, Pet. Beg me to fuck your pretty, pink, tight pussy. Beg for me to make you scream with pleasure," he purred.

"Please?" I replied lamely.

I listened as the rattling inside his chest intensified, and moaned as he removed the pinching pressure from my right nipple to soothe the puckered bud with his mouth. Nipping and then sucking it, his tongue curled around the nipple and pulled it inside his blistering mouth. "I need you inside me, now."

"I need to own you, Syn, to control you. I want to hear it from your lips. Give me this, Pet. You can do better than that," he muttered, before clamping his teeth around my nipple, hard enough to pull a cry from my lips. His mouth released my nipple and attacked the other with the pinching pressure still in place. The combination was enough to create a new storm building inside of me.

His fingers found my mound and entered, but it wasn't what I needed, or what I wanted. I accepted what I could get, and let the storm silently brew until it was sitting on the edge and teetering. "Nice try. Who owns you?" he demanded.

Oh fuck it! It's a dream, right?

"You couldn't handle owning me, Ryder," I challenged him, barely hiding a smile as he prepared to enter me with what I needed him to give me. I wanted him buried inside of me until I was a part of him.

"Is that a challenge?" he purred against my ear.

"Take it however you want to, Ryder," I replied.

"I want to hear it. I want you to beg me to own this

pussy. To punish it with this." He rubbed his massive cock at my entrance again. "Tell me how much you want this cock inside of you. Tell me how bad you need to come. Say it, and I promise to make you come, so many times that you won't remember your own fucking name."

"Fine, you own me."

"Mean it," he snarled as he pushed only the tip of his cock inside of me.

"I'm yours, Ryder," I whispered, licking my lips.

He pushed himself completely inside of me. I screamed from the fullness he created, but the wetness he'd made smoothed the way and allowed him to bury himself deep inside of me.

"Good girl," he whispered, before kissing my lips harshly, his hands running through my hair to hold me still while he fucked my mouth with his tongue and filled my pussy with his cock. He was merciless, and I loved it. He was punishing and pleasuring, and I exploded around him, shaking and breaking into a million pieces as he continued to fuck me through the orgasms. He didn't stop there, and soon, another one crested. He kept going as orgasm after orgasm tore through me, rocking me from the inside out.

There was no one else who could do this to me. There was no life outside of Ryder, no other lover would make my body explode and shatter. My mind knew he was feeding from me, and I didn't care. It was a dream. In the morning, I would deal with reality, but right now I wanted to submit to him—I wanted to be his.

I smiled against his mouth as I felt his body go stiff with his own release. He growled until it became harsh and guttural, like a wild animal. My hands fought to get out of the restraints. "Ryder," I whimpered as I felt something growing inside of me. I moaned, and exploded again, but this time it was violent and shocking.

Something ripped into my neck, and then everything stopped around me, the room was silent. I listened in shock and fear as I felt my blood flow, as if it was being sucked from my neck by a wild animal. I fought against the restraints as stars burst behind my eyelids. My blood pulsed in my ears as the animal lapped at my neck and the blood around the wound.

"Ryder," I whimpered as I fought against the pain. The dream had changed, and in its place was a nightmare.

Chapter
THREE

I woke, drenched in sweat. My hand flew to my neck and relief washed over me instantly when I realized I was safely in my bed. I laughed nervously at my own stupidity. "Jeez, Syn, it was just a dream. Nothing more," I whispered to myself.

I sat up and looked around the room, and then fell back onto the pillows with a soft exhale. I flipped over and winced as pain shot up my leg. I pulled my leg up and scowled at the angry red welt on my left ankle. What the hell? I rubbed it and blinked my eyes open. I wondered if I must have run into something when I was running away from the mansion. My brain usually didn't function too well when I first woke up, so I shook it off for now.

I threw my legs over the edge of the mattress, and growled when I heard the board wince from my weight. "Screw this. I need a date with Mister Coffee."

I tripped down the stairs, set up the coffee maker, and flipped it to brew, before slumping into a chair at the table with my hands covering my face. I needed to figure out how long Adam was going to be down, or if he'd even look me in the eye again after what he'd tried doing to me. I was hoping he wouldn't remember it.

He'd tried to force himself on me. He'd been starting Transition, which no one had seen coming, or expected to happen so fast for that matter. Dristan had told Ryder that the brand on my neck might have stopped my own Transition and kept me hidden as a human. Had it tampered with Adam's, somehow suppressing his Transition? Neither one of us had any idea that we were Fae, not until Ryder had taken me inside Faery and something had affected the brand to make it fade.

Adam hadn't been able to control what he'd done. It scared me to know that, soon, I would be turning into a mindless sex machine. When the coffee maker beeped, I released my face and stared at it. The entire house was silent. The only noises inside it were mine and Mister Coffee's, and he sucked at listening. Maybe I should get a dog to keep me company.

I smiled and made a list of things I needed to get from the store while I was out and about today. After drinking the entire pot of coffee alone, I showered and glared at my leg where there was still a red and angry looking welt. I quickly got dressed and left the house.

It took more than an hour to finish shopping and find the animal shelter. A perky maybe twenty something year old girl smiled and bounced over to me at the counter. "Hi! Can I help you find you something?"

"I think I need a dog," I found myself blurting out to the bubbly blonde.

Twenty minutes later I was leaving the animal shelter with a shaggy dark gray dog that looked like a small wolf that had been left in the wild a little too long, judging by the amount of ribs he was showing.

We discussed names—well, I suggested names, all of which received a firm whine from my four-legged friend. I settled on naming him Mister Fancy Pants, since he had darker colored fur on his legs than he had on the rest of his body.

I smiled and started walking toward home, with Mister Fancy Pants on his brand new leash. I walked slowly, because he wasn't in the best shape, and looked like he could use a few meals to fatten him up. At least he was getting a chance at life—maybe. "I've never owned a dog," I said to my new pet.

He whined.

I'd probably whine too if I was him, since I'd never owned a pet before and it probably showed. At least the shelter had taken care of all that shot stuff and said he was healthy. The rest was up to me.

Why the hell had I wanted to get a dog again? We walked home in silence, which I guess was pretty normal, since he was a dog after all. When we arrived at the house, he wasn't impressed at all. In fact, he showed me just how unimpressed he was by growling at the walls for at least three straight hours.

"Enough already. The wall is not gonna bark back, Mister Fancy Pants!" He growled at me. Maybe he didn't like his name? "Don't pee on my carpet, no sniffing, no barking, and no chewing while I'm gone. Stay away from the coffee—touch it and you're gone." He blinked at me and then snapped his head back at the walls and went back to circling in front of them like a sentry—well, a growling, whining sentry.

My cell phone rang, startling me, and I answered it. I winced as the dog continued to go off at the walls as if they would attack him. "Stop barking!"

"What?" Ryder asked.

"I'm not talking to you. I'm talking to Mister Fancy Pants." I should seriously change his name. It was too long.

"Who the *fuck* is Mister Fancy Pants?"

I snickered as he said my dog's name. Coming out of his mouth, it really sounded bad.

"He's my dog. I got him at the shelter today." I sounded defensive, even to myself.

"Why the hell did you get a dog?" he asked with a hint of horror in his tone.

"You can't tell me what I can and can't get, Ryder." I tapped my foot waiting for his reply.

He laughed. He set down the phone and laughed at me! I glared at my end of the phone, before hanging it up. I waited, wondering if he'd had a purpose for calling, or if he'd just wanted make my life hell, since he'd said nothing important. Why phone me when he could just sift here and torment me in person? The phone promptly rang again. "What?" I shouted.

"Bad timing?" Alden asked.

"Bad day. I'm getting ready now. I will be at *Nightshade* in an hour, and I'll call you with the target's location. Anything else?" I asked, slipping easily back into Enforcer mode.

"Don't die."

I laughed. "Gee, thanks. Really feeling the confidence lately," I said, looking towards the dog as it started barking again. "Seriously! They're walls, nothing is there."

"What's a wall? *Is* that a dog?" Alden asked.

"The walls of the house. And, yes, I got a dog. He keeps acting like there is something on the other side or in the walls."

"You need to get out more, Synthia," Alden replied.

"I plan on it. I'm getting ready right now to do just that."

"I meant that you should go out now. Try to enjoy life before Transition hits, ya know?"

I snorted. "Is this a pep talk, Alden? Because, if it is, you need to stop, now," I paused and laughed. "I am far from normal. I have never been that person, and I'm not about to start now. Transition could happen at any time now, and I need to be practical."

"No, of course you're right. I just think you deserve something normal for at least a little while. You be careful tonight. Call me if you need help."

"Will do, and hey, Alden? *You* should date." I smiled as I listened to him snort from the other end of the phone.

"Fat chance in hell, and I don't need a pep talk either. Point taken," he shot back.

We hung up. The whole conversation was surreal after the way he had behaved at the Guild yesterday. I looked down at the dog, who was now sitting at my feet, still growling at the walls. I took a quick peek at the walls. Nothing different. The wards that circled the room were quiet and still looked like nothing more than a pretty border around the top of the wall where it met the ceiling. I shook my head before heading to my bedroom to change. It was easy to slip back into

Enforcer mode, but the pinch of regret that my team wouldn't be with me this time stung.

"Think you could be my back-up, Mister Fancy Pants?" I asked the now-silent dog.

He wagged his tail and lay down at my feet. I watched his head roll back and smiled at him. "I can do this. I'm strong, I'm fast, and I miss my friends…" And I was talking to myself again. I dug through the small closet and pulled out leather pants and a metal studded belt.

I quickly kicked off the jeans I'd been wearing and slipped into the leather pants, glaring at the dog as he lifted his head and eyed me. "I am *not* dinner, so stop looking at me like that!" I pulled off the long sleeve shirt and slipped into the leather top that hugged my curves perfectly.

I looked in the mirror and exhaled. My eyes were more of an electric blue right now, rather than the azure I was so used to. I had no idea if it was from my body changing to Fae, or if my magic was trying to recharge. Or, worse—a little of both. I applied a touch of blush, some eyeliner, and mascara, before adding the ruby red lipstick to match the Big Apple Red OPI nail polish I was sporting today.

"Okay, Mister Fancy Pants, let's go get you some food and water," I said, talking to the dog, which was wagging his tail and watching me. But, hey, at least he'd finally stopped barking at the walls.

Chapter
FOUR

Nightshade was full tonight. Humans and Vampires mingled together while Vlad once again tended his own bar. I smiled and walked over to him. "Full crowd tonight," I shouted over the music as I took the only free seat at the bar.

Vlad smiled, showing off his wicked set of fangs. "The band is playing, and there's a lot of press in here tonight. I didn't figure I'd be seeing you for a while, Syn. What gives?" Vlad said as his silver eyes took in the leather I wore. "Hunting? Because I hope you didn't come in here, thinking you could take me out." He clasped his hands over his heart and rolled his eyes in mock fear.

"I'm not hunting you, Vlad. I'm wondering if you have seen a new vamp, someone who doesn't care if he drains the blood bank."

"We don't allow anyone to be drained inside my club. *Ever.* Anyone who disobeys the rules inside this club forfeits his life, or *hers*," Vlad replied testily. Great, I'd managed to offend him. Like my day wasn't bad enough, now I'd pissed off Dracula!

I smiled at his play on words. "And what would

be the rules?" I asked, narrowing my eyes as he rolled his.

"Don't hunt inside my club, Syn. You won't like the results. This place is a neutral zone; we don't allow our own to get harmed. Nor do we allow those who come inside to get hurt. If they are dumb enough to leave the premises…" he let his words trail off with the implication hanging in the air.

"So, let's say someone is here, and they're draining humans…what happens then?"

"The Horde takes care of it."

"Without their King?" I replied, lifting a blonde eyebrow in surprise.

He smiled and leaned over the counter with his elbows resting on it casually. "Look, Syn, I respect you. You get knocked on your ass and you get back up swinging. You have every reason to hate me for what I did to Adrian, and hell, maybe you have every right to mark me as a target, yet you didn't. You're smart, so do the math. No one is leaving here tonight in a body bag, and no one from the Guild is being allowed through the doors, so if that was the plan…I already sent your back-up packing."

"Speaking of Adrian, why him? Why did you turn him, and not me?"

"He was the easier target in the coven."

"That's a lie and you know it. Larissa was the easiest target. Try again."

His face shut down and he stood back up, narrowing his eyes. "Adrian was more accessible."

"No, he wasn't. We were all at different locations

inside that parking garage. I was the easiest to get to, second only to Larissa, who was in the van alone. Someone sent you to take him and only him. I want to know why."

His eyes swirled, and he shook his head. "Like I said, you're smart. Leave this one alone, Syn. It isn't something you could come back from anytime soon. This wasn't his choice *exactly*, but the kid's got heart. He's doing the best he can right now, and he needs to know you are okay with it. Your opinion means more than it should to him."

"What the hell is that supposed to mean?" I asked, feeling anger rise within me. He was telling me that Adrian had been handpicked to be turned, but to leave it alone. Was he serious? I was about to argue when a guitar started from the stage. I turned, finding Adrian staring right at me as the band played a few notes doing a quick sound check.

I met his turquoise eyes and smiled until he returned it, showing off his fangs. He'd been my first love, and Vlad had turned him Vamp, because he'd said I'd gotten too close to him. As a warning, he'd taken Adrian, which I hadn't understood. Still didn't understand. Vlad had a secret, and I needed to know who had ordered Adrian to be turned. Adrian set the guitar down on a stand and approached the main microphone on the stage.

He smiled, even though I was no longer smiling. "This first song goes out to my girl, my first and only girl."

The band began playing Buckcherry's *Sorry*, and it took everything inside of me to hold the tears back. I stood before I knew what I was doing, and walked towards the stage. He looked good, even if he was undead. His dark hair was pulled back and hidden in a ponytail. His skin was a little lighter, and he lacked a pulse, but he was still Adrian. He was still the first boy I'd ever loved.

I sang silently along with the lyrics, his lips moving with a cocky grin as he sang. I stopped at the edge of the stage and watched as he moved to stand directly in front of me. I hadn't expected him to stop in front of me, but he did. The microphone was still in his hand, held up to his mouth so it didn't disturb the song he was still singing. His free hand reached out and grabbed mine. I closed my eyes so he wouldn't see the flinch that came with his icy touch. I tried to pull away, but he held me in place as the song slowed and then stopped.

He leaned his face close to mine as if he would kiss me, but instead he kissed my cheek and pulled me against him. "Mark's in the back with a willing victim, and I'm your back-up baby."

I pulled away and smiled at him, but it left my face with the implication his words held. "Adrian, no—" His mouth crushed against mine, cutting off my words. His lips weren't as cold as the rest of him, and I felt his fangs graze my lips, before his tongue pushed into my mouth.

His kiss was gentle, and yet I could feel his urgency…and it was more than just to shut me up. There was fire inside of it. I melted against him, uncaring who was watching, even as the entire club erupted with cheers that he'd gotten the girl. When he pulled away, his eyes narrowed. "You let him mark you?" There was hurt in his tone, and regret.

Unfortunately, I had no idea what the brand on my hip did, but I had a feeling it was to repel all other men and deter them from being interested in me. It sounded like something Ryder would do, since he tended to mark ownership on the things he wanted. It's what I was to him, just a pretty thing to own. Adrian sensing the brand confirmed it and made me want to spit nails at Ryder.

"I didn't let him do anything," I replied crisply, knowing exactly who he was referring to.

"Do you have any idea of what that means, Syn?" he countered, ignoring me.

"I don't care, and as soon as I finish Transition I won't be seeing him again!"

He shook his head as his eyes flashed from turquoise to red. "Good fucking luck with that. You can't just undo a brand like that. He owns you right now, and it's dangerous to play games with Ryder."

"What does that mean?" I asked, unsure I had heard him right.

"He's fucking marked you, Syn, and it wasn't just because he wanted to be able to find you. That mark means no other fucking Fae can touch you. No one can, but Ryder. He made you his own little fuck toy by placing that on you."

"That's bullshit, Adrian. I'm not anyone's toy."

He laughed, the sound was chilling, and so unlike him. His eyes turned turquoise again, but his posture was stiff. "You'd better get going. Your owner just walked in with his crew."

I turned, looking through the crowded club. Everyone was watching us. "I need to go," I whispered, pushing away from him.

"Syn, listen to me carefully. After Transition is done, or hell, even before it is, choose me. I promise to keep you safe. You know I'd walk through hell for you, girl."

"Adrian," I warned as I was surrounded by Ryder and his men.

"She chooses you, and she won't live through Transition, and neither would you, boy." Ryder hissed in warning to back up his words.

"Is it true? Is this thing you put on me more than just some fucking property tag?" He narrowed his eyes and said nothing. "You fucker! You *tramp* stamped my ass!"

"It *isn't* on your ass, Syn," Ryder growled as he pulled me against himself, even as I fought to stand my ground.

"Get away from me. I've lost everything! Everything, Ryder. I'm barely fucking standing on my feet and you just keep taking from me. I signed the fucking contract. You have me through Transition! Why the fuck would you mark me as your whore?" I was losing it.

He crushed me closer to his body and snarled in my ear. "If you ever call yourself a whore again I will put you over my fucking knee and spank your tight ass until you can't sit down again."

"Let me go. Now," he released me, and I felt it. My body sizzling with magic, as anger poured through me and lit up the brands on my skin. I'd thought that I would never see them again. I inhaled and exhaled, wild magic was coursing through me and I didn't have Adam with me this time to stop it. Shit! "I have to go," I whispered, pushing away from him and through the club in a hurry to get to the cool night air, before I went nuclear.

I could feel it building inside of me, pulsing through my veins. The crowd of people split, and moved out of the way, opening a path as I ran through the club, oblivious if anyone was trailing me—or stupid enough to. I didn't have anyone to help take the power, or neutralize it. I could feel it growing unstable, a wild, tangible thing that wafted *from* me.

I rushed out the doors as both huge bouncers parted to allow me outside. The cool air did nothing to quench the power raging inside of me. I felt my heart rate increasing and my throat closing. I was dying, being consumed with power overload, which was almost hysterical, since I didn't have any power ten minutes ago…and I'd wanted it. Ryder started toward me, and then pulled back in frustration, as if remembering something.

"Fuck, Z. Go get Adam, *now*!" Ryder growled.

"Let me through! Now," Adrian shouted, trying to be heard over Ryder.

"Adam's um…Ryder—" Zahruk stopped as Ryder growled an inhuman sound that made everyone stop and take a step away from him.

"Ryder, let Adrian through. He's connected to her too. He might be able to stop it—," Vlad said as the voice of reason.

Adrian was suddenly there, pulling me against him as he took me to the ground. I wasn't drawing in air. I shook my head as panic started to kick in. "Breathe. Come on, Fancy Face, let me in."

I felt his magic touching mine. His was as cold as he was. The powers inside of him were deadly and untapped, as if he hadn't been able to use them without the help of the coven. I watched his eyes light up as they held my own; beautiful turquoise so striking that I allowed myself to get swallowed inside their endless depths. I could feel him connecting to Adam and completing the link that the Coven had.

"That's it, Syn, give me more," Adrian crooned as something growled from behind us. Adrian ignored it, but something inside of my body acknowledged the growl and heat flared up inside of me. I pulled Adrian closer, feeding him more power, until I could sense the others around us.

Something inside of me wanted out, violently. My body was teetering on the edge of something; my core drenched with need from whatever was inside, trying to get out. I shook with the force of it. It was overwhelming and primal but worse, it was out of my control.

"Oh, fucking hell," Zahruk growled.

I heard a scuffle of feet moving and something struggling, but I ignored it as I cupped Adrian's face and kissed him. I didn't know why I did it. Only that I did, and that we both were glowing, raw current flowing through us, around us. He moaned against me and ran his hands through my hair as he deepened the kiss.

And then he was gone, and Vlad was shouting curses violently.

I looked around, stunned. What the hell had just happened? I looked up at the faces of Ryder's men. They looked unsure and worried. Ryder and Adrian were both missing. "No," I shook my head. This wasn't happening. "Get him back here, now! Zahruk, bring them back, now!" I was screaming, coming off the ground quickly as my hair flew around my face with the current running through me as the glow left my body, along with the rush of power.

"Sorry, Synthia, this isn't our quarrel. Ryder will bring the boy back in one piece—I think," Zahruk said carefully.

"No! This isn't happening. I don't know what the fuck just happened, but I need him. I need him alive, dammit. I can't lose anyone else." My voice cracked with unshed tears. I couldn't handle it if Ryder killed Adrian because of something I couldn't control.

"Go home, Synthia, and tell the Guild I took out the problem. Tell Alden if he ever tries to turn another of my *creations* against me, it will be war," Vlad snapped, before he went back inside the club, leaving me alone with Ryder's men.

I turned to Ristan, numb with shock. "Tell Ryder that if he killed Adrian, to never think about me again, to never fucking try and contact me again. I will not be owned, and I will not be Transitioning. Transition can take me to bloody fucking hell right along with it for all I care. Tell him I am no longer his."

Ristan pushed closer, grabbed my arms, and shook me a little. "Flower, snap the hell out of it now, before you light up the entire city again." He got right up in my face, and those patterned eyes swirled at me dangerously. "You've got to stop trying to think he is ever going to behave like a human, Syn. He's not. He is a Fae warrior, and we come from one of the most dangerous places that you couldn't even imagine in your worst dreams. What you saw in Faery was just a glimpse of what we consider relatively safe. He. *Is*. Fae. That means he is a fucking predator that is used to taking what he wants, and he *will* protect and defend what belongs to him by *any* means necessary. And, before you go on and on about how no one owns you, trust me, he does. You just haven't gotten it through your head yet, but your heart knows it's true." I tried to turn away, and he wouldn't let me. He just kept after me until I had no choice but to look in his eyes again. He softened a bit when I did.

"Flower, I know this a big change for you. You will Transition, and you don't have a choice in the matter. You have got to learn our world and ways, and you don't have much time in which to do it. Ryder may wear the mask of a human, but he has only been in this world for a little over fifteen years. That is a blink of an eye to us. He is still trying to adapt and understand this world, and sometimes it gets messy. Now, I am sure nothing permanent happened to your boy-toy this time. Come on, and I'll give you a quick sift home."

I nodded and placed my hand in Ristan's. I was losing control. I'd kissed Adrian, and it hadn't been him who I'd wanted to kiss—that damn growl had made my mind go blank, and I'd kissed the wrong male. I'd also failed to take out the target and, what's worse—I was teetering on the brink of Transition, and I could feel it starting to take over.

Chapter FIVE

When I got home, I could feel the power draining, but it had taken its toll on my body. It had been dark magic, and there had been no light to counter it. I'd been light based, with dark magic as a backup. Dark magic was dangerous, and you had to be careful of using it at all. I'd just done a huge power overload, and now I felt it with every move I made.

The dog was waiting at the door when I arrived, and he growled at me. Great, even my dog hated me. "Mister Fancy Pants, go lay down!" I shouted, frustrated with everything, and scared for Adrian.

The door I'd just slammed closed, flew open. "Get the fuck out here, Syn," Ryder growled.

"Where's Adrian?" I cried, not knowing if I wanted the answer.

"Afraid I killed your boyfriend?" he asked coldly, his eyes turning hard.

Mister Fancy Pants snarled, but stayed beside me. I swallowed and shook my head. "Leave me alone," I shouted back.

"You belong to me, you *kissed* him. You breached

the fucking contract, Synthia," he replied scathingly as he crossed his arms over his t-shirt clad chest.

"I kissed him so you *killed* him? I couldn't stop it, dammit, I couldn't control it. Something inside of me needed to kiss him, not *me*. And it wasn't even him this thing inside of me wanted! It was whatever the fuck was growling! So, yes, I kissed him, Ryder, because I seem to have a monster inside of me! And you killed him! So, fuck you, fuck him, and fuck me! Fuck everything!" I was swinging at the air with tears streaking down my face.

"You're close to Transitioning," he replied carefully, his face still concealed in the shadows of the porch.

"No! I'm *not* doing it. *Period.* No fucking way. I control what happens in my life! I want to know what you did to Adrian!" I hated the fact that when I got pissed, I cried. Most of the time I didn't make sense when it was this bad. It was such a girlie thing to do, and it screamed weakness.

"He's alive, Syn, bruised—but alive. He won't be if he touches you again. No one touches what is mine, and lives. Make no fucking mistake, Pet, you *are* mine."

"I am not *your* anything. You marked me without my permission. So I'm not yours until *I* decide to give myself to you. You can't just piss on my leg and say I'm yours. It doesn't work that way in the real world."

"I didn't piss on your leg, Syn. I fucked you. I claimed you. Regardless of what you say now, you gave yourself to me, and I'm pretty sure you would have agreed to anything I had asked while I was inside your pretty pink folds."

"Bullshit! I am not yours. I'm not something that can be owned, Ryder! I am not a fucking pet that you can just chain to your fucking wall and play with when you want to! I'm a human being!"

"There's where you're wrong. You're not human, you're Fae, and you're changing already. Fast. You broke the contract by kissing Adrian. I could kill you right now, and no one would be able to stop me. Just remember, I have Adam. Be at my club tomorrow night, or I will give Adam over to the women to feed, from *him*."

"You can't do that!" I shouted.

"I can, and I will." He sifted before I could argue with him.

He left me standing at the door fuming. He was the most infuriating male on the fucking planet. Hot one minute and the next, cold as the freaking iceberg that dropped the Titanic! I turned and slammed the door, pretending it was his face instead of empty space.

I showered and changed before calling Alden on the phone number he had called me from, and reported that the target had been taken out by Vlad. "Alden, I recharged…" I said, trailing off.

"And?" he asked cautiously.

"Dark magic, only," I replied.

"That's not good." He sounded worried.

"How bad we talking, Alden?"

"Pretty bad," he mumbled before continuing. "If you have no light magic the dark will consume you. Did you use it?"

"I kinda went nuclear. Adrian calmed me down though. He balanced it out before I could get hurt." *And then he got his ass beat by Ryder...*because of me.

"Adrian isn't connected, *is* he?" he asked quietly.

"Yeah, well with everything that went down, I kinda forgot to tell you that he was. He used the Coven bond to link to Adam and pulled power from me. He got too close, and I used mine against him to tap my line and pull from it. We're connected the same as we were before. His felt deadly though, stronger somehow, as if it had been building up without an outlet."

"That's not good," he said again.

"Alden, I really need good news right now. I'm not sure I can take much more bad news."

"You have magic," he replied chuckling.

"Dark magic, without light...I basically have bad magic that can kill me. Yay me. Any word on the wards inside my house," I asked.

"I have my best people working on it. So far, we only have a few words figured out. I can tell you it protects against the Horde, but not sure if it pertains to a certain caste of Horde, or more. Shawn says it could also protect against a couple of other castes of Fae, like Dark and Light. So we ended up with more questions and only a few hints, so far."

"Great, can you make them hurry up?"

"Listen, Syn. Try not to use any magic unless you have to. I'll dig through the archives and see what I can find on how to harness it. Good job tonight. I know you didn't make the kill, but we'd still be chasing our

asses looking for him had you not gone in. I'll have
Shawn work through these wards and see what he can
come up with. Syn, what Shawn is doing—is for me,
and off the record—the Guild doesn't know, so don't
contact him directly. There is a lot going on at the
Guild right now." He hesitated. "Stay away from the
Guild for the time being. As soon as I can, I'll tell you
what I think is going on."

"I need some sleep. Maybe it won't be so bad with
coffee in me." Yeah, I could actually sleep after a cup
of coffee. I could do anything after coffee.

We hung up, and I stretched before heading in to
get some liquid happiness.

I walked into the kitchen and fired up the coffee
maker. Feeling a bit peckish, I opened the fridge. It
was empty, and it hadn't been when I'd left the house.
I closed it and scratched my head, thinking it was
strange. The wards I'd cast were still up and working
when I'd come in. The dog's food bowl was still full,
along with the water.

I shook my head and went to the living room,
grabbing up the remote and flipping on the TV while
sinking blissfully into the couch. Mister Fancy Pants
sat at my feet, wagging his tail happily. He looked
bigger now and more alive now than he had when I'd
brought him home.

He turned his head and leveled me with clear blue
eyes. I patted his head and his eyes closed, like he
really liked head pats and scratches and wanted more.
I felt something ripple inside the room, and instantly
went on guard. My heart raced as the thought of the
Fae who had killed my parents flashed inside my
mind. I reached into the cushion, pulling out one of
the handguns. This wasn't happening.

I felt someone sift in behind me. I turned and took aim, but Ristan was faster. He disarmed me and swore. "Flower, what the hell are you doing with a gun? Ryder felt your panic."

I growled, but ignored him as I disarmed him and took my gun back. "Something isn't right. Can't you feel that?"

Ristan turned his strange silver and black swirling eyes to the walls that had started to glow red with warning. The wards were reacting to something, and they only did that when something bad was inside the house, or close to it. "I don't feel anything. Your wards on the other hand…" He smiled and lit up his brands.

"Something is coming," I warned. "Mister Fancy—*fuck*!" I shouted as I watched my dog shift.

Into a person.

"No-o-o! You turn back into a fucking dog this minute!" I shouted, stomping my feet as Ristan barked with laughter until he doubled over from it.

"Only you could go to the pound and pick out a Shifter, Syn."

My dog was a Shape-shifter. A twenty something boy sat where my dog had just been, with lanky red hair and bright blue eyes. He was screaming with pain as he changed to his human form and the wards were showing him no mercy. Alden had just told me that the wards were to keep out certain castes of the Fae, most likely Horde…were the Shifters from Faery too, and part of the Horde?

Was Ryder Unseelie—the Horde?

My mind shifted back to what I had glimpsed in his eyes a little over a week ago at the ball—like an animal was lurking there. His face had shifted subtly, and I know I had seen a glimpse of fangs. The rumors about the Dark Prince were pretty consistent about him being one of the most powerful Fae out there.

Ristan watched as I put it together and shook his head. "I wouldn't let your mind wander in that direction, Synthia. Nothing good ever comes from making assumptions."

"Is Ryder the Horde King? The timing is about right. The rumors started about twenty years ago, and Ryder has been here for about fifteen of those years. He can't enter my house, his comments…" I stopped as Ristan turned to face me with cold, merciless death in his beautiful eyes.

"Sorry, Syn, you're wrong."

"No, Ristan, let her assume," Ryder said from the doorway where he stood at the threshold. "The boy needs to get out of the house."

We all looked down to where Mister Fancy Pants was writhing silently in pain. Ristan easily picked the now red-headed boy up and took him outside where it looked like he had immediate relief. I watched Ryder where he stood outside my door.

"You're the Horde King," I whispered.

"Is that what you think, Syn? That I'm the mythical Horde King?" He tilted his head and smiled coldly. Unfriendly.

"The wards…shifters must be part of the Horde, and the timing—it's too right," I smiled, thinking how I'd just hit the nail on the head.

"And you think the wards only work on the Horde?" he asked carefully.

"I think you're the Horde King, Ryder, and that you're after something."

I looked down to where his feet were on the other side of the threshold. He couldn't come inside the house. He'd had to pull me outside yesterday since he hadn't been able to come in, and the wards had landed him flat on his ass once already. "Alden said the wards protected, and that my parents had been hiding me from evil."

"Ah, so naturally you think I'm evil."

"I'm not quite sure what to think yet, Ryder."

He stepped over the threshold and strode inside until he stood inches in front of me. "I already have you, Syn, and as you can see, the wards are not reacting to me. Still think I'm him?"

I eyed the wards and looked back to Ryder. No strain showed on his face. Ristan stood with the naked shifter on my porch as Ryder's men stood on my dead lawn, watching the standoff. "But last time...?" I asked, looking up to meet his eyes.

"Last time the wards must have reacted because a Fae was inside the house. They hadn't been active for a while. Perhaps they reacted to the fact that a Transitioned Fae was inside their protection. Who knows why they reacted to me? Inactive wards are unstable at best. They had been left unattended and un-strengthened for a very long time. You're smart enough to figure that out."

I hated when he was right and had to state the obvious. Especially after I'd just accused him of being the Horde King based on theory alone...

I crossed my arms over my chest as my body reacted to how close he was. "And him?" I leveled a glare at Mister *Not* So Fancy Pants. I also thought of the Fae who had abused and killed my parents. They had been Transitioned, which killed his explanation on the spot.

Ryder's lips lifted as he turned and took in the naked Shifter. "Only you, Syn, only you could find a Shifter inside an animal shelter, and bring it home."

Ristan snorted from the doorway, and asked the Shifter where he now stood on the porch, a safe distance from the wards. "Explain how you ended up in the pound, Fido."

"I was caught by humans after a bad run of luck. Ended up with a few others that had been trapped as well."

"Caught by humans?" Ryder asked, turning beside me until his hand touched my leg from his close proximity. I shivered with the knowledge of how good they felt inside my dreams, which caused him to look over at me with a knowing smile on his lips. I frowned and took a step further away from him.

"Yeah," my dog said, running human hands through his hair. "They injected me and a few others with something that killed most of us. The others had a really bad reaction to it. I eventually shifted to get out of the cuffs and, I was so sick, I couldn't shift back afterwards."

Ristan and Ryder both looked at each other, and I had the distinct feeling I was missing something. "How many humans did you see?" Ristan asked after a brief second had passed.

"A couple, they wore masks though. They called us castes, and, well, *you* know we don't consider each other castes, they kept saying we were test subjects."

"Oh my God! You watched me change!" I blurted out accusingly.

He blushed and scratched his head with a guilty smile on his lips. "Sorry about that, but not sorry for what I saw." He wiggled his eyebrows and smiled boyishly.

Ryder growled low in his chest. "Take him home, Ristan. Eliran will need to look him over to be sure he is fine."

I watched the others sift out, which left me standing alone with Ryder, who I'd just accused of being the Horde King. He turned and smiled as if he could read my thoughts. "You're not the first to think it, Syn," he said, taking a step towards me.

"What are you?" I asked, taking a step back and winced when I felt my back go flush against the wall that seemed to come out of nowhere.

"You really want the answer?" he asked, moving closer until he placed his hands on either side of my head. "You couldn't handle it, and you're not ready to know. When you are, you won't need to ask me because it will be too late for you."

"Too late for me?" I asked before licking my dry lips.

His eyes lowered to my mouth with liquid heat burning inside of them. "I want to fuck you, right here, right now, Syn." Wow, nothing like Ryder whiplash when he wanted to change topics.

I swallowed, and closed my eyes against the lust I'd seen in his. "Ryder..." his mouth crushed against mine and heat flooded my entire body, saturating my core. My hands came up to rest against his cotton shirt, planning to push him away, in a moment, right after I took what I needed…Who was I kidding?

He made that deep rattling sound in his chest again as he growled deeply against my mouth. His hands slid down to rest against my waist as he lifted me up against his body. He was hard and ready. I moaned against him, but managed to pull away from his addictive kiss. "I still have a day, Ryder," I reminded him in a whispered tone, trying to catch my breath.

"Are you scared, Syn?" he whispered back as his eyes changed from gold to burnt amber. He was hungry, and it was making me wet with need.

"To be with you? Yes." I admitted it, which only made him smile. "You scare the shit out of me, is that what you wanted to hear?"

"Because I make you want things that you think you shouldn't," he replied.

I glared, hating that he could read me so easily and effortlessly, as if I were transparent to him. I shook my head, reminding myself that he'd hurt Adrian. "Would it matter, Ryder? You don't want to love me, you want to own me, and I don't want that for myself. You don't actually care how I feel, and that doesn't work for me. I'll show up tomorrow, but only because I don't have a choice."

"You think that boy could bring you through the Transition, Syn? It would take him and about ten others to get you through it alive. That's how many we line up for the females when they go through Transition. And you're right. I like to own pretty things. *I* own *you,* and you like me inside of you. Or did I miss something?"

"Go to hell, Ryder! I don't want to Transition at all! What if it changes who I am? What if makes me evil, like the Fae who killed my parents? Or worse, what if I change into some grotesque monster?"

He smiled gently, and moved closer. "It won't change how you feel, or who you are. You could never be grotesque, either. Vanity isn't something you give a fuck about, so don't start now. You're worried you will have to admit that being Fae doesn't make you evil and that you will have to fuck in order to feed. There are other ways to feed, not through Transition, but after. You can lie to yourself all you want, but don't expect me to buy the bullshit you keep feeding yourself."

"We don't even know what I am! You have no idea what I will change into. No one does. You knew what you would change into when you Transitioned. I don't. Hell, Adam doesn't even know!"

"Dark Fae. Adam is Dark Fae. His brands are fully developed now. He's your familiar, so my guess is that you are as well, which means I'm your Prince fucking Charming." His eyes sparkled mischievously.

I snorted. "My ass, you are. You're not Dark Fae, Ryder. You may not be the Horde King, but you sure as hell are not the Dark Prince. You can sell that lie somewhere else, because I ain't buying."

Chapter SIX

I showered and laid down, ignoring everything…
or trying to, with my brain running at warp-speed.
My dog had been a Shape-shifter and I hadn't even
noticed—well, to be truthful, I didn't have much to
do with Shifters in the past, so it wasn't as if I really
knew what to look for. Everything I knew about them
came from a Guild textbook. According to Ryder and
Ristan, I was starting to go through Transition, and I
wasn't going to be given an option about it. I wasn't
ready. I'd barely processed the idea of being Fae. I
hadn't gotten to the acceptance part of it or that I'd
soon become a fully Transitioned Fae.

I was starting to think it was like the stages of
grief. I hated not knowing what I would change into,
or, worse, who I would feed from for the rest of my
life. I wasn't the type to go from lover to lover. I
wasn't a fucking ride at the damn carnival!

Who the hell abandoned a child? Had I been bad,
or born wrong? Had my real parents handed me off
to my foster parents, or did my foster parents find
me? The Guild was notorious for not wanting to have
anything to do with the Fae, much less cooperating
with them, until my 'interview' with Ryder. Suddenly,
the Guild was BFFs with the Fae, and now they were

back to Guild business as usual.

Looking over happier memories with my parents, they had to have known I was a Fae child, but why would a Guild couple knowingly take in a Fae child? Add that to the fact that my father had been in a very high position on the council. It only added to the confusion I was trying to sort through. I hated not knowing, and I couldn't keep it off my mind. To make matters worse, if Mister Fancy Pants had been right and telling the truth, there was a radical group of humans out there fucking with the Fae—and I'm not sure I could blame them for it, considering how much the Fae seemed to use humans.

I rubbed my eyes and sighed. I'd bought a damn dog so I wouldn't do this, and here I was doing it! My dog hadn't even been a damn dog. You couldn't buy this kind of bad luck. I wanted to blame it all on Ryder, because my life might not have been perfect before I met him, but I'd been in control of it, for the most part. Now, the only thing I could manage to control, was the on and off switch on my coffee pot!

I'd put things together and accused Ryder of being the Horde King…Now, I couldn't put my foot any further into my mouth. He'd withstood the wards, walked right the hell through them. I turned and punched my pillow. I needed to get control, and I needed to do it quickly, before I was so far in that I couldn't climb out.

I closed my eyes again and, the next thing I knew, he was there. His dangerous, sinfully-beautiful, golden eyes laughed at me as he watched me. Gah! The man was taunting me inside my head, and what was worse, I wanted him. I wanted his hands touching me, his mouth seducing me…

I felt myself falling, and tried to right myself on

the bed, as if I'd drifted to sleep and felt that instant of falling through the air weightlessly. I landed, hard, on beautiful, gray and black mosaic tile, with water covering my hands and cascading around me. I spit water out and tried to sit up. I pushed the water out of my face and eyes and let out a startled moan. I was staring right at Ryder's dick.

His deep chuckle made me look up further. I was in a thin Betty Boop pajama short set, soaking wet, on my hands and knees at his feet...in his fucking shower!

"What the hell?" I growled, trying to get to my feet and slipping. Why the hell was he in the shower anyway, seeing that he could snap his fingers and be insta-cleaned?

"You sifted—into my shower. I'm flattered, Pet."

I growled and splashed water. "I do *not* sift!" I had totally sifted and landed at his flipping feet!

"You just did." He smiled and held out his hand. I slapped it away and tried to stand up again, but slipped. "And, to think, I'd almost forgone the shower for a quicker fix...and would have missed this."

"This isn't happening. Wake up, please wake up..." I closed my eyes and looked up again. Yup, his dick was still there. I squeezed my eyes shut again and counted to ten slowly. I exhaled and opened them to find Ryder at my eye level, watching me.

"You look good wet...very enticing." He smiled and pulled me up with him until I was standing against his now growing erection. The only barrier was my pajama tank top and shorts. "First time this has happened?" he asked, with glowing amber shining in his eyes now.

I nodded. I was pouting. I'd sifted. *Into his fucking shower!* "I'm a fucking Fairy. Dammit! Why does fucked up shit always happen to me? What, do I have a fucking sticker on my ass that says *fuck with me*?"

His lips fought against the laugh I could hear bubbling in his chest. "Don't fucking laugh! This isn't funny, Ryder. I can't have anything! I can't have friends, because I get them killed. I can't even have a fucking dog, because I attract trouble like there's no fucking tomorrow. I get the people I loved killed, and I don't even know why. It's not fucking fair. You should have left me inside my mind, Ryder. This isn't fair." I hated admitting this kind of stuff to him.

"Done?" he asked. "I'm willing to check for that sticker now."

"I'm serious. I feel like I have to be strong every fucking minute of my life, because the minute I let my guard down, something bad happens. Maybe that's why they ditched me, maybe I got them killed too."

"Who?" he asked, running his thumb over my chin as the shower cascaded water over me.

"My real parents," I mumbled.

"Syn, I doubt you got them killed. Faery isn't like the world you grew up in. Everyone fucks everyone over. They probably hid you because they had to, or maybe you were stolen by their enemy. It's not something you can just assume. I doubt anyone threw you away. Or that you got someone killed because you have bad luck."

I blinked at him and looked up at the multiple shower heads that were situated around the lavish shower stall, then back at him. He was covered in soap, and he looked pretty damn hot lathered up. I spit out the water that kept pouring over me. "I ruined your shower."

"Oh, no, you made it very interesting. I can honestly say that I've never had someone sift into my shower and land so sexily at my feet before. Plus, you always remember your first sift, which means every time you think of yours…"

"Peachy," I countered.

He threw his head back and barked with laughter, and then pulled me up and against him again, his lips touching my forehead softly. My hands settled on his muscled back and drifted down to his ass. I lifted my head, as he lowered his, to accept his kiss.

It wasn't hard. His mouth was searching and tender, which affected me more than if he'd been hard and demanding. He pushed me against the black slate wall and I allowed it, needing his touch. His scorching mouth was making it so I didn't have to think. It was selfish, but he consumed and demanded everything inside of me. I had no time to think when I was connected to him, which was deadly and dangerous, considering I knew nothing about him.

He picked me up, and I wrapped my legs around him. His hungry mouth deepened the kiss until a fire started inside of me, threatening to burn out of control. His hand pulled against the fabric of my tank top. He found my nipple and pinched it hard, making a moan leave my mouth, only to be captured by his.

"Ryder, we got a problem," Ristan called from beyond the other side of the etched-glass shower door.

"Someone had better be dying, Ristan," Ryder growled when he'd pulled away from kissing me.

"They might be. You need to come see this."

"We will be right there," Ryder called out as I slid down his hard body. He watched me with a smirk and then placed his hand on my arm to move me from beneath the water, so he could rinse off. I watched him, unable to pull my eyes off of his hands as they roved over his body. He was quicksand, and I was sinking.

"Did you say we?" Ristan asked.

I blushed from my head to my Paint Your Toron-Toes Rose colored toenails. I opened the shower door and stepped out meeting Ristan's eyes. "Don't ask."

"How the…did you *sift* into his *shower*?" he asked, bubbling with laughter.

"I said don't ask! It wasn't my fault. I was sleeping!" I shouted as both men laughed even harder. "Real mature guys, just real fucking mature!" I walked out of the large bathroom and headed for Ryder's closet to grab a shirt, since I was wet, and my clothes were clinging to me like a second layer of skin.

Ryder was behind me with a towel wrapped around his hips. I didn't need to turn around to know it. I could smell his intoxicating masculine scent, and I wanted to turn around and take his stupid towel… just to touch him, to feel his skin against mine. Ugh! How was I supposed to think with that much sexual Fae standing practically naked behind me!?

"Need some help dressing, Syn?" he purred silkily.

"Not on your life, Fairy," I quipped, pulling on one of his t-shirts that flowed to my knees.

"In my shower and wearing my clothes," his eyes roved over my body. "All in the same day?" He laughed and dropped his towel. I watched as he used his magic to glamour clothing on with nothing more than a thought. Go figure.

"Are you two done flirting yet? People are really dying," Ristan said impatiently as he walked to the bedroom door.

"People are always dying when I'm around," I mumbled, tearing my eyes from Ryder.

"Not like this. Never seen anything like what the healers are dealing with right now, Flower."

I swallowed and felt the blood drain from my face. "Pieces?" I barely managed to get the words past the lump in my throat.

"No, but just as bad," Ristan's tone turned sober. "I'll meet you two down there." Ristan sifted out without waiting to see if we followed.

I turned and eyed Ryder's brands. Thick intricate Celtic brands that were black in color and beautiful against his dark skin were beginning to pulse with his immense power. "Before we go, please tell me why you were torturing those people." Ryder was quiet for a few moments, as though he were mulling through options.

"I did not want to involve you in this. There is so much that you don't know, that you are not ready for, and so much that we are still learning." He shook his head and continued, "I didn't kill anyone, Synthia. Not yet, anyways. Those men inside my house? They fucked with you. They not only gave Joseph the information needed to find you, they also told him what would probably break you. They signed Larissa's death warrant. I don't allow anyone to hurt someone under my protection. They got to you. I won't let that go, and neither will Alden."

I felt my heart rise to my throat. I closed my eyes

and shook my head in denial. "Was it someone high in the Guild ranks?"

"From what we have been able to find out, more like a group of 'someone's' who didn't like you or what you are becoming. We have been putting pieces together for a few days now, and we are still trying to confirm the information we are getting. Joseph didn't torture it out of anyone, Syn...they willingly gave you up."

I flinched and nodded, suddenly wanting to discuss anything but this. Someone had betrayed me, had betrayed the Guild. "We should get down there."

"I told you that I would protect you. Even if you don't need me to," he whispered, moving closer and pulling me against him. "Some things are worth protecting."

He reached his arms around me and pulled me close, before he sifted us together, effortlessly, just like he did everything else. I still couldn't believe I'd sifted to him. I moved away from him the moment we popped into the medical ward, and gasped. There were around thirty or more Fae in the room, and every one of them looked close to death.

"Oh...my God," I uttered, alarmed and shocked by the sight that met my eyes. As fast as I could blink, most of Ryder's men, healers, and several Fae I didn't recognize, were sifting in to try and help.

"We're going to need God, Danu, and Hecate to fix this," Ristan growled shaking his head as the woman he was helping quaked and cried out. "Ryder, they *are* dying. Eliran can't figure out what the hell is killing them."

I kneeled down, even though I wanted to run

from the stench of death in the room. I scanned the woman's skin and then focused on seeing past the normal human sight while tapping into my second sight. She was a sickly white color. "Where did you find her?"

"They were found dropped off in a field, like fucking trash. Asrian felt their pain and called me to him," Ristan answered. "From the best that I can tell, all the victims are from the compound that was attacked a few days ago. They used a mortar-like weapon full of powdered iron, so it became like an aerosol, and the Fae breathed it in. It made a lot of them sick, and quite a few were reported missing from the compound afterwards. Our healers cured the ones we found left behind, but these ones might be the missing Fae. It looks like they were caught and held for further torment by their attackers."

"Here," I said finding a discoloration on her skin. "Looks like silver was added maybe?"

"Silver my ass. That's full iron. Someone is injecting fucking iron into Fae creatures," Ryder said from beside me. I turned and met his gaze. "Someone is trying to figure out a natural way to kill us."

"That's what Mister Fancy Pants was saying back at my house."

"Who the fuck…the Shifter? His name is Gabe," Ryder finished, standing up and running his hand through his hair in frustration.

"Ryder, I can't fix them. Maybe if we had reached them sooner, but now it has taken over too much of their blood stream and is attacking their internal organs," Eliran said, coming in looking shocked and frustrated.

"That isn't what I need to hear right now," Ryder growled, running his hands through his hair in frustration once again.

"Flush it out," I offered.

"Our bodies are not the same as humans," Eliran explained.

"So, you can't flush it?"

"No, Syn, they can't just flush it, because our blood absorbs anything introduced to it. For most things, it is not a problem, as our metabolism can process it and move it along like waste. But iron will fuse to our cells and spread like a poison, understand?" Ryder snapped harshly, his face a mix of annoyance and helpless frustration as he watched them suffer.

I closed my eyes and nodded. I understood it. They were all dying and we couldn't save them. I was so fucking tired of feeling useless. I groaned in frustration, anger, and a not-so small amount of despair. I felt my magic roar to life, pulsing inside, boiling in my veins. Anger that mixed with magic was one of the worst combinations when you only had dark magic at hand. I tried pushing it down, but it refused to go.

"Ryder…" Ristan warned.

I could hear the blood pulsing inside of me, but, worse. I could feel the blood of every victim in the room. I closed my eyes and pulled it to me. I could smell the iron, thick and putrid. The power was consuming, dangerous, and the smell of their tainted blood was overwhelming. I wanted it gone.

I felt as if I'd left my body, and maybe I had. I felt as I had when I'd lost it the first time and been unable to control it, until Adam had balanced it. Only this time, I had control. I pulled at the tainted cells, wanting them gone.

I just needed them to live. I was tired of watching people die, finding dead bodies and feeling useless when I couldn't help them—always too late to save them. I opened my eyes and cried out as something poured through me, as if tiny molecules were tearing through me, but promptly propelled into the air where they vanished.

"Holy shit," Ryder said barely above a whisper.

It was as if I was able to pinpoint the cells within each victim and pull the iron to myself, then dispose of it through my body like a filter. I could hear them crying and whimpering. I sought those who were screaming and the closest to death, and tore the iron from them disposing of it effortlessly as if I was doing it methodically with my mind alone. When I'd cleaned the last Fae inside the room, I turned to find the three men staring at me with a mix of shock and confusion.

"Did she just clean their blood?" Ristan asked.

"No fucking clue," Ryder whispered, never taking his eyes from me.

"Look at the patients. Either she just killed them all, or she cured them," Eliran said softly, and stepped closer to Ryder as the world spun around me and became very dark.

Chapter
SEVEN

"Syn, it's okay. Look at me." Adam's voice penetrated the haze from which my mind had retreated to. I could see and hear, but everything was out of focus. A buzz still hummed inside my head. It was overwhelming, and the tanginess of blood filled my mouth, but it wasn't mine.

I met his turbulent green eyes, and winced at what I found. He'd changed. His brands pulsed thick black Celtic designs up his arms, and his eyes were changing to the double colored irises most Fae had. His hair was longer as well. "Adam," I whispered, afraid he would disappear if I spoke too loudly. I looked around to those still watching us inside the medical ward.

"I got you. I got you, Syn," he replied, licking his lips and pulling me against his naked chest. He was warm and smelled of wild magic. He whispered against my ear as he naturalized the magic I'd used. I wasn't even sure what I had done.

"The people?" I asked, wondering when I started considering the Fae as people.

"They are alive," Ryder said from behind us. "How did you do that, Syn?"

"Do what?" I swallowed and hugged Adam tighter against me. He'd be lucky if I let him go anytime soon.

"Whatever the fuck you did, Syn, you cured them."

I swallowed past the metallic tanginess on my tongue and shook my head. I hadn't done anything besides get angry. Had I?

"You cleaned their blood, Syn. I felt you doing it," Adam replied. I pulled away and looked at him, really looked at him. His brands were pulsing, and they weren't just on his arms…They were crawling up his neck to a few inches below his face, which had matured since I'd seen him last. He looked one hundred percent Fae now.

"Do I look that bad?" he asked coldly.

"No. No, Adam, you don't look bad. You just look different," I lied.

"Liar. I can feel your response. I can feel you, Syn. Don't fucking lie to me."

"I'm sorry, Adam. It's not bad. I'm just not used to you like this yet." I saw Dristan sift in and approach Ryder carefully.

"He got away, sorry," Dristan explained in a low voice, nodding toward Adam.

"How did he escape?" Ryder asked carefully, quietly, his eyes on me. "He should have been mindless with the effects of Transition still."

"He is very lucid. Claire told me that he has been extremely agitated a couple times since he entered Transition, but this time, he managed to sift. He's way past the time when most panic, so they didn't think he would need the collar anymore. I've never seen a Transitioning male sift from his feeding. Adam, though, was mid-feed and just disappeared."

"I can feel you, Synthia, inside of me. I need you to turn it off, just for a little while. I need to get you out of my head while I finish Transitioning," he sighed hesitantly, and I didn't blame him.

"I wish I knew how, Adam," I whispered and pulled away from him.

"I need you to figure it out, Syn. It's driving me insane. I want things I shouldn't, and I know you wouldn't want most of the things that are slipping into my mind right now," Adam whispered and shook his head. I could see that his eyes were pained before he turned on his heel and walked away from me. I watched his firm, well-defined back as he walked away. The brands on his back had created a Celtic cross covering the middle, etched into his skin with beautiful details. My best friend had Transitioned, and while I'd been oblivious, he'd become full Fae.

"He's adjusting, Synthia," Zahruk said softly from beside me.

"He's going to make it through this. He's strong," I replied, and turned to look straight at Ryder. "So a group is after the Fae and likes to torture and kill. Any idea on who could be responsible?" I asked, trying to put my mind back to the matter at hand, and off of my best friend who was, even now, walking away from me.

"No, but whoever they are, they won't live long. Attacks like this have been happening here and there all week long and seem to be increasing in the level of violence used. These lunatics are growing bolder. Those that you healed are resting now. When they wake up, we will question them," he replied, and nodded to Eliran who stepped up next to me.

"You cleaned their blood. Any idea how you did it? I'd like to be prepared if anymore come in showing the same symptoms."

"No idea how I did it, sorry," I whispered with my mind on Adam.

He nodded his head and turned to Ryder. "Vlad might have more knowledge on this. If she cured the blood, it's possible she could be Blood Fae."

"Blood Fae?" I asked, trying to recall everything I knew about them—it wasn't much though. The Blood King was reported to be very reclusive. The reports I had read back at the Guild said that he and his people were pretty much isolationists that kept themselves away from the rest of the High Fae castes, and were rarely spotted in this world.

"Interesting idea. Ristan, call Vlad and tell him to get his ass down here. Eliran, call me if any of the victims wake up and recall anything. Syn, you need to get some sleep."

"I can rest at home."

"You can rest here," Ryder argued.

"No, I am not staying here. I can rest just as well at home," I growled, feeling my body sway.

"Your two days are almost up. Need I spell it out for you?" Ryder whispered as his hands rested on my shoulders, sending shivers to my toes.

"Fine, but I'm not sleeping in your bedroom." Ryder's lips lifted into his cocky smile, and I wanted to wipe it off—with my lips. I shook my head. "I need sleep, remember?"

"I need to feed," he challenged.

"I don't have to sleep in your bed for that. It's a business arrangement. Not an invitation to use me whenever you want to."

He smiled wider as he nodded to the others in the room and grabbed my hand, sifting us back to his room.

"I said I wasn't sleeping in your room!"

"Who said anything about sleeping? You are going to feed me. Now, take off your clothes and get your ass in my bed."

"Ryder," I whispered, not sure how to respond to him verbally since my body already was silently. Heat pooled between my legs as my hips spread with readiness for him already.

"Take off your shorts, now," he challenged and stepped closer to me.

I exhaled and glared at him. "Fine, do it, feed from me. Just call me your fucking buffet." I bent down and pulled off my shorts and panties and then ripped off the borrowed shirt. I turned and walked back to the bed, feeling faint and tired with everything that had gone down today. I laid on my back and spread my legs, eyeing him.

I watched him remove his shirt and slowly unbutton each silver button of his jeans until his cock jutted out, hard and beautifully proud. He moved closer to the bed, slowly, each step making my mind wild with what I wanted from him. The fact that I shouldn't be doing this pressed against my mind. "Scoot up and get on your side."

I did as he said, moaning as his flesh pressed against my own. His erection pushed against my ass as he wrapped his arm around me. His mouth kissed up the side of my waist until he reached my cheek. "Thank you for saving my people today, Syn," he whispered and lay back down beside me. He pulled the covers over us and brought my body closer to his.

"I'm not even sure how I did it," I whispered, and pressed myself against him. I turned and looked up at him. "Ryder—"

"Syn, I'm barely managing to keep myself still. Turn-over and go to sleep before I forget you're tired and feed from that sweet, tight pussy."

I smiled and turned back to face away from him. This wasn't what I had expected, not from Ryder. This was calming, and even with his skin pressed against mine, I could still feel myself drifting to sleep against his warmth and protection.

"Sleep is good," I whispered through an overly dry mouth that wanted to taste his skin. I closed my eyes and settled against him until his arm came around me to rest over my chest, his fingers inches away from my already erect nipples. We were full of sexual tension. Being naked together wasn't going to end in sleeping.

"This isn't working," He growled against my ear, and I felt an electrical sizzle as fabric spread over my naked skin. He'd used his magic to dress us both. I looked down with a small gasp to see the baby blue silk nightgown he'd conjured.

"If you complain because I used my magic to stop something you didn't want from happening, I'll have you undressed, and my cock buried balls-deep inside your warmth, so fast it will make your head spin, Synthia."

I hid the smile that threatened to take over my face and replied, "I wasn't even thinking it."

He laughed huskily. "Liar," he whispered. "Go to sleep, Syn. The only thing protecting you right now is the fact that you are exhausted, and I can feel it through the brand. Make no mistake—if you weren't tired right now, we'd be fucking. Hard."

I swallowed and closed my eyes, pretending to be asleep. Eventually, it worked because I felt my body growing slack, even as Ryder's hand caressed my palm. For some reason when he touched my palm, I felt it to the very center of my being. It calmed and relaxed me until I drifted off to sleep, wrapped in the safety of his arms.

When I awoke, I was alone in the bed. It took a few minutes to remember where I was, and when it came back to me, I was up and out of the bed as if it was on fire. Husky laughter made me turn back around.

"Running from my bed won't save you, Syn. I put clothes in the bathroom that Ristan retrieved from the house. Get dressed; we have a meeting to attend."

I rubbed my eyes and tried to focus. "Meeting?"

"We are meeting with the Guild about what happened last night. All week long we have been dealing with crime scenes where a High Fae has been tortured to death. You remember what iron poisoning feels like—those Fae died in the most horrific way an immortal can die," he amended angrily, slipping from the shadows where he'd been leaning against the wall, watching me sleep. "Everyone is convening to share information. You wanted to know what is going on, Syn. Here is your chance."

"Mages?" I asked, but it came out silently, barely

above a whisper. I flinched as he moved closer. It was reflex from years of hating the Fae.

"Could be, or a group of human zealots. There are a lot of possibilities—none of them are good." He walked slowly to where I stood and pulled me against him. "You need to get over this fear you have, Syn. Transition is going to happen whether you want it to or not. I won't share you," he growled, lowering his face inches away from mine.

"Only until the contract is up. After that I'm a free agent, Ryder," I replied, and backed up a step.

He smiled, and licked his teeth. "What makes you think you will want anyone else after I bring you over to my world, Pet?"

I smiled and shook my head sadly. "Because you want to own me and, believe it or not, some women just don't want to be owned. I'm not sure when you were born, Ryder, but women these days like to be treated with respect. Wined and dined, not owned."

"What the fuck is that supposed to mean?" he snapped.

"Caveman much?" I snorted, and ended up laughing at his confused expression.

"Are you laughing at me?" He was annoyed, but his lips were twitching as if he was barely managing to keep his own laughter in.

"You should try dating. Get out more often, Ryder." I smirked and, before I knew what I had done, I'd stepped dangerously close to him.

"You should go shower, Syn, before I decide my hunger is more important right now," he said quietly as his eyes roved down the silky ensemble he'd conjured. I tried to step back away from him, but he was faster, his hands pulling me close, his mouth on mine immediately.

He pulled away, smiling. "This caveman just made your panties wet with a *kiss,* and you're the only item on the menu that I want to dine on."

A delicious shiver crept down my spine. "I'm *not* food."

"You're right, Syn. You are so much more…and I wouldn't want word getting out that I like to play with my food."

I pulled away. "It's not funny, and I'm not a fucking Fairy happy meal, Ryder!"

"A fucking Fairy happy meal…Go shower, Syn. I'm losing my patience and my tolerance for your sassy mouth. Unless you want me to find something for it to do, you had better get away from me."

"I thought you liked my sassy mouth," I replied with a smirk.

His eyes landed on my lips. "I do, and I like it better when it's busy…sucking or doing other things…" He let the words hang on the end of his tongue like silk.

I turned and basically ran to the bathroom, because something had happened to make him grow harsh and angry. He'd turned cold again, and I'd seen it in his eyes before I'd left him standing in the bedroom. He hated that I still flinched from him, but it was habit. I knew I was safe with him, and yet I was afraid that I was getting too close to him. I'd let my guard down, and he was reminding me of why it was dangerous to do so.

I slipped into his shower, not bothering to remove

the nightgown until I was behind the etched glass. I turned on the water and stepped beneath it, showering quickly so we could get down to the urgent problem. People were dying again, and if we could stop the killers, I was going to help.

I jumped as the shower door slammed open and Ryder walked inside naked, his smile all predator, with no trace of the gentle creature who'd held me all night and made me feel safe. I had just finished washing my hair, so I stepped back as he crowded me, until I felt the cool black slate tiles against my flesh.

"I'd run, little girl, before I decide the sight of your tight, wet body is too much for my puny little caveman brain to resist."

"Seriously, did you climb in here just to tell me that?" I challenged with a glint of anger in my eyes.

He was baiting me, provoking me—and it was working. His eyes glanced off to the side for a second, and he seemed to get more annoyed.

"Your boyfriend is waiting for you in the club," he snapped, and dismissed me as he grabbed the soap.

"Why do you even bother with a shower? That neat magic trick you do is a lot faster."

"Faster isn't always better, it's just more convenient. Sometimes, Syn, this feels…better on my flesh. Like other things, I like to feel it, and enjoy it." He smiled wickedly and ran his eyes down my body…slowly, hungrily.

With hungry eyes I watched him lather his body. His hands slow and methodical as they dipped lower to stroke his cock with the soap. I mewled as my eyes feasted on him until I heard his dangerous rumble that ripped my eyes back to his. "You're staring at my cock again, Syn. I need you to either get on your knees and fuck me with your mouth or get out."

He was a bastard. I pushed past him and tried to leave the shower, but his hand snaked out and pulled me back into the water with him. His eyes watched me expectantly, waiting. I pulled my arm away and turned to shove the door open, leaving him and his bi-polar ass behind. I was beginning to think that he did it on purpose, that he was trying to push me away.

Chapter
EIGHT

Adrian wouldn't even look at me, let alone talk to me. I didn't blame him for it. This was my mess, and I'd dragged him into it. I'd kissed him, unable to stop myself while trying to fight against something I couldn't control.

Everyone assembled in the mansion's foyer. The air was tense and no one was making eye contact with me except Ristan. The Demon was the only one who seemed to want to push Ryder's buttons. "Looking ravishing as always, Syn, or should I say *ravished*?" he waggled his eyebrows and smiled impishly.

"Neither?" I offered, feeling eyes lock onto my back.

"You slept in his bed. Interesting turn of events," he continued.

"Your point is? I'm assuming you have one." I growled.

"Oh, I don't have a point, not one I'd volunteer while you have Ryder's brand on you. That would be suicide." The last word was tossed in Adrian's direction.

"Oh, Ristan, I didn't know this was a show." I stepped closer to him, grabbed his shirt and pulled him close to my face. "You sure you don't want a taste?" I licked my lips and watched his eyes lower to my full mouth. "Just a little one?" I was teasing him, and he knew it.

"Tempting, Flower, but you won't find me losing my neck just for a kiss—it would have to be much more for me to take that leap."

I pushed him away, just in time to feel Ryder's eyes on my skin. I turned to catch him watching me with murder in his gaze. "Trying to catch flies with all that honey, Pet?"

"Just getting in some practice for when this brand comes off."

"Is that so?" he challenged, stepping closer to Ristan, the threat visibly clear.

I glared at him. "Blame me, Ryder, not the ones I'm trying to catch."

"Make no mistake, Synthia, I will blame all the guilty parties involved," he challenged me, crossing his arms over his chest.

Ryder's amber eyes scanned my face as if to say this wasn't over, and he was right. He didn't own me, and he damn well wasn't going to tell me who I could fuck if he planned on going all caveman every time I didn't swoon at his feet. I was adapting to the best of my abilities.

I smirked at him, knowing he'd witnessed my display of teasing Ristan.

"Fucking try me, little girl," he growled, the rattling noise returning from deep inside his chest.

I blinked, seeing something shining from within his eyes, as if something besides the man, was staring back at me.

"Should I get on my knees and beg, Ryder? Would that please you?" I asked, feeling sweat bead on the back of my neck. I didn't know why I was trying to antagonize him. Only that I was, and I couldn't seem to stop myself.

"I promise to make you beg, later. In the meantime, try keeping that fucking snarky mouth to yourself, Pet," he growled in warning.

"Make me," I shot back.

When Ryder got pissed, I could see something beneath his cool façade. He was always in control—except around me. And I wanted to know what it was he was hiding. He moved in closer, the rattle intensifying. "You don't want to challenge me. I like to win. I like to play games, just so I *can* win."

I shivered and pulled away from him. "Promises, promises, Ryder," I taunted him before I turned to meet his men's shocked faces. "What?" I barked, fed up with the testosterone level in the mansion.

"We are gathering and meeting your Guild at the Darklands," Ryder said, holding out his hand for me.

"I can sift by myself!" I snapped.

What the hell was wrong with me? I was irritated, and my skin felt on fire. I blinked and shook my head, and ended up throwing out my arms and holding onto Ryder for support as I lost my balance. He scanned my face and narrowed his eyes on me. "What's wrong, Syn?"

"I'm fine. Just a little dizzy. It's probably from not

eating today."

"Sift then," he said, stepping back, while everyone in the room watched us. I closed my eyes and imagined his club, but my mind latched onto Ryder and I didn't move. I waited for the weightless feeling I'd experienced in his shower, when I'd sifted to him before. Nothing happened. I snorted and shook my head and tried again.

This time the weightlessness came and I smiled, until I hit something hard and bounced off of it to the sounds of laughter and snorts. I opened my eyes and looked up from where I sat on the floor of the foyer—at his feet. "I sifted," I said proud of myself, even if I had only sifted to Ryder.

"That's twice in one day you landed at my feet, Synthia. I think I preferred the first time in my shower," Ryder replied wickedly, watching me as his words brought heat to my cheeks.

Adrian gave an angry grumble next to Vlad, who was quick to check his attitude. "That's enough, Adrian."

I swallowed past the pinch of regret and looked up to Ryder, who held his hand out. I slapped it away and got to my feet, closing my eyes. I sifted again and, this time, the entire room erupted into laughter with the exception of mine, Ryder's, and Adrian's. I felt hot tears pushing against my eyes, but I held them in check as I climbed off my ass again.

I ground my teeth together and held out my hand for Ryder to sift me. He shook his head and took it, pulling me in close against himself. "Sifting takes time," he whispered close to my ear, before he sifted us inside his elegant club. It looked the same as it did before the bomb had gone off and killed seventeen

Fae. Ryder had blamed it on my Guild, but, in the end, I'd proven it wasn't and prevented a bloody war.

"Thanks," I said when I had my bearings, and tried to step away from his touch.

"It's sexy, Syn," he whispered, refusing to move away from me as I tried to put distance between us.

"What's sexy?" I asked, even though I was afraid to know the answer.

"That every time you sift, you land at my feet." He smirked and turned, walking away as he left me with my mouth hanging open.

I looked around the club. It looked so different during the daylight hours when it was closed. It was still elegant, but something was missing without the music, flashing lights, and partying people.

I rubbed the back of my neck and found it drenched in sweat. Maybe I had picked up a flu bug somewhere. It would be just my luck and, considering I was supposed to be immune to everything, getting sick would just be the icing on the cake.

"You look like you could use a drink," Vlad said from behind me. I turned and looked into his beautiful silver eyes. He led me over to the bar while the rest of Ryder's group fanned out to the tables to meet with a few of the Fae that were waiting for them. I didn't recognize any of these Fae.

"Is Adrian okay?" I blurted anxiously, since I felt I'd been the one to get him beaten up by Ryder. I slipped onto one of the bar stools, while Vlad made his way behind the bar.

"He's tough. Some lessons have to be driven home. He knew you were off limits. He made a choice, and that falls on his shoulders—not yours."

"I kissed him, Vlad, he didn't kiss me," I argued.

"So you did, but he didn't pull away from you. He took it further by placing his hands on you when he knew better. That makes it his fault. He's been warned against doing it many times."

"Contract or not, Vlad, I'm not a piece of property, and I'm not some fucking animal that Ryder can collar and claim as his own. He had no right to brand me."

"Be that as it may, Syn, he did, and it can't be undone unless he removes it. Drink? Gin and tonic right?" Vlad said, but he had already turned and was diving into the endless bottles behind the bar.

"Please, make it strong," I mumbled, turning away from Vlad to take in everyone who was in the bar. I was surprised to find Alden sitting further down the bar by himself, watching me carefully with a sad smile. He was surrounded by a few Guild-issued guards who stood just far enough away to give him a little breathing room.

Alden nodded and started towards me, settling on the seat next to me as his elite guards took standing positions close enough to protect him, but again far enough away to give him some semblance of privacy.

"We gotta stop meeting like this," I said with a quirky smile.

"This one is bad not saying the last one wasn't," he rushed the last words in when I glared and opened my mouth to say just what he had. "This one looks like it was more than likely radicals. Hate crimes are unstable and unpredictable. I'm relieved to know you are with him." Alden nodded in Ryder's direction and continued. "He won't let anything happen to you.

The National Guild in Washington D.C. wants us to assist the Prince on this one. I told them I had my best working side by side with him, Synthia."

"Did you tell them I was your best?" I looked right at him and saw his hesitation. "Figures," I said. "Wouldn't want them to know I'm on the job, anyway."

Not that I had known I was.

"Are you okay, Synthia?" Alden asked when I wiped the sweat from my forehead and neck yet again.

"I'm fine," I growled.

"Don't use that word on me, girl. I taught you to say it, and I know you better than you think I do. You're sweating profusely, Synthia Raine." He held his hand up to my cheek and swore. "You're burning up."

"I'm fine, just coming down with something," I snapped, tired of being told what I was and wasn't.

"Drink this, Syn. It might help," Vlad said setting the glass down on a napkin and pushing it closer to me. I accepted it and threw back the glass, drinking it all, and enjoyed the burn as the alcohol slid down my throat.

"Another one," I said, sliding my tongue over my teeth.

"Your wish is my command," Vlad said, eyeing me carefully before looking past me to where Ryder sat with his men, poring over what I assumed were crime scene pictures. Vlad quickly made another drink and pushed it to the place where the empty glass still sat. "Syn, when you cured those people earlier— what did it feel like?" Vlad asked, leaning against the bar and using his folded forearm for support on the glossy surface.

"I don't remember. I just remember being pissed that we couldn't help them. I was pissed at feeling useless, and was tired of death. It's stupid. I don't understand why someone would do that to another being—even if they are Fae. I'm tired of people pretending to be God and deciding to end someone else's life, just because they can!" I was shouting, and the entire bar had gone silent. I slumped down and shook my head—this wasn't me. Normally I could control myself better.

"The blood called to you?" Vlad continued, as if I hadn't just had a mini-meltdown.

"I don't know. I just knew I could do it. Knew if I removed the iron they would live, or hoped they would, anyway. I have no idea how, or why I did it, Vlad, I only know that being helpless isn't something I like or will accept."

"You removed the iron. You saved everyone in that room, Syn. My question is—did you *feel* the need to taste it?"

"You mean did I want to rip into their necks and suck the blood?" I narrowed my eyes on his silver ones.

"Something like that, yes."

"No, I'm not a vampire." *Ewww*....

"But, you cleaned Fae of iron—from their *blood*. And you seem to have won over Ryder's men by doing so." He replied, reaching over for the empty glass, before tipping his head to where Sinjinn sat, smiling at me invitingly. Sinjinn was another of the men who was always close at Ryder's side.

"And?" I blinked at Sinjinn and shook my head.

"And that's not an easy feat. They are loyal to one and one alone. Yet, you have them looking at you with respect now."

"I'm supposed to care?" I snapped, feeling my head swim as heat seemed to pool into one central location, and it was pissing me off.

"Syn, are you okay?" Vlad asked cautiously.

"I'm fine, just feel weird."

"Feverish?" he questioned, while handing me yet another drink. I nodded, and he shook his head and looked back to where Ryder was sitting.

I shook my head and grabbed the glass from the bar. I walked to where Ryder was sitting with a few of his men and a few Fae I hadn't met yet. Heat blossomed from my core and flared through me again, making me halt dizzily for a moment. I ignored the heated looks I got when I interrupted the conversation by placing my glass on his table. Ryder's nostrils flared as his eyes locked with mine and lowered, sliding lustfully down my body. "Like it?" I purred and enjoyed the shock in his eyes as they flew back up to meet mine.

"Syn, are you feeling okay?" he asked, coming up to stand beside me. His eyes scanned the men in the club, who were all now looking at me. I felt sexual and erotic. His eyes lit up as he took me in.

"I feel fine. Why does everyone keep asking that?" I replied in a raspy voice.

"You're sweating, and you look…"

"Hot?" I asked, smiling impishly.

"Sick." He didn't agree with me, which made me tilt my head awkwardly.

"I'm on fire," I whispered and closed my eyes, feeling the room tilt around me.

"Sinjinn, go get Eliran," Ryder mumbled from where he stood next to me as his eyes took me in carefully, seductively.

"I feel amazing," I said reaching for him and pulling him closer to my body.

"Syn..." Ryder warned as he scanned the club. "Fucking hell, woman," his voice trembled.

I turned my heated face around and found every male in the place watching me with lustful looks— well, with the exception of Alden and his guards. They just looked really confused, unsure of what was happening. I felt like the sexiest bitch on the planet. Fucking hell was right...

"Ryder..." I growled huskily, not sure if I wanted to throw him on the table and ride him like a fucking horse, or curl into the fetal position and cry. I was in Transition.

"Syn, don't fucking move. Just hold still and stop rubbing your..." His eyes dropped down to my hand, and I followed his gaze as his words trailed off. I was grinding myself on my own hand. What the hell was wrong with me?

Ryder stepped closer to me, his eyes glowing golden amber before the thick lines of obsidian swallowed them. "I claim you, Syn. Agree?" His voice almost sounded strangled.

When I didn't agree, he growled a sound so inhuman that I found myself intrigued, and I wanted to see what was inside of him; to see the layers of this creature bared before me. I licked my lips and stepped closer. "I'm so hungry, Ryder. Help me."

"Dammit, Synthia, focus," Ryder pleaded. "Don't make me fight my own men. You have to choose, them or me. Now," his voice softened.

His men? The thirteen hard-bodied men that currently were surrounding me? Ooh, and there were a few other Fae closing in as well. Oh, fuck yeah. That would be a ride… I purred, throatily, considering it. I could take them—all of them. I closed my eyes and inhaled the musky masculine scent of the Fae around me. All were now throwing some serious fuck-me vibes my way. I wanted them all and, I wanted them now. My inner naughty girl was telling me to choose them, while, somewhere deep inside I fought against the overwhelming rush of hormones that were trying to control me.

"Ryder…" I couldn't get more than his name out.

"Say it," he snarled and stepped closer to me.

I opened my eyes and stepped away from him. I could hear the others growling and pushing past each other, trying to get closer to me. I growled, hungrily, wanting each and every one of them to take a turn. I wanted to feed from them all. I shook my head, trying to dispel the things running through it. He placed his hands on my shoulders and tugged me close to himself.

"Pet, listen to me very carefully. I won't force you to choose me. But I won't allow my men to take you. They will hate themselves afterwards. Do you understand what I'm saying?" Ryder was talking, but it wasn't penetrating inside my brain.

I wanted sex, and I didn't care who fucked me right now. I shook my head. That wasn't right. I shouldn't think like that. I wiped my face with my hands and moaned as I felt the touch of my skin. I shook my head harder and met his eyes, black and deadly.

My Ryder.

I reached out, and my vision swam and doubled. Ooh! Two Ryder's...hot damn. "I want you both," I whispered through my dry mouth. Two Ryder's—I'd won the fucking lottery! Jackpot baby.

"Both of us? Both of *who*, Syn?"

"I want both of *you*, Ryder!" I replied, already trying to remove some of my clothes.

"Fuck," he gritted out, scrubbing his hands over his face. He pulled me against himself and struggled to gain control of my hands. I didn't understand why he wanted me to stop. Didn't he want me naked? "Choose, or I'm going to break my own fucking rule with you, Syn. I'll fuck you right in front of them and show them who you belong to."

The males in the room growled with approval, and my inner naughty girl smiled. My hips flared as moisture pooled between my legs. "I want you to feed me, Ryder, both of you."

"Syn, there is only *one* of me."

"So you say, but I don't think the Gods would be so cruel to only make one of you, when two could be so much fun."

His lips jerked up at the corners of his mouth. "You couldn't handle two of me, Pet. You can hardly take me as is. You need to decide, before you start a fucking riot."

I smiled and bit softly into his neck, enjoying the animal-like rumble that vibrated through him. "Woman, you are going to be the death of me," he whispered and grabbed my hair to pull my face back.

"I want you, Ryder."

I blinked as his eyes closed in relief, his forehead leaning against mine as he released my hair. "Say it louder so they can hear you, Pet."

"I choose you," I growled hungrily and closed my eyes, feeling the world spin around me as I did so. When I opened them again, I was standing across the room from Ryder. Zahruk was smiling down at me with something more in his eyes than should have been there. Had I just sifted? *Without* landing at Ryder's feet?

"I say we take turns; she can handle it. One of us at a time, at first, then both. Until she's so full of cock, she knows nothing but the need to ride it harder."

I blinked and shook my head, trying to find Ryder.

"Z," Ryder warned.

"Ryder, she's woman enough to fuck us all. I want my cock inside of her at least once before tonight is over."

"Not going to happen, brother. She's *mine*. She *chose* me."

"I want her," Sinjinn said, sifting back in.

"I want her as well," Savlian said, smiling wickedly as he strolled even closer.

I was starting to get whiplash, along with the distinct feeling that I should have sifted my ass to safety because it was in danger of being violated. I turned, watching Ristan stroll up with a smile on his lips.

"I should have made popcorn for this shit. It's about to get real in this bitch, *finally*," he said and slid into one of the booths close to Ryder.

"Ristan…are you good?" Ryder asked with marked strain on his face.

"By good, you mean I don't want to drive my cock inside the petals of my little Flower?"

Ryder nodded.

"Yeah, I'm good. No intense need to fuck her. *Yet*."

"Good. Make sure they don't kill themselves then. When they come around, send them out of here. You and Z are in charge. Let me know if there are any leads or if anything comes up—especially from the healers. We stay on top of this. I need to be kept in the loop." Ristan snorted at that statement.

"Like you'll be in any condition to attend to anything over the next couple of days," he smirked.

Ryder's eyes narrowed angrily at Ristan. "You and Z know what to do for the time being. Send Asrian and Sinjinn to watch the field, in case those assholes come back to drop off any more wounded. Have them trade off with Cailean and Aodhan, if need be. This is a scouting mission only. No one is to take unnecessary chances without me present. If you find any more wounded or dead Fae, you are to notify me at once. I need to know right away if anything happens. These are our people dying, and it is our job to protect them if we can. Figure something out for the rest of them to do to keep busy, Vlad?" Ryder asked as I moved closer to him, watching the men do the same.

They were stalking me; I moved, and they all followed. I smiled and continued to move, watching as they followed me like a pack of wolves cornering prey. I giggled like a drunken school girl, even as Ryder shook his head.

"Ryder...you need to get her and that fucking sweet musky scent the fuck out of here. I only have so much fucking restraint, Man!" Vlad growled from the bar where his fingers were white from holding himself in place.

"Vlad," Ryder sighed. "You liaise with the Guild if need be."

Others were grabbing themselves in inappropriate places with sweat beading on their foreheads and wild looks on their faces, reminding me of the night of the Wild Hunt. Adrian was one of them, and the pain in his vivid blue eyes floored me. Ryder noticed it as well and pulled me closer.

"They will be all right once I get you out of here, Synthia. It is a natural instinct for us to react when a woman goes into Transition...This is why I wanted you close to me."

"Take me out of here if I'm hurting them," I whispered, feeling another wave of heat as it started to spike inside of me. He smiled and pulled me closer as we started towards the elevators that were no longer guarded. The guards stationed near the elevators hadn't been immune to me either and were currently straining to stay upright against the wall, away from their post, and had such pain and longing in their eyes that I had to look away from them.

Chapter
NINE

We took the elevator down several floors below the club and quietly exited out into a fairly dark hallway. We passed several doors and stopped before one that was fairly ornate and had wards in a beautiful, elegant script above the door frame, sealing the room. Ryder passed his hand over them to disable the wards, and the door popped open. He gave me a small smile and motioned for me to pass through into the darkened room. I peered around the room and couldn't see anything—no furniture, just a blank, dark room. He waited until the door closed before he turned to look down at me. His eyes were glowing from his hunger, the gold having finally returned to them. He stepped closer as I took an involuntary step backwards.

"Second guessing your choice, Pet?" he smirked, his body dripping with sexual confidence.

"No," I said honestly. I had no doubt that Ryder was the right man to fuck me silly, or that he'd get the job done. He'd save me from myself, if need be.

"Looks like I'm getting that little fucking Fairy happy meal after all," he smiled impishly as he watched me.

"I ache everywhere," I whimpered, ignoring his comment as another wave of blazing heat shot through my body.

He sniffed, and licked his teeth hungrily. "I'm going to enjoy this."

"We need some ground rules," I shot back at him as the butterflies began to fight inside my stomach.

"No rules. Not for this—not that kind, at least. You won't be able to follow them soon anyway." He turned and passed his hand just above the door frame to set the wards on this side of the door.

"Ryder," I whined as my hands swept down, and ran over my wet, sleek heat. Ryder moved in closer to me and pulled me into his arms, resting his head on top of mine. This was pretty effective for helping me keep my hands to myself.

"I need to make sure you understand what is about to happen to you. Do you remember how out of control Adam seemed to be when he attacked you? By that point, he was in full Transition. If my men hadn't stopped him, there's a very good chance that he could have killed you. Because you hadn't Transitioned yet, he would have fed until he'd drained you of soul and mind, leaving nothing of you when he was finished. You're going to be the same way soon."

I shivered and nodded. That part, I knew. "I won't hurt you though, right?" I asked.

"No. I will have to restrain you at first to make sure you don't hurt either of us. I also need you to answer something for me honestly. Do you trust me in this room?"

"What's that got to do with anything?" I mumbled, unsure where he was going with it.

"I want to dominate you. That need doesn't ever stop for me when I am around you. Here and now, though, you will need me to be gentle. Soon, you will be the one trying to dominate me. You're going to only have one thing on your mind, Pet, and that's the need to feed. I need to know if you trust me, Synthia."

I shivered at the intensity of heat in his eyes. The problem wasn't that I didn't trust him; I did. Well, inside this room I did. Outside, we were still shady. "In this room," I replied watching his lips tensed in wait for my answer. "I trust you, Ryder, in this room."

His lips turned up at the corners, and it made my heart flip in my chest. This beautiful creature was about to bring me over to his world, to our world. I watched as he ran his hands through his hair and nodded.

"Will you let me have control of your body? Will you let me control your pleasure, and rule it for Transition?" he asked as he stepped closer.

"Define control," I demanded through trembling lips.

He gave me a lopsided grin. "It's almost the full moon outside, Pet. In Faery, we call it the Fae Moon, because it creates a fever of hunger in each one of us that fights to be let loose. This makes sex off the charts for our race, and is going to add to your Transition. In order for me to control your pleasure, I need to be in full control of your body—at least until you go mindless, at that point you will do anything to get what you want, and need."

I shivered and shook my head. I didn't want to become a mindless fuck machine. It was bad enough that my entire life had been flipped upside down, but now I was going to go crazy and Ryder was more than willing to become my victim. "You have it, Ryder, for Transition only."

"Good enough for me," he whispered and stepped closer to me. My mind was running different scenarios, overburdened with what was coming, and what was going to happen soon. I felt my eyes burn as tears fought to push through. "Don't be afraid, Syn," he whispered and smiled reassuringly. "We are good together. I promise not to hurt you, or to let you hurt me. I'll keep you safe, I promise."

His thumb wiped away the tears, and he kissed me. I moaned hungrily against his mouth. I tried to stop the sob, but it was out before I could. He pulled me against himself until he cradled my head against his well-defined chest. "I got you. You're safe."

"I can't do this," I cried softly, trying to push the weakness away. This wasn't just about Transition. It was what I would be afterwards.

"Look at me," Ryder whispered thickly.

I met his molten gaze, and gasped at the strength I found there. He stood at arm's length, giving me room to panic if I decided to. I was afraid of what I was becoming. He could see it, as he saw everything, as if he was in sync with my emotions and mind.

"It's okay to panic if you need to, Synthia. I understand. You were not given a lot of time to come to terms with what you are. Most are born knowing what they are, and accept what they will go through."

"I am not panicking. I don't panic. Why would I panic?" *Shit! I was so-o-o panicking!*

He snorted, but the grin that lifted his full mouth told me he was not mocking me. I probably would have laughed at myself, if not for the dire situation.

"Of course you don't. You're Synthia and, from what I have seen, you can handle pretty much anything that gets thrown at you."

"What do we do now?" I asked lamely, letting the fear show in my eyes.

"Well, you can get on the bed and start, or I can help you get there. Soon, your hunger will take over, and you will need to feed. Right now, I'm trying to give you choices so that this is as easy for you as it can be," he said calmly, bringing his arms up behind his head and locking his fingers together. He shook his head and smiled gently, his muscles straining against his cotton shirt. "I'm here to help you, Synthia, not hurt you. This isn't something you can do alone, or even control. It's going to happen whether you want it to or not."

Something about Ryder and the word "bed" coming from his lips made my lady parts get all wet. I groaned. "Great, so I'm going to turn into the horny version of Cookie Monster?" I squeaked, trying to lighten the sober mood.

He smiled and kissed my forehead. "Tell me when you're ready for me. Right now, you smell like the most exotic drug, and I'm a fucking addict. Understand?" he replied hoarsely.

"Am I going to be like Adam was?" I asked, not bothering to hide the fear in my eyes or voice from him.

"I have no idea, but I'm all for you forcing my cock into every place it will go." He wiggled his eyebrows even as I blanched.

"Seriously, who says shit like that at a time like this?" I asked out loud, but he just laughed. The sound was strangely comforting.

"Transition isn't something that happens a lot anymore. Our people struggle to keep their children alive. Often they do not survive infancy, much less make it as far as Transition. Those Fae upstairs, they were all willing to fight just to prove they were strong enough to feed you—it's twisted into the fiber or our being, and branded into our souls. No female in Transition should ever suffer. It's the greatest gift a male of the race can ever receive from a woman."

"And you laid claim to mine. Isn't that kind of like cheating?" I asked, lifting a brow pointedly.

"Pet, I'm not above admitting to the fact that I cheated to get what I want. I want you right now, and that should scare the fuck out of you. I have never wanted anything as badly as I want to be buried inside of you. Yes, I cheated, and yes, you agreed. You might hate me after this, but I promise to fuck you until you need no other man inside of you. I promise to be what you need right now, and more. By the time I am done with you, I will know you inside and out, and you will know how absolute pleasure feels."

"What are you, Ryder?" I asked, lifting my eyes to meet his.

"I'm the one who is going to bring you into my world, Syn, into *our* world. I'm the one who's going to make you scream my name, very soon."

I rolled my head on my neck. Sweat was beading on my forehead, and the nape of my neck was wet with it too. I felt on fire, and it scared me. I was changing. My pulse was spiking as blood hummed inside my head, my ears listening astutely to the beat of it. It caused my body to sway along to the beat seductively. I must have closed my eyes at some time during the overwhelming sensations, because a throaty growl made me open them.

Ryder was standing in front of me. His shirt had been removed, and he was holding a thin silver necklace in his hands that looked somewhat like an elegant collar. His eyes searched mine for an answer. "It's beginning. Can you feel the call of it?" he asked, watching me closely.

"I'm afraid," I repeated my earlier words. "I'm afraid of what will happen. I'm afraid that I won't remember it."

"I'll walk you through every moment of it, if that is what you want when you come through it." He offered.

"What if I turn into a monster?" I asked, failing to keep the hesitation from my voice. I could turn into anything, and knowing I could wake up and be part of the Horde, was mind boggling.

"You won't be a monster, and if you do change into one—you will still be mine. Personally, I like a woman with horns and a sexy little tail."

"I think I have a fever," I replied lamely, not wanting to even consider the fact of being a monster.

He smiled roguishly, his lips kicking up in the corners as he stepped forward. "I need to get this on you before you get further into the Transition. This will keep you from sifting out. The chains on the bed will allow you to move, for now, but they will allow me to keep my distance if need be."

"So, you can torture me by refusing to give me what I need?" I asked, confused.

"Oh, Pet, I plan to feed you everything you need, and much, much more. I'm not going to make you hurt, or torture you in any way…unless it adds to your pleasure," he grinned knowingly as he bent over, placing my nose entirely too close to his masculine scent. I growled hungrily and felt something pushing inside of me, trying to get out.

As he secured the collar around my neck, I felt a strong pulse of magic swirl through the room, and a candle flared to life. Then two, three, and five—then more as they lit up, all in ornate holders set into the walls at different points around the room. It created a shadowed effect. I scanned the room carefully, my eyes landing on the bed. It was big enough to fit several people on it, just like the rest of the beds I had begun to associate Ryder with. However, this one had a modern feel with its thick, black metal frame surrounding the mattress and four rail-like posts that rose above the bed several feet, bending to a graceful curve that ended in a square black rail canopy that was slightly smaller than the mattress. The canopy was topped with small brass spires where it met each post. Black silk sheets covered the mattress, and an amazing supply of pillows was stacked in front of the headboard. Attached to each post were long, silver chains that were secured to sturdy looking thick, black leather cuffs.

Vases filled with red and white roses, were set randomly around the room. I looked at him and caught a hint of unease, as if this wasn't something he did often—if ever. I took it in slowly, knowing I'd soon be unable to appreciate the beauty. Ryder cleared his throat a little.

"Transition only happens once, Pet. I believe you said that women liked to be—what was it you said—wined and dined?" I had to smile at the thoughtfulness of Ryder trying to set me at ease with everything that was going to happen. It was so out of character for him, and, yet, it tugged at my heart that he was trying.

"Thank you," I said softly, at a loss for anything

else to say.

I was running out of time, losing a battle with whatever was inside of me. I walked slowly towards the bed. I wanted it to be my own choice to be chained—not because I *had* to be, but because I *wanted* to be. I bent low on the black sheets and crawled across them until I was in the middle of the bed.

"Okay, Fairy, let's do this." My voice sounded a bit shaky.

"Fairy is it?" he asked, lifting a single brow.

"Yup," I whispered.

He smiled, and sifted. He reappeared between my legs, his huge frame holding mine down gently. He sank further into the mattress with a naughty grin on his mouth. "Scared?" he asked, watching me tremble. I didn't need to answer him. He could see it in the way my lip quivered, and the way my body trembled with the unknown. He reached over and gently secured one wrist with a thick leather cuff, and then did the other one. The chains attached to the cuffs jangled a bit, which startled me, but sent a coil of heat pooling to my core. I was at his mercy, and he had none—not in bed, at least.

"You are coming into our world not knowing very much about us, and for that, I am sorry," he said softly. "As I promised in the contract, I will try to teach you what I can. For now, I will let you in on something that the Fae do not talk about and the humans would love to know of, for sure. Do you know why humans choose to take Fae to their beds, Synthia?"

I shook my head. I'd felt it up close and personal, but I did not truly understand what the Fae did to them to make humans crave them so badly.

"Because we can feel their need—we can sense what they want, before they even know it themselves. We can hear the tempo of their hearts as they increase, beating with need and fear of the unknown. We can smell the wetness between their thighs; know when they are ready to be fucked, or when they need more pleasure to get there. Our abilities let us know right where to touch them, and what they need the most. We can feel the orgasm as it builds, as it grows. We can prevent it from happening multiple times, creating one that will shatter their entire world. We can choose to take their souls, or feed it back to them. Our tongues have saliva ducts that are a bit different from humans. Our saliva secretes liquid that turns their most sensitive places to pleasure zones unlike anything they will ever know again. That's why humans seek us out and keep coming back."

Well holy fuck buckets!

"And the multiple orgasms? How do you manage to give those so easily?" I asked, growing more curious as his voice continued soothingly.

"We can give those at will. I don't even have to touch you to fuck you. I only have to make you think I am. That day in my bedroom when I made you come, I never left the door. I only projected an image to your mind that said I had. I watched your sweet body gyrate from orgasm, and I have never wanted to be buried inside someone more than I did at that moment. *You* make me lose control."

I swallowed at the memory of that day in his room. It seemed almost a lifetime ago now, when in fact, only a little time had passed. I'd been positive he'd been lying over me, making my body betray me. "Can all Fae do that?" I asked carefully as I lowered my eyes to his mouth.

"Not all can," he whispered, before he lowered his mouth and claimed my bottom lip between his teeth sensually. I felt heat flush through my entire frame at the connection. "I'm better at it than anyone else I know." He released my lip, and I moaned. The feel of his heated flesh over mine was intoxicating.

I could feel the skin that he'd made sensitive. He smiled as his brands lit up, until thick black swirling patterns covered his arms. He reached over me as he sat up on his knees. I watched him pull on the length of chain and double check one cuff, and then the other, carefully. The cool rush of air and silk on my skin was refreshing as he removed my clothing with a single thought.

I was chained and exposed to him. I wasn't afraid, though I knew I should have been. Something was buzzing inside my ears, and I closed my eyes against it, as if that would help. The stars that erupted behind my eyelids failed to help as perspiration beaded at the base of my neck. This was it; there would be no going back now. I was standing at a crossroad; one that would change me forever. On one side, I was human, and on the other, I was what I'd hated the most not too long ago—Fae. And I was staring it down, knowing I would lose this fight. I'd be full Fae when I reached the other side.

Chapter
TEN

His eyes lit up as he lowered his mouth to my body. "I'm going to taste every inch of you, Synthia," he half growled, half purred.

"Is that a threat, or a promise?" I asked, watching his mouth as he swirled his tongue around my oversensitive nipples.

He laughed, and I felt it to my bones. He was beautiful, and his sudden gentleness was something I hadn't expected from him. It was such a change from his normal gruff, alpha self. His tongue darted out to dip into my navel. I cried out as the wet, hot heat made my body buck with need.

"The first orgasm you will have is going to be hard, fast, and intense. It might scare you. Your body is going to go into overdrive, and your mind is going to go with it. Just remember that I'm here with you, and I won't let anything bad happen."

"Um, can you stop the Transition?" I joked, which caused his lips to twist into a blinding smile.

"Funny girl, let's see if you find this funny shall we?" he asked as he lifted my hips until my core was bared before him.

I swallowed and whimpered as his mouth landed on my wet, slick heat. He growled as his tongue came out and lapped lavishly at the juices his words had caused. "Oh God, right there. Don't stop, Ryder," I cried as he smiled against me. He growled as he devoured me, the vibration sending the climax to impending readiness. I felt it, the vibration against my core as he growled hungrily against my heated flesh.

I felt his magic pulsing through the room, wafting over my skin as I felt something filling me where his mouth was. I groaned as fullness filled me until I could take no more. I rocked my hips in his hands, pressing myself harder against his mouth as he rumbled with approval. The storm that was building was scary; the intensity was sizzling my insides, turning me inside out until my body shook from it.

When I exploded, it was anything but normal. One minute Ryder had been between my legs, and the next he was pinned to the bed beneath me. I'm not sure who was more shocked, him or me. When had he allowed the chains to loosen? How had I missed him doing so, and why the heck did I care? I felt my mind going empty as I watched him hungrily, my entire body still riding the wave of desire he had created.

"Let her out to play, Synthia, I can handle her." He spoke low, but his voice was coming out in layers.

"You are mine." Yeah, that slipped out of my mouth in the same multilayered voice. My eyes narrowed as the room was shut out, and my attention centered on Ryder and his movements, right down to his heart beating in his carotid artery. I could see everything, and yet focusing wasn't happening for me.

I could smell his need, and knew what he wanted. I lowered my mouth, but didn't touch him. In this state, I could smell his rich masculinity, addictive and erotic. I sniffed him and smiled. No freaking wonder he knew what I was feeling and what I needed.

I could smell him right down to the salty bead of pre-come on the tip of his cock. I whined softly, needing to know every inch of him, every curve of his body. I watched his eyes turn black until it swallowed the gold. "I'm going to enjoy this," I repeated his words from earlier back to him.

"Take what you need, Pet."

"Oh, I plan to."

I laughed, enjoying the sound of my voice as it resonated off the walls and came back to me. I ran my fingers through his hair, testing the silk of it as I fisted my hands in the thick strands. I lowered my mouth and flicked his lips with my tongue. He groaned his response and, before I could blink, I was down, pinned against the bed once again.

"You are fucking amazingly beautiful," he whispered as his pants melted off and he parted my legs with his. He entered me slowly, his eyes locked with mine. I needed him to move fast, and hard. He didn't though; instead, he was slow and gentle as he watched my face and the emotions splayed across them. "That's it," he said when I started moving with him slowly.

His hands lowered until he cradled my face, his mouth locked with mine, and together we moaned until the second orgasm ripped through us both. He smiled against my mouth as he continued to move inside of me, his cock already growing with need again.

"What's your name?" he asked carefully between his mouth kissing and nipping my lips hungrily.

"I'm Syn, and you're Ryder. You're my fucking Fairy, and you're wrong," I purred throatily.

"Why?" he inquired, sinking further inside of me.

"You're *my* fucking Fairy happy meal," I smiled, and pulled at his soul. He watched me as I tried to pull it out and into my own body. He only allowed me to take a sliver of it, but what he allowed was beautiful—it tasted pure.

"You think you are in control, Synthia?" He shook his head, and pulled at mine back. I felt it as he fed me more of his, as he took small pieces of mine. The beauty of his soul as it mingled against mine was overwhelming and intoxicating. I was shocked he had allowed it, and pleased that he had let me in, let me see it. I released his, and felt as he pulled at mine with brutal force. I felt empty and cold—lifeless.

"What's your name, Syn?"

Hot tears pushed at my eyes. I was almost completely empty and blank inside. He'd left me just enough so I knew what was happening, and that he was in control. He wanted to show me what I could do, and I understood it, but I didn't like it. The panic of what had happened to my mother came rushing back. He felt it as well and quickly stopped.

He held my soul only a moment, and then he started feeding it back to me, but he fed it back to me slowly, erotically. I felt his soul as it searched mine inside of me, until I was once again completely whole. He was showing me the difference between taking ruthlessly and giving while feeding. He was also showing me the power he held right now. The power I would soon hold. He was showing me everything I feared about being Fae, and I was glad he'd showed me this when he didn't have to.

"What is your name?" he asked gently, watching me.

"Syn," I whispered, relieved but glad he had shown me what I could do if I pulled at someone else's soul.

"Who do you want?" he asked quietly, his hard golden eyes reaching in to caress my soul and reassure it.

"You," I whispered the single word with absolute conviction. I smiled and bit my bottom lip to hide the grin that was forming.

"Fuck, you're so damn beautiful," he whispered, and began to move faster between my legs until I had no choice but to hold on and allow him to intensify my need. I rocked against him and watched as the gold of his eyes circled the black obsidian color, taking full control of it.

"That's it, take what you need," he encouraged.

I did what he said and fed, pulling in the energy he was giving off, feeling it fill and strengthen me. The Fae had not been playing with words when they said that sex was the best way to generate emotion—it was pure, untainted energy to us. I felt his magic pulsing to life, and the pressure came again. Only, this time—I felt it everywhere, kissing my flesh, suckling my breast, nipping at my skin, and then it was there, hot like a mouth licking across my clit until I could no longer contain the scream that tore from my lungs as I exploded with him.

I was still trembling from the release when he placed me on my side. He started moving with that delicious friction again, and this time he fed. He took what he needed as though he were savoring every bit and storing up for a marathon. Somewhere, between him coming, and when I joined him, everything changed. I began to fade in and out of awareness and only saw and felt what was happening in glimpses. One moment my mind would blank, and the next moment, what we were doing would crash into my consciousness in blaring color and surround sound. I tasted blood, and knew instinctively that it was Ryder's, that I'd taken it from him, and that he'd allowed it several times.

It hadn't been violent, and he'd exploded inside of my mouth, feeding both of what I had craved. He was primal in his need to dominate, and yet gentle in doing so. He was unlike anything I had ever known, or would again.

His magic felt as if every single inch of my body was being explored at once. Even as I explored his, his magic touched mine in places no one else had ever been allowed to.

Ryder was in control, and yet he allowed me to believe I was. He encouraged the hunger and challenged it with his own. He was an enigma, gentleness mixed with his need to dominate, and yet he held back from it. He took his time to ensure I felt everything he could give, and yet I could feel him holding something back. He was ensuring that I felt no fear, that I felt treasured, and I wasn't sure how to process it. I was sinking in quicksand and, for once, I wasn't afraid of it.

~~*~*~* Ryder *~*~*~*~*

She's so fucking beautiful. Her will and strength define her, but her beauty comes from within. I held her soul inside of me and wanted to keep it. To keep it, and feel her inside of me forever. She has a moral compass most people would die to be able to have.

She moves against my cock, and I purr, like a

fucking kitten. She undoes me unlike no other woman ever has. Those sweet noises as she takes me inside her body; the look that fills her eyes as she's stretched for more. Unfucking believable. Every time I think I have her figured out, she changes. She's like a puzzle with missing pieces.

She grinds against me and I help her. I send my magic out to kiss and lick her gently on every nerve ending until I watch her shatter over me, pulling that scream of absolute pleasure from her lungs. "That's it, Pet. Fuck, that's so good."

She moans louder as I feel her juices slicken across my cock. She's so wet, so sweet, as she rides me again, already hungry for more. Her eyes glow beautifully, exotic as the woman they belong to. Her supple body rides me again, allowing me to lay back and watch her as, once again, I send my magic out to nibble on her high-tipped nipples and suck her clit. Fuck, she undoes me, she isn't afraid of my magic now. She's undone by it.

She purrs as the magic wafts across her skin, kissing her neck and filling her lips as if my cock was pressing against it. I could fill her entire body with a single thought, but, right now, I just want to watch as she undulates on my engorged dick. Her body trembles against mine, sending her scent of need through my entire being.

She's a goddess right now, her body a vessel of desire. I growl and move her beneath me. With a single thought, I push inside of her haven of bliss. She sighs, and I watch her as she says my name, over and over. The beast raises his head, and I smile. Masculine pride sinks in deep as my name is whispered from her lips, rolling off her tongue like silk, like a plea. Soon, soon she will be past the brink of blackness that takes hold of the mind during Transition, and then I will allow him to feed from her. I listen to her blood pumping through her veins; the scent of her orgasm hangs in the balance.

I hold her legs apart; and come to my knees so I can feed her more inches, more length of my hard cock. She's close to coming again; her body is now covered in a fine sheen of sweat. I move my hips until I find the rhythm that will send her over, and I prepare to feed.

The chains clank as she tries to move her hands to me, but I tightened those moments ago. I plan to ravish her sweet nectar with my mouth after she comes for me. She's addictive; her body makes me weak with need. I fucking hate it, and yet I no longer want to hurt her, to punish her for this ceaseless craving she's created. I want to save her, protect her. It's a weakness I can't afford.

She mewls, and I smile as her core grows wetter with the impending orgasms I have planned. I watch as her head thrashes from side to side, her nipples tightening into taut buds that demand to be caressed— and I do, with my mouth. Magic could have been used, but I love the taste of her, the feel of her coming undone from my touch.

I claim her mouth hungrily and she cries against mine, her need growing precariously close. I nibble against the tender flesh of her lip, licking and teasing her until she moans against me. Her legs spread farther apart and I sink deeper inside of her welcoming heat.

My hands sink into her hair testing the sensitive follicles until the exact pressure is applied, and pleasure meets pain. She cries out, and I relent until I see the heat flash in her beautiful Fae eyes. I send magic out, seeking her nipples; touching her clit until her body quivers for me. I'm in full control of this beautiful woman, *my* woman.

"That's it, Synthia, come for me. Let me taste that pretty pussy as it grows wet for me."

Never has a woman made me need to give her pleasure as much as this one. I find myself slipping around her, dropping my shield that I've erected. I find myself needing to let her in, to show her the beast and see how she reacts.

I pull out before her climax, but I leave her filled with magic. She's full and unaware that I've left her body. I watch as her young body rides my magic. I can feel it as if it's still me inside of her, me she's riding with wild abandon. She's open and exposed as I lower my hungry mouth and apply pressure to her welcoming folds. She tastes like ambrosia, the finest wine of the Gods.

I lick slowly, tasting, teasing as her body continues to be fucked by nothing more than magic. Not many can manage this trick, not many can do so without ripping out the soul of the feeder. I stroke my cock as I fuck her sweet nectar with my tongue, adding to her pleasure. Fuck it's good to be me right now. I feel like the luckiest fucking creature alive.

I nibble her clit with my teeth; feel as my fangs slide down from my gums. Fuck it, I sink them into the delicate vein of her petal-soft pussy, and suck her blood into my mouth. I feel her inside of me as I swallow her life's essence. I stop and seal the wound, the saliva evolving it from pleasure into more intense pleasure that makes her cry out with the need to be filled again. I soak her sweet pussy with it, and watch as she comes undone.

Her body trembles as cries of ecstasy explode from her lips. I lap greedily as her come fills her sweet folds, and I drink it all in, feeding like a fucking animal as she rides my face, rides the orgasms that rip through her until I feel them turning painful. I stop them and allow her to recover. The moment she does, I start it all over again.

Fuck, I can't get enough of her. How had I ever thought I would? She's my drug, and I need more. I want to be high on her forever. The taste of her blood and her climax linger in my mouth like nothing else I have ever tasted. The beast smiles and growls his need for the woman before him. Up until now, I had only let him loose with Syn in small increments, and reined him in tightly. Now, it's time to let him out, to give him a bigger taste of her endless perfection, and see what he does with it. I smile and allow him to see her through his own eyes.

She's his match.

She's everything to him that he has ever wanted.

Our cock grows in size, and we smile as we nudge it inside her tight sheath. We pull back a few inches until we're no longer inside her and then we thrust sharply, impaling her until we push against her womb. Encased in her warmth, we move, slowly at first to ensure she can handle us.

When she bucks back, we let loose. We hold her legs apart with our hands, holding her feet up. We push harder and close our eyes as her whimper of desire caresses our skin. We feed her more until we feel her pulling back, away from it. We pull out with what she needs and watch as her sweet pussy moves to invite it back inside. We lunge and catch the scream from her lungs with our mouth, smothering it.

I allow him to take control, fucking her hard and slow. He snarls hungrily as she accepts him in her mindless state. He licks near her carotid, but I snap at him. He's had her blood once tonight; it's enough. He snarls, but listens to the advice. We don't want to hurt her. We want to give her pleasure—absolute, unrivaled pleasure. We agree on this.

He sends his magic out, and I marvel at the absolute control he has over her. She's exploding around him until her body is wrapped in ecstasy. She rides him, giving him back what he gives her, and he purrs. He fucking purred! He's an endless killing machine, and right now he's reduced to a fucking kitten, lapping at cream!

I watch them from inside my head, watching as he kisses feathery-soft kisses over her delicate flesh. "*Mine,*" he snarls.

"Ours," I growl, answering him.

"*Yes,*" he snaps hungrily and smiles as he continues to drive our cock inside of her. He wants to touch her soul, he wants to consume her, and own her. I watch him, ensuring he pulls back from what could hurt her. I rumble a warning and watch as he pulls our magic back from her body.

"*So good,*" he whispers, and my eyes bulge. "*Need to, have her!*"

"We have her," I answer. "She is ours now. You marked her flesh."

"*Not enough; need to possess her; need to be here, like this, forever. Understand?*"

He thinks I'm the weaker half. "My turn. Give me back control. She's not ready for you, yet."

"*Need her. Want her. You have to chain her for control. I can tame her, make her need me!*"

"She's chained for her protection. I won't share her; she could sift out and be hurt by others. Smell her, smell her utter fucking perfection. What Fae could walk away from that, even with your mark on her?"

He sniffs, and I feel our eyes turn obsidian. *"Need to taste her,"* he replies and pulls out, and fuck, if he doesn't go to town on that sweet, pink flesh. He is sucking, licking, and fucking her with his eight inch tongue. She comes instantly. He can't control secretions as I can. He makes inhuman noises; as does she as she rides his face greedily. I feel our hand go to our cock and stroke the hard, silken flesh.

I'm fucking her without touching her. She wanted to know how I did it. This is how. I'm not alone in this body. I can do things other Fae can't. I can do bad things, and really fucking good things. I watch as our cock explodes, pumping juices on the sheet. Her body quivers as it continues to come for the beast who is feeding at her core gluttonously.

He pulls away and howls hungrily, even though he is sated and fed from her sweet juices. *"So good, so pure. Need to go deeper, to own, control, fuck! Mine! She's mine."*

"Ours," I remind him. I trade places with him. He goes, but not willingly. Like a child denied his favorite toy, he sulks, and I shake my head. She's the only female he has ever let live. It rattles me and makes me wonder if I shouldn't set her free.

Magic ripples through the room. It's not ours, it's hers. She's turning. I want, *no*, I need, to be inside of her as she changes, to see it unfold as I take her. I push inside her, watching as her head rocks from side to side as I feed her more inches. She spreads her legs and begs for more. She's so wantonly glorious; her folds are soaking wet because *I* made them that way. She's turning Fae, even as I watch her. She's losing the fight, and I bide my time riding her body, fucking her hard, and making her come over and over, until she's boneless. She won't feel the pain from the change; I won't allow it.

So far, the only thing changing is her beautiful eyes. The purple is light, the color of freshly bloomed lilacs in spring. The blue is now as electric as its owner. The black ring surrounding it marks her as royalty. As I watch, crimson brands begin to appear and pulse beneath her skin as she wiggles her tight ass impishly against me. I nudge it against her ass and watch as her eyes grow hooded with need.

I move to watch her Transition; those red brands are growing darker as they set in against her skin, until they are such a deep crimson they almost look black. They will lighten later as she comes into her full power. They continue to appear and spread out, thin, delicate brands that grow up her arms and around her torso. Dainty little Celtic knots of womanhood sit on her shoulders, beautiful against her pale flesh.

She's Blood Fae, I think with a smile. *She's mine, and I own her, every succulent fucking inch of her.* I pull her up against me, bringing her to her knees as I flip her over on the bed, before I push her back down until her ass is exposed. I bring her bound hands out, releasing the chains as I hold her hands behind her back and enter her body slowly.

"Syn," I growl, needing to hear my name on her lips, but knowing she's too far gone to know who is taking her.

"Ryder," she whimpers, and I freeze in shock that she knows I'm inside of her.

"Pet?" I ask again, and close my eyes as no reply

comes.

And then it does.

"Move, Fairy. I'm hungry. I need you, Ryder, please," she replies as her beautiful backside sways invitingly.

"Who is fucking you, Synthia?" Un-fucking-believable! She's aware of what is happening to her, when she should be utterly mindless with need.

"You are, Ryder. I need to feel you moving inside of me," she cries, her body trembling with need.

I sink inside of her, amazed that she's coherent. How the fuck!? Not even I managed to understand fully who was riding my slick cock through Transition. She's utterly amazing.

"Synthia, I plan to keep you forever," I whisper softly as I rain magic kisses all over her body.

"Mmm," she sighs as she moves against me.

She's fucking mine.

We both struggle, pushing, riding each other, and then we collapse in a mess of limbs and exhaustion. I smile against her hair as she rubs her ass against me again. She turns over and smiles like a cat in need of having its tummy rubbed. Her eyes flicker to my cock that's already growing from the sultry look of her eyes. She pushes me down and lowers her head. I swallow a groan, watching as her tongue strikes out and runs the full length of my cock.

My hips buck and she moans, taking my cock inside of her mouth, relaxing her throat until she can take no more. She pulls away and slides her tongue down the hard length of it, sending pleasure to my balls. I feel it then, her teeth. Canines—she has fangs. I should be taking notes; instead, I'm at her command. Her teeth drag over my flesh, and I groan from the intense pleasure. She takes the head in more and I run my hands through her hair, growling with approval. And then her fangs sink into my flesh, and I explode in her mouth, her hungry moan the only sound in the room.

I swallow another groan that tries to tear from my lungs. Eventually, I pull her off and looked into her glowing eyes. She has fangs; they're tiny, but there. I smile as she wipes the blood from her chin and climbs up on my body.

"You took my blood," I accuse huskily.

"I want more," she replies, smiling as her tongue tests her new fangs.

"No one takes my blood, Synthia, ever."

"Planning on killing me then?" She's teasing me.

Fuck! She's amazing. I push her back down on the bed and my cock enters her greedy warmth as she smiles impishly. Too bad she won't remember any of this. She's the most erotic thing I have ever encountered in my entire life. She moves, and I moan as her cries join mine.

I feel my chest tighten as I watch her. Something feels like it is cracking inside of me and allowing her in. I should push her away, make her hate me. The thought of it makes my chest tighten, and my stomach drop. Fucking hell! I shouldn't feel this shit—it's deadly, and she's deadly to me.

Chapter ELEVEN

She sleeps, oblivious to the fact that she's finished her Transition in neck-breaking time. Ristan watches her closely from where he stands, beside the bed that Syn and I lay on together. "Anything?" I ask impatiently.

"She's like a blank fucking slate. I can't see tomorrow, hell, today is blurry. She Transitioned in less than three days. From the brands, I can tell you she's some kind of Blood Fae, but you already knew that. She's very strong and exceptionally beautiful," he finishes, ignoring the growl that rips from my throat. He smiles and turns to level me with his silver and black eyes. "You need to curb that shit now. We don't have time for it if we are going to save Faery and figure out who the fuck is killing our kind."

"You think I haven't tried? She accepted him. She fucking fed him, and she baited him for *more*."

His eyes grow large and round. It's almost fucking comical. "And he allowed her to live?"

"He more than allowed it, Ristan. She made him purr like a fucking kitten. My beast fed from her, and he backed off instead of feasting. He didn't want to hurt her. He even pulled away when he thought he was close to doing so. He's never done that before. He has never wanted anything as much as he wants her."

"Are you sure she won't remember him?" Ristan asks carefully, his eyes guarded.

"Why the fuck do you think I called you in here? It sure as fuck wasn't so that you could stare at her naked!" I scrub my hands over my face in exhaustion. She had fucking worn me out, and I loved every minute of it.

"She's an enigma to me. I'm not even sure how she managed to live this long. I can't see enough of her future to even know if she actually has one. I'm not sure what you want from me here. Either she's being shielded from me seeing it, or I'm not supposed to. I could sit here all day making excuses, but the truth is this, I can't get shit from her."

"How can that be? She's here, I claimed her, and you can't see her with me at all?" I ask, growling in frustration. I wasn't losing her. Not after what we'd just done.

"I have no idea why I can't see her future. I'm only shown what I need to see most of the time. This could mean any number of things that range from you not being able to claim her, or that you free her to choose and she leaves—I don't know. Maybe there is a specific reason I am not supposed to see hers or Adam's futures. I'm trying to figure it out, but, again, it's not like I can just tap in and ask Danu why she won't allow me to see their futures."

"Try to figure it out. Send some feelers out. See just how many of the Blood Fae have missing daughters. Check the larger as well as the smaller clans. If she's pure Blood Fae, I could potentially keep her for myself, seeing that we have a rather convenient feud with them right now. I could lay claim, and no one could challenge it. Nothing is ever that simple with her, though."

"What if she isn't? What if she's only half?"

"If she isn't, then she still belongs to me. Otherwise, her family could put up one helluva fight to get her back. Let's not get ahead of ourselves, though."

"Would you fight for her? I could understand you wanting her as a pet when you thought she was human, but she's Fae now. It's a game changer. What if fighting for her means giving up the fight for Faery?"

"I can fight for both, and she's more than a pet, Ristan. I'm finding it hard to stay away from her at all. She's like a drug in my veins."

"And if she doesn't want you? What then, Ryder?"

"She wants me; she just hasn't come to terms with it yet. If she were just Blood Fae it would make this a simple thing. She's got royal blood in her though, and that might cause some issues." I'd planned to keep her when we'd assumed she was human, and even took steps to ensure that I could, but he was right. This changed everything. Can I actually keep her now that she is Fae? I have no plans of letting her get too close to me, and it really isn't fair to her. My past is dark, filled with things that still haunt me. I'd done things that she would cringe at, because she was raised as a human, and if she ever catches a glimpse of it, she'll willingly walk away from me and not look back. I've done things that I now regret, and if she finds out, she'll hate me for them.

In her eyes, I will be a fucking monster.

"Is that something you are willing to risk, now

that we're so close to being done here? Could you give up who you are, and lose the advantage we have struggled to keep, just because you like fucking her?"

"No, that's not an option. I'll figure it out when the time comes. She also has the look of a few of the Light Fae, so let's cross that bridge when we get there. We need to worry about who is killing Fae. You and Z didn't reach out, so I assumed nothing happened."

"They didn't find any more bodies. No one came back to the park either. We've been out searching, but nothing has happened in the last few days. It's been pretty quiet. We've been lucky in that aspect, since you had a Transition to deal with. You made the right choice trusting the men with this. It gives them a sense of responsibility. They need it now that we are close to being finished here."

"Good. We need to see if this is connected to the Mages, or if it is connected to whoever is trying to kill off Fae. Ristan, if it is the Mages, I want Syn left out of it. She's going to be unstable after Transition, and she isn't going to like it. I'm not sure I can control the beast if she is harmed again. I almost lost control when we found her in that apartment."

"Are you sure he hasn't chosen her for more than just food?"

I wince at the thought. "If he has, we're fucked. I can easily keep her, but I can't force this on her. Syn is too strong to be bent to anyone's will, including mine. It isn't the easiest thing to admit. Not to mention it would breach the laws of our people. You have seen some of my future, and you know I always do what is right for our people in the end."

"And if she willingly chose you?"

"You think she would want me? If she knew *who* I

was, and what I have done in the past? No, she'd run. She's unpredictable. Fuck, Ristan, she went into full Transition with me standing beside her and I didn't *feel* it. I felt the tension and aggression, and *then*, I felt her need. There is nothing normal about her, or anything surrounding her for that matter. Someone went through a lot of effort to keep her existence secret. I want to know why and who it was. She's mine for now, either way."

~~*~*~* *Synthia* *~*~*~*~*

My entire body felt as if I'd run a marathon. I blinked and lifted my head before laying it back down as the room started to spin. I brought my hand up and tried focusing, but it was a blur, like everything else in the room. I could make out voices, but couldn't see where they were coming from. I felt no different in my body or mind; unless you counted the '*unable to see shit,'* part.

"Hello?" I asked the room in general.

"Synthia, you shouldn't be awake yet," Eliran said from somewhere beside me.

"I can't see," I whispered through parched lips.

"You need more sleep," Eliran continued.

"How much more sleep does she need?" Ryder's rich baritone sounded from right beside me, making me jump. "Easy, Syn. I took the collar off. If you sift right now, you could easily be hurt."

I must have blushed over my entire naked body. I turned toward his voice and lifted my hand to find his face through the blurry vision. "Did I change into a monster?"

"I would like to say a three-headed one," he said

with his mouth against my cheek.

"Well, shit," I said for lack of anything better to say about turning into a fucking monster.

"I'm teasing. You held human form the entire time. You are Blood Fae, or at least half—fangs and all."

I felt my stomach churning. "Fangs?"

"Sexy little ones that felt un-fucking-believably hot on certain body parts."

I groaned at him and pulled the sheet over my head, trying to close out the world and what I had done. I remembered some of it and some of the things that fell out of my mouth, like telling him his dick was the best treat and that I'd rather have it than chocolate. I mean, c'mon, I gave his dick a better rating than *chocolate—who* does that?

"Can we pretend it never happened?" I asked when he had stopped snorting.

"Not on your fucking life. Not when you said my dick was better than—"

"Okay, Ryder, she looks good, healthy. I'd say she needs more sleep so her senses could come in, but she's a stubborn patient. I'm going to go and give you two some room," Eliran said a moment before the door closed across the room.

"—Chocolate."

"Seriously, I'm at a disadvantage here, and I might have to apply for a handicap sticker for my ass."

"Your ass doesn't need a sticker. I promise it was just as amazing as the rest of you."

I swallowed and shook my head. "Did you also kick my ass while you were at it?" I asked, feeling each and every muscle cry with the slightest movement.

"It got rough; you got rough. It should go away after your body heals with sleep."

"Ryder, where exactly did I bite you?" I asked, pulling off the sheet and blinking as I tried to gain control of my eyes.

He laughed; it was deep and husky, as if he was remembering it with way too much fondness. "You really want to know?" he replied when he had finished laughing at my expense.

"Sorta," I whispered and swiped my hand at his shoulder as he started to laugh again. "This is serious! I need to know how bad I was."

"You weren't bad, you were sexy as fuck. You took your first blood from my cock." I could just barely make out his mouth smiling wickedly as he enjoyed torturing me with the explicit details.

"No," I shook my head in disbelief. "There's no fucking way I did that. I bit your cock? Did you scream at least?" I was shocked and kinda glad I couldn't remember that part.

"No, your fangs are for pleasure. They're not the same as Vlad's. You're at least part Blood Fae, you can control blood and anything to do with it. Vlad's are to feed, and if necessary, fight. His father was Horde."

"So I don't need to drink blood?" *Oh hell—say no. For all that's holy, say no!*

"No, but you *will* take it for pleasure. How are you feeling, besides being sore?"

"Like I should hide my face. How many times did we…you know?"

"I lost count after seventy," he whispered heatedly.

"That's a joke, right?"

"No," he replied as his lips touched my ear. "I fucked you in every position, in every way I could, and you begged me for more. You took everything I gave you. You begged me, and it was the hottest fucking thing I have ever seen in my life. You fed perfectly."

Heat flooded my body as I turned and watched the blur of peach color that moved closer. "You suck," I mumbled.

"No, baby, *you* suck, and you do it very fucking well." He kissed my lips and held my face in place as I tried to pull away from him. "Oh, I don't think so. We've been together in every way possible, and you think you can pull away now? You're going to have to feed, and it's going to be every few days until you can balance your system out, or you could die. Who do you plan on feeding from?"

"You; duh, Ryder. I'm not the type to sleep around, even if I am a fucking Fairy now."

Chapter
TWELVE

I stared at my reflection, unable to look away. I had high cheekbones, higher than they used to be at least. My face was smooth; the small scars I'd earned by enforcing the laws were gone. My eyes had the thin black line around them that Ryder's had. Otherwise, they were the same blue and purple two-tone coloring my eyes had changed to after my first meltdown, minus the glow shining back at me from the mirror. I blinked and took in every fine detail. I was changed. I had perfect skin now, and my hair was thicker and a little longer than it had been before Transition.

My brands were now formed, with delicate lines that kissed and caressed my flesh. They flowed up my arms and settled on my shoulders. They were dark red, and beautiful. The brands had also formed a Celtic triple spiral knot at the top of each of my shoulders. I remembered in some of my studies back at the Guild that this type of knot represented three stages of a woman—maiden, mother, and wise woman.

I licked my fangs and shook my head. I had flipping fangs. I looked up from my little self-discovery session to find Ryder watching me. He'd put on jeans that sat low on his sexy hips, but had left his shirt off. His smile drew my eyes up to it briefly. Hunger drew them down to his sexy six-pack, and lower to the thin, dark kiss of hair that led into his pants. That happy-trail led to what my hunger wanted.

"Not the monster you thought yourself to be?" he asked, moving across the room to stand behind me. He pulled me back against himself, and I felt his already hard cock press against my bare backside.

"How do I make the fangs go away?" I asked, trying to make my mind work past the feel of his desire.

"They will go away on their own, Pet. They will come and go with the hunger though."

"I can't just make them go away like Vlad does?" I asked. I wanted them gone now. They were a reminder that I had changed, as were the ache between my thighs; which reminded that he'd abused me in ways I'd enjoyed.

He smiled over my head as I watched our reflection. We looked Fae, and I wasn't sure how to process it. I was now immortal. Or, basically, it wouldn't be official until I was fully out of Transition. I could already feel my hunger growing for this man, and it had little to do with actual hunger.

"Mmm, already hungry, Pet?" he said wickedly against my ear.

"How often do I have to feed?" I asked, turning around in his arms to face him.

"Every few days. Right now, your body is changing and needs to feed often. Later, you will be able to go for weeks at a time between feeding. Without it, you would become sick, and eventually you would succumb to hunger and, yes, you would die. Starvation is one of the few ways Fae can die."

I nodded and met his eyes, watching as his glow crept into his beautiful amber orbs. I swallowed and considered my options. I was hungry, and he'd feed me. I wasn't ready to ask him for sex, though, because, well…it felt weird asking him for anything.

"You are so beautiful," he whispered softly, dropping a reassuring kiss to my forehead. It made my heart flutter in my chest. "Are you done hiding in here?"

"I wasn't hiding," I whispered as I placed my head against his chest and closed my eyes. I listened to his heart beating and wondered what it would be like if it beat for me.

"You have been in here for a while," he murmured, wrapping his arms around me.

"I was trying to figure out how to shut off the second sight. I see everything too bright. It's giving me a pounding headache."

He laughed and pulled away. "That's not second sight, Syn; that's how we see."

We.

"All the time?" I asked, looking up at his face. He was even more beautiful now. His skin was perfect.

"All the time," he confirmed.

"So, before, when I was still human…" Why the hell would I ask him that? I'd been about to ask him if he thought I was beautiful before I'd Transitioned.

"You were beautiful then as well, Pet. You are strong and stubborn, but that soul of yours is undeniably beautiful. I know, because I've felt it from the inside when you stole part of mine. My soul was addicted to yours from the moment you stole it. I felt the untainted beauty of it. It only made me want to taste you more."

I could have given some smart ass retort, and it might have gotten him to release his gentle hold. But, right then, I only wanted him to hold me and reassure me that I hadn't become some fanged freak. "It's not pure. I'm not a good person," I whispered and looked up into his face.

"Why? Because you've killed those who failed to follow the rules of this world? That doesn't make you a bad person."

"I'm not talking about the Fae," I whispered and tipped my face up to his.

He smiled and lowered his mouth to mine. His kiss was gentle, and I felt myself melting against him like butter in a frying pan. He picked me up and carried me easily into the bedroom. He didn't take me to the bed. Instead, he pressed me against the wall and captured both of my hands in his much larger one.

The moment he had them above my head, he pulled away from my mouth and watched me. His sexy, self-assured smirk was back in place. "Is it bad that I want to keep you here, in Transition? I don't want this to end," he said, before he trailed kisses over my collarbone softly.

I didn't answer him, because to do so would be to admit that I wanted to stay here with him too. I liked being with him and the problem with that was I was falling for my enemy. He was hiding something from me. I'm not sure how I knew, but I had a feeling that when I discovered it, we'd forever be changed. He was more than he claimed to be—so much more.

"Are you sore?" he asked as he allowed me to

slide down his body until my feet were on the floor.

"Yes," I answered him, watching his eyes as he still held my hands above my head.

"I can fix that," he replied, allowing his hands to glow with power. I instantly shivered and gasped. It was the second time I'd ever seen his hands ignite with his powers. The first time, he'd been using it to hurt people.

"No, leave it, please," I whimpered as I felt his power start to enter my body.

"If you're sore, Syn, I can fix it easily."

"I like the feel of it. The reminder of what we did."

He shook his head and claimed my mouth again, growling his approval as he did so. When he pulled away, I cried out from the loss of his mouth on mine. "Someone wants to see you, Pet," he said grudgingly, as if it pained him to say it.

"Adam is out of Transition!?" I squeaked in half panic, half joy.

"He is," he answered, and he kissed my neck again, as if he couldn't get enough of me.

I brought my hands up and threaded them through his silky hair. "Is he okay?" I questioned him, even as his hand moved between my legs to press against my sensitive flesh. "He's fine, he lived. I gave him my best girls to get him through it." He smiled against my neck and whispered against my ear, "I like knowing your flesh is tender because I fucked it."

I smiled and then watched as he sucked against my nipple while his eyes met mine. He pulled his mouth away, but only far enough that I could watch as he licked and ran his teeth over the pink tip. I moaned and felt moisture pooling as he continued.

He lifted his head and smiled. His magic wafted through me as he cleansed my body of all signs of Transition, and I noticed a shirt now covered his torso as he pulled away from me.

"You should get dressed before I end up taking you back to the bed and spend the rest of the day between those pretty thighs of yours. You have an entire gathering up there awaiting you."

"Huh?" I asked, confused as I pushed off of the wall.

"Your boy toy is up there. He's not very bright," he whispered.

"Adrian is upstairs too? Can I see him?" I asked carefully.

"He is. I'm only going to say this once, Syn—keep your lips to yourself. He's been warned now that you are mine. For as long as I have my mark on you, no one else will take liberties with you. Be careful with hunger, Pet. It belongs to me, for now. Remember that, so no one else will get hurt."

"Ryder, get a grip. I'm not going to lose control this time. Last time was a mistake, and if I had been myself, it never would have happened."

"So you say, but women are fickle creatures. I don't share what is mine, and, right now, you are mine. Some women are free with their bodies. You are not to be one of them, understand me?"

"Not everyone works like that. Some need and want to be loved by one man *alone*. When I love someone, I give them everything I have and don't expect to get anything back in return for it. I'd never tear you down, Ryder; not if you were mine. Besides, you told me once before that love was worth fighting for." He shook his head as his eyes narrowed. I wasn't sure how we'd gotten into something this deep. He'd told me from the beginning that he wasn't that kinda guy.

"I never asked for, or offered, you love, Synthia," he snapped defensively.

I smiled sadly and stepped closer to him until I was close enough to kiss him. "That's a shame, because this is what you could have had," I whispered before claiming his lips and putting everything I had into the kiss until I heard his sigh and felt his hands tremble as they landed on my waist, pulling me closer.

I didn't want this. I wasn't supposed to love the enemy. My hands came up to cup his face as I deepened the kiss, before pulling away to stare into his beautiful eyes. "That is what people spend eternity looking for. That's why men go to war when they lose it."

"You're still thinking like a human. I'm Fae, and we don't fall in love easily, if ever. We marry for gain, or to end wars."

"I wasn't asking for your love. I was showing what it would be like if you had mine," I growled, before pushing away from him. I watched his angry back as he walked into the bathroom and closed the door so hard that the wood cracked in protest.

I stood rigid and finally moved across the room to dress. It took several moments to make my mind function and find the bag of clothes at the foot of the bed. I heard him re-enter the bedroom as I pulled on a black bra, thong, and jeans and slipped quickly into a black long sleeved shirt before turning around to face him. He had a mask on his emotions and stood stiff and rigid. Angry. "I already have you, Syn. I never asked for love."

"Good, because I couldn't give it to you while you owned me anyway. It would be missing the whole point of giving *freely*. You take because you can; because it's how you are. You have had me in every possible way, and, yet, you haven't had *me* yet. That's what pisses you off about Adrian. He's had me, all of me. He's had all of me willingly—without having to own me to do so."

"What the fuck makes you think I care who you fucked freely? It only matters to me who you fuck while I own you, Synthia. Right now, you are mine. Don't confuse fucking with any other emotion. I fuck, I feed. I don't need to make excuses for what I do to anyone. You need to get it through your stubborn little skull that I am Fae, and not one of your pathetic little humans."

I pushed the angry tears away. "Good."

"Good," he growled back.

We walked stiffly together to the elevator, and stopped with him standing directly behind me. I stood firm and inflexible as his hand reached over my shoulder to punch in the code to get to the higher levels of the club. Neither of us said anything, but I could feel his eyes burning into my flesh at the back of my neck.

"Do you still love Adrian?" he asked quietly after a few moments had passed.

"Yes," I replied crisply. "He was my first love. I may not love him as I did then, but there will always be love between us. Even when I marry, or he does, love doesn't just go away. But, don't worry… I'm no longer *in* love with him, but I will always love him."

"Not if I got rid of him," he growled, forcing me to turn around and face him.

"Jealous? Because, right now, you sound like a jealous lover. Why would it matter if I loved him? I'm your whore right now. Your contract said I couldn't have physical contact with another person sexually. I'm following *your* rules. You can't control what I feel and what I don't. Your contract said nothing about emotions, Fairy."

"I don't get jealous often, and, when I do, I take care of the problem, and right now his mooning over you is a problem."

"He's looking for closure. We grew up together. We were kids. Stupid kids that thought we could make something work. He isn't in love with me. He's probably in love with the idea of being in love."

"And yet you admit that you still love him." He narrowed his bronze eyes on me.

"Yes, I also love Adam. I love Alden, and I loved Larissa. I still love Larissa; she's dead, but that doesn't make the love I have for her just shut off. If you had ever known love, you'd know this. Nothing can force love to go away. You grow apart, or grow up, but it's still there. You still care what happens to them, and if you make Adrian go away over that, then you're just showing how stupid you are. Even without him near, I'd still love him."

"I'm not sure what I want to do more right now; strangle you, kiss you, fuck you, or all three."

"I don't suggest you try any of them right now.

Right now, I'd do the first to you and forget the rest, Fairy."

His smile was impishly sinful and dark. "I'd be careful. You could end up chained to the bed inside the room you just left. You're still in Transition. I'd be within my rights to keep you locked up until you learn to sift without landing on your knees at my feet."

"Go ahead! It doesn't mean I would need to feed while chained. It would only prove you need to own pretty things, Fairy. You think being Fae gives you the right to own me? Well, it doesn't. The only thing holding me here is the contract, and it's almost up. Remember that."

He grinned, but it was anything but friendly. "It hasn't slipped my mind, I assure you."

I stepped into the elevator when the doors opened and turned to face him with challenge lit inside my eyes. His smirk was gone and in its place was tension. He was already trying to figure out how to lock me into another contract. "I won't sign another one. Not even to save myself or anyone else. So, before you go threatening anyone I love—know this. I will not be owned by you anymore. I'm not a fucking pet, so stop trying to own me like one. If you want me, you need to start thinking like a human male and stop thinking like a fucking Fairy."

"Keep in mind a few things. You will need to feed every few days for the first couple months following Transition or you can quickly starve and die—that is a fact. I will not allow that to happen while you are under my protection, either; not when it's so easily fixed. You are a casteless Fae; by rights I can claim you. Unless you know where your family is, or where they come from. Hell, I might even be able to broker a deal to buy you."

"Why the fuck *would* you?" I leveled an angry stare at him.

"Maybe I like fucking you," he purred, letting his eyes trail down my body slowly.

"You have a hand, Ryder. I suggest you use it. I promise you won't like fucking me if you force anything else on me. I might be Fae now, but I'm still myself, and I still won't be your toy."

He stepped forward and forced my back up against the glass wall of the elevator. His hands landed on either side of my head, and his face lowered to mine. "If I want you, nothing in this world or any other one will stop me. And, right now, I want you."

"I want someone who actually wants me for who I am. Not someone who just wants to fuck me. You don't want me; you want control *of* me. I'm not sure why you fail to see the difference. It's an easy thing for me to see, but then I'm still thinking human," I shot back at him.

"You have me, Synthia. What's wrong with wanting beautiful things? All men want something beautiful in their lives. What's wrong with controlling your body when we both know you like what I do to it?"

"Because, I don't have you," I hissed. "Why won't you let me see beyond your shields if I have you? You think I can't see that you're holding me at arm's length? I'm not an idiot. I know you have secrets that you don't allow anyone else to see. I know you think you're good at hiding them, but eventually all secrets come to light, and we all have skeletons in our closet. The only difference between yours and mine is that you forced mine onto the table, and you don't trust me enough to let me see yours."

"Careful, Syn," he warned.

"Careful, my ass. You keep taking from me, and in return I get owned! I'm not a dog that you can just chain up like a fucking pet. Eventually, I'm going to be done with the contract, and you're going to see me walk away."

"And if I let you in, and show you all my secrets? What if I'm the exact thing you hate most? What if my past is bathed in blood and my deeds are so evil that you end up hating me; what then?"

"It's in the past, unless you are still doing it. Whatever it is you did, it's in the past as far as I'm concerned. It's what we do with the future that matters. If you plan on continuing to do whatever it is…you know what? This is stupid; I don't even know what the hell it is you did. I'm not asking for marriage. I'm just saying I won't be owned. You want me, ask me. Stop demanding it, expecting it, or eliminating the competition."

"You're thinking like a human again. Fae take what we want and always look to see how we can stack the odds in our favor."

"So, I should club you over the head and drag you to my room and chain you? Ya know, since I turned all Fae cavewoman and shit."

He smiled. "Interesting idea, Pet."

I snorted and shook my head. The man was impossible, but that was the problem. He wasn't a human and I kept expecting him to act like one. "Can I borrow your club?" I asked, smirking up at him.

"I don't need a club," he replied.

"Of course not, you just write up a contract and

I end up signing it. I guess I'll have to put my new brain to use and figure out a riddle that ends with me owning you this time."

"Is that so?" he growled smiling.

"It is."

"You couldn't handle me," he challenged.

"Is that so?" I shot back at him.

He growled throatily.

I licked my small fangs and rolled my eyes. "Any news on the group that are killing Fae?" I changed the subject. Yes, it was chicken shit of me, but it was getting way too deep, too fast.

"Not that you need to know about," he said, searching my face. "You need to concentrate on figuring out how to sift and what powers, if any, you acquired. I'll handle what's going on with my men."

"People are dying, Ryder. I'm not going to sit on my fucking thumbs while they do so. I'm not that girl."

"You really are the most infuriating woman on this entire fucking planet!"

"And you're the most annoying fucking Fairy on this planet," I shot back with a twisted smile on my lips.

"I think I should chain you and give you another example of just how well I can fuck," he purred.

The elevator doors slid open as it stopped. I quickly ducked beneath his arms and practically ran down the hallway, headed to the short stairway that led to the club below. Obviously not fast enough, since I could hear his boots close behind me as they padded on the floor. I stiffened my spine and took the steps that lit up beneath my feet as I stepped onto them.

At the bottom of the steps, I paused, wondering how everyone would react to my new appearance. I couldn't pretend to be anything but Fae with the telltale glowing eyes and fangs I was now sporting. I gasped as Adam came into view.

He was beautiful. His vivid green eyes met and held mine. They were now the emerald and lime green double iris I had seen before and held the same thin obsidian black circles around the iris as mine did. His hair was a little longer, as was mine now from Transition, and it was the same dark brown it had always been. He was taller and wider in the chest area. His t-shirt showed his own brands pulsing like mine were beneath the sleeves of the shirt I wore to hide them.

He smiled with perfect white teeth; no fangs, though. I stepped closer to him, but he was faster. He could sift now, and, before I'd even placed my foot on the floor, he had me in his arms, crushed me against his massive chest. "Stop thinking that I could ever hate what you are. You know better than that," he whispered roughly against my ear.

"Adam," I cried and wrapped my arms around him.

"I remember what I did to you, Syn. I'm so sorry. I was afraid you'd hate me for it," he whispered.

"As *if*," I smiled to reassure him, and winced as his eyes grew huge.

"You have fangs," he laughed uncomfortably.

"Baby ones. Ryder said they'll go away," I replied

self-consciously.

"You plan on hoarding her all to yourself?" Alden asked from behind Adam.

I pulled away from Adam and looked at Alden, waiting for disgust to show on his face. It didn't come. Instead, he smiled and held his hands out, which I accepted and allowed him to spin me around once. "You look beautiful, Synthia. You shouldn't fear what we think, and before you start telling me you're not that girl, remember, I raised you. You're still that same girl inside, and that is what matters to us."

"Thanks, I—" The lie I meant to say— *'don't feel any different,'* —froze on my tongue. I did feel different, and I felt a pull to Adam that hadn't been there before, as well. I could hear every heart that beat, as well as the blood that flowed inside of every person in the room. This was an in-your-face reminder that the Fae really can't lie—even over stupid things, and another reminder as to why they were masters at manipulation.

He smiled as if he knew I'd tried to tell a lie, but didn't comment on it. "Glad to see you're okay. I wasn't expecting you to accept it so easily." He smiled sadly.

"Who says I accept it? I'm still me. I may be Fae, but I'm still an Enforcer by blood, trained by the best Guild in the nation. Changing into something else hasn't made me forget my priorities, or what I was taught."

"You're royal Fae, Synthia—this whole time you've been under my nose—you and Adam here are both royal Fae. This is something I should have noticed. I failed the Guild in that aspect and I have a feeling that there will be hell to pay for it."

"I'm always here for you, Alden," I mumbled.

"I know that. I raised you to be a proud woman. I also made sure you would be able to handle anything life threw at you. I couldn't be more proud of you," he said. His eyes misted with tears as he smiled.

"If you ever need me, you only have to ask."

"Thanks, but I can handle this, Synthia. You focus on what you need to, and stop whoever is killing the Fae. That's what's important right now. So far, no more Witches or Fae have turned up dead over the past few days, and I think I can handle the Guild for now." He smiled as he patted me on the back and then headed back to his seat at the bar.

"Nice fangs, Fancy Face. Sexy as fuck," Adrian said, stepping closer.

I smiled and wrinkled my nose. "Mine will go away."

"That's too bad. They really are fun." He smiled, showing off his own.

I blinked at his words and shivered as the whole room faded to nothing. I was once again back inside the candle-lit room with Ryder, biting him for the first time. I blushed profusely at the memory, and swung my eyes back to his, where he stood behind Adrian. His mouth turned into a sexy smirk as if he knew exactly what had just flashed through my mind.

"I'm glad you made it through Transition in one piece," Adrian finished. Vlad moved in beside him and the tension built inside the room.

I tilted my head, listening as Ryder's heart rate increased and the brands started to pulse violently across my arms and chest. "It's the call of the blood,"

Vlad said from beside Adrian.

"What?" I asked, feeling Adam's hand slip inside mine.

"The blood flowing through the veins of those in the room. The hearts beating to a tempo. You hear it all—use it. You will always know when someone is lying, or scared of you."

I blinked at Vlad. "That's creepy."

He laughed, wickedly. "It comes in handy. Trust me."

Chapter
THIRTEEN

We spent some time with Ryder, Z, and Ristan, going over what Adam and I should and shouldn't be able to do, while the rest of Ryder's men sat around us listening. I had to laugh when Ryder gave us the snippet of Fae advice, *'just because we can do something, doesn't mean we should.'* Most of the Fae adopted a 'don't use magic unless absolutely necessary in the human world' attitude to help cut down on a lot of the suspicion and hate that the Fae were encountering from some of the more right-winged and prejudiced groups that had been cropping up. All the information was daunting, but I could manage it.

What a relief! Food was still on the board for us, as it turned out the Fae could and did eat; it just didn't have the same nutritional properties that the emotional feeding gave the Fae. Zahruk let us know that the old stories about humans eating the food of the Fae and becoming bound to the Fae who tricked them was very true, as this was the old way that the Fae used to lock humans into staying with them forever. I had to raise an eyebrow at Ryder for this revelation, as the giant fink had fed me in Faery, and I had forgotten that little tidbit of Hades-Persephone-esque lore of the Celts. A little smirk from Ryder confirmed my suspicion that he had indeed fed me *food of the Fae*. I rolled my eyes at his sneaky attempt. That this was one more way he had tried to lock me into being his pet while I was still human.

Ryder had insisted that no one else would teach me how to sift, since it could create an appetite. It was part of Transition, so he was within the agreement of the contract to demand it, just like he did everything else.

Ryder insisted we all retire to the mansion as soon as our little Fae class 101 was done for today. There was still a lot more to learn, and a great deal more that they were hiding from us. Adam and I were hanging out in the room I'd been in the last time I'd stayed with Ryder—he may have assigned the room to me again, but I wasn't staying there long term. The minute I could, I was going home.

"You don't think it's weird that Ryder isn't a little more pissed that Arianna wasn't the Light Heir?" Adam asked, sitting on the edge of the bed. Arianna had been a Witch who'd ended up killed by Joseph, and used against the Fae in a deadly game of cat and mouse. We'd discovered she'd been nothing more than pieces from several victims, sewn into one body.

"I find it weird that he's pretending to be something he isn't. I also think there's more going on around here than we can see; more than what they are telling us. Ryder isn't the type to let something like being engaged to a fake heir go unpunished, and I have a feeling we're going to end up in the middle of a flipping war."

"You actually think the Light Fae were in on the deal with Arianna and the Mages?" Adam narrowed his eyes as I smiled in reply.

"I can't help but think they were. It's the only way she could have gotten close to the Dark Prince, and both castes seemed really eager for an alliance of the Dark and Light Heirs. I think these guys are messing with each other, because, Adam, some of what I have seen and heard doesn't add up. I don't think Ryder is the Dark Heir—I think he's something else."

"No, I am *not* the Dark Heir, but Adam is," Ryder said from the doorway making us both jump like naughty children with their hands in the cookie jar.

"What?" I asked, hiding my shaking hands.

"Adam, I need you to come downstairs." Ryder ignored me as I came off the bed wide-eyed.

"Okay, give me a minute, unless Syn is allowed out of her room?" Adam asked with a mischievous smirk.

"It's better if she stays up here for right now." Adam nodded to Ryder and kissed my cheek, before walking out of the room. "Stay put, Syn, unless you need to feed. If that's the case…" Ryder let his words trail off as his lips curled into a dangerous smile.

"I'm good. Why did you say Adam was the Dark Heir?"

"Let it be for now, Pet—I'm sure he will tell you when he is ready to."

I shook my head as a sick feeling engulfed me. "He's my family."

Ryder nodded, but his face showed no emotion. "He had one before you claimed him as your familiar. Try to remember they lost him so that you could have him when you needed him."

I swallowed the retort that sat on my tongue. "I'm going home tonight. End of story."

"You stay with me until you're able to sift home. Besides, Gabe wants to meet you in person and—clothed, preferably."

"Gabe?" I asked, before sitting back down on the edge of the bed.

"*Your dog* would like to meet you. If you'd like to go out for fresh air later, I will arrange it. Other than that, you're stuck here. I'll be leaving in an hour to take care of something that needs my attention. Ristan is staying to keep you busy."

"You mean to babysit me? I don't need a fucking babysitter, and what if I get hungry?" I asked with a devious glint in my eyes that I allowed him to see.

"Ristan will let me know if you need my assistance. Or, we could take care of it right now and solve the issue before it becomes a problem for you."

"Nice try. I'm sure I'll be fine with my *sitter*. You'd better be teaching me how to sift tomorrow so I can go sleep in my own bed."

"I like you in *my* bed, Pet."

 *~*~*~*~* Adam *~*~*~*~*

I have a father. I have an entire family. And Syn had been right. Ryder wasn't the Dark Heir—*I am*. As if it wasn't fucking bad enough that I'm Fae, now I'm royal, as in *ruling family* fucking Fae. I can't function with the things going on in my mind. I can't get her out of my fucking head. I'd almost raped her, and she'd selflessly forgiven me.

She should hate me; would hate me if she knew

how I was imagining bending her over and fucking her until I couldn't feel her anymore. Larissa would hate us if she was around. She'd hate me. I fed gluttonously without a thought of her. I'd wanted to spend my entire life with her, and not once had I thought of her—only Syn.

This is fucking ridiculous! I can't get her out of my head. Her emotions run through me. I'm a fucking filter. She's my world, and I filter her shit and, yet, I can't blame her, because we're linked. Like a fucking machine. She's my other half, and without her there is no balance.

"Cadeyrn, you need to come with us. You belong with us in Faery," the stranger before me said, not for the first time. He is at least as tall as I am, with the same frame I now have. His sky-blue and sapphire eyes seem to snap at me with restrained humor. He has hair that's so black, it has blue highlights; sort of like Ryder's, only it's shoulder length like mine. Just barely visible above his collar is a detailed Celtic cross brand on the side of his neck that is similar to the one on my back. If the familiarity of his features isn't enough, there's also the feeling like something settled into the depths of me and clicked into place—a puzzle piece that had been missing from me for a long time. This man is definitely my father.

"My name is Adam," I growl, not really able to deal with this new round of shit, when Syn is upset just upstairs.

"Your name is Cadeyrn, the Heir to the throne of the Dark Fae. You are needed at home, Son." My father's eyes seem to be searching my face for some sign of recognition, his frown showing the only sign of emotion on his face.

"I belong here now," I argue.

"Your mother has yet to recover from your disappearance, and you have a sister and brothers who also miss you. You have a responsibility to the Dark Fae, and we need you to come home. Ryder has been searching for you, in addition to his other responsibilities." His voice lowered briefly, a twinge of fear and sadness in his tone.

"I really don't care. I'm staying here. I have a life here, and responsibilities."

"Adam, Syn will be okay without you," Ryder said, throwing in his two cents as if anyone fucking wants it, or needs it.

"She's mine," I snarl, hating the fact that he's had her. She is falling for him, and she's as oblivious to it as he is. I can feel it though, and it worries me.

"You think she is. You balance her out, Adam, but you don't want her—you feel the need to please her because you can taste her emotions. She's inside of you, Adam, and everything you think you feel for her is only because you are connected. It isn't real. You don't want to do anything other than be there for her. You are as much a part of her as your hand is a part of yourself."

"Thanks for the education. If *I'm* the Dark Heir, Ryder, then who the *fuck* are *you*?"

"Cadeyrn, you have twelve brothers and a sister. All of your brothers carry the title of Dark Prince." My father looks amused with himself as he watches me absorb the implications. I shake my head. No fucking way. I turn and look at Ryder who's also watching me with a cocky-ass smile on his face. This has to be a fucking joke; he was *not* my brother.

"Adam, it's best for you to go home right now.

You have a lot to catch up on, and I have a job to do here beyond just finding you. The Light Fae are not what they appear to be, and we can't just accuse them outright. They are denying they knew what Arianna was. Everything points to them being a bunch of self-absorbed pricks that are helping the Mages. I plan to eradicate the Mages once and for all, Adam, so I suggest you get in line with me, or stay the fuck out of my way. I don't care which one you choose, but you had better do one or the other soon." Ryder's tone is becoming increasingly angrier, and his eyes are starting to glow.

"And Syn? Where the fuck does she fit in? Or is she just something you plan on using until she's served her purpose, b*rother*, or until you have had enough of her?" I growl back.

"What I do with her is none of your fucking business. She can be yours when I have had my fill of her. Until then, stay the fuck out of my way. She's mine by contract. She breaks it, and I will own her for eternity. She's immortal now, so I'd be careful what you say to her."

"She's nothing more than a toy to you. She is so much fucking more, Ryder, so much more, and you don't deserve her if you can't see that."

"I don't answer to you, *Cadeyrn*. She's a way to pass the time in this cesspool. I have made her no promises beyond training and protection. When I have had my fill of her, I'll let her go. Until then, I suggest you stay the fuck out of my business, *boy*."

"Did you tell her that, or better yet, why don't you tell her that you had Adrian killed so you could fuck her!?" I shout, tired of playing word games with this overbearing prick.

~~*~*~* Synthia *~*~*~*~*

I gasped as my hand flew over my mouth, and I leaned heavily against the wall to keep myself from falling over. Ryder was an asshole, and I was still reeling about him and Adam being brothers. I turned, heading back to the room as fast as my feet would go, and silently closed the door with shaking hands. I had to get away from him.

I don't know what I had expected from him, but I wasn't his to use as he saw fit. This was taking things too far, and I was tired of it; tired of everything. Adam wasn't even named Adam! Seriously! It was like waking up with someone else's life, and no matter how much I wanted it to change, it wouldn't.

Ryder had killed Adrian, or at least he'd had a part in it. More than likely, he ordered it and Vlad carried it out. Either way, I was done with Ryder the second I was finished with Transition. I couldn't trust him. He was up to something, and it wasn't as if he planned on sticking around, other than to finish his business and head back inside Faery.

"You shouldn't be eavesdropping, Flower," Ristan said, startling me. Damn Demon was just lying around on my bed and making himself at home.

"People should just tell the fucking truth around here then," I snapped, frustrated with the entire situation.

"Why can't I see your future?" Ristan sighed, swinging his feet off the bed to sit on the edge.

"No clue. What's Ryder's assignment in this world?" I tossed a question back at him.

"He will tell you sooner or later. Tell me, my little

Flower, what do you remember of the men who broke in and murdered your foster parents?"

"*Parents*. It takes more than sperm and an egg to become parents. They raised me," I said, seething with anger. After what I had witnessed with Ryder and Adam, this questioning had me off balance, and there was a Demon that was gonna get his ass kicked if he wasn't careful.

"Touché. Tell me what you remember of the men who killed your parents then," he repeated as his eyes took me in slowly.

"You saw everything I remember with Z's little 'regression therapy' session. I don't want to remember that shit," I snapped.

"Ah, but I think you do. I'll bet that's why you got the tattoos on your arms. You spelled them so you would never forget what happened."

"Why did Ryder keep from me that he was Adam's brother?" I ignored his question and asked another.

"I don't think that was intentional. We suspected that Adam was the Dark Heir when he broke out of Transition early, and the Heir brands formed. The Dark King came here today to confirm Adam's identity, as every Fae father is linked with his child. For some reason, Adam's link was not working as it should, and I suspect it has something to do with your tattooing. Now, what else do you remember? It might help us solve the mystery of who you are—or *were*, before."

"It doesn't matter to me who I was, Ristan. The only thing that I care about right now is finishing Transition, and getting the fuck out of here. I am who I was before. Just because I'm Transitioning doesn't mean I actually changed the core or character of who

I am. I'm still me and being Fae doesn't change me; it changes my DNA only."

He smiled and messed his long inky-black hair up as he ran his large hand through it. "I don't like mysteries, and, right now you and Adam are the only wild cards in my life. I can see pretty far into everyone else's future—hell, I can tell you most of what will play out for the next week, but not the two of you. I can't even tell what you will have for dinner."

"Ryder. Because he owns me, I'll be having Ryder for dinner, right up until the very second I'm done with his contract. Then, you can bet your ass that he won't be on my menu. Besides, the future is never set, because a single choice can change everything."

"Exactly, Synthia. Hence why I need to know where you fit in. I don't like the fact that I can't see your future or where you fit into Ryder's—"

"Ryder's *what*?" Ryder asked from the door.

"Ryder, I was explaining to Synthia why unknown factors shouldn't be left as unknown."

"She doesn't need to know any of this, Ristan," Ryder warned with his eyes on me.

"Yeah, I get it—knowing too much is dangerous. And anything that doesn't fit in your plan gets itself killed. But then, you'd know all about that now, wouldn't you, Ryder?" I sneered, before turning and leaving the bedroom. I slammed the bathroom door and considered sifting out, but then I'd probably land at his fucking feet and defeat the purpose. Besides, I was almost out of his fucking contract and then I'd be gone for good.

Chapter
FOURTEEN

The next few days were spent learning to sift, which mostly consisted of me landing on my knees in front of Ryder, whom I wanted nothing to do with. I reached up and wiped the sweat from my face, before huffing in frustration and trying again.

I'd been ignoring him since the day I'd over heard his little conversation with Adam. It had dug its way to the top of the box inside my head, and every time I looked at him since, I could hear him telling Adam I meant nothing to him. I'd been putting distance between us, and no matter how hard I tried, I failed at it. I should hate him, but the truth was I didn't. I was hurt and angry all the way to my soul, but I didn't hate him.

Ryder had been silent and brooding as I ignored him. There was a tension around the mansion that was palpable. Even his men gave him a wide berth when he walked through the room. I hadn't brought up what I'd overheard because it probably wouldn't change anything, or change how he felt for that matter.

My goal now was to finish Transition and figure out my next steps, without including Ryder. I was getting too close, feeling too much for him, which I should have known better than to do. I was becoming the type of female who wanted a mate in her life and, even though I did want love, now wasn't the right time, and Ryder had shown me he was absolutely *not* the right man.

"Focus." He growled. "Picture what you want. Put it inside your mind and visualize it," Ryder said from where he stood across the yard.

Adam was my focal point. It should have been easy. It wasn't. I had been at it for days now, and the hunger was becoming all I could think about, and I wasn't caving in. I wouldn't give in and allow Ryder to use me. After his little speech to Adam, I'd made a vow to myself that I wouldn't be used by him again. If anyone would be used, it would be him. But it would be on my terms, and I'd make damn sure he knew it.

I closed my eyes and tried again, and groaned when I felt the wet grass beneath my jeans again. I pushed off the ground and spun around, ignoring Ryder as he held out his arm to grab me. When I was across the yard again, I closed my eyes, shutting out the world. I'd tried everything, and either I was defective or I hadn't found the power within, as Ryder kept calling it.

Adam could sift with ease. He'd done it on his first attempt perfectly. I was distracted by everything inside my mind and everything going on around me, and everyone trying to keep me in the dark was making matters worse. I tried to send out my senses and pulled them back, afraid to tap the leyline. I opened my eyes and caught Ryder's cocky smirk as he looked from me to the ground that had actual imprints from my knees.

I was tired, and cramping from hunger. Frustrated and pushed to my limits, I closed my eyes and tried to focus on my magic, the magic I was used to.

Everything was colliding together. Hunger pushed at me as my mind grasped what it could. I smiled as power suddenly rushed through me. Shouts erupted from Adam as he felt me tapping the leyline. My mind had been so jumbled that I hadn't even realized that I'd even tapped it. I opened my eyes as Ryder snarled and sifted to me, shoving me to the ground.

Ryder's men were instantly surrounding us as I released the line, realizing the mistake I'd made. Ryder was the first to speak as his men closed in around us. "What the fuck, Syn?"

"I didn't mean to!" I cried, shaking with the knowledge that I'd just jeopardized everyone here with my carelessness.

"You never tap a fucking line unless you know where it leads!" he shouted at me furiously, and I deserved it. I was trained better than this.

"I'm fucking sorry!" I cried back through angry tears.

"Ristan," Ryder growled as his Demon's eyes flashed red.

"Something's coming Ryder, something big," Ristan said with an eerie calmness that didn't match his words.

"No visual of what it is?" Ryder asked, pulling me up and closer to his body.

"Whatever it is, Ryder, it's coming for her alone," Ristan said as his eyes went back to black and silver.

"Savlian, Dristan, get these two inside the house. The rest of you, get ready," Ryder said as he pushed me away from himself and toward Dristan.

I watched as those who surrounded Ryder shimmered momentarily and then solidified again, only now they were dressed in dark cloaks and tunics, with wicked looking weapons held in their hands. All of them in their Fae battle gear looked like something out of the books I had read back at the Guild ready for war or whatever it was that was heading our way.

"Ryder, be safe," Dristan said.

I didn't say anything as those golden eyes met and held mine captured. I couldn't. This was my fault. Savlian pushed Adam toward Dristan and grabbed my hand. "Stupid girl," he growled.

"Enough, Savlian. Take her to her room and guard the door until I say otherwise," Ryder snarled, leveling me with a dark stare as his eyes changed, and his cloak materialized around him. It was the same one from the Wild Hunt, and instantly he'd changed from the beautiful man, into the beautiful, dangerous creature I saw in Faery.

"Sure thing," Savlian said, holding his hand out in front of us to indicate we should precede them. I started forward, but only because I was about to pass out. I needed to feed, and I was being stubborn, but I had never imagined it would lead to anything like this.

Upstairs, I entered my room as Adam, saying nothing, started toward his own. "Adam?" I called out, hoping he'd turn around and say something, but he just shook his dark head and kept walking. I spun on my heels and went after him. "What the hell, Adam?"

"What do you want from me, Syn? Because I'm in the same fucking boat, on the same fucking pond, and right now, we're both sinking!"

"In the room, you two," Savlian said as he folded his massive arms across his chest.

"We are not sinking, Adam. It's called surviving. If you want to go and do whatever, do it. Don't stay because I need you. I'm a big girl and I'll be fine. I need you to be happy. I don't want you to stay because you feel obligated or anything stupid like that."

"Syn," Adam said when I spun around to leave. "Stop dammit. I'm just—shit! How the heck am I supposed to stay when the only thing I feel right now is the need to be *with* you?"

"Adam, I need to be with you as well," I whispered, and reached for his hand, but he jerked it away as if I was diseased.

"No, Syn, I actually want to be *with* you. Not by you, not around you, I want to be inside of you, and it makes me sick. I loved Larissa, and, yet, I can't even feel her death anymore. The only thing I feel is this need to help you. To take that internal fucking hunger away and make the pain stop, because I feel it every fucking minute of the day. It's driving me insane!"

I took a step back and shook my head, confused. I wasn't sure what to say other than *shit*, and a few other choice obscene words. "Adam—"

The house shook as something exploded outside. Adam caught me before I could fall to the floor. I cried out as I realized that whatever I had brought to us had just detonated some sort of explosive outside where Ryder and his men were.

"Get downstairs, now!" Savlian shouted, and Adam obeyed by grabbing hold of me. We sifted to the basement where Dristan and Savlian were weaving a spell against the wall.

"Get inside," Dristan shouted as Savlian pushed us inside a make shift shelter, and before we could respond or ask what had happened, they'd sealed us inside.

I couldn't speak past the lump that had formed in my throat. Guilt crept up my neck. Something was happening out there because I'd tapped the line and I'd brought whatever it was back to me. I turned and looked at Adam. "This is my fault," I whispered, and looked around the room. A large bed was positioned in the corner of the room and actual lanterns sat on a dresser, already lit. I scanned for anything, weapon wise, and jumped when Adam spoke.

"This isn't your fault. We're stumbling through it, Syn. While we know what I am, we still have no idea how to get your powers open. Think of it like a box, one you have to unlock. You have to want it to open, and right now you don't know how to get to that place in your head. You're starving, I can feel it; you want to go home, you want everything to stop and just go back to the way it was. It won't. We both know that. Ryder said that these feelings—"

"I heard him, I heard everything. I know he ordered the hit on Adrian. What I don't know is why?" I left out the part where he was using me, because it hurt still, and I didn't want to hear it, didn't want to feel it—or worse, to have Adam feel it through the bond.

"I don't know. Hell, all I heard was Zahruk saying he would kill him again if he couldn't keep his hands off of you. My guess is that Ryder's been trailing us for a while. That he's been watching and waiting. Watching you, Syn. Alden said Marie left a letter saying that in the event of her death, Alden should contact Ryder. What I don't know was why she would think he could help you."

"Ryder told me that Marie sent him a letter a few years ago too, but it just said something about protecting me, and that I was different from the rest of the Witches. You think she knew what we were?"

"I think she at least suspected it, or why leave the letter? Unless she thought she was helping you, she wouldn't have left it. She loved you. She loved us all. She was well respected and an elder and I'll bet she covered Alden's ass from the get-go about us."

I nodded considering it. "You have a fucking Fairy family," I said with a cheeky grin after a minute of silence.

"So do you, Syn; somewhere. I can't imagine they hid you for spite. The Guild doesn't allow Fae to hide their own within the ranks unless someone pretty fucking important had asked them to. Even then, it would have had to have been something that involved the Guild for them to have lifted a single finger to help."

"Or, someone took me and lied to the Guild. It's the Fae, Adam. They are notorious for lying and fucking each other over. They get off on it. They don't trust one another, and war is always looming on the horizon for them. Eventually, it will bleed over into this world, and then God have mercy on us because the Fae won't."

We sat for what seemed like hours, talking to ease the unease. The mansion shook several more times before anyone came down to the room, and, when they did, it wasn't with good news. Zahruk stood in the doorway covered in blood, his face nicked in several places from fighting.

"Get ready to move. We have injured men. We are heading to Faery to be safe." He glared at me before sealing up the entrance to the shelter behind him, as if we'd escape if the seal was down.

My heart hit the floor. What the hell had I done? How could I have been so stupid to tap the line, even if I hadn't meant to? This was my fault. If I hadn't been so tired and denying the hunger I felt, this wouldn't have had happened at all. I felt hot tears as they dropped from my eyes to run down my face. They were tears of shame that I'd been so childish to place others in danger over my own stubborn pride.

"They'll be fine, Syn. They are immortal," Adam tried to reassure me.

My heart had sunk in my chest, and for a few moments I wasn't sure it was even beating. I felt sick to my stomach and almost numb with disbelief. This couldn't be happening. What the hell had I been thinking to tap a line? I felt tears falling down my cheeks, even as Adam kissed them away.

Ristan came to the door and weaved his hands before he stepped through, and looked right at me with the most sober face I'd ever seen on him. "We need to go to Faery. It's the only place with the medical supplies to heal the men."

"Ristan, get the boy. Syn...you get to be *my* Pet, for now," Zahruk said with a wicked tilt to his mouth.

"Who is injured?" I asked, and felt hot tears pushing with the need to be released.

"It's nothing you need to concern yourself with, Synthia. Right now we just need to get to where it's safe, so we can take in the extent of the damage and evaluate the information we gained about these assholes."

Chapter
FIFTEEN

We sifted from the shelter into a room that was dark, swallowed in shadows. The room was elegant, even in the cover of darkness. I could see a medium sized bed pressed up against the wall, as usual. Blue silk sheets that looked inviting and soothing adorned it. I could smell Ryder's masculine scent, and watched as Zahruk, stood awaiting orders. I was wary about being alone with Ryder, since I'd caused his men injury that could have easily been avoided had it not been for stubborn pride.

"Leave us, Zahruk," Ryder said from across the room.

"I'm sorry," I whispered into the shadows, knowing he would hear it.

"Come here, Synthia," he replied without emotion, which sent butterflies to my stomach as chills began to race down my spine.

"Ryder, I said I was sorry." Shit, I sounded weak! I strengthened my resolve and squared my shoulders.

"You are used to being able to depend on your coven, but, as Fae, you will have to depend on us for the foreseeable future. What happened today can't happen again. I have to hear the words from you; that you understand what was so wrong about today. I need for you to promise me that you will not allow this to happen ever again," he said gently.

"Ryder," I murmured.

"No, Syn. Not this time. You need to learn some humility from this. Mistakes like this could have killed someone; as it is, some of my men were hurt. I take responsibility for their injuries, as we could have sifted out at any time, but I took this opportunity to try and learn more about this enemy. You have to take responsibility for drawing them to us with your stubborn foolishness."

"I said I was sorry. What do you want from me? If I could go back and undo it, I would in a heartbeat," I whispered, before stepping closer to him and into the shadows. I knew what he wanted, and my hands shook with it. My eyes adjusted enough to see Ryder leaning against the far wall of the room, eyeing me like the predator he was. He was in his full Fae form, which I had only seen once before, when I had been in Faery.

"I want you to fucking mean it! I want you to get over this anger or whatever the fuck has you staying away from my bed. I've given you room. I've stayed away from you so that you could adjust. I thought maybe you needed time, but it turns out you don't need time. You're too stubborn to fucking admit when you need to feed, or when your body is weak!" He snapped angrily, his eyes narrowed on me, his arms still lazily folded across his chest.

"You killed Adrian!" I cried, feeling the angry tears as they welled up in my eyes.

His face went cold and blank, instantly. "Who told you that?" He asked in a deadly tone.

"You did. I heard everything you and Adam said to each other. Why? That's all I want to fucking know. Ryder, why would you do that to me!?"

"Because I wanted you," he replied, dropping his arms to his sides and shaking his head as if in denial still.

"So you gave the order for him to be killed!? Do have any idea how crazy that sounds? We were just kids!"

"You keep expecting me to behave like a human. I'm not; I'm anything but human. I saw the way you looked at him, and I watched you for quite a while. Adrian wanted more power. He wanted to be stronger than you and Adam. In this, he is no different than a Fae man wanting to be the one that others look to for protection and strength. I knew if I got it, he'd be out of my way for a while. It was the perfect chance to get him out of the picture, and for me to get close to you. I did what any other Fae would have done. Only, I fucked up by thinking I would be done with you by the time he'd been fully changed over to my world. I fucked up by thinking that a short amount of time with you would be enough."

My jaw dropped. "You killed one of my best friends and that is what you reply with?" I was floored, and a little pissed that he couldn't even say sorry.

"I didn't kill him. I made him stronger."

"You had to kill him to turn him! And even if Vlad did the killing part, you gave the fucking orders. You ordered your competition to be *killed*! You didn't even try to get me first. You just took him out because you could! You don't even want me. You told Adam to stay out of the way, and when you were *done* he could have me!"

"Yes," he said, stepping closer. "Who says I will ever be done with you, Synthia?"

"I do, because I'm going home. I can sift, and even if I do land at your feet every time, at least we know I won't starve to death. I won't be some play toy. I can't do it. I won't."

He swallowed and nodded, and I felt my heart flutter to the floor. I closed my eyes as the tears dropped, angry and unabashed. He'd actually killed Adrian, and I'd blamed Adrian. I'd blamed him for not fighting harder to stay with us. Adrian always did have a chip on his shoulder about the amount of power he wielded compared to Adam and me, even though Adrian was extremely powerful in his own right. Offering Adrian more power would be the one thing that he would never refuse, no matter the cost. I guess Adrian had been telling the truth when he said he had no choice in the matter. I questioned how much truth there was to the rest of what Adrian said about the night he 'died.'

"You can go home when you can prove you can feed; when you can show me that you will continue to feed—even without me. I won't let you go just so you can starve yourself. I can't change the past, and I'm not going to play on words and say I'm sorry for what I did, because I'm not. I'm Fae; it's how we are raised. Had you been raised with us, you'd see that this is how we get what we want, and how we show who the better mate is."

"You were not in Faery, and I was raised by humans. You can't expect for me to react as someone who was raised in Faery, any more than I can expect you to act like someone who was raised here. We just need to end this before it gets too complicated. Adam found his family, and I'm happy for him. I'm not staying with you, though. I can't play cat and mouse anymore. You shouldn't have killed Adrian, or ordered his change. I'm not even sure where we go from there. You're not in this for me. You're in it because you want me. Believe it or not, there is a difference."

"I want you," he growled and ran his fingers through his hair. "I know that much. It's not just going to stop, because you tell me to. I take what I want, always have. I told you when we started this, Syn; I make no excuses for what I am."

"You had my boyfriend turned into a *Vampire*," I snapped.

"And you just almost got my men killed by the same group that tried to take out the Fae compound."

"That was an accident. You gave an order! You wanted something like a spoiled fucking child, so you took out anything in the way to get to it," I barked angrily, and heat fused in my cheeks with guilt.

"I wanted you, and I went for it with everything inside of me. I'm not some fucking little boy that will stand aside and wait for what I want. I did what I have been taught. I set events in motion so I could have you. I wanted you from the moment I saw you, Synthia Raine McKenna, and I did what I had to do to make it happen."

I shook my head. I couldn't expect him to act like a human, because he was anything but. Still, I wasn't sure I could forgive him right now either, so I wondered where we went from here. "I need to feed," I whispered. "And then I need to get away from you." I fought against the tears, but they fell, regardless of how much I tried to stop them.

The tick in his jaw was hammering wildly; his brands were pulsing in perfect tempo with them. I walked to the bed, ignoring him as I did so. I removed my shirt slowly and tossed it on the floor, before unbuttoning my jeans and stepping out of them.

"You can't leave without someone to feed from, Synthia."

"I'll figure it out, but at least that will be my choice. I need to get away from you. I need time to figure out what to do."

"And if I say no?" he asked, narrowing his eyes as he stepped closer.

"Then you won't like what happens. I have told you, repeatedly, that I'm not a pet. I can't just be leashed just because you want to keep me, or because you enjoy me in your bed. I need more than that. I need someone I can trust, and who can trust me. That's not us. We don't trust each other, and I'm only yours until you are done. The truth is I'm not even sure why I agreed to allow it to happen the first time. I should have run faster in the hunt, and I should have been smarter and told you no."

He growled, but he didn't move closer. Instead, he sifted from the room, so suddenly it left me breathless. Obviously, it left me boneless as well, because, the moment he was gone, my legs gave out and I cried. He'd told Vlad to change Adrian, and he hadn't considered the consequences of it.

I wiped angrily at my eyes as the hunger pangs clenched agonizingly inside of me, but, once again, I tried to push it away. It's how we'd gotten here in the first place. I was gulping down huge sobs when Ryder sifted back in violently, sending a wind through the room in his haste. He picked me up off the floor, and cradled me against his chest as he sat on the bed.

"Fuck, Syn. It wasn't supposed to be like this. You were supposed to think I was the better man, but I didn't even stop to think of you. I don't take humans to my bed. You were the first I had to have. I'd never thought this far ahead; I only thought as far as getting you into my bed. I fucked up. I was only buying time with you by sending Adrian away. I was stacking the deck in my favor so that I could make us happen. I was the smarter and better man; it should have impressed you. Instead, it broke you. I was supposed to be done with you by the time Adrian was done with his change. Instead, I only wanted you more after I'd had you. I hated that I wanted you; that someone like me could be obsessed with something like you. You were human, a Witch, and beneath me. It should have been a simple thing to get you out of my system. Instead, you rocked my foundation and made me need you. My mistake was expecting you to react like a Fae. Because of that, you will end up hating me."

"What else have you done?" I asked, turning my face further up so that I could see his eyes.

"I made Alden send you to me. I knew Arianna wasn't the Light Heir, but I knew that asking him for a decoy would get you close. I asked for the best, because I knew he'd send you to me. I had my men watching you and Adam from the moment you pulled up outside of the towers, but you were smart enough to figure that part out. I watched your eyes as you told him to abort. You already knew I had your team, but you just couldn't let it enter your mind. I watched you sleep inside your bedroom before that. I watched you touching yourself, soothing the need you wouldn't allow another to fulfill, because you were still mending from a broken heart; one I had created."

"The wards inside my room," I said. He'd been in my room watching me. How many times had he done it? It was unnerving to know how easily he'd gotten inside, and not to have known I was in danger at the time.

"I changed them to think of me as an exception, a non-threat. I'm Fae. Your wards were child's play for me and easily manipulated."

"Larissa?"

"I had nothing to do with that. I liked Larissa. I'd already watched you suffer from grief once by that point. I'd never be a part of it again. I meant it when I said I'd protect you. I'm not going away just because you want to leave me."

He wiped the tears from my cheek, and I let him. I inhaled deeply and let it out slowly and evenly. He was right; I was going to leave. I was leaving this world and going back to mine, one way or another. I needed time to think, to process. He'd done too much; he'd given an order for something that could never be undone. I wasn't sure it could be forgiven either.

"Anything else?" I asked, afraid of the answer.

"Isn't that enough?" he responded, wiping away another tear.

I shook my head, not because it wasn't enough, but because it was too much. He'd done too much to get me right where I was, in his arms. In his world, this was how you got the woman; while in my world, it's how you made them run screaming for the hills. I punched him in the arm, and he growled, but took it.

"What about the way you treated me, Ryder? You hated me as much as I hated you."

"I punished you, because I wanted you. I've never wanted anything I couldn't have. You were the first woman to tell me no, Synthia. You called me names with that sexy fucking mouth, and all I wanted to do was kiss it shut. I hate that you got beneath my skin, where no one else has been."

"You lied. You're Fae, and you lied to me. You told me you didn't know he was alive," I said, struggling to get out of his arms and upright on the bed.

"I didn't lie, I played with words, Syn. Adrian wasn't dead. He's undead. He got what he wanted; he has more power now. He is no longer regretting his decision to change. In the end, he got what he wanted, what he craved; it just turned out he wanted it more than he wanted you. You ended up being the only victim with the way this played out, and I failed to see that as a possibility. I never expected you to break, and I'm sorry for my part in that. Fae do not grieve the same way humans do, and I didn't know how to react to what I had done. You broke, and I wanted to pick you up and put the pieces back together. In the end, I just watched you do it on your own, and it drew me to you more than I could have ever expected."

"Exactly how long have you been watching me, Ryder?" I asked, narrowing my eyes as I sat back down beside him.

"Since Marie sent me the letter a few years ago. At first, you were young and looked just like the other humans. I watched you train, and I watched you grow into a woman. It wasn't until I saw you in the arms of Adrian that I knew that I wanted to know how it would feel for you to touch me like that. I should have realized then that it had become more than just some twisted infatuation. You wanted my secrets, Synthia, and I warned you that my past was messy. I told you that you'd end up hating me if you knew."

He had. He'd warned me about this. I didn't hate him, though. I couldn't believe the lengths he'd gone through just to have me, but, at the same time, I couldn't hold him to the same sort of accountability that I would hold a human to. He wasn't human, and everyone had been warning me this entire time to stop thinking of him as one. He'd crossed the line, though; one I wasn't sure he could come back from.

"I don't hate you, Ryder, but the things you did… I'm not sure I can forgive you right now, if ever. I need time away from you to think. At any time, did you actually want me, or was I just something to pass the time for you?"

"You weren't supposed to be more. From the first time I danced with you, I knew I was in over my head. Holding you in my arms and watching you smile set things into motion that I'd never thought possible. As I got to know you better, I knew that when you figured out what I had done, it would be the end of us. I didn't want you to find out like this. You deserve someone who can give you what you want; someone who can be what you need. There's a problem with that, though, because honestly, I'm not sure I can let you go."

"That's no longer your choice. I'm going home without you. Ryder, the contract is over. I'm going to feed from you to show you that I can, and then I'm leaving here. I need to know you'll stay away from me when I do."

"It's not safe," he argued.

"That's my problem now. I am out of Transition. I can sift, and even though I might land at your feet when I do so, it's still sifting. You have one night left with me. It's all I can give you. It's less than you deserve, but we both need to feed. I'm sorry that I got anyone hurt because I was upset and refusing to feed. I learned my lesson. I'll start looking for someone to feed from when I get home."

His jaw popped, but he kept quiet and nodded, then fisted his hands against my skin. I could feel him breathing shallowly as the rattle deepened in his chest. "Fine, if that's what you want."

"It is, Ryder. I need to be alone to think."

"You need to feed, and then, when it's safe, I'll take you home."

I turned to look at him, really look at him. Here was this beautiful, deadly creature, who'd done what his culture thought was right, just so he could have me. He'd been doing what he'd been taught from birth, and I had paid the price for it. I could feed from him, because the truth was, I'd never been more sexually or physically attracted to another person or creature.

"Fine," I said reaching up to remove my bra, realizing I'd been arguing this entire time mostly naked. He was faster though. His magic wafted through the room and instantly we were both naked. I allowed my eyes to take in his masculine beauty, memorizing everything in case I never saw him again.

The rattling that had started deep in his chest intensified as he pulled me closer. His hands were gentle, but I could feel his urgency to feed match mine. I allowed him to bring me close and capture my mouth. I was giving myself to him for this night. Tonight, I was his. Tomorrow I was leaving, with or without his help.

He pushed me down on the bed and rained magical little kisses all over my skin again. The entire room was wrapped in his magic, stronger than it had been in the human world. The scent of him was wild and primitive here; dark and sensual, like the creature it belonged to.

He pulled his mouth from mine and whispered in a strange language, his eyes watching mine for a reaction. His voice had been gentle and endearing. I wondered if it was an endearment, or if it was something I should fear. I knew he wouldn't brand me again as he had the last time he'd spoken in this language. This time, I felt no connection from the words, and as his hand lowered and stroked my naked sex, I gave in and just felt him. It would be the last time I would be with him like this. He'd given me his secrets, and they'd proven to be just as he had warned—too much to come back from. But, I didn't hate him. I hated what he was, what I was. That couldn't be fixed with words, or sex. I needed time to heal from it.

I whimpered with need as he continued to touch me slowly, leisurely as if we had all the time in the world. Time was passing around us as I reached down to grasp his cock, stroking the velvety softness in my hand. He gasped at the connection and moved his hips so I could better please him. We said nothing, both just lying there pleasuring the other until it became too much, and he took control.

His mouth found mine as his hand continued to work my sensitive flesh. He pushed me back against the bed, pinning me easily. He gave me a sad smile as he parted my legs with his knees and entered me swiftly. He was hard and fast until we both exploded and fed from each other's release.

He pulled back, and his golden eyes locked with mine. He began to move around the slickness of my pussy, until he found the perfect tempo again and continued it. I struggled to make him move faster, but he was intent on doing it slow and gentle this time.

My heart clenched along with the muscles gripping his cock. He lowered his mouth and licked the hard peak on one nipple, and then the other. When he raised his head, his eyes had changed to obsidian, and it was as if something else had taken control.

I felt my heart race as the change took over his face, and he became even more beautiful. Gold lights blazed in the obsidian of his eyes like stars, and the room vibrated with power that made the fine hairs on my arms rise up from it. It was raw, vibrant, and deadly power. Instead of standing by a single power line, it felt as if I was standing inside a power plant; one that had raw power surging unchecked through it.

"You're *mine*," he said in the multi-layered voice, his body moving faster until I could only hold on to him as he pounded inside of me until he exploded. I pulled from his orgasm, and moaned with pleasure, and fear as his powerful orgasm entered me violently. I vibrated from the inside out until I was sure I glowed from it, and when I thought he was done, he turned me onto my stomach and entered me again from behind.

"Ryder," I moaned, but he ignored it and entered me again, making the words die on my lips. My hands gripped the silk sheets as the sound of flesh meeting in lust echoed through the room. I exploded, and still he continued to fuck me until one after another, the orgasms took me over the edge of sanity and left me hanging there. I was barely awake when his teeth sank into my flesh and drew from my artery while his cock continued to drive home inside of me.

The sound of sucking and something else was flittering along my brain, as if I knew what it was, but couldn't think past it, or around it to figure out what it was. I heard arguing and the sound of animalistic growls, combined with Ryder's voice in that strange language again. To my fuzzy brain, it was as if he was fighting against something for control. Then everything went blank, and darkness swallowed my mind.

Chapter
SIXTEEN

I awoke to Vlad looking over me. His silver eyes scanned my face as he slapped my cheek. I tried to make words come out to tell him to stop, but my mouth was dry and unusable. I squinted and slapped him back. He smiled, and I glared at him. Why the hell was he slapping me?

"She's going to be fine. She just needs some rest," Vlad said, standing up to his full height. His eyes were gentle, but there was coldness to them that hadn't been there before.

I tried to make my eyes fully focus, but the moment they did, I wished they'd stayed fuzzy. Dristan, Ristan, and Vlad were all inside the room. I had been dressed in a dark-blue silk nightgown, and I struggled to recall what had happened last night between Ryder and me.

"What happened? Why are you all in here?" I questioned. Normally, if they were inside the room, something had happened. "Where's Ryder?"

"What do you remember?" Vlad asked, watching me closely.

"Fighting," I said, remembering that we'd fought over what he'd done.

"That's all?" Vlad persisted, and I searched my mind.

"No," I admitted and blushed profusely. I'd been having sex with Ryder. I realized I wasn't hungry anymore. For the first time since Transitioning, I felt really full. "Did I hurt him?" I asked, fighting through the sludge in my mind. My neck hurt, but as I ran my hand over it, it seemed fine. He'd bitten me! The memory came rushing back. As he'd been inside of me, he'd taken my blood. Holy shit, Ryder was a Vampire! "Ryder's a Vampire?" I asked in disbelief.

"Is that what you think?" Vlad asked with a laugh, as he sat down in a chair I hadn't noticed before.

"He bit me. What else should I think?" I countered him.

"Ryder is not a Vampire," Dristan said, lowering his lime and emerald green eyes to meet mine. For the first time, I noticed that Dristan had a thin black ring around his two-toned eyes. I'm not sure if it was my new Fae sight, or if it was being here in Faery that I noticed it now. His full Fae form was painfully beautiful to see. Even Vlad and Ristan were breathtakingly gorgeous inside of Faery.

"He's not a Vampire. So what, he just goes around biting people when he's—ya know?"

"No, please tell us, Flower," Ristan said grinning wide.

"Figure it out," I said, hating that I blushed even more.

"You look good in red," Ristan said as he laughed.

"Shove it, Demon," I quipped.

"Only if you help me," he continued.

"Children, if you're done," Vlad said. "Syn, what else do you remember?"

"I remember arguing with him. I remember arguing with him because he told you to change Adrian, in fact." I leveled him with an accusing look and sat up. "I argued with him because he thinks he can own me."

"You challenged him," Vlad said.

"No, I did not. I told him I wouldn't be owned, and he calls me his pet! I'm not a dog, and he had my boyfriend changed into a vampire just so he could get in my bed!"

None of them even blinked at the words. No shocked faces, no utter horror. Just three faces that waited for the catch. I rubbed my hands down my face. I had at least expected Vlad to understand why I'd be upset, since he'd spent most of his life around humans—but no such luck.

"And?"

And there it was. The looks on their faces changed into words. I growled and shook my head. "And nothing! I need to get away from him. He's done things I can't even fathom, much less process. I need to go home so I can think without him making me want him! He's impossible to be around because every time he is, my brain shuts off, and my vagigi turns on!"

"Vagigi?" Vlad asked as Ristan laughed outright at me and Dristan let out a strangled noise like he was choking on something.

"Yes. He walks in all tall, dark and deadly, and my brain turns me into a sex addict. I know I have to feed, but if I don't get away from him I'm going to go crazy. I need space. I just need to think."

"No, go back to vagigi. I want to know why you named your vagina vagigi—spare no details," Ristan said between laughs.

"Grrrr…Is there a reason you Three Stooges are here, or did you just come to drive me insane? Where's Ryder?"

"He's checking your house," Vlad said calmly as Ristan smirked.

"You actually told Ryder you were leaving him?" Dristan asked.

"Yes, I told the caveman I was leaving. He had my boyfriend—or ex…whatever—changed into a Vampire just so that he could get in my pants. You may not think that's a bad thing, but I do. You keep telling me to give him a break because he's not human, but you forget the fact that I was raised by them. What is okay for you guys is not always the same for me. I didn't take Claire's ass out just to get to Ryder, nor did I have her turned into anything." Claire was the woman I'd caught Ryder with right after I'd given him a lap dance. He'd had her bent over his desk in his office and it had been educational to say the least. "Oh, not to mention that I also found out he's been stalking me for years, and watching me in my bedroom, and seeing things that no one, and I repeat no one, has ever seen!"

"Were you dressed?" Dristan asked as heat entered his jewel-like eyes.

"Eyes up here, Buddy. And, does it matter!?" I said pointing my middle finger up as I held it at chest level, where his eyes were currently looking.

"Please, tell me what you were doing inside your

bedroom," Ristan purred silkily.

"I prefer lower," Dristan said, smiling roguishly, continuing his own conversation.

"I'm with Ristan on this one. I want to know what he saw, and exactly what you were doing," Vlad said as he smiled wide, which showed off his fangs.

"I prefer to go home," I countered.

"You will have to discuss that with Ryder when he gets back," Vlad said, his eyes no longer hard.

"Am I a prisoner?" I asked as my eyes narrowed on him.

"No, Synthia. You are a guest. Those men came through that leyline to kill you. He won't let you go back unless he is assured you will be safe. Don't be that girl; you're smarter than that. You are as hot-headed as he is. It's best to let him make sure you are safe."

"What girl?" I asked, offended, but not sure why.

"The one who runs home crying and gets dead."

"Oh." Well yes, that would suck.

"Flower, you're upset. We can see that much, but he did what any of us would do. At the same time, though, you have a right to be upset. Just let us make sure you are cared for and that it is safe for you to go home before you run off."

I nodded. "How are the wounded?"

"Feeding," Ristan said impishly. "They are not complaining, Flower. No one was so injured that they needed more than a good feeding and some fresh Faery air to heal. We all have grown attached to you, so none of us harbor ill feelings toward you for what happened. We could have sifted out and ended the fight before it had begun, but, then again, we would have lost an opportunity to learn more about these Fae who want to kill you. You are an infant in our world, and you are learning. It takes time, and we respect that. Do the same for Ryder," Ristan said, serious for once.

"I don't even know if it's me who wants him, or if it's the fact that everything is turning upside down and he's something to hang on to. That's not being fair to him, Ristan. I told him what I heard him say to Adam. He doesn't want me for more than what we have right now. I'm not built like that. I'm not someone who will go from one man to another. It's better if I get away from him now. We go at each other hard; we fight more than anything. I'm not even sure we actually like each other, because it's been one thing after another since Larissa died. He's not my happily ever after. He told me that from the start of this. Fairytales are full of shit, as far as I'm concerned. There is no happy ending to this. I get it now. I just need to go home and figure out where I am now."

"Welcome to the club, Synthia. Life isn't a fairytale," Vlad said with a faraway look in his eyes.

I wanted to know about his past. I mean, who got to ask the real deal about Dracula's past? But I needed to go home, where my brain could put everything together and; make sense of it all. I was still in shock, and processing it all here wasn't an option.

"So, you remember nothing else, except that he bit you?" Dristan asked.

"Nope, only that he went crazy and bit me. Again, should I remember more?" I asked him yet again.

"No," Vlad said with a small smile on his lips. "You should try and rest a bit. Ryder will be back soon to talk to you about going home."

Great! That's all I needed—Ryder coming in here and us going at it like rabbits, which we seemed to do every time there was a bed near us. As if my panties had a mind of their own, which was attached to Ryder's will—they just slid down or dissolved at his whim. I was a smart person, unless I was facing Ryder. From the moment I had met him, I had stopped thinking anything through. I had started doing stupid things, making mistakes, like signing a contract without reading it. Normally, I wasn't that girl. I was a badass Witch who did as she was told and protected people. What I did meant something, and now I had no idea where to even start rebuilding my life.

"Flower, we need to talk," Ristan said, sitting closer to me on the bed.

"Go away, Ristan. I don't want to talk about this anymore," I replied.

"Did you tell him how you feel about what he did to Adrian?" he continued to question.

"Yes, but inside his head it was the right thing to do, and I get that. It hurts knowing he did this to me, to my friend. He stalked me, Ristan, and while I could overlook that, I'm not sure I can ever forgive him for what he did to Adrian. I just want to go home and start living. I need time to heal."

"Could you?"

"Could I what?"

"Could you go back to your life now that you are Fae, and could you forget him so easily? If it was only because he was using you, you wouldn't be upset. It's because you have feelings for him, and they always get the better of us."

"I'm not admitting to anything but distrust and anger right now."

"Cheater. You are upset, because you think he hurt someone you loved. You're upset, because you have feelings for him, and it pisses you off that, even after learning about everything he has done, you still want him. Ryder won't love easily; you will have to fight for him if you want him, Flower. He's a good man, though stubborn and very self-disciplined, and yes, he knows what he wants, and he gets it, no matter the cost. You're applying human rules to him when he isn't. He is what he was always meant to be."

"Is this another pep talk? I told you, I need time. If Ryder can't give me that much, then he isn't the person you think he is. What he did was over the top and uncalled for, Ristan! He shouldn't have done this, period."

"You're missing the point. Shit, you're as stubborn as he is. There's something bigger going on right now, Syn; bigger than you both. You brought the Mages along with that group of Fae to the mansion, and they were ready for war—we weren't. He could have blamed you, but he didn't. He protected you while he was looking for answers, even though he could have been killed. His worry was for your safety. He sent us to protect you, which left him without his main bodyguards, so you could be safe." He stopped and placed his fingers under my chin to lift my face to his. "I think you are tied to his destiny, and that's why you are in my blind spot. I've never once met someone who has no tomorrow inside my head, Syn—until you and Adam." His silver and black eyes narrowed, and he shook his head. "Tell him, Syn. Tell him how you feel."

Ristan left soon after that, and I replayed his words over and over in my head. I watched the time go by on my watch slowly as I lay in the bed, wondering where Ryder was, and if he was okay.

Time passed endlessly, before Adam came into the bedroom radiating anger. "Let's go, Syn. *Now*."

It was the only words I needed to stand up and accept his hand.

"Follow," he said, pulling me with him as he rushed from the room and took me down a long winding hallway. We stopped at a railing that overlooked a magnificent courtyard full of trees, flowers, and fountains that put the most beautiful parks in the world to utter shame. "Those are all his, Syn, all of them. He owns each and every one of them." My brain finally wrapped itself around what his heated words implied.

I felt a sob rip through me and managed to hold it in as I saw all of the women that were in the courtyard, dressed in nothing more than silks. He had an entire harem of women to pleasure and feed him. They were all beautiful, and Fae. Why would he ever need me? He had so many women that I couldn't count them all.

"They all belong to Ryder?" I squeaked through the tightening of my throat as it choked from tears.

"They do. Some are used for guests, his men, and others he keeps untouched by any but himself in a separate part of this place."

"Take me home, Adam, please," I whispered brokenly.

"I can't go with you, Syn. I'm under contract. The only way I have out is to go home to my father."

"Will you be okay if you help me get out of here?"

I asked, not wanting to get him in trouble for helping me.

"I'll be fine, Syn. Will you?"

"Just take me home, Adam, please."

"Come. I have been exploring what little I can since I got here. Most of this place is heavily warded and sealed off from me, so there was only so much I could see. I did find a portal that I am sure was not meant to be found by us. This place is a maze; one meant to keep people in it. I can get you home through the portal. I need to know you will be okay, Syn. As a friend who is going through the same thing, I'm worried about you."

"Huh, you had a crazy Fairy turn your ex into a vampire and watch you do naughty stuff inside your bedroom, too?" I joked, which made Adam laugh. It had been my aim, even though my heart was breaking.

Ryder had a courtyard full of beautiful Fae—why the hell had he wanted me? I felt my heart drop to my feet, and I stepped over it to enter the portal that would take me home without my Dark Prince of secrets by my side.

Chapter
SEVENTEEN

It had been six days since I'd left Ryder and Faery behind. And, even though I'd left him behind, it felt as if he was still with me. When I slept at night, I could still smell him and feel his arms wrapped around me. I dreamt of him watching me sleep, and even though he never responded to me in the dreams, his presence was strangely soothing.

It shouldn't have been. After everything he'd done to me, I should have hated him. The problem was that I was new to this life and still slightly under contract, since I couldn't sift. It was a lot to take in; that he'd been watching Adrian and me, and had given the order for Adrian to be changed just to have me. I wasn't even sure I'd actually processed it all yet. I wasn't sure what was worse; the fact that he'd watched me inside my bedroom without me knowing he was there or that he'd admitted to it.

Marie had brought me to his attention, but why? Had she known? I hated that every time I found answers, those led to more questions. Worse yet, it normally led to the dead, which couldn't answer them for me. My entire life always pointed to the answers that only the dead, who couldn't speak, could provide.

I'd spent the entire morning tearing through boxes trying to find something that could point me to my birth parents. My mother had been impeccable at keeping records. I soon learned she'd kept a detailed record of everything *but* me. By noon I had given up and started packing the room back up.

I'd tried eating like I used to before Transition, since Ryder and his men had assured me that I could. I gave that up fast and turned to comfort food like chocolate, and then ice cream…which led to me sitting at the table cussing at the endless calories that did nothing to sate the hunger pangs started to gnaw at me like a fire burning out of control in a dry forest. At least I'd had several days reprieve before the hunger had started in on me again.

I was settling in to a routine; a very unhealthy one. I glared at my own reflection. It was a stark reminder that I was no longer human, and that I couldn't even try to act like one now because of it. I also noticed that I had the same glow that the Light Fae had—was I half Blood Fae and half Light, or was it just the dye Alden had injected into me at the Guild that had somehow jumped to the brands I'd inherited since Transition? These types of little things would lead my mind down the path about my origins that I did not want to go down. And then there was Ryder. He was on my mind twenty-four-seven, or so it seemed, and I knew that wouldn't change anytime soon. I was actually missing the overbearing caveman!

I could have been an ad for drugs; only not so much for the drugs…It seemed like I was addicted to Fairies. *This is your brain before Fairies*…Then I could play the part of the brain after Fairies had played with it. I was moving through the motions of living, but Ryder had been right—I hadn't been living. I'd been doing what I thought I was meant to do. I'd been damn good at pretending to be happy, and, if I was honest about it, I really hadn't been.

I couldn't complain too much. I'd had amazing friends. I'd been loved. Even though Larissa had been hard on me and had kept things to herself, in the end, I knew it had been to help me. I couldn't go back to what I had known my entire life. I had no idea where I fit in now, if not with Ryder. I was pathetic, and I missed him.

I was needy, and it pissed me off to no end. I should hate him. Hell, I had plenty of reasons to hate him. Yet I felt pathetically alone. I'd been to the cemetery twice now to dance with the dead. Where it used to comfort me, now it was a reminder of how alone I really was.

I was in the kitchen when Alden arrived. He'd been calling nonstop trying to figure out why I was home alone, as if I wasn't supposed to be here anymore. I smiled as I set down the coffee mug and lifted a brow. "Come to make sure I was still alive?" I asked as I stood to move over and pour him a mug.

"You stopped answering my calls," he said by way of explanation.

"I did, but only because *'are you eating humans'* was bound to come up in the conversation sooner or later. The answer is no, I have not started to demolish the human food chain yet."

He snorted and shook his head. "Ryder said—"

"Zip it!" I shouted and slammed the mug down onto the counter. "We do not say *his* name in this house. And don't look at me like that! Don't look at me like I'm a cup short of crazy," I barked when his eyes narrowed. "If it gets that bad, I can shoot myself in the head and just wake up tomorrow."

"You sure you could do it?" he asked as he looked

at me carefully.

"Alden, I'd have to. I won't feed from humans. Kinda hard to when I've spent my entire life learning to protect them from monsters like…me." I scrunched my face up distastefully as if the words tasted dirty on my tongue, and I laughed, even though I found nothing funny about it.

"You're not a monster, Synthia. I need to talk to you about something, and I need for you not to explode when I tell you this."

"You knew Ryder had given the order for Adrian to be changed, and you also knew he was still alive," I said, hoping he'd say that I had it all wrong. I knew he wouldn't though. Over the past several days I'd started putting the pieces together. The problem with pieces was, when they lined up right, you had to find more to finish the puzzle.

"I suspected it. I told your team to report to me after that happened to keep you three safe. I knew someone was tailing you, but it didn't make sense why someone would be only trailing you and not the other teams. You were just an Enforcer, and you held no real power inside the Guild. Those who seek revenge come looking for me or someone higher up in command. They don't go after the ones who only take orders; they come after the ones issuing them. I had another team whose job was to tail your team to see who it was. After a while, I had to pull them off or take the chance of someone above me questioning my intentions."

I blinked at him. How bad-ass was I? I hadn't even noticed I had two tails chasing me! I shook my head and took the seat across from him. "Why? Why chance another team for me, Alden? The Guild states that in our contracts, if we are compromised, we go away quietly. If I was compromised, and someone was tailing me, I should have been on my own with it."

"Why do you think? It's because I raised you, Synthia. Hell, you were the only family I had left. You are like a daughter to me, believe it or not, and I wasn't going to lose you. I was doing my job protecting you from harm, as anyone who had a raised a child would have. Never thought it would become this big of mess, though. I knew you were different, and Marie's actions confirmed it. Marie kept you and Adam close to her at all times. I'd never thought anything of it, until Adrian was killed. We had known your coven was being tailed before that, but whoever it was, well, they were smart and impossible to find. It wasn't until Marie was killed that I started to get really worried."

"By a radical," I replied as my eyes took him in. He looked tired and disheveled. It was out of character for him, and I knew there was more he was going to tell me, and I wasn't going to like it.

"No, that's just what we told you. She was killed in the catacombs beneath the Guild. No marks, no indication of a struggle. She looked as if she'd just sat down and died, but in our line of work we never take anything at face value."

"Magic? Was there any leftover residue from magic being cast in a closed area? Was it one of *us*?" I asked as my heart sank in my chest. I'd been inside those catacombs. It was a cramped space at best. There wasn't enough room down there to manage spells, let alone hide the residue of one.

"We found nothing. At the time, we had nothing to explain it. We decided to tell the children that she was killed outside the Guild to be safe. We couldn't have that many children panicking because we had someone killing high ranked members inside our protected walls."

"No magic, no marks. That makes no sense. She was healthy, Alden, very healthy. What was found on the autopsy?"

Alden nodded in agreement. "She was healthy, and her autopsy proved it."

"But there is nothing else you can tell me about it, right?" I asked as I mentally filed away the information to think about it later when I was alone. He was a good man, but he wouldn't tell me more. I was smart enough to know when I was being told only the basics. "So, let's go back to Adrian. You knew Ryder was most likely behind it, and you still sent me to him anyway." I crossed my arms and leveled an angry glare at him.

"Synthia, when the Dark Prince of the Fae comes inviting you into the Dark Fortress, you go. He didn't want just anyone, and when he started asking for my best…well, I had a feeling it had to do with the letters Marie had mailed to him right before her death. It wasn't my idea to send you, but when I sent the query up the ladder to the higher ups, they said I had no choice. So I actually had little choice when it boiled down to it. I haven't had much choice since the new elders took their places at the table, either."

"Wait, so you didn't agree with me going?"

"No, I thought it was too risky. You scored higher on the magic scale and in hand-to-hand combat than any other Witch to date. Sending the only one who could potentially save the one we sent in was a risk we shouldn't have taken. If anyone could have gotten those who got caught by Ryder out, it was you and your team. I wanted to send in Ilea's team."

I pinched the bridge of my nose in confusion. "So they sent me to Ryder, and you told them it was a bad idea from the start? That I was the only one who could get in to save the team if they got caught, and they still sent me. Like…a sacrificial lamb to the FIZ slaughter." FIZ was what the Fae called the humans after they'd digested the soul and left them as mindless meat sacks.

"Why do you think I was there waiting? I was told to stand down and let it play out. I couldn't take that chance; not with you. I brokered the deal with Ryder to be on the same floor for the interview. I knew Chandra was going to die, because it was just another test by the elders for all of you. I did not trust her, and I suspected from the very beginning, when she was sent to us, that she was a Guild plant. I did know that if she turned on you, you wouldn't hesitate to take her out. It's how I'd trained you, Syn. I'm sorry for that by the way; placing it on your shoulders to carry out what I should have done myself. You are a tough shell, Syn, but even with time, it's hard to fix the cracks."

"I didn't know any of that, Alden. I thought you were getting money hungry and abusing power. You should have trusted me enough to tell me this from the beginning. I wouldn't be in this mess now if you had," I said, and blinked when I realized what I had said. "That came out wrong!" I tried to fix it, but he smiled and shook his head.

"That tongue of yours is unable to tell a lie now, Synthia. I knew what it was beginning to look like, and that's why I'm here. I have been watching my fellow Guild members for quite some time now, and I did not want to say anything or involve you until I had enough evidence to do so. I need you to get word to Ryder that the leaders of the Guild are now publicly taking sides in this fight between the Mages, and the Fae. They have been spreading propaganda that the

Mages are true ancestors of the Druids, and they have been actively singling out anyone who has friendly contact with the Fae for...*early retirement*, he said, his fingers curling into air quotes around the last two words.

"Um, are we speaking of the ancient Celtic Druids; those Druids?" I asked, trying to stop my legs from shaking at the mention of the Mages.

"Yes, the very same. You're a smart girl. I'm sure you are already placing and sorting through the implications."

"Yes, Alden, I get it. We *are* the fucking Mages."

He nodded and stood up to leave.

"Wait! That's it? You just drop a bomb in my lap and leave? What are you going to do? You can't go back there. Stay with me; I can keep you safe. If the Mages are inside the Guild and turning the Guild against the Fae, then you're in danger. Let me help you."

"Synthia, someone has to stay inside to get word back to you," he argued.

"That's shit, and you know it. You'd be in the enemy's den. It's suicide."

"Synthia, *we* are the ones who killed Larissa. The Seattle Guild knew it while they stood beside us at her funeral. There were no reports of the girl who played Arianna ever going missing. I started to wonder soon after she was exposed, since something like that would have been reported to us as well as to the rest of the Guild Covens. I started to wonder why—because if you had gone missing, I'd have gone to the moon and back looking for you. I'd have sent a line out to every coven I could until I had found you. They didn't even contact us for it, let alone warn us that there was an issue. Not until others went missing, ones who had families that would have reported it. No, I need to stay and make sure it doesn't happen again. I can't live with knowing I did nothing to prevent what happened to those girls. I have to stop this from repeating itself. This is something I need to see through, before I am *retired*."

"Alden, I'm always here if you need me," I said numbly.

"I know, Synthia. I also know they had me train some of you to become Druids. I didn't know it at the time, but if it comes down to a fight, you and what is left of your coven have all been trained for this. If it comes down to it, *you* could fight against the Guild."

"How is that even possible? Wouldn't we have known it?" Even as the words came out of my mouth, my jaw dropped to the floor as it dawned on me. "… Oh shit!" *Ink.*

"I trained you, Adam, and Adrian in the Dark Arts. I injected ink that made it stronger inside of you; intensified it. You three have the ability to prevent the Mages from harming more innocent people. You also know how the Guild works and functions. I can't allow them to hurt, or kill anyone; I won't allow that to happen again."

"So…I'm a Druid Fae?" I almost laughed, but the implications of it were just straight-up messed up.

"Technically, your Fae DNA cancels it out. The ink only increases the magic you use. Sorry, but you're still only Fae. I need to know something, since you can't lie now. Did you ever think of me as a father?"

"In a way, yes, but I've always kept my father in my heart, and your sister, my mother. I love you,

Alden, and you've made me into what I am today…
minus the Fae part."

I thought about things for a few moments, reeling
over the information that Alden had dropped on me. If
the Guild was being infiltrated by the Mages and they
had ordered Alden to send me to the Dark Prince…

"Alden, given my past history with the Fae, do
you think that the Guild was hoping I would snap on
the assignment and assassinate Ryder?" I asked softly,
afraid to hear him answer what my mind had already
processed.

Alden nodded sadly, confirming my suspicions.
So, his being there, close by that day, was to save me
from myself if need be….

"Do you think the Guild killed Marie for being
close with the Fae?"

Once again, Alden nodded. Yep, shit soup was
being stirred and it was simmering now, and getting
ready to be served with a side of crunchy crackers.
Once the soup hit boil, this was going to get ugly.

He sat back down, and we talked for over an hour
about what else was going on inside the Guild. He'd
explained a lot that he wouldn't have under normal
circumstances. When he left, it was hard, because it
felt as if we were saying goodbye for the last time.

Chapter
EIGHTEEN

It had only been about five minutes since Alden left, and I was still sitting at the table, unable to make my mind work past the idea of the Guild being the enemy. How could this even be possible? My Guild—which I'd loved, grown up inside, and given my faith to—was the enemy? They had thrown me out because I'd been Fae, and, even though I wasn't a part of it anymore, I still felt the need to defend them. And I still had yet to get up from where Ryder had knocked me down with his word games and trickery. I must have had a sticker on my forehead that said, *Please dump info here*, because I was getting it by the truck load today.

I had been trained, unknowingly, by Alden to massacre Fae. I looked at the cell phone in front of me on the table. What the hell was I supposed to tell Ryder? *Oh, hey, by the way...I am the enemy! Or I was. Oh, and by the way—the Guild was hoping you would trigger me to have a massive freak-out, which would result in your untimely demise at my hands.* Yeah, that would go over like a truckload of Goblins in a daycare center. I glared at the phone and played out the conversation in my head several times, and it never ended well.

I eventually picked up the phone, deciding I needed to get it over with, but a noise in the front room stopped me cold. I shook my head and started towards the front room, wondering what Alden had forgotten and come back here for. That was when I saw him.

He was exactly as I'd remembered him. He was tall, reaching a little over six feet, with long muted blonde hair and dead black and gray eyes. He wore no human clothes, and there was nothing human about him to stave off the fear of what he was. He was cold, everything I hated in the Fae. He was the entire reason I'd started hating them. I stepped back, realizing he hadn't seen me yet. Fear stuck in my throat, making it impossible to speak or cry out. It was probably a good thing, considering this was the leader of the Fae who'd killed my parents.

He was dressed in a dark, blood-red cloak, a black tunic, and pants, but he'd already removed the hood of the cloak before I'd discovered him inside the house. He must not have gotten the memo that he'd blend in better wearing Dolce or Armani. I looked at the wards, realizing they were not going off with his arrival. I stepped back so I could watch him for a moment more. He was looking for something. He growled gutturally and stepped closer to the picture of my family.

I barely contained the hiss I felt when he picked it up and tossed it carelessly to the floor. I couldn't tap a leyline, because there wasn't one here. I pulled my magic to me and smiled as it slithered through my mind. I cracked my neck as the tanginess of electrical power filtered through me. It came without having to think about it; just the fact that I'd needed it had brought it to my palms. I pulled the energy to me and allowed it to light up my brands.

He turned those lifeless eyes toward me as I

launched a powerful ball of blue-white energy right at him, but he was faster. The fireplace exploded as the ball of blue magic shattered the bricks and mortar. He moved out of the way in time to miss getting hit by the debris. He was up and moving toward me quickly, but I was fully prepared for it and fired another wave of magic at him. It connected, and sent him crashing against the wall. I sent one ball of energy after another at him.

He snarled and sent his own flying at me, but I easily dodged it and threw another back at him. Blood spattered the wall behind him, but he didn't stop fighting. I felt my magic as it began to wane and at the same time, something inside me was pushing to get free, as if something stronger was buried there. I showed no weakness, keeping the energy balls in both palms locked and ready as I allowed him to pull himself away from where I had pinned him against the wall.

"You shouldn't have come here. Now I'm going to kill you, bastard."

He smiled coldly, and looked me up and down slowly in a way that made my skin crawl. He wiped the blood from his lips and spat it onto the floor as his eyes continued to take me in. I wanted to throw up as I remembered him giving my mother the same look before he raped her. "So, finally we meet," he growled and tilted his head to watch me as he pulled his own magic around him.

"You killed my parents. I want to know why," I said, never removing my eyes from him or my magic from my hands as I stalked him, precisely and effortlessly.

"They were expendable," he shrugged as if it didn't matter what he'd done. "Although your mother was a *sweet* meal," He smiled, but it was a diversion. I knew the moment he planned to attack, and I sifted, easily avoiding it, shocked that I had managed to do so. He smiled wider, revealing perfect white teeth with pointy baby fangs, just like *mine*. "You discovered what you are," he said as he stepped closer.

"Why them?" It was the only thing I needed to know before I took him out.

"Because you—" His eyes looked over my shoulder, then he immediately sifted out without finishing his sentence.

I turned my head and locked eyes with Ryder and his men, who had sifted in behind me. I didn't drop my magic. I didn't know who to trust anymore. I stepped back and turned toward Ryder with my hands glowing from my magic, as I'd seen Ryder's do before; bright, beautiful, and deadly magic. *My* magic.

"Syn, drop the magic," Zahruk said as he stepped in front of Ryder slowly, protecting him from me as if he needed to.

"I didn't invite you in," I snapped, angry that I'd been seconds away from discovering the one answer I'd needed since that grisly day so long ago; only to have it ripped away when they'd sifted in.

"I didn't ask," Ryder said, pushing Zahruk out of the way.

"You have no right to be here. Not after what you did," I seethed, but dropped the magic since it was taking too much strength to keep it up. I wasn't suicidal. Ryder was king of badass, and I was a daisy next to him.

"I do if you're in trouble, Synthia. You are still mine to protect."

"I think you've done enough protecting me, Ryder. I seem to get hurt more around you than I do on my own. If I'm not mistaken, your second in command stabbed me. You stalked me, and killed my boyfriend, and then bit me...Stop me if I'm off here."

He just stood there, staring at me with no emotion on his beautiful face. I wanted to scream. I wanted to hit him, but in the end I really just wanted to hold him. And I think that part pissed me off the most. His eyes held caution, as if it was taking everything he had to stand still.

"You need new wards on the walls. Yours didn't keep him out. He was the one who—the one who attacked your mother," Ryder said quietly as his eyes turned gentle.

"Raped my mother; he turned her FIZ, which should be easy for you to say." I watched his expression shift. He smiled coldly, and I felt my pulse quicken. I was such a fucking masochist.

"So he did. You tapped a leyline?" he asked, distant and cold. I wanted to scream at him. Why wasn't he trying to pull me to him and check for wounds? Anything would be better than this cold asshole that was suddenly treating me like a fucking stranger.

"There isn't a leyline here. If there was, I'd still have my parents," I replied, stopping the pain in its tracks as I forced it down.

"He just showed up?" Ryder asked, not bothering to turn around as Ristan sifted in, late to the party.

"No, Ryder, I opened the fucking door and asked him if he took sugar with his tea! What do you think happened?"

He growled, and I almost smiled—almost. There

was the emotion. Maybe it was bad, but it was better than nothing.

"Next time, I suggest you kill him," he replied.

I lifted a brow at his words. "Um, hello! I was trying until an army of men *sifted* in and scared him away! I had him right where I wanted him until you got here."

"Maybe strike before asking if he'd like fucking sugar in his tea next time," Ryder snarled.

"I thought it was Alden coming back in; he'd just left. I never imagined that the Fae who…" I swallowed. "That he would sift right in and start breaking shit!"

"Well, he did, and he could have easily killed you. He's not some just newly Transitioned Fae like you! He could have killed you! I told you that you needed to fucking stay with me until you learned your powers," Ryder snapped.

"Or, I could have killed him! We won't know because you keep thinking you have some right to protect me, when you don't."

"You could have fucking died!" Ryder fumed as his jaw ticked wildly and his nostrils flared.

"But I didn't. I was holding my own against him just fine until you showed up and scared him away! I get it. I'm nothing more than a child in your eyes, Ryder—and I wouldn't survive a week in *your* world! But, right now, I don't trust you—actually, at this point, I don't trust anyone except Adam, and he's not here right now!"

He nodded, but said nothing before he stepped back to talk to Zahruk. "Station Savlian and Sinjinn at both doors. Ristan, try to get a reading on the Fae who was here. Dristan, put his ass through every record we have and see if you can match his features, cloak, and brands. Call me if you find anything that goes bump in the night around here. And do not let Synthia leave this house alone at all. That's an order."

"Excuse me? You don't control—" He sifted to me and pressed me between his hard body and the wall.

"I will not let anything happen to you. I'm not a fucking saint, Synthia. I'm not a fucking human either, so stop confusing me with what you think I'm allowed to do. I told you from the beginning of this that I wasn't human. I don't play by human rules." His eyes lowered to my mouth, and came back up to lock on mine.

"Let go," I whispered.

"Make me," he challenged heatedly.

"Ryder," I warned.

"How's the hunger?" he asked, removing his hold on me and backing up to allow me space enough to breathe.

I met his eyes and flashed him just how hungry I was before turning and leaving the front room. I sifted the moment my feet hit the stairs, without realizing I'd done so. I'd only wanted to get away from his men and their probing gazes. I needed a moment alone to collapse and, the moment I hit the bed, I did. I inhaled slowly and exhaled even slower. I did it for several moments before I noticed that I wasn't alone.

"Are you okay, Synthia?" Ryder asked as he leaned against the door.

"I'm fine," I whispered as I moved onto my side

to look at him. The man was a sex God from any position.

"I may not be human, nor have I spent an extensive amount of time in this world, but even I know that 'I'm fine' coming from a woman is normally code that she's about to cry. You just faced the man who killed your parents. I'm here if you need me, or to feed. Use me, please," he said softly.

"I have to be fine," I said. I'd said it for so long that now it was my motto.

"For who? Who says you have to be strong anymore? You are allowed to fall apart, because I will hold you through it. You can crumble, and I'll hold the pieces together until you can pull yourself out of it."

"You had Adrian turned into a *Vampire* because you wanted inside me, Ryder, and I'm not sure I can forgive you for doing it," I said as I looked up to meet his eyes, and watch as he shut down once more. "You don't get to put me back together when *you* shattered my world just to sleep with me. You took too much, and you won't offer me anything in return, besides sex. You keep telling me that you want me, and yet, you turn around and tell me you are not in this for the long run. I can't keep doing this to myself. I need someone who wants me."

"I take what I want, and I wanted you. I made a stupid fucking choice according to the rules of this world, Syn, but I'd never wanted anything more in my entire life than I wanted to have you. I shouldn't have stolen him from you, or fucked with you at all. I can't give you what you want. I can't be the man you need, Pet. I can only be this. I'm Fae, and, while it might not make sense to you, you have everything I can give freely of myself. I'm leaving Zahruk inside the house tonight. It's not up for discussion." He smiled roguishly and sifted over to the bed. He kissed my forehead so gently that it shocked my heart. I'm pretty sure it stopped beating for a moment while his lips pressed against my skin.

"Ryder," I whispered brokenly, but he'd already sifted out.

Chapter
NINETEEN

I lay curled beneath the covers, even though I wasn't cold. I felt chilled to the bone with the information running through my head. If the Guild was picking a fight, then they were going to be up a shit creek with a lot of unneeded collateral damage as their paddles. It could send the entire world into a war that the humans would lose.

I should have told Ryder what Alden had said, but my brain was already running on overload, and today's events had only made it worse. My surprise visitor was making it hard to think of much else. With him came the memories of that night.

The presence of Ryder's men did give me a level of comfort that I wouldn't have had if he'd listened to me and taken them with him.

I'd have to thank him next time I saw him, which kind of sucked.

My brain was bouncing from his gentle kiss on my forehead to my parents' deaths, that horrible night. I now knew that they had died protecting me from whoever that blond Fae was. It hurt to know I had been right; that they had died for me.

I turned over in bed and shook my head at the sudden bout of dizziness that made the room spin. I felt a bolt of fire race through my body. Before I could even think, I was off the bed and running to the bathroom where I emptied my stomach violently. Strong hands helped me as I sat back away from the toilet. Calm, soothing fingers pulled my hair away from my face and a cold cloth was placed against my forehead softly.

"Syn, what the hell did you try to eat?" Ryder asked as he sat with me cradled against his chest, on the cold bathroom floor.

"Food," I whispered, fighting another wave of nausea. How the hell had he gotten here so fast?

"Your body should be able to digest food without any problems. Food didn't cause this. Are you done?" he asked softly.

"I need to brush my teeth," I replied, trying to stand up, but he was faster. He pulled me up against himself, and I felt his magic cleansing me from head to toe as he walked me back to the bed slowly.

"How long have you been sick?" he asked, helping me back into bed.

"I'm not sick. I just threw up."

"Try to sleep. I sent the others home to sleep as well. I'll make sure you are safe."

"You sent everyone else home?" I asked, wondering how long ago they'd left.

"Yes. You need to feed soon, and the scent of your Transition can still affect the men. You need to rest tonight. Tomorrow, I will show you how to feed without sex, if you are strong enough. Most newly

Transitioned Fae can't feed without the sex, so don't get your hopes up." A small smile tugged at the corner of his mouth. He was actually teasing me, which was unlike him. I was so used to his demands and his orders that it caught me off guard.

I crooked my arm under my head and watched him as he sat down in the overstuffed chair next to my bed, removing his shirt. My eyes slid down his torso to the small dark patch of hair that led deeper into his loose fitting jeans. "Alden came by today. He said he thinks the Guild is siding with the Mages who are attacking the Fae. He also said that the Guild is spreading propaganda that the Mages are the true ancestors of the Druids." I kept my eyes leveled with his and waited for the explosion that would surely follow my words.

His face gave nothing away as he replied, "I know. I've always known the Guild had a part to play in the Mages' game. I have been watching them for a long time, sizing up the enemy, and seeing what cards they held. I always stack the deck in my favor."

I shook my head. "How do you always manage to be one step ahead of everyone else, Ryder?"

"I do it by studying my enemies, and being the better player at the game. I approached the Guild fully aware of the Guild's origins and history that they don't teach their young. Keep in mind that all propaganda, as you call it, starts with a grain of truth. So, what Alden told you is right, but not quite. The history goes back farther than you have been taught—farther than humans realize. The Fae came to this world long ago and stayed mostly out of curiosity. Humans are full of emotion, and it is something that we tend to lose over an immortal existence. It draws us. This interaction created a problem as humans at the time were quite primitive, impressionable and extremely superstitious. You mix that with magical beings that are far more advanced intellectually and culturally, and it can become a very big problem. Many of the so-called *Gods* of early human history were, in fact, Fae that had challenged the ruling castes in Faery and broken the sacrosanct rule of not interfering with humans. They did this by setting themselves up as Gods." He smiled at me as his words lulled me with the history of our kind.

"The Fae spread out and unintentionally influenced cultures wherever they went. The Dark Fae tended to frequent what is now known as Scotland, whereas the Light Fae favored England, and the Blood Fae drifted towards Ireland and Wales. The ruling Castes in Faery did not mind the Fae that liked to visit and amuse themselves in this world, as long as the rules were maintained. Not interfering with humans, as I mentioned before, was one rule, and the second was not allowing creatures of the Horde into this world." Ryder looked at me intently as he measured his words.

"Syn, there are some creatures from the Horde that do not belong in this world. They are far too dangerous, and they have no control over themselves. As you may have guessed, both rules were broken many times over, and there were many tragic situations that occurred by bringing some of the more dangerous and unstable Horde creatures into this world. Many Changelings were born as a result of the Fae taking humans as their lovers. The challenge, as you speculated with me before, was that the Changelings really had no place to belong. They were powerful in their own right, but they were not human, and they did not like the fear that the humans had for them.

"They entered into Faery and banded together for protection and to learn from each other and the Fae. At first, they tried to belong with the Light Fae. The Light Fae, knowing that the Changelings were part human, rejected them quickly and quite violently. They then tried the Dark Fae, but Mauricio, who was King back then, rejected anyone who was not of his lineage." His eyes started to glow faintly. Before he spoke again, he had sifted beside me in the bed, and he pulled my body closer to his hard, warm skin.

"The Blood Fae would not have accepted them either, but the Changelings never asked them because by then they had decided to strike out alone. They hated that the Blood Fae and the Horde were Unseelie. They rejected the two castes and returned to the human world."

"So, this was when they became the Druids?" I asked, trying to think past his naked skin that rested against mine. When I had gotten ready for bed, I'd only changed into a small pair of shorts and a thin tank top that read 'Sassy' across my breasts and rear end.

I felt him smile against my neck. "Yes, Pet. The Changelings became the Druids of England and Ireland that the Guild would have taught you about, but as time moved on; they slinked back to the shadows, just as Fae tend to do. We kept watch over them, because they were only children who were hurt and felt as if they did not belong. As the human world evolved, they evolved with it. When they took the titles of Witches and Warlocks and created the Guild, we took note. They seemed harmless enough, and the elders of the Fae thought it cute when the Druids took up arms and vowed to protect the human race from us. A more radical group formed within their ranks and became the Mages, and they were a different matter altogether. They could not let the rejection of the Light and Dark Fae go and move on with their lives. They have been operating within and outside of the Guild ever since. Their agenda, as best as we can tell, is revenge at any cost. Some Guild members, like Alden, don't know all the facts, while others are extremists, working in the shadows and moving the Guild in the direction they want it to go in with those who would reject this fanaticism being none the wiser."

"So we are Fae?" I asked, turning over to face him.

"Not you, Pet. You are full Fae. They are Changelings; half human and half Fae, born of a union between Fae and the human race. The Horde would have welcomed them, had they asked them to. They chose to leave, though. Only a small portion of those inside the Guild know of what is happening deeper within the ranks."

"How can you be so certain that it is only a small portion, and not more of them?" I asked, narrowing my eyes on him. It resulted in them lowering to his full, gorgeous, skillful mouth. "I mean, how do you know that I'm not involved?"

"Because I had you in my bedroom inside the club for thirty minutes before I allowed Adam in to collect you. I could have taken you then. You were so fucking beautiful sprawled out on my bed. I tranced you, and asked if you were involved with anything off-the-books with the Guild, or any group inside that was off the grid. The only thing you admitted to was cheating on your diet to eat chocolate. You had no secrets; none that were real anyways. You were the first human who seemed to be real. Go figure, you weren't even human," he replied, smiling.

"You tranced me the day I signed the first contract?" I asked, not sure how I felt about him messing with my head without me knowing it.

"I had to know. Z's gift only allows us to see events as they happened, not as they are perceived by the human mind. Our group is very effective at getting information and not all need the type of interrogation tactics like you saw at the mansion. I also needed to know how far you'd go to protect the Guild if they were the ones killing those poor, mutilated women."

"I wouldn't protect them if they had done it."

"I know. You're a fierce protector, but only when what you are doing is right," Ryder said, smiling wickedly.

"You shouldn't have killed Adrian. How am I supposed to trust you now?" I asked softly, already having to fight the need to kiss him.

"You shouldn't trust anyone, including me. If I thought sacrificing you would accomplish my goals, I'd do it in a heartbeat. I'm not here to make friends, or to build a life. I'm here for one thing alone, and stopping Fae from dying needless deaths is a part of why I am here. We are not so different in that. We both fight for the weak and vulnerable who can't do it themselves," he whispered softly, but with enough force I knew he wasn't bluffing.

"They sent me to kill you. Alden admitted that he thought they were hoping I'd have some sort of PTSD attack and kill you. I wonder if Arianna was a back-up plan. You knew what they were up to, so why didn't you just kill me?"

Ryder nodded and ran his finger over my bottom lip. "I didn't kill you because I knew when I tranced you that you had nothing to do with the Guild's plans. Arianna is a very different matter. We think that she was planted by the Mages and the Light Fae to kill either me, the Dark King, or both of us. We just can't prove it, or accuse the Light Fae outright of conspiring with the Mages. Syn, now that you know more about the Guild, you need to know the rest of what we found out. Larissa was a message. Joseph was under orders to convert you to their plan or kill you. He was obsessed with killing; he got off on it. He took it farther than they wanted it to go. He was obsessed with you because you took from him what he had built. I killed him tonight. That's what I came back to tell you, one less thing you have to worry about now."

My heart skipped a beat; I'd wanted that kill. I didn't feel better knowing he was dead and wouldn't hurt anyone else ever again. It didn't give me closure to the way Larissa was killed, and it sure as hell didn't lessen the pain of her loss. "Did he suffer?"

"He's suffered since the moment I found him trying to cut you open. He took from you, so I took his flesh. He died screaming in a very bad way. I removed his beating heart for you, and Ristan ate it, consuming his soul while Joseph watched."

"Ristan *ate* his heart?" I asked, and waited for his nod before finishing. "That's disturbing on so many levels." Ryder smiled as my own filtered across my face.

"He took from you, and even though you may think I don't care, Pet, I do. I have a mission here, and thousands of innocent Fae are depending on me. None of the other Fae seem to care, minus Adam's father."

"And your father," I said, watching him.

"Yes," he said, looking right at me.

"So, he is your father?" I'd hit on something.

"You're fucking Adam's brother, yes."

"I'm not fucking you," I said, smiling impishly up at him.

"You will be. I can smell your hunger, Pet, and your eyes keep dropping to my mouth, which is why I keep talking. The more you look, the more you want me. All I have to do is wait it out."

"I don't feel good," I said as my body started to burn again. "Shit," I said, sifting to the toilet and retching again. I didn't even have time to be glad that I could sift to somewhere else besides his feet.

"I need to know what you ate, so I can tell Eliran when he gets here," Ryder said from behind me as he pulled my hair away from my face.

"Just normal food. I ate chocolate and drank coffee. I've been drinking coffee since right after Transition though, and nothing like this happened."

"Birth control, Syn?" he questioned as he pulled me up into his arms, and carried me back to the bed.

"Still active from the Guild; I have three more months of it left in my system."

"Good," he said, and my heart dropped. It shouldn't have, but it did.

"Wouldn't want my child, Ryder?" I quipped and instantly regretted it.

"A sassy little girl with a mouth like her mother's?" He smiled and my heart missed a few beats. I didn't smile back though; something inside of me was sinking further into despair. "Syn, I don't want children; not until I've finished what I set out to do. I have a few other responsibilities as well before I can play the role of parent. I'm not sure I'd make a good parent anyway," he said, the last statement almost as an afterthought.

"Eliran, come inside the room," Ryder said,

already stepping away from the bed as I noticed the healer standing in the doorway with Ristan peeking over his shoulder.

"We got problems, Ryder?" Ristan asked cautiously.

"No clue. That's why I called Eliran, so he could find out."

"You didn't use a phone," I said as I struggled to sit up in the bed.

"He's telepathic. He sent me an image of what was happening, and I sifted in. I hope you don't mind, Synthia, as you did not invite me yourself," Eliran said, smiling.

"It is fine. You are welcome here, Eliran," I replied softly as I watched him materialize several small medical devices and sit down beside me on the bed.

"I need to know what you ate."

"She ate chocolate and coffee," Ryder said from across the room.

"Ryder, Ristan, get out. I need to run some tests, and she deserves some semblance of privacy," Eliran said, looking at me carefully, which only caused me to blush.

"Excuse me?" Ryder said with a deep growl.

"Ryder, you called him. At least let him do his job," I said, meeting his penetrating golden eyes.

"Fine, I'll be downstairs," Ryder huffed, but it was more like a child pouting because he couldn't have his favorite candy from the store.

When the room was cleared, Eliran pulled out a

needle and laid it on the bed. "When was your last menstrual cycle?"

"It's been a month, but it's said that traumatic stress can affect it. Plus, I'm on still on the birth control from the Guild."

"Good. That's good. So you have been throwing up. How many times?"

"Twice. It just started. I thought I was immortal now, so why would I be throwing up?"

"Immortal only means that you don't die easily or of old age. We still get sick occasionally, and sometimes we do die. You also haven't completed Transition yet, so it is a little different for you. I need to take some blood," he said, tying the plastic band around my arm. "Make a fist a few times," he said, and nodded when I did it correctly. I squeezed my eyes closed when the needle poked through my flesh. "Okay, I'm done. You can open them."

"Sorry, I think I've seen enough blood to last me a lifetime this month already."

"Understandable after everything you have been through. Okay, I'm going to run a few more tests and take it all back to be processed."

Chapter
TWENTY

Soon after Eliran had left, Ryder came back in, still shirtless. He looked around the room and then looked back at me. "How are you feeling?"

"I'm okay. He did a few tests and took the samples back with him."

"You should try to get some sleep," he said, coming over to lie on the bed as if he owned it.

"You gonna hold me through the night and keep the bad guys away?" I said jokingly.

"Among other things, yes. That was my plan tonight, if that's okay with you."

I hadn't expected his response, and almost moaned when he wrapped his strong arms around me. "Close your eyes. I've got you, Pet. I'll keep you safe; I promise. Nothing will happen to you."

"Ryder, you said you would teach me how to feed without sex. How would I be able to do it?" I asked.

"I'm not sure you can, yet. We will worry about it in the morning, or when you are strong enough. Right now, you need to get some rest."

~~*~*~* *Ryder* *~*~*~*~*

I watch her sleep—so beautiful, so fucking perfect. She isn't in my plans, and, yet, I find my entire world wrapping around her more each day. It's dangerous, and I lost control of *him*. She wants more than I can give her, and a better man would let her go. I'm not a better man. I'm also not above cheating to keep her. It is how we are. We take out what gets in our way. We kill to prove we can control what we want. She's still thinking as a human. If she wasn't, she'd know that by me getting him out of the way I was proving to her that I was the smarter Fae, the better man that I was willing to fight to keep her.

He growls inside of me; pacing, watching, and stalking her, even now. He wants to be inside of her, but I'm afraid of what he might do to her. He took over so quickly, and I was unable to stop him or protect her. I fought with him and regained control. Normally, I am aware when I allow him to take control. This time, he completely blocked me from seeing what he did until I was able to wrestle control back from him. All he will tell me is that he made sure that she would not need to feed from another while she sorts her mind— so we can give her the time she wants. Asshole, he still thinks he can control her. He seems confident that she will forgive me, but I'm not so sure that forgiveness will come anytime soon. I'm still not sure what else he has done to her. It scares me to think about what he might have done, and nothing scares me.

I could keep her; tie her up and fuck her as I desire. But she's Syn, and I love her fight—her inner strength is undeniable. Her lust is addictive and, bloody hell, even lying beside her while holding the nightmares at bay is driving me into a stiff state of need. My cock presses against her, demanding to sink into her sweet honey until I'm balls deep in it.

My hands splay over her nipples, just to watch the sweet tips grow hard with the need for my mouth to devour them. I'm such a fucking prick. I couldn't stop the need to be around her, to control her need. The first night I'd seen her had been a shock to my system. Nothing has ever drawn me in as her electric eyes did that night, and the pain I saw inside of them. That same pain made her fight hard, and love even harder.

She'd been with him when I had first laid eyes upon her. Her eyes had been on him as she watched him fill his lust for power, but she'd been blind to it because of her love for him. Fucking kids; they'd been in love. She'd been staring at him as if he was the most amazing thing she'd ever seen. I wanted her to look at *me* like that. The way she'd smiled at him, with no fear hidden behind her luscious eyes. Her mouth smiled so beautifully that it made my cock respond. He wanted power, and he had it right fucking in front of him. She had been his anchor, his power. He'd wanted more, and she'd never caught the look of dissatisfaction that shined from behind his mask. She'd been blind to it, happy in her assumption that he was happy as well. He wanted her power, and, eventually, had I let it, it would have consumed their relationship. Jealousy is a bitch.

I watched her pleasure herself, and nothing had ever made my cock harder than the sight of her legs spread open wide as her small hand worked herself over. Those sweet fucking noises she made had sealed her fate. They haunted me when I'd left her, right until I sifted back in the next day in hopes that she'd do it again. Eventually, I helped her feel the need to; pushing Fae aphrodisiacs into the air, just to watch her until she fell asleep, sated from her own hand. Like some fucking low ass pervert, I'd watched, her, unable to leave. I had never wanted a human. I'd stuck to a strict code to never meddle with them, until *her*.

I'd actually given in and kissed her once, and she woke up. She doesn't remember it. I erased it from her mind. A fucking kiss! I'm a monster, and the one thing I had to have from her was a taste of those red fucking lips against my own. She'd awoken confused, disoriented as to who I was. I almost made love to her and allowed her to think it was a dream. But I couldn't. I wanted her to scream my name when I fucked her tight folds. *Needed* it, like I needed fucking air.

I couldn't take from her what countless others beg to give me. I can't even think of fucking anyone else without the sweetest pair of electric blue and lilac eyes popping into my mind. She's in my dreams when I sleep, sweet and saucy, begging to be bent over and fed greedily. And I do fuck her in my dreams. Every. Fucking. Time.

I tried to let her go. I let her leave Faery, leave me. I sent guards to watch over her in disguise and keep her safe. I spent the entire time struggling against the beast for control, and when I slept, I would visit her in our dreams. Zahruk had brought women in, stripped them naked and took them in front of me like we used to do a million times before. The men even brought in a new one to fuck as a group. Eventually they gave up. Where it used to excite me, to see women screaming to be filled, the only scream I wanted to hear wasn't even in the same fucking world as I was.

I wanted to come back here and erase her from my memory and me from hers. Easier said than done. To not hear her say my name in desire would be the same as death. I hate that I want her, that I can't get her out of my system. It scares me to feel his need for her. He's a fucking monster, one she's made purr. But he's temperamental, like his owner. Deadly.

I growl as I feel Ristan's presence before the door opens. "What?" I snap, because the beast doesn't like anyone close to his sleeping treasure.

"You can't erase her memories. You could end up changing her destiny, or, worse, yours," he says.

"I can do anything I want. If I do it then the only one who would remember it is the beast. Then, it will be easy to walk away from her," I bark, trying to do so quietly.

"Will it be that easy, Ryder? Do you think the beast will let you?" Ristan asks, with his eyes glowing red as they begin to swirl.

"Fuck. This isn't the time to be having a fucking future walk, Ristan!" I scream at him through the mental link we share.

The room fades away until we are standing inside Faery. The dead litter the ground. On the ground is mostly children and infants that the land has rejected; it's starting to reject even more as times goes on. Ristan is just as floored as I by what we are shown by Danu. Faery is nothing more than a cemetery.

"When is this, Ristan?" I ask, making his eyes focus on me.

"Soon, too fucking soon. We have to stop this. Look at the ground," he says with his true language coming out in layers just like mine.

Blood covers the ground. Faery is drinking it; trying to fix itself. Hundreds of corpses litter the ground. Adults cry from across the field, mourning their loss as the Deadlands claim them for their own.

"Does it present a cure to you, Ristan?"

"The Heirs, always the fucking Heirs of the four houses and the four relics. It's the only way. We need those fucking relics, and the Heirs like *yesterday*." He finishes his words, and once again we are inside the bedroom where she sleeps.

"We will complete mapping out and retrieving the relics. At least one of the Heirs we need has surfaced. The others have to be somewhere we can find them as well. No more fucking around. It's time to finish what we came here to do. Do you have any idea how far off that vision was?"

"No, but it could be next week for all we know, Ryder. The land is growing weaker, and more and more children die because it can't accept them."

"Go to the club and bring me back the maps of the relics' locations. Sinjinn and Zahruk can start reconnaissance in the morning on the ones we have located but yet to retrieve. Keep the others out searching for ones that we haven't found yet. Wake me up if you see anything else. I can't leave her alone. If that asshole comes back, I am going to kill him without the answers she seeks. I can't chance him getting to her."

He silently sifts out of the house, and I pull her body closer. Time isn't on our side. Soon, she might not even remember me. Erasing her memory is the last thing I will do, and only if there is no other option. I want her too fucking much to let her go, and the beast will not allow it.

She moans against me, but my body doesn't rise, nor does the beast. For now, he is content just being close to her. The lifeless eyes of the dead children in my world drift through my mind and the disturbing images Ristan showed me tonight play over and over. I have to stop it, no matter what the cost; even if it means giving up everything I want, and my own life for theirs.

Chapter
TWENTY-ONE

The next morning was surprising, and unlike any morning I had ever had before in my life. I woke up wrapped in Ryder's arms with my head nuzzled against his chest. I smiled against him as his warmth melted me. His chest rose and fell in sleep. I didn't want to move or disturb his sleep. I felt safe in this moment, cherished, even if it was just an illusion.

I placed my hand on his heart, listening to his even breathing. In sleep, he almost looked human—if you ignored the pulsing brands on his beautifully bronzed flesh, and the electrical zing that was in the air around the bed. I closed my eyes, inhaled deeply, and tried to hide the smile it brought to my face.

He was every inch the Dark Prince, and he was sleeping in my bed, holding me. Not because he had to, but because he wanted to. I heard him growl, and my eyes shot open and darted to look up into his eyes that were still half-lidded from sleep.

"Molesting me while I sleep, Pet?" he asked with a tired, sexy smirk lifting his lips.

"There was no molesting going on," I retorted.

"You just smelled me, your face is rubbing against my chest, and I'm pretty sure you just made my nipples hard."

I considered it for a moment before I smiled guiltily. "Okay, I'm guilty of those things. What's my punishment?" I asked, shocked the words had come out of my mouth. I was supposed to be mad, and I was failing miserably. My brain was once again high on Fae.

He smiled brighter, and my breath hitched in my lungs. He looked like a man just waking up to the most beautiful woman in the world. I swallowed and smiled back at him. "I think someone is ready to feed," he whispered, before he pounced and pinned me to the bed playfully.

"As *if.* You promised to teach me how to feed today. And I'm pretty sure you said it was *without* sex."

He smiled down at me. "But, I like sex *with* you."

"Okay, who are you and what did you do with my Ryder?" I asked playfully.

"*Your* Ryder?" he whispered as he lowered his mouth to mine, not expecting an answer. His mouth met mine, and I didn't stop him as I should have. Instead, I opened to him and allowed him inside to caress my tongue with his.

We were just kissing. He wasn't seeking more. He was giving me room to move away as well, not that I needed it. When he finally did pull away, it was because a knock sounded from the bedroom door.

"Yo, Ryder, it's late," Savlian said, with his deep, rich baritone shaking the wood of the door. I looked at the clock and was shocked that it was far later in the day than I thought. I was never one to sleep in late; at least, I hadn't been until I'd met him.

"I'm awake," Ryder yelled back and turned his face back to mine. "I have to go. I'll be back tonight to teach you how to feed. I'm leaving a small group of men here to keep you safe."

"I don't—" His lips crushed against mine, stopping my protest. When he pulled away, I glared at him. "That was dirty, Ryder."

"Who knew kissing you was all it took to shut that sassy mouth up?" he whispered playfully and rubbed his hard cock over my groin invitingly. He wiggled his eyebrows at me. "You will allow me to protect you. I will not be distracted from my objectives by knowing you are unprotected and alone. Give me this, at least until we know who it is that we are up against."

"Fine, but they better clean up any mess they make," I whispered, afraid to look away from him and miss this playful side he was showing this morning.

"Duly noted, Pet. If the hunger gets too bad, tell Ristan. We have a mental link, and he can easily get word to me. Don't push yourself today. If you feel sick, have Ristan take you to Eliran."

"Okay, you can't tell me Ristan ate a guy's heart, and then have me ask him for medical help, ya know. That's just not going to happen."

"He's a Demon, and one I'd trust with my own life. You can trust him, Syn. He'd die to keep you safe."

"I'm not worth dying for," I said as I chewed my bottom lip. He started to reply, but I kissed him hard. I pinched his bottom lip between my teeth. Then I gently replaced my teeth with my lips and sucked his bottom lip into my mouth, enjoying the groan that broke as I did so. "Hmm, works on you too."

He laughed the sound vibrating through him as he watched me. "If you keep kissing me, Synthia, I'm not going to be leaving this bed for the next week."

I licked my lips and sighed dramatically.

"I have to go, Pet. Stay inside today. Give me time to figure out who that was in the house last night. Let me protect you, for now."

"Fine," I said, watching as he stood up and glamoured a new shirt on. His thick, dark hair hung close, framing his face. He looked sexy with the sleep still hanging onto his eyes, making them look heated and languid.

I got dressed and headed downstairs a few minutes after Ryder had left. I'd made it half way down the stairs when I heard voices discussing something; discussing *me*. I stood perfectly still, listening, unaware of who the voices belonged to.

"I'll bet he's feeding from her again. When she has satisfied his hunger, I'm sure he will give her to us as he does the others. I, for one, can't wait to get my dick inside of her."

"She's different; I'm not so sure he will release her. He will probably keep her in the private pavilion. Remember what he did to Sierra?" the other male asked.

"Sierra was different though; she liked us all riding that sweet slit of hers."

"You really think he's going to let us fuck her?

She's got his mark on her right now, and he didn't let us in for Transition. I don't foresee him letting us anywhere near that sweet peach."

"Maybe, but I think he will, and I, for one, want to be first in line to hit it. Besides, he was talking to Ristan about her earlier; about taking her memories of him from her. Maybe he's done with her already."

"What the fuck do you think you are doing?" Ristan's voice was angry and held a hint of malice in it. His anger was palpable, even from the distance I stood from them.

"We were just talking. No harm done, Ristan."

"No harm done? Synthia, why don't you come down the stairs the rest of the way," Ristan growled.

I did, only to find Sinjinn and one of the other men—I think his name was Aodhan—looking at me in surprise. I ignored them both as I headed into the kitchen to escape them and their words. Would Ryder really try to remove my memories? No way in hell was I going to allow that to happen. I poured myself a cup of coffee and slid into a chair at the small table.

"Syn, don't think anything about those fucking idiots," Ristan said, coming into the kitchen.

"You all share women," I said, making it a statement instead of a question.

"We don't live by the same code as humans do, Syn."

"The girl they were talking about...Ryder was with her when you all were—together?"

"Yes," Ristan said calmly, with a gentle nod of his dark head.

"When was this?" I asked carefully, trying to school my emotions.

"Years ago, Flower."

I chewed on my lip, considering how much information I could get from the Demon. He was being open with me right now, and I needed to know more about Ryder while he was in such an accommodating mood.

I sat at the table, thinking over everything I had heard. I could flip out, which would totally be the girlie thing to do. But I wasn't hot-headed. I could do a lot of things, none of which would make me feel any better. Why would Ryder take my memories?

"Brewing over what the two jackasses said?" Ristan asked, hauling up a chair to sit with me.

"How many women has Ryder shared with you?" I inquired, straight to the point.

"Many; but you need to understand something first, Flower. We grew up together, and we are not human. We feed from what is available, and, as you have noticed, some of the men are not that bright. Probably starve to death, because they got nothing but shit for brains. Anyway, that wasn't my point. We only share because we grew up together. They feed and I fuck. I like to fuck—a lot. Women love it—well, most do anyway. We are not human, and we have different views on what is normal. They fuck to eat. I just like to fuck. Very seldom do we keep women to ourselves for sex alone, as Ryder is doing with you. In short, we grew up together, so sharing isn't an issue for us."

"Will he ever want to share me?" I asked as I looked up to meet his patterned eyes.

"No, he won't. You, he is different with; very

territorial and possessive. If he'd been planning to share you, he'd have left that door unlocked at the club when your Transition began. He wouldn't have warded it against *us* coming in. He is different with you and has been from the very beginning."

I didn't know he'd done that. "Can I ask you something…um…well, can I ask you something that's a little uncomfortable, Ristan?" I swallowed down the uncomfortable feeling that was causing my cheeks to fill with heat. Now was as good of a time as any to get this out of the way.

"It is uncomfortable how, Flower?" His eyes lit up with mischief. "Are we speaking toys and nipple clamps kind of uncomfortable, because I'm an expert with that shit, or are we speaking your vagigi uncomfortable? I'm game to look at it, play with it. Hell, Flower, I'm pretty much open to it all. Lay it on me." He smirked, and his eyes laughed at me.

"No, this has nothing to do with that…" *Mental Note: Ristan is a freak!* "Uh, yeah, there was a courtyard that I saw in Faery." I couldn't make eye contact, but I noticed that he'd stiffened and sat up straight in his chair. "There were a lot of women there, and Adam was told that they all belong to Ryder." I heard Ristan sigh.

"That's the reason you ran, Flower?" he asked softly as he reached over and lifted my chin. I met his eyes and nodded. "Yes, there is a pavilion; you heard the idiots referring to it earlier. The women there do belong to Ryder. Most are there voluntarily, and some are there for protection." He shook his head and moved the hair from my eyes with the tips of his fingers. "Ryder hasn't been inside of it since he took you to his bed, Synthia." His lips jerked up in a wicked smile. "You locked him into a contract as much as he locked you into one. You made him agree to only feed from you while he had you under contract. Smart, but useless. He wouldn't have touched anyone else while he had you. He's protective of you, and he's also different around you. He's a good man to have at your back. He's the one person in this world and any other that I'd give my life to protect."

"So, he hasn't been with anyone else since we started this…whatever it is we have?"

"You have to ask?" He shook his head.

"Why would he erase my memories, Ristan?" I asked as I lowered my gaze to the smooth wood of the simple table. I felt conflicted about knowing the answer.

"He won't. I'd have seen it if he'd intended to go through with it. He talked about it; thinking it would make it easier to leave you if he had to. You gotta understand, Synthia. He has an objective here in this world. A lot of people depend on him. You're a distraction; one that no one saw coming."

I narrowed my eyes on him. How the hell was I supposed to respond to that!?

"Obviously, I weighed the outcome and decided that, while you *are* a distraction, you are also a part of this mess. I'm not sure how I know, but I do."

"I'm not sure why you think I have some sort of an important part to play in why you came to this world."

"I'm not sure either, but somehow you do play a part in this," Ristan replied as he smiled impishly.

"So much shit is happening. Everything is changing so fast that it's hard to take it all in. I'm not sure where I stand anymore. I'm not even sure who I should stand by." For some reason, I had always found it easy to talk to the Demon, even if he was a huge, demented pervert.

"The Guild? So he told you then," Ristan said as he eyed me cautiously.

"That's why he treated me the way he did when we first met, isn't it?" I probed.

"Yes and no. He wanted you; still does. It pisses him off, Synthia. He's been through hell, and I think you are something he knows he won't be able to let go of, but he also knows he needs to. He has set his goal on finishing this mission and getting home since day one. Now, you walk in all sexy as fuck and throw a monkey wrench in the whole thing. You're this beautiful fucking mess, and it draws us to you. You have so much emotion pouring through you that we could feast off it alone, endlessly. You are unlike the Fae in Faery, because of the way you were raised. Ryder won't erase your memories, but I don't think this will work out as either of you hoped it would, either. I am afraid you both will be fucked up when it ends, and I don't see it ending well, either…Not that I actually *saw* any of this; it's just my opinion."

I didn't need to turn around and look at him to know he was there; I felt him. I felt him as I felt my own legs connected to my body. As if he was a part of me. The air grew thick with the electrical tanginess he created when he entered a room. The rich scent that was unique to him filled my senses, intoxicating me. I could sense him anywhere, but in a room this small, he took it over. Where it had been a kitchen minutes before, it was now filled to the brim with his presence.

"Ristan," he said from directly behind me. His voice wrapped around me like a silken caress.

"Any luck?" Ristan responded.

"We found one, but there's a problem. We need to find more information on the items, as well as someone who can easily pass through so as not to disturb them."

"What for?" I asked Ristan, since he was more likely to answer my question. He didn't, of course— not with Ryder standing directly behind me.

"I told you this wasn't your fight. You have enough shit trying to kill you right now. The Guild has closed ranks, and, from the sounds of it, they are weeding out those opposed to turning on us. My guess is they are going to make it very public, very soon as to which side they are choosing."

"That's shit! They don't have the right to do that. Alden would never...*Oh shit*. We have to get him out of there, now!"

"He chose to go back inside, Syn. If you go in to get him out, they will know for sure which side he is on. Right now, they have no idea he's our inside man," Ryder said gently.

"No, screw that. I can't lose him too," I said as my heart dropped to my feet. My hands gripped the coffee mug hard enough that it cracked, coffee leaking through slightly.

"He chose this," Ristan said softly "He's a good man. He's strong and very capable. He raised you to be strong. Have some faith in him."

"Fine, but I want in on whatever you have going on then. I'm not just going to sit around idly while there's a potential war hanging over our heads," I snapped angrily.

"This isn't your problem," Ryder growled.

"No? Then whose is it? The Fae? The Guild? I'm kinda 'all of the above' at the moment. I was part of that Guild, and I still have friends inside of it. I'm also Fae, in case the three day sexual marathon we had slipped your mind!"

He growled beside my ear, so close it tickled my flesh. "Hard to forget that, Pet. Still, my answer stays the same. You need to stay where I can keep you safe."

"Ryder, I'm not the type to sit around when I can help. I can help you. I'm trained to get into places and get out of them. You've seen me do it. I can help you."

"And I said no," he warned.

"And I said I'm doing it, Fairy!" I growled at him.

His lips pressed against my ear as he whispered softly into it. "Come upstairs, Pet, and I'll show you how much of a fucking Fairy I am."

I turned, catching his lips and biting his lower one, sucking it into my mouth before releasing it. "Not now, Ryder. We're fighting," I said, pausing as a smile crossed my face, "and I'm winning."

"No, you are not," he growled.

"Are you two done fucking around? You're making my cock hard just watching this shit." Ristan laughed boyishly.

"I'm going up to shower. When I come down, I expect to be included and filled in on the details. I'm either with you, or against you. Figure it out and let me know," I said, standing up and turning to meet his golden eyes. "Soon."

"Are you giving me orders? I think you need another example of who is the master in this relationship."

"Relationship? Who the fuck said anything about a relationship? You can't give me one, remember?" I glared pointedly and headed up the stairs.

I made it to the middle of the stairs when I felt it. You know how they say that you can tell when death picks your number; how you can feel it as it wraps its cold arms around you? It's true. I felt the thickness of the air, and turned back to look down the stairs as I felt it. The air grew cold, as if it too had felt death's cold clutches coming for me. The entire house grew silent. Not even the birds outside the house made a single noise. A window broke downstairs, shattering the silence. And then it all came back with a vengeance. The sound deafening and damning as my ears exploded from it. I gasped, knowing I wouldn't make it out alive.

The entire house shook around me, and the sound of wood splintering erupted as the house started to shake with force. I watched the blurriness—something moving fast up the stairs—right before it hit me. And then the feeling of weightlessness sank in.

We sifted into Ryder's club. It was filled with people dancing and drinking. Right up until we'd sifted in, they'd been having fun. I blinked as Adrian looked right at us, and Vlad, who had been behind the bar, moved using lighting fast speed to stand in front of us.

"What's happened, Ryder?" Vlad's voice boomed over the music, which made it stop on the spot.

"Someone just blew up her house, with us inside of it," Ryder growled, holding me against his frame as my legs threatened to give out. As if he was afraid to let me go. I was glad he was holding me as I had no doubt I'd hit the floor if he released his hold.

"Adrian, get Syn seated and get her a drink. The rest of you," Vlad's eyes swept the room with a grim look that promised retribution, "follow."

Vlad's voice was cold and sent chills racing down my spine. I almost felt sorry for the asshole that blew up my house—almost. Ryder turned me in his arms and planted a firm but gentle kiss on my lips before sifting out with the others. I looked around the club and blinked; everyone except Adrian and a few humans had left.

Chapter
TWENTY-TWO

I turned to Adrian, who moved swiftly to embrace me. "Are you okay, Syn? I know how much you loved that house."

"I didn't love the house, Adrian. I loved the memory of my parents that I had inside the house before it was turned into something darker. It's gone now. Everything I had of them was inside of it. I don't even know if Ryder's men made it out alive."

"No, Syn, you have them inside of you, here," he said, placing his hand over my heart. "They can't touch how you feel, or the memories you made with them. No one can tell you to forget that, or even replace it with something else. You choose what you remember."

I blinked at him. He'd gone off topic, and I had a feeling he was referring to us. "I need some water, please."

I walked to a booth as he moved to the bar to grab the bottle of water I had asked for. My hands shook with the realization of just how close I'd come to being nothing more than a pile of ashes. If it hadn't been for Ryder, I would be nothing right now.

Tears rolled down my cheeks as I considered the fact that he'd gone back to the house and was in danger there. I had a feeling that Adrian wasn't quite sure what to do with me. He had a frown marring his beautiful bronzed skin, and the crease between his eyebrows showed he was trying to figure out how to make me stop crying.

"I'm sorry," I cried even harder, unsure how to make myself turn off the waterworks. It was just too much, and everything was crumbling around me yet again. I kept getting knocked down, and it was getting harder to get back up each time.

Adrian smiled, and pulled me to my feet. He wrapped his cold arms around me, and whispered that it would be all right. I buried my head in his shoulder and hugged him back, as the reality of what had just happened overwhelmed me.

Adrian was a vampire.

Adam was the Dark Heir of the Fae.

Larissa was dead.

Alden was facing danger to help us.

I was homeless, jobless, and attracted to the one thing that would surely kill me in the end.

The reality set in that I had even lost my dog, and now my life was just one tragedy away from becoming a sad country song.

Reality sucked.

I cried harder, promising myself that this was the last time. This was the last time I cried over my life. Tomorrow, I'd pick myself back up, kill the asshole that did this, and move on. In that exact order. I was getting ready to pull away from Adrian and ask for the water when Ryder sifted in, and growled an inhuman sound that made my spine stiffen and my heart race.

I turned, and leveled him with a pointed look. "Did everyone get out? Is there anything left?" My voice hitched and cracked as I said it, which made his eyes soften a bit. He nodded, lifting my hope. "How bad is it?"

"House is a total loss. We managed to save a small portion of the clothes, pictures, and anything pertaining to your parents that we could find."

"Wait, you went back to get my stuff?" I asked, incredulous that he would risk anyone's life for things I cherished. On the one hand, it was sweet; on the other, it was stupid.

The tick in his jaw was working overtime now. "Yes, I took *immortals* inside a fucking inferno for your stuff; things that I couldn't replace, or anyone else could for that matter. Fae can't undo that kind of damage, or turn back time, but we can recreate what we have seen. We just don't know what was in there so that we could reproduce it for you, so we tried to save what we could. I know how humans like to keep memories from their past."

"Thank you, thank you all," I said, looking around to find people covered in soot from the fire. The scent of smoke filled the room, wafting from their bodies. "Next time, Ryder, screw the stuff and kill the motherfucker who did it. Don't risk anyone's life for *things*. They are only items, and even if they can't all be replaced, I'd choose safety over things any day."

He stared at me openly as if I'd just shocked, confused, and made his day all in one sentence. I moved closer until I was standing on my tiptoes, and kissed his untouched cheek. "And thank you for saving me." Because I, like a ninny, had forgotten I could sift. And he'd known I would, predicted it, and saved me from death. I wasn't quite done with Transition yet, and this could have put a damper on my future as an immortal.

He wrapped his arms around me, pulled me closer, and whispered in my ear, quiet enough that only I could hear him. "You almost got killed yet again, Synthia. I'm about to wrap you in fucking bubble wrap."

I smiled against his chest. "I hear plastic isn't big in fashion these days and, besides, it wouldn't last long since I have a weakness to pop the bubbles."

He laughed, but it wasn't the musical one I wanted to hear. I could hear his heart hammering wildly inside his chest. My own was matching his in tempo. "Someone openly tried to kill you tonight, Synthia. Come back to Faery with me where I can keep you safe," he said, possessiveness flooding his tone.

"No, someone tried to kill me. Tonight, I'm upset. Tomorrow, they die. I won't run from a fight, and this guy needs to be dealt with," I smiled sadly as I pulled away. "I'm not hiding. I'm just not that type of person, Ryder. They want me? They can come and try to get me."

"They just fucking did. They blew up your fucking house with you *inside* of it! If I hadn't been there," he paused, and shook his head as if dispelling the thought. "You'd be inside that burning fucking mess."

"But I'm not, because you saved me. They failed, because the guy at my side is the biggest, baddest boogeyman on the fucking block. They failed, and if I hide they win. I can get knocked down, but what I can't do is stay down. Don't ask me to, because the answer will be *no*, every fucking time."

He shook his head and grinned. "All right, then we need to figure out who is trying to take you out. It could be same asshole who keeps showing up at your house, or…Could it be someone from the Guild or, perhaps, one of the fanatics outside of the Guild?" he asked, raising a brow.

I crinkled my nose and nodded. "It's possible. If they are making a list and collecting information on those who were sympathetic to the Fae inside the Guild, I'd be on that list by default."

"Drinks, come sit at the bar," Vlad said when he noticed it was going to be awhile; I was shaky on my legs at best right then anyway. I guess almost getting blown up had that effect on a person. I sat beside Ryder as his men circled his back.

I'd noticed that anytime he couldn't put his back to a wall, they became the wall that stood at his back. He was always guarded and never alone; unless we were inside a room together. I was willing to bet that someone stood close to the door guarding it as well. He was important to his men; even if he wasn't the Dark Heir, he was definitely a prince who was extremely important to his people. He had an elite guard of men he cared about, who worked like a well-oiled machine. He was fast enough to remove me as a bomb went off in my house, and strong enough that people listened without questioning him. He was primal, sexual, and deadly to his very core.

"We're out of tonic right now. Gin and seven, ok?" Vlad said, and my stomach pitched and rolled with the sound of the drink.

"Just a bottle of water please," I replied, smiling when he cussed.

"This is a bar. I can't do my stereotypical bartender moves if you only order water." He winked, joking with me as he tried to lighten the mood.

"Do I need to throw up everywhere? Because right now the only thing I can stomach is water," I countered and watched his face turn to a mask of disgust.

"So rather you didn't. Water it is."

"Okay, so we know the Fae who showed up at the house knows you. He said as much, and he was in your memories. What we don't know is if he was with the group of Fae that were with the Mages who attacked the mansion or if he is also the one who blew up the house," Ryder said as he brought me back to the reason we'd sat down at the bar in the first place.

"Yes, he was there. He raped my mother, and he's the one that killed my father. He also had fangs—like mine," I whispered past a lump as the memories flashed to life inside my mind. They were no longer as painful as they had once been.

"He knew your name as well, Syn, and he didn't set the wards off. It's curious that he got through while they instantly seek anyone else out. Question is, who is he and why does he want you dead? He's definitely after you alone. It's possible he was sent to kill you." Ryder said.

"No idea. Considering we don't know who I really am yet, I have no idea why anyone would want me dead."

"We need to figure it out. It might help us determine who is trying to kill you."

"Alden said that the wards might have been guarding against the Unseelie, but since there are hundreds of different kinds, it would be impossible to narrow it down to just one caste." The entire club went silent with the word, as if it was taboo to speak it out loud. You could have heard a pin drop from across the room. I looked around, and back to Ryder, since the most I could see was a wall of backs guarding us.

"Could be, but that doesn't make sense. What would the Unseelie want with you? You are not even of our world, and most of the Unseelie are not allowed into the human world."

"It took you to your knees the first time you came in; maybe you are Unseelie," I pointed out.

"That happened one time, and we discussed why that might have happened." He smirked boyishly. "So, there goes that theory."

"Okay, but why hide me from the Unseelie? It makes no sense."

"It makes no sense in a human world, but in ours every caste is always at odds with another. One clan could have hidden you from another. Stop thinking as a human, and start thinking as what you are, Syn. Nothing will ever make sense if you keep thinking as a human. We just need to figure out why they wanted you hidden to begin with. That might lead us to who is trying to kill you."

"Okay, so say they did. How do we tell which caste he's from, or me for that matter?"

"We don't. We set a trap."

"With what?"

"With someone who looks like you," he replied.

"Why not just use me?"

"Fuck. That."

"I second that," Adrian shouted over the wall of men.

"I'm not some damsel in distress, and you'd all do well to remember who I was before I changed, because I'm still me."

"You're also sick, Synthia. Something is making you unstable; you have yet to tap into the powers you were born with."

"Maybe it's too much testosterone arguing with me?" Everyone inside the club snickered at that.

"Only way you're going out as bait is if I'm standing right fucking beside you."

Chapter
TWENTY-THREE

Several hours later, we sifted into Ryder's club basement, forgoing the elevator for the more direct route. My house had looked exactly like you would imagine a house would look like if a bomb went off inside of it. Alden had shown up soon after Ryder had sifted me in to see the wreckage so I could see the damage for myself. It had been heartbreaking to see it destroyed, but I'd refused to cry or show any more emotion, since it was only a house and no lives had been lost in the destruction.

Alden had been glad to see that he didn't have to dig me out of the pile of ashes to bury me properly. He'd also reported that the Scribe had made progress on the protection wards that were now destroyed. He had requested more pictures of the wards to determine exactly which caste we were up against, but that was now a dead lead for us.

I yawned and peeked at Ryder as he walked beside me. I just wanted a bed and to sleep for days if I could. The look in his gold eyes told me he wasn't planning on sleeping. I bit my bottom lip to keep from smiling.

He leaned over and whispered seductively in my ear, "Don't bite that lip too hard, Pet. It makes me want to do very bad things to it that would feel really good." He pulled away with a wicked grin tugging on his beautiful mouth. I looked at the walls of the corridor, which had begun to glow as we walked through it.

"After your little visits, I had the entire corridor warded. It's only visible right now because I allowed it to be," Ryder said, waving his hand to light up the ward in front of a familiar door, before turning it off. He pushed the door open and stepped back as he motioned for me to precede him in to the room. His eyes met mine invitingly, and something like anticipation flashed in them as he waited for my response to his silent request.

I stepped through willingly, my eyes taking in the details of the room I had Transitioned in. The bed was inviting, and the thought of Ryder and what we would be doing soon was even more so. Right now, I needed him; needed him to erase the shock and anger of what had happened. Hunger was also playing with my mind. I needed to feed, and I wanted it to be only from him. I didn't want to find someone else to feed from, and the realization of that was frightening.

"Syn, are you okay? You've been through hell tonight," Ryder said gently from behind me.

"It was only a house," I replied, but my voice had cracked with the words.

I felt his breath fan against my neck enticingly as he moved closer. "It was more than a house to you, Synthia. It was the home you loved. You felt more for it than you are letting on. I can feel it from the mark you bear."

"Still, it was only a house. I'm grateful no one was injured in it. I'm only here because you saved me." I turned to face him, my eyes telling him I was his for tonight, in any way he wanted me. "Ryder, I need to thank you…" I let the meaning hang in the air precariously between us.

"I told you that I would protect you, Pet. You don't need to thank me for saving what is mine," he replied, but I could see his eyes lighting from within. I knew it had little to do with hunger, and everything to do with me submitting to him.

"I know, but I want you right now. No walls, just barebones right now, please. Tonight I'm giving you me, just me. Unless you don't think you can handle it, Fairy," I challenged him. I knew his touch could make me forget everything that had happened tonight.

"I can handle it. The question is, are you sure you want what you are asking me for? If we do this, I'm going to make you scream for me, and I'm going to want to keep going until I'm sure you want no one else but me ever again. I'm drawn to you in a way that I've never been to another person before. I don't want to feel this for you, but I can't shut it off either."

"I want you. Just you, Ryder," I whispered, not backing down from his challenge.

"You want me, and you already know what I want. You know what pleases me. Show me that you want me as much as I want you right now. No walls between us, and I promise I'll give you no pain this time."

I shivered as the magnitude of what I had requested settled in to my system. He stood there, dressed in his clothes, and, for once, I didn't want him to use magic on them. I wanted to undress him, to reveal his beautiful body to my eyes slowly and kiss every inch of him as I did so.

I stepped closer to him, enjoying the electrical tingle that came from standing too close to him. I reached up with my hands as my eyes lifted to hold his. I smiled shyly, which made no sense. He'd had me five ways from Sunday, and yet, every time seemed like the first to me.

I finished unbuttoning his shirt and removed it from his shoulders, discarding it on the floor carelessly. I licked my lips hungrily as I undid his belt, and worked his zipper to reveal his magnificent cock. It sprung out, hard and ready to be kissed.

He hissed, and a feral growl built inside his magnificent chest. I raised my hands to test the silk of his chest and the taut skin of it. My eyes took in every brand and beautiful curve of his tight abs. I lowered my mouth until I was close enough and then I kissed his nipple and allowed my tongue to flick against it, enjoying the moan that broke from his lips as I slowly worked at seducing him.

I was a glutton for punishment, but there was something magical about seducing a beast such as Ryder. I clamped my mouth around his nipple and sucked against the puckered flesh. I scraped it gently with my teeth as he continued to make sounds of pleasure that clued me into how much he liked it. My hand lowered and sank in to his jeans.

I pulled his erection the rest of the way out so my fingers could curl around his cock, and his moan was the sweetest sound I'd ever heard. I smiled wickedly as I lifted my eyes to meet his, and continued stroking his need. This man was made for sex—it showed in his size and in his need that was bared in his gorgeous amber depths.

"What did it feel like when you watched me in my bedroom?" I asked, watching him sift away from my seeking hands to the bed, as if he needed to put distance between us to think. He settled onto the enormous stack of pillows and laid his head down on them before turning those burning amber eyes toward me again.

He swallowed before he could answer, and it made me smile. He let his eyes trail down my body before he snapped his fingers, and I was entirely naked before him. "I'd never wanted to be buried balls-deep in anyone as much as I wanted to be inside you."

"You could have taken me at any time you wanted to, and simply erased my memories. Why didn't you?" I was curious. He'd gone to some pretty extreme lengths to get me to his bed, and yet he could have easily taken it from me, and I'd never have known the difference. He hadn't though. Instead, he'd waited for me to say yes. That alone told me he wasn't the monster he pretended to be.

"Because I wanted you to remember me, to remember I'd had you," he replied openly as he reached down and began stroking his need while I watched. I was breathless; with every stroke he took of his magnificent organ, it became harder to breathe.

"But I was only a mortal back then. Why would some glorious creature like you want me?" Yes, I was fishing, sue me. I wanted to hear him admit that he wanted me. Right now, I needed to know that I mattered for more than just sex to him. I needed to know he didn't do what he had done just to get laid.

"I honestly don't know, Synthia. I just knew that I had to have you. You were this exception to everything I knew of humans. You never sought anything for yourself, except that little pleasure you gave yourself at the end of the night. You lived to make this world safer, even though no one knew you were doing so.

You took no glory in killing the Fae, even though you could have. You were the most beautiful creature I'd ever laid my eyes on, and you didn't even know it. I wanted you to know that I was inside of you, and I wanted you to be mine. I wanted you to know the feel of me fucking your tight pussy, even if it was only the one time."

I felt his magic clamp down on both of my nipples at the same time, and a gasp exploded from my lips. I allowed his magic to once again take over and pleasure my body as I stood bared before him. It pressed harder on my core, creating a maelstrom of pleasure as the incredible sensations started to build inside of me. I felt it release, and I met his eyes in wonder as the intense sensations started again. His eyes watched me from where he lay on the bed as my body shook from the pleasure he was giving me while I still stood near the door.

I wanted to know what he'd looked like as he'd watched me. Had he stroked his cock while he'd watched me doing the same to myself? Had he needed to because I'd driven him insane with need? I was losing the anger from what he'd done, and when he'd saved my ass tonight, it gave me appreciation for what he was.

I walked slowly in the direction of the bed, giving him a full view of my body as I stopped right before the mattress. I smiled shyly as his eyes slid down my body, hungrily. There was no hiding his desire for me, and even if he wouldn't admit to having feelings for me, he wanted me. Maybe it was shallow, but tonight I wanted to feel needed. I wanted to feel his need for me, in more ways than I could admit, even to myself.

My eyes lowered to where his hand stroked still, and I licked my lips, not bothering to hide the fact that I wanted them wrapped around his engorged cock. I wanted to taste him until I knew him from his flavor alone. I lowered myself onto the bed and crawled toward him slowly. I took my time as his eyes watched me heatedly through slits. I smiled at him as I lowered my mouth to where his hand slowed.

I stopped inches from the glistening tip and held my hair out of the way with one hand as I lowered my head to do as I wanted to. I licked the bead of come from his cock and watched as his hips bucked from the pleasure of my tongue. I didn't take him into my mouth. Instead, I licked him slowly, tasting his flesh and listening to his breathing as it hitched in his throat.

"Good girl," he purred as I pressed my tongue hard against his sensitive flesh, never removing my eyes from his. "Do it, Syn, take what you need from me," he encouraged as my fangs grew slightly longer.

I was empowered by his need and unsure how to do what he wanted. I wanted to please him, and it startled me at just how much I wanted to. I let my fangs trail against his flesh and paused as he growled and hissed at the same time. I didn't want to give him pain, only pleasure.

I watched as his vein pumped to the beat of his heart, and, before I knew it, I'd cupped his balls and sucked the side of his massive cock, unable to fit my lips fully around the side. My thoughts flew to what Vlad had said about the blood. I also remember what Ryder had said that the Fae could control pleasure with our saliva. I was part Blood Fae, and I could give him pleasure. If I could control the blood and the saliva—I could give him the ultimate release. I instinctively cut my tongue with the tip of my fang, and then I hesitantly pressed against his cock with the tips of my fangs, and they melted through his silken flesh like butter.

It wasn't until I tasted his blood that I felt my body accepting it and feeding it back to him with my own blood cells and saliva inside of it. He moaned and bucked against the assault of my blood invading his body. I pulled back, fully intending to stop, but I felt my essence inside of him! I fought to control my breathing as I sent my little experiment in search of his pleasure zones.

He shouted my name as hot come shot from his cock within a moment of my exploration. Holy fuck buckets! I watched him explode and fed gloriously as he writhed for several moments in exquisite torment until he sagged against the mattress, spent from his release.

"Holy shit," I whispered with a smile so big the Cheshire Cat would have been jealous of it.

"Yeah, holy shit," he agreed with shaky enthusiasm and a wide smile on his beautiful mouth. "My turn, Pet," he said with a gravelly tone.

I was on my back before I could consider what he'd said. His hands held mine down, locked above my head as his magic assaulted me. It was touching, kissing, and caressing my naked skin everywhere as he watched me from his position stretched out above my body.

"I've never allowed anyone to tease me, and I'm not sorry I let you be the first to do it," he whispered.

His legs spread mine apart, and I instantly felt full, even though I could see him and feel his massive cock resting against my hip. The man had a recovery rate that was shocking. I moaned at the fullness, knowing he was filling me with the use of his magic alone. Knowing he was inside of me without touching me was both thrilling and a little scary. The look on his face was complete pleasure, mixed with wonder. *I'd* put that look on his face. *Me*! Not any other woman. Not some other fucking Fairy happy meal...Me, Synthia Raine McKenna.

"Fuck, you're so beautiful when I'm inside you," he whispered throatily.

"You're not inside of me yet."

"I'm not?" He smiled, and the fullness dissipated briefly, only to come back with a vengeance, pounding inside of me until I was helpless to do anything but feel him as he magically fucked me. Sweat beaded on his forehead and slid down until it rested on his nose. I was jealous of that bead of sweat because it was touching his flesh.

He finally released my hands from where he had pinned them above my head, and I threaded my fingers through his hair and brought his lips down to meet mine. I kissed him as if there was no tomorrow, because for us, there might not be. When I allowed him to pull away from me, his eyes said he too was thinking the same thing. Even with his comments about keeping me, we both knew that probably wouldn't happen.

"I'm going to show you something, Pet. I need you to trust me, and not panic."

"I think I can handle that, Fairy," I shot back.

He pulled away from me, taking his magic with him. When he was sitting on his heels with his hands in the air, I felt his magic pulsing around me. I'd felt his magic during sex, and it was mind-boggling. I was about to tell him that when it started. I had something...no, I had things, pressing against every fuckable hole in my body.

I felt the need and started to open my mouth instinctively, but he stopped me with his eyes and words. "Just feel, Syn, don't react."

Easy for him to say; he wasn't the one with something trying to press into every place it could fit! I shivered at the feeling of his magic invading my body, my senses. I could feel him inside of me, and, yet, I could see him and knew he wasn't. I could taste his come in my mouth, and whatever was inside of it. It was pressing against my throat, and so I imagined what it would be like to curl my tongue around it. His magic felt and tasted just like he did. He moaned as if he'd felt it, or maybe I had the ability to do the same thing as him with my magic. I continued imagining caressing him with my tongue, but no other noise of pleasure broke from his lips. It had been worth a shot anyway.

The one between my thighs entered me and began keeping the same slow, steady motion of the one in my mouth. The one aimed at my ass didn't move, it only pressed against it with the impending threat of penetration. I felt myself teetering on the edge, my body trembling with the impending orgasm, but he held it off and wouldn't allow it yet.

"I'm inside of you, everywhere. I can take you any way I want, at any time. I can make you feel more than any other creature in this, or any other world, can."

I moaned at his words as fear trickled down my spine at the thought of his full dominance and how he intended to use it on me. I wasn't a sub. I wasn't even sure I could pretend to be one very well. I wanted what I wanted, and I did not like waiting for it. Ryder wasn't the type to boast either; when he said he could do something, he did it. The man was a sex god, and I was his with only one look from him. I could hate him one minute, and the next, I was in his bed naked.

His laughter was dark and sexual as he took in the look of unease, and pleasure mixed on my face. "I plan on doing so, but not tonight. Tonight, I just want you to learn to trust me again. I fucked up, Syn, and I'm sorry you got hurt in the process." The magic mimicking his cock in my mouth eased out. It was a good thing he couldn't read my mind, or he'd know I was a lost cause with that simple look of dominance he got in his bronze eyes.

"I'm learning to trust you, Fairy. In this room, I trust you, always have. It's outside of it that we don't work. You keep secrets from me. You hide who you are from me. You are no better than I am, Ryder. We pretend to be what people need from us, what they need us to be. People like us have no future. We live our lives for other people."

He shook his head as he spread my thighs apart. "Not tonight. Tonight, I'm living for *you*. I'm making a choice to treat you as my woman," he whispered as his magic left my body, and he replaced it.

I moaned as he pushed into me; the feel of his flesh was more than any magic could ever replace. I had tears in my eyes, but not because I was sad. They were there because he'd just told me he cared for me. Ryder, the freaking Sex King of the Fae, had just told me I was worthy of him in his eyes.

He was slow and gentle, and when he rolled us over so that I was sitting on top of him, I moaned in response to the depth he had reached in that position. I moved my hips slowly, allowing him to go even further inside of me.

"That's it, ride me. Gods, you're so fucking tight around my cock. I can feel your pussy tightening around me, caressing me from the inside."

I moved a little faster, gasping as I did so. He was too big, and in this position he was buried deeper than before. I knew it was taking a lot for him to give up control. Ryder was a control freak, and I loved that about him. He loved to control my pleasure, and I loved it when he gave me releases unlike anything I'd ever known before.

I was stretched wide to fit his incredible size, and while a twinge of pain shot through me, I knew it would be worth it in the end. I was wet for him, which helped with riding him. I felt the storm increase in strength, so I moved in a frenzied tempo to crest the storm and exploded, still impaled on his shaft.

He didn't allow me to come for long on him. Instead, he sifted from inside of me, his mouth replacing his cock at my soaked core, and he started lapping at it intensely, and working me over with his mouth.

The noises he made while he ravished my soaking core made the orgasm continue, and his magic was inside of me again. It fucked me from the inside while I rode the orgasm, feeding him as I did so. When the orgasm began to wane, he was behind me, shoving me down as he entered me hard, and fast.

"I love that you are so wet for me. Your body knows who it belongs to. It weeps for my touch, and parts so readily for my cock. Can you feel me, fucking you, stretching your sweet flesh for me? Can you feel my magic kissing every inch of your beautiful flesh as I control your pleasure?" He growled it out between clenched teeth as he pounded himself deep inside of my wet sheath.

His hand reached up and pulled my hair, hard

enough that my head was forced back so he could watch my face as he continued to fuck me. His magic nipped greedily on my breasts, as if his teeth were there, biting them softly. Hot magic fanned across my clit before pressure was applied, and I cried out. His wicked smile told me he was well aware of the effect his magic was having on my senses as he released it to control every nerve ending that was connected to my passion.

I moaned and felt him growing inside of me as the wetness his magic created allowed him to penetrate my body further. His eyes were lit, and he pounded inside of me relentlessly, his body moving inside of mine with perfect movement. His magic sucked at my clit and abused my nipples sinfully.

"You are *mine*, so fucking mine."

"Yes," I whimpered as he increased both the magic and his assault. The only sounds inside the bedroom were flesh ignited in passion and muffled screams of our mutual pleasure. I fucking loved it.

"Who controls your pleasure, Pet?" he asked.

"You do!" I screamed as another orgasm threatened to take over.

"Who am I?"

"Ryder," I moaned.

"Who am *I*?" he asked again, and the question made me think, which I didn't want to do.

"You are my Fairy, and I am yours. Now shut up and fuck me harder." I said the last hoping to ignite his anger, because with his anger came hard sex. I loved it hard, and I loved sex with him.

His hand came down and slapped my ass hard as the other pulled at my hair, sending the nerves inside both regions into overdrive. He rubbed the area that he'd just spanked and repeated it. "That's for almost dying on me again, Pet," he growled. His hand pulled me up by my hair until my mouth was close enough for his kiss. "This is for pleasing me." He kissed me, without any walls. He held nothing back as he took me from behind, and his mouth assaulted mine in a hard demanding kiss. When he released my mouth, he gave one final deep thrust and his release came out as a strangled groan. I fed from it until we could do nothing more than lay there, entwined together and catching our breath.

When we'd both recovered, he wrapped his arms and body protectively around me and smiled. "You're so beautiful. So fucking perfect," he whispered and leaned over to kiss my forehead gently. Tears shot to my eyes, hard and relentless. I shoved them away, knowing they would disrupt what was occurring between us—whatever it was. We had found a semblance of peace tonight, and I didn't want to ruin it.

Chapter
TWENTY-FOUR

I felt like I couldn't walk the next morning. He'd taken me until my legs trembled, and the only thing I could say was *more*, and *yes please*. I felt painfully full, and fully sated. His only response when I'd tried to crawl away from him had been that he wasn't done with me yet. He was insatiable, and every time I'd tried to crawl away, he would just pull me right back to him and make me want him more. When he finally allowed me to sleep, I'd slept like the dead, wrapped in his arms and safe, which seemed to hold the nightmares at bay.

I was currently watching him sleep. Once again, he looked much younger, and peaceful. He'd watched me for at least three years, and he'd designed our fate. He'd arranged it all and ensured we'd meet, and, in the end, we had.

I wasn't sure whether I should be upset or impressed that he'd actually gone through everything he had just to be with me. Most people would run. Hell, I should be running and putting as much distance as I could between us, but I couldn't.

I wanted him to look at me with that intense heat burning deep in his golden eyes. I wanted to feel his touch on my soul. And he *had* touched my soul. He hadn't even been trying, and yet, I caved in to him every time he touched me. I wanted more than he could offer, or was willing to.

This wouldn't end with a happily ever after. It would end with me becoming his sex pet, and that wasn't something I would ever accept as my future. I wanted more than that, more than just to be his bed mate. Besides, I wasn't sure in which direction my life was going. Everything was out of control. I mean, someone had just blown up my house.

I may have changed into something else, but my principles were the same as they had always been. Right now, I was sleeping with the enemy, and, no matter how much I tried to tell myself I needed it, my heart was going to end up broken. Today, I would start looking for another source of nourishment, and cut ties with Ryder before I fell any deeper into whatever it was I felt for him. I was teetering on something dangerous with him, and every moment I spent in his company, I was getting more attached—and that was dangerous. I wasn't sure I wanted to delve deeper into my feelings for him. It wasn't safe.

He smiled and opened his eyes to look directly at me. "Sore?" he purred with his eyes low and fused with heat already; a self-assured grin lifted his mouth into a sexy smile. They were beautiful when heavy from sleep. Unguarded was the best way to describe them.

"Very," I whispered, and sat up, trying to dispel the heat that rose inside of me from looking into his endless golden depths.

"Good," he replied with a low growl, watching me as if he was stalking his prey. I could feel his gaze penetrating me, even without turning to confirm it.

"What's the plan?" I asked, getting straight to the point and to veer away from a topic that would only boost his male ego. As if the man needed it.

"You are staying here with me. At least until I can figure out who is targeting you, or why they are. It was too close last time, and in order to prevent it from happening again, I want you here, protected."

"You want me to stay here, inside, until you can figure it out?" Was he serious?

He nodded and smiled as I groaned inwardly. "That was not what I agreed to. I agreed to be your happy meal, not your prisoner. Locking me up to keep me safe is the same thing."

"Someone is trying to kill you. They blew up your fucking house. Give me some time to look into it. Please, at least give me this. I need to know you are safe before I allow you to leave. Besides, where would you go?"

I wanted to say no, but that would just confirm how stubborn I was. Or worse, it would show him I was afraid to be close to him. People had almost gotten hurt because someone had tried to kill me. "Fine, you have a week. If you can't draw them out by then, you have to promise me that I get a try at it."

"No—"

"Ryder, they are not just going to come out if I'm not used as bait. They came when I tapped the line. They knew where I'd be immediately after. These are the same people who killed my parents, or at least one is for sure. Don't ask me to stay idle through this, because I can already tell you it won't happen. I want him dead. I want them all dead, in a real bad way." I didn't often want people dead, but when I did, I went all *Goodfellas* in the brain. I wanted them dead, I wanted their memory dead, and I wanted them to die in a real painful way.

"Blood thirsty wench. I think my dick just got hard."

"I'm serious, Ryder; you have one week. Then, we do this my way without a single complaint from you or anyone else. Agreed?"

His eyes narrowed, but I wasn't backing down. Not on this, not with the ones who'd killed my parents. This was my fight and mine alone. People could get killed, and I'd carry the burden on my soul because it was how I was shaped. He was lucky I was giving him a shot at them without me being present at all, and he knew it.

"Pet," he looked right at me and paused. He must have seen the determination in my eyes, because he changed the direction of his thoughts. "One full week, with the agreement that you try to learn your new Fae abilities so you are prepared for whatever happens. I want you ready for them, Pet. On this, I won't bend," he said, pulling me back into the bed, and leaning over me.

"Fine, one week. You train me on how to be a Fairy," I whispered, swallowing as he lowered his mouth to mine and captured it passionately.

"One week," he repeated, before kissing me again gently, with softness he didn't normally use with me. When he pulled away, he smirked wickedly as if he'd just won a huge prize. "It's time to learn how to use magic to dress, Pet."

~~*~*~*~*~*~*

We settled into a routine. He was gone at night—he

wasn't specific on where he was going or what he was doing, but I suspected it had to do with the Mages— and I'd learn how to use magic during the day. I was making progress, and could become clothed with a single thought—as long as I wanted to wear leather, which seemed to give Ryder some enjoyment.

He acted almost like he had a normal relationship with me, and was surprisingly gentle in the few days it had taken for us to settle into a routine. It was comfortable, and the atmosphere was amazing when he'd drag me to bed to feed me after draining my energy during my Fairy training. He smiled more and would become almost human until he'd go out at night, leaving me in his bed like the entire day had meant nothing to him at all.

Each night, one of the men would knock softly on the door, signaling him that they were ready to go, and his entire demeanor would promptly close off and become detached, cold, and distant as he left for the rest of the night. We would go back to normal when it was time to train. Nights I used for planning how to call out the person who wanted me dead. As time dwindled down, I was becoming more agitated.

"Pull the magic around you. Focus," Ryder said from across the room.

We trained in the room where my entire existence had been altered by him, the same room where he'd asked Zahruk to replay my past, only his powers had made the room larger. "Ryder, this is pointless. How am I supposed to know the difference between Fae magic and the same magic I have been using all my life?"

"One is wild magic, the other is dark magic. Try not using the dark magic," Ryder smirked as he once again leaned against the wall and folded his arms across his chest. He continued to watch me fumble through the training. I was beginning to think I would never learn how to use Fae magic, and frustration at failing plain sucked. My confidence was already battered and still bruised from failing to save Larissa.

I grumbled, but tried again. The entire room grew thick with electrical current from the power radiating through me. *Dark Arts*...I cut it off and shook my head. Several more tries and I still couldn't pull the power out that Ryder thought would be inside of me. I was still trying to pull the correct magic from within when Ristan entered the room.

"Keep trying," Ryder said while nodding to Ristan, who walked to where he stood and leaned against the wall with him.

"Anything?" Ryder asked, turning to look at Ristan.

"No, I have a small group out scouting, but I can see nothing. How's the magic training going?"

"She's unable to pull it out," Ryder said softly as I continued to try.

"So, she isn't progressing?" Ristan asked.

"No, she isn't trying hard enough. She's still using the magic she was taught at the Guild. She should be able to do it naturally, with just a thought. Right now, she isn't tapping into anything besides my patience."

"Oh I wouldn't say that." Ristan grinned widely. "She's tapping you nightly."

"Ristan, figure out who is trying to kill her. I want to know who it is by tomorrow night."

"You got it. But, Ryder, whoever it is; he's doing

a damn good job hiding from us. There's no scent to follow, not a single trace of him."

I turned my back on them, shutting them out as I tried to pull out more magic. It was hopeless. I'd been using magic since I could remember, and nothing was coming but the magic I'd always used. But that wasn't the magic I needed. Casting came easily, but the only thing coming was what I couldn't and shouldn't use. Not without the help of a coven anyway. Dark Magic could kill or do damage to the caster if not leveled and kept balanced by a full coven.

"Ever consider that she's already tapped into her Fae magic and that maybe, just maybe, she's been using it all along?" Ristan said to Ryder, making me spin on them.

"How is that possible if I've been blocked by the brand on my neck? Wouldn't you have felt the magic?" I asked as I narrowed my eyes.

"If she's been using it this entire time, we'd have felt it," Ryder agreed, even though he'd tilted his head, which he did when he was thinking. "Unless the actual magic is being shielded. She has always smelled of wild magic, even if she wasn't using it."

"How old were you when you first used magic, Syn?" Ristan asked softly.

"Three was my first memory of using it," I answered him smoothly.

"She can't lie," Ristan said, causing me to lift an eyebrow in confusion.

"Why would I? I have nothing to gain by lying."

"You're also fully Fae now, Synthia. You couldn't lie if your life depended on it," Ristan mused with a cocky grin on his lips.

"Point?"

"Age three is extremely young for a Witch to start casting. What else could you do at three, Syn?" Ryder asked as he pushed from the wall and let his arms drop to his sides. I watched the muscles in his abdomen as they tightened with his movements. He'd come shirtless today for the lesson, and I hadn't complained one bit until now.

"Simple things; I could control the heat of my bathwater, food that I didn't like I could change into something simple like fries, and clothes—shit!" I stopped cold and blinked. I'd changed my clothes, and even my mother's on occasion with a simple thought—but I hadn't used spells then. I realized that I had begun believing in the power of the spells instead of the power inside of me when I had moved to the Guild.

"You could change clothes," Ryder said, tilting his head with a devastating grin. "This whole time you have been struggling to materialize cotton, and you could do it at three. That's an impossible feat for any but a select few Fae at that age."

"You thinking what I'm thinking, Ryder?" Ristan asked from where he'd stayed leaning against the wall.

"That Syn is the real Light Princess, whose mother must have had an affair with one of the princes of the Blood Fae, giving us a little Syn?" Ryder smiled wickedly as he watched me closely.

"I'm *not* the Light Heir. You said I was Blood Fae."

"She's about the right age, and it would account

for why she would have known Adam and bound him as a familiar at such a young age," Ristan supplied. "Blood Fae had a compact with the Light, as well as the Dark, twenty-one years ago. They could have easily met at the Samhain feast, and typically all three castes would have been present."

I felt as if I was drowning and couldn't breach the surface of the water. It was horrifying to even consider it, since the Light Fae were the most obnoxious of any caste, with their air of superiority.

"The glamour you cast when we first met, Syn. How long could you have worn it?" Ryder asked quietly.

"Not long, I guess; it would have drained my magic," I replied as I absently fisted my hands at my sides where they had started to shake. It was one thing to know I had family out there, and another to actually have someone figuring it out in front of you.

On one hand, it was exciting, considering I had lost everything, but scary to think he could actually figure it out and take me to them. What if they didn't like me? What if they thought I was a freak since I could still summon the glow that Alden had pigmented into my skin? There were way too many things that could go wrong. Hell! They could turn around and sell me to Ryder, since the Light Fae had an army of daughters.

"That was before Transition, though, so it stands to reason that she would drain easily if she used it too long," Ristan said casually as if we were discussing a nice family vacation in the South.

"So you're saying I'm a royal bastard who came from an affair, and that the entire time I was supposed to be pretending to be the Light Heir, I *was* the Light Heir?" They both laughed. I was the only one who didn't think it was funny. It would be my luck, though. If it weren't for bad luck, I'd have no damn luck at all.

"Could explain why someone is after her though. There were rumors for years that the Light King had been trying to find the Light Heir so he could kill her." Ryder looked at me with a smirk. "Just so you know, that was why we didn't question it when Arianna's guards said there were assassins after her, not that we were stupid." I glared at him for omitting that little piece of information from me before.

"This makes absolutely no sense, you know that, right?" I grouched, already feeling the resulting hunger from hours of practicing magic today.

"Because you don't want to be a bastard? Or because…?" Ryder asked with a frown on his face.

"Because it's one thing to be Fae, Ryder, but it's an entirely different thing to be Light Fae. They're the worst of the fucking Fairies. They're a bunch of nauseating, sanctimonious prats that think they are better than every other caste of Fae. I'd rather be Horde than one of those pricks!"

Something silent passed between Ryder and Ristan, and then he leveled me with a stare that could have lit a wet branch on fire. "It doesn't change the fact that it fits—*you* fit, Syn. It gives us a lead on who is trying to kill you as well. Now all those rumors are taking on different meaning. It would make sense that she'd dump her offspring if the heir was not legitimate." Ryder smirked. "Looks like some of what Dresden said was the truth."

"I don't give a crap if I'm some royal bastard. What bothers me is that I don't want a family. I don't need them. They didn't want *me*. I don't need them to figure this out, and I sure don't need them to want me because I'm an heir. They threw me away, and whatever their reason was for doing it, it changes nothing. I had a family, and I know who I am without the Light Fae, or them claiming me for that matter."

"You don't want to meet your mother?" Ristan asked guardedly.

"No. I watched my mother be slaughtered by Fae, and nothing and nobody can replace her. She gave her life to protect me, Ristan. She was my mother, and she proved it with her sacrifice. It changes nothing."

"We still need to know who's trying to kill you," Ryder pointed out.

"So figure it out without telling the Light Fae you found me, or I'll figure it out. I never agreed to a flipping Fairy family reunion. I agreed to give you a week; that was it, Ryder. If you push me, or push this, I will leave. I promise you that; I don't want anyone coming to claim me."

"And if I can't find the guy who is trying to kill you?" he asked.

"Then I will."

"Give it up. There is no way in hell I am allowing you to go hunt the bastard down. I'm going to figure out a way to kill him, and, when I do, it will be without you being used as bait." He gave me a knowing little smirk. "I suggest we use this time to feed."

Chapter
TWENTY-FIVE

Later that afternoon, we were summoned up to the top floor of the club. Zahruk watched us closely as we approached the closed off entrance of the VIP section. He nodded to me briefly, and then we all started up the winding stairway that led to the private rooms of the club.

"Reconnaissance is complete on the first one, we have the extraction plan formulated, and we have men on the other sites, Ryder. I know you don't like it, but it's time to call in the contract," Zahruk said carefully as he watched Ryder react to the news. Ryder nodded grimly, turning to me.

"Syn, I will release you and Adam both from the contracts I hold if you help me recover the relics that will help me secure the future of Faery. This goes against my better judgment, as I did not want to involve you in this, but I need someone who can easily get in and out of tight spaces, which I know you can. After that, I will let you both go. These won't be simple tasks, and it's going to take us awhile to retrieve them all. I want your answer, now."

I felt my throat grow constricted as the idea of being away from Ryder registered in my brain. I hesitated to answer him, and jumped when Zahruk's voice boomed from ahead of us.

"Syn, answer him," Zahruk demanded.

I turned my eyes to Ryder and nodded. I couldn't speak; I was fighting against the pain that came with knowing Ryder would walk away from me soon. I had known, eventually, that the peace we had found would be shattered. I'd known this would end, but I hadn't expected it to be anytime soon. The thought of being without him made a weird tightening sensation form in my throat and stomach.

"So, what do we have to do?" I asked him quietly.

"Zahruk will explain the operation. You will need black clothes, and make sure they are tight," Ryder said looking up the stairs to where Dristan had poked his head out from the curtain at the top, back to where I stood awkwardly on the stairs. "You getting this?" he asked pointedly. I nodded again and watched as his hands balled into tight fists at his sides.

We walked into a room that had a model set up, along with a blueprint of a building. Ryder's men stood silently by the wall, with the exception of Ristan and Z, who were now explaining the plan for tonight.

"Okay," Zahruk said. "This is the point of entry." He pointed to the section of the blueprints that showed the room of a building. "Our intel says it is heavily guarded, but I think we can work around them. We enter through here," he continued, pointing things out to me carefully. "The window will only have a few sensors which we can easily disarm before entry. Inside, there are alarms that we won't be able to shut off; those are the first issue we need to deal with when we are inside. We should be able to get in and out during the shift changes; with the right timing we should miss the guards. This," he pointed to a group of squares on the map, "is where the scepter will be secured. Inside the case are more sensors that will need to be dealt with and not triggered. If they go off, the bars on the ceiling and the doors will seal shut immediately. There are dummy cases set up; basically the entire room is full of traps and tricks that were designed to keep the relics from getting back to the Fae. Ryder will be with us to point out which one is the right one, and which ones are the fakes."

"What does it do?" I asked, lifting my eyes to Z's, and then Ryder's.

"It is a very powerful scepter that was stolen many centuries ago by a group, thinking it was a way to control the Fae and gain power as well as immortality, but they never figured out how to unlock its powers. Wouldn't have mattered anyway; it only comes to life in the right hands. Our time is running out, and we know that once we start retrieving the relics, they will immediately move the other relics, and this will force us to start the search over again. We now have people in place to prevent this from happening when we strike tonight," Ryder relayed before he turned and started toward the door. I watched his wide back as he left the room, leaving me alone with Ristan and his men.

Twenty minutes later, I was dressed in a snug leather jumpsuit that I had materialized myself. It was similar to the jumpsuits I had worn on jobs for the Guild. I'd dug through the remains of the items they had saved from my house and almost squealed with happiness when I found my mission pack. Next to the OPI collection, it was one of the items I'd mourned the most, since it was a gift from Alden when I'd graduated. It came with a silver belt that had a few secret items in it that a girl just couldn't live without.

I shoved my feet into the soft-soled knee high boots, pulled my hair up into a tight ponytail, and headed back up to the club's VIP lounge. I smiled as I took in the faces that registered from shock to humor at my outfit. They could laugh all they wanted; this type of outfit had saved my ass a hundred different times. It also fit the description of what Ryder had said to wear. Oh sure, with a lot more concentration and work I could have created the black, Guild-issued fatigues, but leather was so much more fun.

I felt better the moment I caught the look on Ryder's face, until he shook his head with a wicked smile on his full mouth and anticipation dancing in his eyes. "I didn't say *that* tight."

"You said tight. Besides, this kind of outfit has saved my ass more times than you have, Fairy."

He rubbed his hand down his face and closed the distance, holding out his hand. I looked at it, and back up to him. "So, what is the real job? I know how you guys work, and I need to know what's really going on."

"It's not a job, Syn, and we told you the details that you need to know. There's no deceit in tonight's plans. We are going to take back something that should have never left Faery to begin with. Period," he replied carefully.

"Give me details other than just telling me it's a scepter. I noticed that the building is an old Masonic Temple, but what I don't know is, why there and what is their involvement? I need more than what you gave me, and I'm smart enough to know that more is going on than you are telling me. I've read about the Masons, and, from what I know, they are not the bad guys—normally."

"Politics aside, Pet, you are right about that—normally they are not. The group has had many evolutions before they were the Freemasons. The group that stole the scepter was the Knights Templar, who were, for all intents and purposes, thought to have been disbanded shortly after the Crusades ended. They are still active today secretly, behind the scenes. And they are a lot like the Guild Enforcers. They are trained to kill, but, unlike the Guild, they only do so to protect their secrets, along with those things they are invested in. What they stand for, and the symbol they have been using since the Crusades are the only constants, no matter which evolution the outer group goes through. They are trained to be no more than rumors. Deadly, efficient, and not people you would want on your bad side. Normally, they stay out of other groups' business unless they fear it endangers the humans or their own tenets."

"Okay, so what's the backup plan? Because planning on missing them is option A. I need to know what option B is for worst case scenario. Do we fight? Do we run? I need to know these things, so I'm not responsible for starting a bloody war, unless you want one."

"We are Fae; we don't believe in a plan B. And no, we don't want to start a fucking war with them," he mumbled, and looked at his hand.

I lifted a brow at that, and placed mine inside of his as he pulled me closer and we sifted. When we materialized on the roof of the Templars' building, I was fully inside his arms with his lips touching my forehead. I'd felt it before we'd materialized, but I'd thought it was only my overactive imagination. "Stay close to me, Synthia. Watch where you step; there are sensors on the ground to alert the Templars to intruders," he whispered, taking in our surroundings.

"How the hell did the Templars get the scepter anyway?" I asked, letting my curiosity out, instead of the nerves in my stomach.

Ryder's lips kicked up into a mischievous smile. "Ah, so more story telling for you, eh?" He smirked a little at me. "The four relics we are looking for are ancient relics of our people and thought by many to be magical weapons. Our people would keep them in the strongest caste's realm, and at that time, the Light Fae were the strongest caste outside of the Horde. Anise, who was the queen of the Light Fae, was incredibly powerful, but she had a daughter who was very foolish and fascinated with humans. She became infatuated and thought she was in love with one who belonged to the Knights Templar. Even though the Knights themselves were supposed to have taken vows of poverty, chastity, piety, and obedience to their order, we know that the Knights Templar were one of the groups that the Mages had infiltrated, and we believe that they encouraged this young man to return her affections. She thought the Templar Knight truly loved her, and he, probably prompted by the Mages, asked for a sign of her love by giving him the relics. Now, the Light Princess may have been foolish and blind. However, she knew that he would not be able to use the relics. She stole them for him, thinking she could get them back at any time and return them to her mother. When she returned to her Knight with the relics, his order captured her and took control of the relics. Eventually, she obtained her freedom, but by then the relics of the Fae had been scattered to hell and back. I want you to help me find them, and bring them back to our people."

"And when they are all gathered and placed together again, what will they do?" I wasn't an idiot, and I'd heard stories of those ancient relics as part of the Guild teachings. Alarms went off in my head.

The idea of Ryder wanting the relics had Han Solo whispering in my ear, *"I got a bad feeling about this!"*

"It is nothing bad for any human or Fae. That's all you need to know for now, Pet," he said, leaving what the relics would do a mystery.

He dismissed me, so I did the same to him and watched as his men circled around us. There was a slight breeze blowing, which told me we were not as far up as I had originally thought. The night's sky was filled with beautiful stars and a half moon. I felt Ryder's eyes on me, so I turned toward him. He smiled back and lifted his hand to touch my cheek before he gave off orders to his men rapidly and efficiently, in a voice I could only describe as a stage whisper.

"Z, Savlian, and Aodhan, you're on point. Ristan, any hiccups you have seen?" Ryder asked.

Ristan narrowed his eyes on me and shook his head. "None," he replied slowly. I narrowed my eyes on him and grinned. Even though he knew my skills, he was probably thinking I would be a problem, and I wouldn't be. I was in my element here. Well, I was, unless it was another set up.

The men all got down low, so I followed their lead. We moved forward with everyone crouched low until they rounded a large, dark, square sunroof. Ryder placed his hand on the glass and whispered something in that strange language that I had heard him use a couple of times now, which made the glass vanish. I blinked and tilted my head a little. Ristan smiled at me as he took in my look of surprise. They were all talking in hushed tones, and I caught the word *warded* and smiled.

"No, it's completely warded. It was only supposed to be pressure sensors. Fuck! They have it warded against Fae. You try and go down there, and we will have every guard in the building on our asses in a heartbeat," Ristan said to Ryder, who shrugged as if he couldn't care less.

"We need that fucking scepter, period. We can't see whatever bullshit magic they are using without it. No matter which way you look at it, Ristan, we need that scepter to finish what we came to this world to do. If we don't get it now, they will try to move it. We can't take the chance of losing them again," Ryder argued.

I listened with one ear to the two of them whispering at each other. Knowing they had a mental link, they must have been hissing out loud for the rest of us in the hope that someone might have a constructive idea for this clusterfuck. No plan B my ass. I rolled my eyes and quickly took in the lasers inside the room, gauged the distance to the floor and how hard it would be to get there, and took in the time calculation of how many seconds I'd have before I needed to move from each spot. I started unraveling my belt as I continued to count them, and stopped only to look around for the heaviest thing on the roof to secure it to. I smiled as they continued to argue in heated whispers over how they would get in.

They were still arguing when I started from a dead run and flew through the air over Savlian, who had come back to see what the issue was; he had just leaned over to look at the problem.

"Synthia!" Ryder let out a strangled curse as I hooked my leg in midair and looped it through the thin rope that had been hidden inside my belt. I looked up at the shocked faces of the fourteen men and smiled. Ryder wasn't smiling; he had an alarmed look on his face, until I flipped and landed on my feet perfectly between three lasers. I wouldn't set the wards off because the sensors would not recognize me as Fae. Or, at least, that's what I hoped after Alden's revelation about me being some sort of Druid Fae; that it would make me different enough and get me in undetected.

"That was fucking hot as hell," Sevrin said with a small grin. He looked up to catch the glare Ryder had leveled on him. "What? It was!"

"If you guys are done, I need you to point out which scepter you want, since they have twelve down here," I whispered as I looked up into angry golden eyes. Twelve glass display cases mounted to solid wooden pedestals were interspersed throughout the room, and each held what looked like an eighteen-inch long oak branch displayed in each case. Based on the plans, I had expected the room to be like a storage room and, instead, it looked more like a museum.

"Second case to your left, Syn. Be careful, it's connected to an alarm wire." Ryder exhaled slowly and shook his head as his eyes warned that my ass would be pink after this little escapade.

I looked across the room and counted the cases with my fingers in the dark room. I didn't move, though. I'd studied the room and had a feeling about what was coming, unlike Ryder, who almost called out as I went flat against the floor from a full standing position, as glowing red laser shot out of the wall and ran a waist level scan of the room.

"Close," Zahruk whispered.

"Synthia, are you okay?" Ristan asked.

I didn't answer, as yet another laser beeped and shot through the room. This one was lower than the first, and it searched more of the room as a whole.

Shit. Another laser shot out, even lower, until it touched the lasers I now lay beside. I waited for it to finish scanning before I carefully looped my leg back through the rope. Another laser shot out, lower again. I waited. Another, lower again. Still waiting. The next one would give me away.

I jumped and twisted my body up through the rope rapidly as a laser blinked to life on the spot where I had just been, then slowly faded out as it found no threat. "Three minutes. They run a scan of the room every three minutes," I whispered, hitting the ground again and moving through the ones on the floor while I made my way to the display case. I was almost there when a door opened and closed across the room. I crouched low and backed up against a display case.

"Room five is empty. Doing a reboot of the system now; over," a voice said into the room as the lasers turned off. The sound of heavy work shoes walking across the marble floor started, moving closer to where I was hiding. I listened to his footsteps, counting them as I rounded the display case the moment he would have seen me on the other side. I swallowed, holding my dark magic to me to keep the rope, which was moving with me, invisible, while praying that what little magic I was using didn't set the wards off.

When he had walked the room, he turned and took a secondary route back. It caused me to have a small heart attack. I quickly moved around the small display case and looked up to find only a pair of shining golden eyes watching me. I smiled and winked up at him, before I blew him a silent kiss. He shook his head at me, and I could have sworn I heard him growl inside my head.

"All clear; rebooting system," the guard said, and I felt my heart drop. Well shit, this was going to suck. I waited until I heard the door open and close before I dared to breathe.

I couldn't sift, because I'd set off the Fae wards. I peeked around the case and found the guard still punching buttons on the wall panel. On reboot, it was going to run every laser inside the room, at once. I took off at a quick crouched run toward the side wall that had a corner in it. It was the only wall I could get to that the guard wouldn't see me. I was lucky this room had been built in an odd shape for the purpose of displaying artifacts. I placed my feet on both sides of the wall so I could hold myself up and away from the multiple lasers.

I managed to jump right as the first ground lasers started up. I didn't breath, I didn't move. I held Ryder's eyes for support while the system ran at full capacity before they returned to their original routine.

I inhaled slowly, so slowly that my lungs didn't fully inflate, and watched the lasers on the ground before silently placing my feet back on the floor and taking a step forward, and then another. "Which one?" I whispered again since my sense of direction was off. Ryder pointed it out, and I made my way to it. I held my breath as I found and disconnected the red alarm wire to the display case and then crossed the blue to the green to give it a false safe reading. No alarm went off, but I wasn't stupid.

I raised the glass display case off the pedestal and looked inside, smiling triumphantly. I found a trip wire that would sound an alarm the moment I picked the scepter up and separated it from its mounting. I whispered a spell to make the glass levitate as I reached in and counted wires. I swore as the lasers started up again, making me scramble to lift my body, with the help of the rope, high enough to miss them. When they'd run their course, I lowered my body and made sure my feet missed the ground-level ones. I inhaled and exhaled slowly before reaching in and twisting wires until the pressure was enough that I could lift the scepter without tripping the alarm. Once it was free, I shoved it into my belt and slowly returned the glass case to its pedestal.

I kicked my feet up quickly and crawled feet-first, up the rope until Ryder grabbed me and set me down on my feet. "That wasn't the fucking deal," he whispered heatedly.

"No, but I could get to your stupid club, caveman, and *you* couldn't," I said nonchalantly. "So I did. Get over it, Fairy. I came to help you guys, and we got what we came for," I whispered back as I withdrew the wooden branch, err scepter thingy from my belt.

"Good, hand it to me," he said, holding out his hand for it.

I eyed it uneasily for a moment, noticing it didn't change as I held it. When I handed it to Ryder, I immediately felt butterflies of unease set in. I saw his eyes flash with anticipation as it changed from a solid branch of oak, into a beautiful, platinum staff that almost stood as tall as he did. A ruby that was bigger than my fist was nestled in an elaborate platinum setting on the top of it. His hand wrapped around the staff, caressing it much like he did my skin when we were alone.

"Why do I feel like I just handed you something that I shouldn't have?" I asked.

His lips lifted into a grin. One that was a little too dark and a little too deadly for my taste. "Ristan, take Synthia back to the club, please. I'll meet you there, Pet. I need to secure this where no one will find it."

I narrowed my eyes on him, but he sifted out,

leaving me standing there to angrily stare at the empty patch of roof where he had just been.

"Flower," Ristan said, holding out his hand.

"Demon," I replied.

"Shall we?" he asked as I curled my fingers into my hand.

"What happens if I say no?" I joked, knowing I didn't really have a choice.

"Then I would take you back anyways. I like my women feisty."

Chapter
TWENTY~SIX

Adrian was with me today. Ryder had allowed him to come to the club to keep me busy. Ryder noticed the walls closing in around me as I waited for him to turn up any information on my would-be assassin. Outside of the little field trip last night, I'd been kept inside, and it was driving me insane. I wasn't as bothered by staying inside as I was by being idle. I wanted to be doing something helpful, and all I was doing inside was sitting and waiting. Waiting sucked. I'd tried not to let it show, but some of it must have, because Ryder had allowed my ex-boyfriend to come in and keep me company while he'd gone out to hunt today.

"So, how are you adjusting?" Adrian asked from where he sat across the table.

We'd ended up sitting at one of the many booths on the club's ground level. The club looked abandoned in the early morning hours, and the only people inside were Ryder's crew. Mazzy Star's *Fade Into You* was playing softly over the club's music system. "I'm adjusting," I said as I lifted my eyes and met his vivid turquoise ones. My world used to revolve around those eyes, until he'd left me to think he was dead for years. I was tempted to confront him about his stretching the truth about the night he 'died' and the choices he'd made, but I wasn't really ready to rip that scab open yet.

"Cute fangs," he said, smiling as he reached up to move his spiky bangs away from his bronzed skin.

I grinned impishly. "I'm not going to say the same thing about yours."

"I didn't figure you would." He smiled and licked one fang wickedly with his tongue.

"You know you're an ass, right?"

"Always. You expected it to change?" he asked, raising a brow.

I smiled softly and shook my head. I was glad he was here, and, yet, I felt uncomfortable under his close scrutiny. It wasn't the same as it had been before, when we'd been together. "No, I always knew better than to think you'd change." I grinned, and toyed with the tea bag in the glass mug that sat untouched before me.

Ryder had ordered the tea before he'd left today. He had been a little overprotective since I had gotten sick back at the house, but I hadn't had another bout of losing my cookies since that awful morning. I knew already that when I tasted it, it would be perfectly made. He knew exactly how I took my tea, and that worried me a little bit. I hadn't drunk it around him before, so he shouldn't have been able to figure out that I liked it with sugar. I brought the mug up, and inhaled the soothing chamomile scent. The light scent of sugar made my lips quirk up. I tasted it, and a smile broke across my face.

"Wish it was me who brought that beautiful smile to your lips, Synthia. I'm thinking it wasn't though," Adrian said with a soft, comforting smile on his mouth.

"He ordered my *tea*, right down to the two teaspoons of sugar," I said as if he should know how it made me feel, or that I was a little worried that Ryder knew it.

Adrian gave me a confused stare for a moment, before moving it to the glass mug. "You like tea?"

A smile tugged on my lips. "And coffee," I answered.

"I knew you liked coffee; had no idea you liked tea though," he replied as something behind me caught his eye. "We got company."

I turned, watching as Adam, his dad, and Ryder's men approached us. "Syn, this is my dad. He has a few things to talk to you about," Adam said with a little more formality than I was used to from him.

I blinked. I had no idea how to address a King, and Adam's father was just that. He was the freaking Dark King! "Uh," I faltered. Even dressed like a human in jeans and a button down dark green shirt, the man had a regal bearing and radiated power like a generator. His height and frame were exactly like Adam's was now. However, his facial features, like the sky-blue and sapphire-blue two-toned eyes and blue-black hair that was much like Ryder's, set them apart.

"Synthia, it's a pleasure to meet you. I have heard nothing but good things about you from my son," the Dark King said with a patient smile and ancient eyes that probed my face.

"I haven't heard much about you at all," I replied honestly.

"May I?" the Dark King asked, indicating a chair

next to the booth we sat in. I watched him pull it closer, waiting for my answer.

"Of course," I replied, not sure which I wanted more at the moment—to run from the Dark King or to hug Adam. I met Adam's gaze and smiled. "You're okay?"

"I've been through hell, but I think I'll be okay. You?"

"Same; been through worse."

He smiled and nodded before sliding into the booth next to me. Zahruk stood at my right with a guarded look in his eyes, which was doing little to ease the uneasiness I felt within this group's presence. Dristan was standing across the club, observing, and I wasn't stupid. They were here to guard and protect me in Ryder's absence.

"There are a few things I would like to discuss with you, if that is permissible?" the Dark King asked gently.

"Okay," I replied, straightening in my seat.

"Ryder said that he believes you might be the Light Heir. Do you understand what that would entail?"

"That I stand to rule the Light Fae, which won't happen." I was *so* going to strangle Ryder for going against my wishes. If he reached out to the Light Fae too, there was gonna be some fried Fairy for dinner tonight.

"You think it would be so easy to just say no?" he countered, folding his massive hands on the table in front of him.

"No, but the current Queen is healthy, as is her

King. I see no reason why I would be forced to claim the crown. They abandoned me. Oh, yeah—I heard the stories when I was in the Guild, that the Light Princess was stolen, but I don't believe it. If I am her, they got rid of me because I'm more than likely illegitimate, since they have quite a few children they kept, and, personally, I'm okay with that."

"Your mother has been known to be unfaithful, and her king also has a wild streak." He nodded as if it was nothing new.

"The Light Fae are not a faithful caste. They think that they're above tradition, and above any other caste of Fae for that matter. To put it bluntly, they are self-absorbed asshats."

He smiled and nodded, before looking past me to Adam. "I see why you like her, my son. She is blunt and doesn't play with words. Straight to the point, and doesn't beat around the bushes."

Adam smiled and grabbed my hand softly. I beamed at him and noticed something was missing in his eyes. He was the same Adam I'd grown up with, but he'd lost the innocence he'd had. Maybe we all had after losing Larissa. I prayed that he would be able to come back from this. I missed my wisecracking best friend.

"If I may, I'd like to explain some of our traditions, politics, and a bit of history so you can better understand my true purpose here today. I am not sure how much you have learned from Ryder and his men over the past few weeks; however, Adam has been going through an intense crash course in everything he missed out on since he has been gone. If our speculations are correct, it is important to bring you as up to speed as fast as we can." The Dark King took a deep breath before he continued. "Synthia, if you are the Light Heir, it stands to reason that you'll gain the crown. Normally, children of royal families in Faery are betrothed early in life, and some even before birth."

I nodded.

"I believe you met Adam, and he became your familiar, at one of the Harvest Festivals. It's a huge celebration held on Samhain where truce is declared, and all castes of Fae come together for a few days to celebrate the birth of new children, riches, and other developing things such as strength of a realm. At least, it makes sense that you and my Adam became linked there, based on everything I have heard about you and your history."

"Why would she take me there if she planned on ditching me?" I interrupted, pointing out the obvious.

"I don't think your mother did. She has many children. I think she wouldn't have cared who the father was, but I do think if the Light Heir was birthed of another caste, the Light King would have wanted you gone immediately. You see, an Heir is first identified when a Fae child of royal birth begins using magic at a very early age, usually under the age of one. Most Fae children do not begin showing magic until they are older, about ten or so. You can feel the magic's presence within Fae children, but they are unable to use it until they are a little older. She may have intended to keep you, as she has done with her other illegitimate children, until you showed signs of being the Heir. Once that happened, they would have wanted your death at the first opportunity. Placing you in a human setting would have assured that you would perish without having the blood of their child on their hands. Or it should have; but the people who raised you took certain steps to keep you thriving, which the Light King couldn't have counted on. I think when he found out you hadn't died, he sent those Fae in to kill you."

The hair on the back of my neck stood up. "Because another heir wouldn't be born until I was dead."

He smiled. "Smart as well. Impressive. Not many born outside of our world would have put that together."

"I've spent a large part of my life learning anything I could to kill those who killed my parents."

"I don't blame you for that. I do blame the Light King, as his actions stole Adam from us as well. He disappeared from his bedroom one night—one minute he was there, and the next he was gone. The pain you felt had to have been tremendous for you to take him. It breached the barrier of Faery to bring him to you, and could have killed him at that age. It would be easy to blame you, but you were no more than an infant yourself at the time."

I watched him and nodded as he continued.

"You must keep in mind that we knew Adam was our heir. He showed promise from the beginning when he began bursts of controlled, deliberate magic at seven months of age; anything from materializing toys to summoning his mother if he was peckish." The Dark King chuckled at the memory, and Adam looked slightly embarrassed. "I knew he'd become a familiar to one of the children in attendance at the Harvest Festival about twenty one of your human years ago, but it would have been impossible to pinpoint which one with the hundreds of children that are brought to the Harvest."

"Fae like to fuck each other over, so I'm going to take a gander and say that this festival is more a look-see to figure out who they wanted to dish out trickery the most to that year." He smiled as a sparkle similar to one Adam often had lit in his eyes.

"That would be spot-on my dear. We do love to play games. As it was, after Adam disappeared, we searched, but we just couldn't find him. I never stopped looking for him because the chances that he'd sustained injury from sifting at such a young age were very high, and we refused to believe that it killed him. He was so small when he disappeared, almost ten in human years when he went missing, and I knew it had to be one of the other heirs who had claimed him. We kept it very quiet; only family and trusted servants who were sworn to secrecy knew he was gone. The last thing we wanted was to jeopardize his safety by announcing that my heir was somewhere out there unprotected. The Blood King was in attendance that year, as was your mother. Light was the most sensible option, since the Blood King is alpha, only surpassed in strength by the Horde King who normally chooses to skip the Harvest," he said, watching my face.

"Why would the Horde not attend when they have more strength than the other castes? It would stand to reason he'd want to get in on the games that would be played."

"The Horde doesn't need to play games. The Horde is more inclined to stand back and watch as we destroy ourselves. He knows he can take any caste down, so no reason to see who is coming up when he knows he can easily tear them down."

"Why couldn't I be Horde? I'd take them any day over the Light Fae," I asked, striking one caste off the list. Out of the castes I had to choose from, the Horde was the only one that accepted everyone. Ryder had said as much anyway, and, right now, they were looking like the one in which I'd fit in best.

"You have a remarkable resemblance to the Light Queen, but not the Horde. The other option was that you could be from the Blood Fae, but the only female infant of royal birth born around that time died. She was given funeral rites at the second Harvest of her life. Her parents would not speak to anyone that year and handled everything through emissaries. I did, in fact, see the small darling before she was given funeral rites and entombed."

"So, not only is it a celebration, but they also bury their dead at the Harvest?" I asked, letting the curious little monster inside of me out to play.

"Sometimes; we struggle to keep children alive inside of Faery. It has become much worse and far more dire over the last thirty or so years. In short, Faery is dying." My heart must have stopped at that moment.

"That's around the time that the Fae made their big announcement that they were in charge of the Otherworld creatures and that the humans were no longer alone," I said, remembering back to what we had been taught.

"Otherworld is just another name for Faery," he mused with a small smile. "It was easier to encourage the humans to believe that there was a world other than Faery that Shifters and other creatures were coming from, rather than one world. Feeling that you are under attack from one front is less intimidating than feeling like you are being overwhelmed from multiple fronts. We knew there would be fear; however, we wanted to avoid the whole Inquisition or Salem Witch Trials type of backlash if we could."

"But Ryder told me that the ruling castes were against interfering with humans—it's like one of the number one rules."

"That was my doing. I forced the other castes hands in this matter, as we no longer had any choice but to become more active in human affairs. Synthia, Faery is at least triple the size of this world. Many of Faery's denizens are very hazardous to this world. If Faery dies, where do you think all of the inhabitants of that world are going to go?"

"So that is what Ryder is doing. He's here trying to stop this?"

"Yes, but until we can figure out all of those parties threatening our world, we cannot stop them. Healing the land is important, since it is rejecting the infants when they are presented to the Goddess Danu. If Faery does not accept an infant, then the child's lifespan is limited, as any ailment can kill them. Not only has Faery stopped accepting them, the world itself is dying. Huge tracts of land that are ruled by the Dark, Horde, and Blood are withering and showing signs of death."

"And you think it has something to do with the Mages, or the Changelings who you all thought weren't a threat before," I supplied, wondering if this was why Ryder would be sticking his nose into it.

"We suspect that they are at the root of it, but I didn't come here just to discuss the problems of Faery, Synthia. I came here to discuss you."

"What about me?" I asked, feeling my walls close around me as my defenses went up.

"Please, hear me out before you say anything. When one Fae is bonded to another, as you are with Adam, we betroth them or handfast them to one another. Adam was betrothed to the Light Princess by proxy when Ryder agreed to marry Arianna. I don't want to go into all of the details, but it was my hope that it would draw Adam, or the people I thought might be holding him, out of hiding. At this time, he is to marry the Light Princess, Caitlín, to unite the kingdoms."

"It would make sense, since an alliance is usually made through marriage to broker peace, or, for gain," I replied, finding the logic in it.

"Exactly," he said, watching me carefully.

"So—wait, what?" I asked as my head started spinning with what he had just said.

"Adam will marry the Light Princess, Caitlín, which is the true name of the Light Princess that Arianna was impersonating. If you are the missing princess…that would be you."

I choked and then laughed until I snorted in a very unladylike matter. I alone was laughing. "Oh holy mother of fuck buckets, you're serious!"

"Syn," Zahruk warned in a stern tone.

"He's like a brother to me. This is crazy! You understand that, right? Adam?" I looked at him for help and found nothing but acceptance. He just sat there and watched me. "We've been friends forever, and I think of you as my brother, dammit." *Marry Adam? The one who I count on because we worked together? We were as close as any siblings, and now I'm supposed to marry him? No flipping way.*

"Would marriage to me be so bad? We know each other inside and out. You grew up with Adrian, and yet, you developed feelings for him. What happened between you two could happen with us. We would be a strong, steady couple."

"Adam, I love you, you know that. But *marriage*?

We don't even know for sure if I'm the Light Heir; it is all just speculation right now. It could be possible, yes, but we don't know for sure."

"I get it, Syn. I do. But if marrying you will bring peace to an entire kingdom and save them in the process, I could marry you easily," Adam said, staring me down in challenge.

"And if we got married and I wasn't the Light Princess? What then?"

"Dammit, Syn, I don't know. I just know you ripped me from a life I should have had, and I have a family that I don't even know. You owe me. We could help Faery. Doesn't that mean anything to you?"

I felt my heart drop to my stomach. "You've been with them this week, with your family."

"Yes," he replied, tightening his grip on my hand.

"I'm glad—or happy for you. Still, I can't marry you because I don't love you in that way. I'm not sure what you guys came here for today. But if this was it, I'm sorry that you wasted your time."

"Synthia, there is more to it than just uniting two kingdoms," the Dark King began. "You were raised in the human world, so this will be difficult for you to understand. At least, this is what Adam has told me. Sometimes we have to rely on the most improbable course when looking for answers to our problems. Some call this faith. We are all children of Danu, and she does not want Faery to die any more than we do. Being a Goddess, it is not like she can just tell us outright what we need to do, as the journey is just as important as the answer is, and sometimes you have to have faith that she knows what she is doing. She has given us several prophesiers and seers who have had visions to help guide us to heal Faery. There is one prophesy about a child born of the Dark and Light Heirs who will complete the healing of the world that the returned relics began."

"No pressure, right?" Adam said, with the first genuine smile I'd seen on him today.

"This isn't fair. This freaking sucks! We just barely found out we were Fae and now we get this tossed into our laps?"

The Dark King continued. "The only other option for your heritage is that you are a second heir—which has happened before, but it's extremely rare. We have no way of knowing, since the Light Fae, like any Fae, only allow us to know what they want us to, and of course what information they allow can always be misinformation. A good example of this is the situation with Arianna. The Light Fae offered the Light Princess, Caitlín, to us because they knew that we had been looking for her as part of the prophecy. They said that they couldn't completely vouch for her because she was illegitimate and, therefore, the paternal bond between Fae father and child couldn't be used to verify her identity. Of course we thought this was a bit off, with the huge uproar and accusations that were flying around after she went missing; that miraculously, after all these years later, she would suddenly turn up and they immediately offered her to us. When you combine this situation with all of the rumors of the Light King sending assassins out for her, you can understand why we were quite suspicious of her. Now, we did accept her, as it suited our needs at the time, and our plans did work, by the way; but you can see how the chain of misinformation can be problematic." He rubbed his chin thoughtfully for a moment before continuing. "You can't be part of the Horde, because you show no signs of their brands. Blood Fae yes, you carry their brands, but, at the same time, yours are unique. Almost too unique. No, once you add up everything, it makes the most sense that you are Caitlín. We have many royal Fae, Synthia, every caste does. We don't die easily once Transition is complete so you can understand why we'd have so many. However, heirs are a very small percentage of royal Fae as the Goddess herself chooses them."

"Maybe they should find some Fae birth control," I mumbled under my breath.

"Nature takes control of that my dear. Our females can only breed within the first year immediately after our Transition, and every ten to fifteen years after it. Time is of the essence, which is why you would only have a short time to consider Adam's offer."

"Adam's offer?" I asked, narrowing my eyes. Adam hadn't made an offer, and I was afraid of him making any offers now.

"Syn, we've been friends since the day I came to be with you maybe even before that and I'd like a chance to court you; see where this could go. If you are the Light Heir, you and I can help save Faery. If Faery dies, they will come here. We need to consider the consequences, and we need to make the right choices to protect both worlds. We are part of something that could save thousands of innocent children."

"So, you want to make a baby?" I replied bluntly. Brilliant! "Can't we just do like some Fae ritual, put a funky headdress on, and call this Goddess down for a chat or something? Anyone?" I looked around at the faces in the club. Nope, no one was going to say yes to that! Damn.

"No, I want to save the world, and maybe save Faery while we are at it. And I don't think you can just call a Goddess down to have a chat," the Dark King replied sternly, even though his eyes flashed with a hint of suppressed laughter.

"Okay, this is too much. One, I don't want a baby with anyone. I'm not mother material, period. I'm screwed up, and everything I love ends up killed or tortured. Adam, you already know that, so why the hell would you want me?" I asked, confused and a little panicked that this wasn't an offer but a demand. Sure, they could say it was an offer, or call it anything they wanted to, but it was still a demand.

"You're not cursed, Syn. Bad stuff happens in life. You taught us all that. You know what the Fae coming into the human world could do to it, probably better than anyone. Is that something you could allow to happen because you think you're cursed, or is it because you're scared?"

Damn right, I was scared! I wanted to scream that this wasn't fair. As if finding out I wasn't a Witch— that I was one of the creatures I hated most—wasn't bad enough, but now this? "Adam, in the last month alone I have found out that I was adopted, I got the two humans I loved and cherished the most killed, and my ex-boyfriend came back from the dead. I had to work beside the enemy to bring down a serial killer, which resulted in getting my best friend killed. My other best friend and I turned out to be the same race as the enemy, and we both went through Transition. My house got blown up. I'm jobless, homeless, and I have lost everything. You can't just walk in here, drop this on my head, and expect me to say okay."

"You left out the part where you were tortured," Adam said, pulling me closer to him. "Syn, I can give you things I couldn't before. We can be together, and this need I feel for you might finally go away."

"You feel it because you're bonded to her, Adam,

not because you love her in that sense," Adrian said from across the table, finally speaking.

"It could be, but what if I actually love her? If we can save the world, then isn't it worth a try?" Adam growled.

"You just said children were dying, right?" I asked as I turned to the Dark King.

"Yes, and you can call me Kier."

"Okay, Kier, so say we have a baby and it dies because the land rejects it. What then?"

"I don't think that will be the case, but if that happened you would need to try again until one lived," he said with a sadness set deep inside his vivid sky and sapphire blue eyes.

"So we just keep trying, going until we have one that lives. I can't lose anyone else. I'm sorry, I really am, but I couldn't do it."

"Fertility is not as big of a problem as getting them to Transition alive is. We have every available resource being put into a cure. Even the reclusive Blood King has begun to send healers and scholars to help in the fight for the cure while still battling the Horde."

"Why is the Horde battling the Blood Fae? I mean, if their king is *missing*, who is leading them?" I asked.

"The Horde King has many sons to lead his army. The Horde does not produce females often, and they are overrun by strong sons, which allows the King to be gone for extended periods. It seems that the two castes had a nasty falling-out, and the back and forth between the two of them had gone on for a very long time. I understand that they had finally reached an agreement, and the Blood King reneged on his promise, so they are back at it again. As the Dark Fae are allies of the Horde, it puts us in an uncomfortable position of choosing sides."

"Do you know where he is?" I asked, narrowing my eyes.

"No, I don't have any idea where he is," he replied, looking at me directly in the eye. Well shoot, I was hoping he would know, seeing that he and the Horde King were friendly.

"What did Ryder have to say about all of this?" I asked, holding his eyes level with my own.

"He has no say in this. Synthia, you and my son are bonded already. If I petition the Light Fae, they will give you to Adam. They are trying to avoid war with the Dark Fae after what they did with Arianna. The Dark Fae are a good deal stronger than the Light Fae, and they would prefer to avoid an all-out war with us. The Light Fae would prefer to publicly behave as if they are our dearest friends, and, in secret, they are always looking for a good place to stick a knife into our backs. The Light Fae deny that Faery is dying because this plague, for lack of a better word, strikes the stronger castes first, so they have not felt the full impact of what the rest of the castes have. My sense is that they hope the rest of the stronger castes will succumb to the affliction and then they will be the strongest caste by default. I only speculate this because they have done everything they can to stall or stop our efforts, so we are forced, for the most part, to go around them. At this point, our relationship with them is becoming more and more contentious. Eventually, they will wake up to what is going on and need the cure as much as the rest of us do. However, my fear is that it will be too late by the time they wise up and stop deluding themselves. We will give you time to decide, but, since you are almost fully through Transition, you won't have long to give us an answer. We would need to have the marriage blessed soon, and a child produced as quickly as could be managed."

Chapter
TWENTY~SEVEN

I was curled up on the bed in the room I'd been sharing with Ryder as I waited for him to come back. I'd sifted here directly from the meeting with Adam and his father to be alone. Unable to hold the emotions in any longer, I'd lost it and cried until I'd felt drained. Childish, probably, but it was as if life was throwing every curveball it had at me. It was getting harder to duck when they came sailing at my head.

The clock was ticking by with agonizing slowness as I waited. I could hear the minute hand from across the room, and sleep wasn't coming. I'd opted out of comfort from Adrian, not because I didn't need it, but because I had to think. Or so I had thought, but thinking wasn't helping. What I needed was for Ryder to show up and tell me he wouldn't allow this to happen.

I had a sick feeling in my stomach that said he wouldn't this time. That, even though he'd said I was his, with the fate of Faery in the balance, he'd let me go. Hell, he'd probably hold the door for me and help me pack what meager belongings I had. We'd become more than just lovers over the past week, and it was breaking my heart to even think about leaving him. When the hell had I started thinking like that!?

Tears welled up in my eyes again, and I allowed a few to drop. I wasn't sure I could do this. I loved Adam, but not in a way that this would ever make sense. I couldn't honestly walk away and let children die either. What the hell kind of a person would I be if I did so? Was it bad that I wanted to be that person who could walk away and say *not my problem*? It was overwhelming and just plain sucked!

I was still awake when Ryder came into the room. I sat up slowly, wondering if he'd heard the news. He wouldn't look me in the eye at first. That alone told me that he did, in fact, know what had occurred.

"Ryder?" I asked, pushing the covers off and throwing my legs over the edge of the mattress. He turned those beautiful eyes on me, and my heart dropped at what I saw. He wasn't going to help me. "I can't marry Adam, Ryder. There has to be a different way to save Faery."

"Don't you think I've fucking tried, Syn? I've been searching for it since I got here." He dragged his fingers through his hair and let loose a string of curses before he turned and sifted out of the room, leaving me to stare at the empty space he'd just been standing in.

He wasn't going to save me, and, even though I knew it, it hurt. I crawled into a ball on the bed, and silently cried myself sleep.

"Ristan," I growl, letting them hear the inner rattle of the beast as he tries to get out.

"I can't change what I've seen, Ryder. Syn and Adam secure an heir together. I've seen him with her and the child. You did the right thing by telling Kier the truth of it," Ristan said.

"You said you couldn't see her future, and now you can?" I snarl, barely resisting the urge to throw the Demon across the room.

"I don't control how this works, or what I see. I can only tell you what I see. I do wish it were otherwise. I know how much you want to keep her. It's best you let her go. This is part of what we came here to do. We know the Mages are working within the Guild. We have identified most of the other groups they are hiding behind. We just have to flush them out and kill them now."

"I fucking know that! She wasn't supposed to be the fucking Light Heir. She was supposed to be some nobody I could keep. And you're positive it's Adam's child she has?" I ask carefully.

"They are in a room together, and she's presenting him with a son. It's Adam, not you, and it's not as if I would be giving you this shitty news if I had another option."

"You better be fucking sure, Demon. I don't like to lose. Period. Does it give Faery a fighting chance to heal?" I want to break shit. I want to tear the fucking club down around me. Mostly, I want to sift back to that room, wipe the uncertainty from Syn's beautiful face and hold her. I want a lot, and with every fucking word the Demon spews out, I want to sift back in and take her away from it all.

"It's two interlocking pieces of a bigger puzzle. We don't know what the future holds even with this new development. We can only pray to Danu that it works. If we don't allow this to play out, we may be taking away the only chance Faery has. So far every vision she has given me has turned out to be the right path—well, not as we thought the path was going to turn out, but the end results of following the visions were successful. We still need the relics, but if Syn and Adam produce an heir that lives...they could save Faery. We could do exactly what we came here to do by giving her to Kier, washing our hands of her and Adam in the process."

"And the Light Fae? What part do they play in this? Can they even be trusted to be close to her? She's potentially preventing Dresden from producing his own heir. We have been hearing the rumors for years about the assassins who are after the Light Heir, which was why I did not think anything about Arianna's guards asking for more assistance," I growl. *She's mine to protect. I won't send her in to be slaughtered by those presumptuous, self-serving bastards.* She's right; the Horde *is* better than those egotistical pricks.

"Dresden would want her dead, in a very bad way, yes. She can never be alone with them, which is a no-brainer. He'd kill her without remorse and without so much as blinking an eye. As it stands, Tatiana will be lucky if he allows her to remain as his Queen."

"I won't allow him to succeed. I'd take out the fucking Horde King himself for Synthia."

The men gave amused smirks and snorts of agreement. This wasn't going down the way I'd planned it. I'd vowed to make her mine. Now, I had to shove her into the arms of another man. Would she go willingly? Would she give him the soul searing kisses she'd given me? Fuck! "Zahruk, send men out to get feelers on the Mages; I want them buried in the ground before we leave this place. Ristan, if this vision changes, and you see anything, I want to know immediately. You will also need to show Syn what is happening. She won't go into this easily without knowing what she would be walking away from. She will need to see the future you have shown me in order for her to make the right choice."

I exhale as my chest rattles from the beast within. He's pacing and growling, shaking his cage violently to get out. He's enjoyed her body, mind, and so much more. Her wicked little fucking smile, her sensual heat that envelopes her eyes when she explodes on my cock. Fuck!

Adam would marry Syn, and they'd have pretty little babies. Pretty little babies that could potentially save our fucking world. It was a cruel fucking joke the gods were playing on me. Ristan had seen it, he'd fucking seen it. Fuck! I'd known she was special from the beginning. The beast inside of me had known as well.

I have to get her out of my system, purge her from it brutally. Hard to do, when all I want to do is bury myself inside of her warmth and stay there forever. My entire life is one cluster fuck of endless denials, and now I have to hand over the only woman who has ever fed the inner beast hell, she left the fucker purring like a sated kitten!

"Sinjinn," I growl angrily, not bothering to shield them from the displeasure I feel.

"What's up?" Sinjinn asks, coming instantly to his feet.

"Prepare the men to be ready to leave this world for our own by the end of the week. I want to be out of here as soon as possible. Start preparing for the club to be handed over to Vlad for safe keeping. He can just as easily send word to Faery if he gleans any information we need. I won't be coming back. Have Zane gather the others and tell them it's time we go home."

"And Faery? Will this actually work, Brother?" Dristan asks with confusion in his green eyes.

"Syn will save it. Ristan has seen it. She'll marry Adam and have true heirs who will bond to the world and start the healing process. In the end, she will save it," I snarl, unhappy with admitting it. Fuck, it tastes like shit in my mouth. Saying it makes my chest hurt. She's under my fucking skin. She burrowed her way under the steel shield that had grown around my heart, and she's gotten in to it.

"She doesn't love Adam she won't go for this," Adrian snarls, coming to his feet to challenge me.

"She doesn't have a choice, boy. Children are dying because the realm of Faery isn't embracing them. Someone fucked with it, and she is the cure. Get it? If I have to drag her fucking ass to him, she's doing this!"

"She'll hate you. If you were going to toss her aside from the beginning, you should have let someone who loved her fight for her!" the kid shouts.

I smile coldly. "Who? You? You jumped for the chance to become the undead. Did you fucking tell her that? That you didn't have to be asked twice? Or were you happy letting me take the full blame?"

"Vlad offered the deal. I chose as you knew I would. I wanted power—but I'm not stupid enough not to put the pieces together. You knew I'd take it. I died for her to *live*, so I could protect her. You planned it all just to have her, and now you're sending her away. If you won't fight for her, *I will*."

"Think it matters? She's going. End of fucking discussion. People are dying, kid, and she can fix it. What do you think she will do; walk away from them? Not fucking likely. So understand this: it's not a choice *I* can make. You know she will choose to help, because deep down she will always strive to be someone others can believe in. In the end, she will always choose to help innocent people. It's who she is. Like it or not, that's what attracts us to her. She's selfless and pure—unlike us, *boy*."

"Adrian, go back to the club. I'll meet you there soon," Vlad said, placing a hand on the kid's shoulder.

I hate that I respect the little shit. He'd cut off his fucking legs for Syn if he was asked to. It made it hard to hate the little fuck. I pushed him, and he pushed back. He'd be a warrior of worth if he lived long enough to train. Chances were he'd mouth off to someone and end up dead before he reached that status. "Vlad," I nod in greeting.

"Ryder, I'll handle the club until you want it back. I've got one club; don't need two. If you ever come back, it's yours," Vlad says with a look of sympathy in his silver gaze. I fail to hide the pain. She's inside of me now. They can see it. Fucking hell, I cannot afford to show weakness.

"Not sure I'll be coming back, Vlad. Eventually Dristan might, but I have responsibilities that need me. It needs to be done and it's time to face it, finally."

"If you need me, you know how to contact me."

"I do, and the same goes for you, Vlad. If you ever need us, I mean ever, send word and we will be there. You've been a big help. You will be greatly rewarded for your services."

I shake his hand and take a long look around the club I'd built. So much information gathered here, right under the Light Fae's noses. Years of living in this world, and it is quickly drawing to a close. It is time to go home and let the beast run free. He'll need it when Syn is gone when she belongs to someone else.

I hate it, fucking hate it. If it had been anything besides my fucking homeland, I'd fight like a starving fucking wolf to keep her. I can't fight this, though, not even for her. The entire world depends on it. Too much could be fixed from her and Adam's union to ignore it.

Chapter
TWENTY~EIGHT

I felt his eyes watching me before I fully woke up. He was leaning against the wall with his arms folded over his chest as he watched me sleep. I sat up slowly, sensing he was going to talk about what had occurred with Adam and his father this morning. As he continued to stare at me, my heart flipped once before it shattered inside my chest. He was going to choose Faery over fighting for me.

"I need you to know that if there was another way, I'd take it in a fucking heartbeat, Synthia. The fact of the matter is...right now, this is all we have to work with. I need help finding a few more relics which, when secured, will help heal the land and allow it to help the child you will give birth to." He stopped, as if saying it tasted foul on his tongue. "It will help the child that you and Adam have," he paused and closed his eyes so briefly that I wasn't sure I had seen it, "bond with the land," he finished painfully.

"You think the same thing that they do?" I asked, carefully schooling my emotions. I wanted to scream and cry, deny that I'd go. In the end, we both knew the truth.

"Unfortunately, yes. It's what Ristan has seen. He

has shown it to me. You give Adam a child; a son."

"So, you expect me to just go along with it?" I snarled, tired of everyone telling me what to do. I wanted him! I blinked at the realization that I wanted to stay with Ryder. I swallowed the cry that tried to gain passage from my lips. I was so stupid. He had a harem of women waiting for him, and here I was, falling for him. Stupid heart! Stupid emotions! Why did they always show up too late to be useful?

"There's something Ristan needs to show you. After that, you can decide on what's the right thing to do, Synthia," Ryder said softly.

Ristan materialized by the door a moment later, as if he'd been waiting for Ryder to just say the words. His demeanor was sad and uncharacteristic of his normal, smartass self. "Syn," he said softly, bowing his head to me slightly. His patterned eyes said what his lips would never say I'm sorry.

I watched him walk over to the bed and sit beside me. He held out his hand as if he expected me to accept it. "What?" I asked, unsure of his motives, or if I wanted to actually see what he would show me. It was so much easier to walk away, oblivious to what was happening around us, but knowing could set me on a path I didn't want to walk.

"Synthia, allow him to show you what you would fix," Ryder said, still leaning against the wall with his face now hidden in the shadows.

I placed my hand inside Ristan's much larger one and met his swirling gaze. "Beam me up, Scotty," I whispered, terrified of what I was now bound to see.

"Remember, it's only a projection and no one will know we are there, Flower."

One minute we were in the bedroom, and the next we were standing in a large medical facility. It looked like something from an apocalyptic movie. Women sobbed as they held lifeless infants against their breasts, men watched them with helpless defeat marked on their brows. Healers and their assistants looked around, hopeless, while infants wailed from small makeshift cribs. Death hung on the air, holding close for the next victim to pass away.

"Why is this happening to Faery? The Mages? Why aren't the healers doing anything?" I asked, turning to find Ristan watching me closely.

"There's nothing they can do, Syn. Our world is rejecting them because it's been poisoned. The Fae who were injected with iron…The same sort of thing was done with Faery. She's dying now, and the infants and children perish because the land can no longer welcome them. The visions I get—well—they show the heirs giving birth to the next generations of heirs— ones who can bond to the world and start healing it from the inside out. The Mages poisoned it, and Danu will not assist us in healing it unless we make the first move. By going with Adam, you would be doing what is necessary for this world to begin healing. You can stop this, Synthia. I had, at one point, thought you were against us, or some sort of distraction to throw Ryder off his goal, and that was why I couldn't see your future. Now, I know it's because you are a part of the cure, and Danu made me wait until the time was right to see your future."

"This is crazy. This is happening now?" I asked, unable to take my eyes away from the horrifying scene in front of us.

Ristan shook his head and grabbed my hand. No longer were we inside the medical pavilion; we stood in a forest surrounded by ancient oak trees. "This is the heart of Faery," he said, when I looked at him.

I moved from him, looking all around us at the ancient, dying trees. I turned as I felt Ristan's hand reach for mine, and, once again, he sifted us somewhere else. This place took my breath away. Water covered the ground and, even though we stood above it, you could feel it on your flesh. Moisture completely saturated the air, creating a pureness from its beauty. A thousand tiny fireflies lit up the night sky, as smaller ones covered the trees, giving them a luminescent glow.

"It's beautiful," I whispered holding my hand out for one of the many flying bugs.

"I wouldn't do that; they bite," Ristan said, acting as if he was shooing the small creature away. It wasn't a bug; it was a Fairy.

They were trying to heal the land. Thousands of them worked together to protect the ancient forest, but they were fighting a losing battle. "I can fix this by marrying Adam," I whispered through thick tears that tightened my throat.

"You can, but you'd have to let Ryder go, Syn. It's not going to be easy for either of you. He is trying to walk away. You need to let him go so he can do it. This is going to hurt you both, but, eventually, both of you are going to do the right thing for both worlds."

No, it wouldn't be easy. I didn't know if I could do this. Not even to save one world from dying. I wasn't a selfish person, but Adam? Marry Adam to save the world.

Okay, it wasn't the whole marry Adam part that got me...It was the produce an heir part. Sex with Adam. It was laughable. We were as close as siblings, or at least on my end we were.

"You're asking a lot. You are asking me to sleep with someone that I've considered a brother for most of my life. I'd be giving up my life for your world, Ristan. One that didn't want me."

"I know, but I also know it's not inside of you to just walk away. You cured the dying in the medical ward because you were tired of death; tired of being unable to save people you cared about. Imagine what would happen if the entire Fae race was to descend upon the human world. Only one percent of our world has left for Earth so far, and billions more would make the jump if they had no choice but to do it in order to live. Would you stand by and allow that to happen if you could help us stop it?"

"No, but you guys knew that. Ryder knew what choice I would make if I saw this. It's why he had you bring me here. Dirty. Plain and simple, Ristan. You just took my choice away from me. Bravo, now take me back." It was the truth. Those faces of the dying would haunt me if I chose to walk away. I'd see them in my nightmares, and every other moment of the day. They'd known. So, to make my choice, they'd brought me here to show me, up close and personal, what I would be walking away from.

"We knew, yes. We had to have you see what was happening so you would understand that we are doing what we have to. This isn't something that would go away for either of you. We came to your world to find the heirs, secure the relics, and gain a foothold against the Mages. You've already helped us in that department. It's not fair of us to ask more, but it's also not fair for us to walk away when we can ask you to help stop this."

"I just need to know what makes you so sure that

I'm the Light Heir; that I'm the Heir that the prophecy spoke of. Don't these types of visions have to be interpreted anyway?" I was grasping at straws, I knew it, but I had to try. Ristan nodded solemnly.

"Yes, they do normally, but it isn't exactly easy since often the vision is the path that we need to take to get to the solution. Sometimes, what is shown gets us to the solution; just not the way we thought we would get there."

"How so?" Demon lingo was making my brain itch with more questions than I had intended to ask. He didn't seem to have a simple answer.

"Well, most recently, I had a vision of you and your friends in a late morning setting, in front of a crowd of dancers in a courthouse. You saw Arianna there and became violently ill at whatever you had witnessed. That vision fast forwarded, and I could only see a flash of the newspaper headline of the Guild being cleared in the attack on the club. I could not see what you did at that moment, but I knew that, even though we did not understand what the Light Fae end-game was with Arianna, the vision told me that I had to free you from the mansion so we could get to the bottom of what it was. I had also hoped to do so before Ryder tore the Guild down, seeking revenge." Ristan closed his eyes and did a little mock-shudder. "When I saw her on the ballroom floor after you used her for target practice, I knew what the vision meant. Before that one, I had a vision of the newspaper announcing that Ryder offered a marriage contract to the recently-recovered Light Heir who had been named Arianna. Then the vision flipped, fast forwarding a short time frame later, and showed Ryder and Kier together in the foyer of the mansion. He had an expression of wonder on his face as he felt the paternal-bond clicking into place when the true Dark Heir was returned to him. I knew our goals, I knew that Ryder wasn't the Dark

Heir, and I knew that the only missing Light Princess was named Caitlín. So when the Light Fae approached Kier and offered him the missing princess, who was going by her adoptive name of Arianna—well, you know what we did after that. I never saw Adam in the vision with Kier and Ryder, and you and I both know that it happened just as I described it, Flower."

"What would you have done if you were wrong; if you'd misinterpreted the vision?" I couldn't help but ask since it was my life that was now riding on his visions.

"Fortunately for Ryder, some Fae engagements can last a really long time. The visions always lead us to where we are supposed to be. It's the journey that can get challenging and often times it takes a while before we understand Danu's overall plan. I know we are asking you to put your faith in something that is really outside of your comfort zone and frame of reference, but this can't continue, and you know deep down that this is the right thing to do. You're a gentle soul, even if you do bite sometimes, Flower. We already know that you'll do the right thing here, because I've seen it."

I glared at him before sighing. He was right; this couldn't go on. I was smart enough to understand that what I was seeing was the truth. Faery was dying, and with it, so too would the human world when they made the jump. They fed from us...err, from humans. It was a no-brainer to guess what would happen when that came to pass. "And the relics Ryder needed?"

"We still need them. Ryder was hoping you'd help us find them before your marriage to Adam, but time is short. Your womb clock is ticking. The Dark King will demand you go to him, so that you can be prepped for your role in our world. Ryder will no doubt be able to work a deal with him as to your involvement in helping us find the lost relics. Adam will be needed as well."

"Take me back to Ryder, please."

Ristan's projection faded, and we found Ryder sitting on the bed beside us, his head resting in his hands. He looked up as we came back to ourselves and our surroundings. Pain was carving out my chest, making the path ready for my heart to be ripped out with the decision I would make. I'd lose him; my beautiful golden-eyed Fairy. "Leave us please, Ristan," I whispered.

Ryder lifted his tortured gaze up to meet mine from where I sat next to him. He swallowed and tried to look away, as if the sight of me brought him pain. "You saw it. What is your decision?"

"You," I whispered brokenly. "My choice will always be you, Ryder." I sat up and captured his face between my hands, forcing him to look at me.

"Synthia, sometimes what we want and what we have to do just don't align, and we have to do what is right. I have been doing my best to stay on my path and follow the fucking rules, except with you. When it came to you, I couldn't leave it alone. Couldn't do what was right and just fucking walk away. You weren't something I could have ever prepared for. Your sassy mouth," his eyes locked with mine as his arms pulled me closer. "The devotion to those you love, Pet. You are the most selfless person I have ever met. Your soul, while it may be stained, is pure and beautiful."

"Did you fall for me, Ryder? The sassy mouthed little Witch, who drove you crazy?" I joked, but his eyes held no humor.

"No, I didn't fall in love with you," he whispered, and my heart shattered a little more.

"Good, because that would probably make leaving you impossible," I whispered and started to pull away from him. He didn't allow it. Instead, he pulled me closer until I had no choice but to straddle to his lap. "Ryder," I shook my head, fighting the tears that threatened to fall.

"You've left a mark on me that will never be replaced. I'm incapable of loving anyone. You have turned my world upside down, Pet. I want you—the visions don't change that. Let me make love to you, Synthia. Let me show you what you make me feel. I need to be with you now. I need to feel you beneath me. I need to touch your soul and leave my mark on you, so that you never forget me."

His mouth was soft and searching as he kissed me. His hands held me immobile in his arms. His warmth sank in to my bones as his erection pressed against me. His power vibrated through me, and I didn't want him to stop. I didn't want this to stop, this, well, *whatever* we had together. I wanted him to keep me. I wanted him.

His mouth drove me insane as his tongue caressed mine as his clothes melted away with his magic. He didn't remove mine with magic. Instead, he took each piece off slowly as if he was trying to commit every fine detail to memory.

I captured his head with my hands and opened myself for him to ravish. I spread my legs in open invitation, and he growled hungrily with approval. We were together in this moment, and the vision could wait. In this place and time, we were living in the present, and not with what we both knew would happen soon.

Chapter
TWENTY-NINE

I was scheduled to meet the Light Fae in the presence of Adam and his father. Ryder and his men would also be present. I wasn't looking forward to this, and, personally, I could have gone the rest of my life without meeting them. I'd worn a skirt and a sleeveless blouse at Ryder's request, but had skipped putting on any make-up, since I had absolutely no desire to impress the Light Fae. I was sitting at the bar waiting for the inevitable to happen when a strong hand landed reassuringly on my shoulder.

"You look like you're about to throw up, or run away. Which one is it, kid?" Alden asked, seating himself beside me.

"It might be both. Why are you here?" I asked, wondering how he'd gotten away to come here.

"This old man has ways of finding things out, Synthia. Besides, I couldn't let my only family meet her *other* family without me here to support her," he said before reaching for my hand and squeezing, after shooting me a reassuring look. "I'm here for you, kid, always and forever. I told you, McKenna's stick together, kid. It doesn't matter if you're my family by blood or not. You're my niece in here," Alden thumped his heart and smiled reassuringly. "That's all that matters to me."

"Thanks," I said, grinning into his gentle, smiling blue eyes.

The commotion at the club's doors wiped the smile from my lips as a huge group of people entered. Adam and his father were close to the doors, and were first to their feet with the arrival of the Light Fae. Ryder swiftly walked over to stand in front of me as the crowd came in.

They were all impossibly beautiful. Their hair was varying shades of whitish blonde, while their eyes ranged from shades of sky blue, to my own electric blue and lilac colored eyes. Power radiated from them, but it lacked Ryder's raw current that sometimes resembled a downed power line.

"Only address them if they speak directly to you. Let me do the talking," Ryder hissed against my ear, before he grabbed my hand, and pulled me across the room to stand by his men. Once again, they created a wall around me.

"You had better have a damn good reason for calling us here. Kier, this is a direct breach of etiquette. Next time you summon us, it had damn well better follow the rules of protocol," the tallest of the group growled out to Kier who was, even now, waiting to greet to the Light Fae.

"You wouldn't know protocol, Dresden, if it slapped you upside the head and said hello," Adam's father replied innocently. Oh yes, he had been waiting for this showdown for a while.

"I see you haven't changed a bit. So tell me, what has you breaking protocol this time, Kier?"

"I found something you lost," he said with a mischievous smile on his lips.

"And what would that be? I didn't come here to play word games with you. Spit it out already," the Light King demanded.

"Your daughter. The real one. We found her."

"I see, and why should we believe you? Considering we have already had one imposter trying to pass herself off as my wife's child, I'm hesitant to buy another so easily," Dresden said with his own lips lifting into a sardonic smile.

"Because we have a seer among us, and he has seen the union of the Light Heir, and the Dark Heir, my son. They are to have a child that heals Faery of the toxins induced by the Mages. Ristan, would you care to explain what you have seen to them?" Kier asked, tilting his dark head toward the Demon who stood and nodded his agreement.

"Your majesty, I can see the past and the future. Sight is granted to me by Danu herself, and she has shown me that this girl is the Heir, and she has shown me her part in fixing our world," Ristan said, bowing his head to the Light King.

"You seem rather full of yourself. Are you sure you want to continue?" Dresden taunted silkily.

"We think you knew that Arianna was one of the Mages' puppets," Ristan said, smiling coldly and losing all pretense of friendliness.

"Obviously you're mistaken on interpreting what you see, Demon," the King said snidely.

"I didn't interpret much of this particular vision. It showed me that you willingly sent Arianna to the

Dark Fae with emissaries that could lie, because you knew she wasn't your wife's child. The vision showed me that Arianna was sent by someone to do harm to the Dark Fae, so you thought that you would let it play out. Two birds with one stone and all that. But then we knew you were up to something. We had heard enough rumors over the years about you searching for her. Not to bring her back to her mother; no—you wanted to find her to kill her. Why, after all these years of searching, would you suddenly offer her to us instead of keeping her with her family for a while, or killing her immediately? We decided to watch and wait. Even the botched attempts from the assassins seemed to show they were pulling back and waiting for something. We figured out what that something was when it was discovered that Arianna was just a meat puppet. So, if you want to get into breaking protocol, by all means, let's take this to the Fae council."

No comment this time from the Light King, only a slight narrowing of his baby-blue and lapis eyes.

"This is outrageous," the Light Queen interrupted quickly, with a sheltered look in her eyes. "We are not held to the humans' laws. My husband was within his right to dispose of the child from a union that was not his. I am responsible for this, and, as the mother, I can seek to have the child disposed of."

The Light King glared openly at Ristan, whose eyes had begun to swirl in his telling of the story. "You are making some very serious charges. Make your point. I'm low on patience, Demon."

"I just did. Kier will take it from here," Ristan said.

"This is why you called me here? For this? I am within my rights to kill any illegitimate heir my wife sired from another, if that were the case. I am shocked at these allegations you are making, you *filthy* Demon! There was more than enough evidence to support that Arianna was my wife's missing daughter when we signed the contract for her to wed the Dark Prince. We were tricked as you were, Kier."

"You may not have said she was the Heir—I think Arianna started that nonsense however, you knew that she was not the missing Light Princess when you offered her to us. You thought she would take us out, giving you full rein on both worlds, because you assholes have been trying to find a way back to the most power since Anise lost the relics," Ryder growled, finally coming into the fray.

"I signed a binding contract with you. You also turned out to be not as you appeared. Seems we were both wrong, Kier, so it stands to reason that the contract is no longer binding. Now, let me see this child you claim to be my wife's daughter. I'd like to see the new imposter with my own eyes."

"She's under my protection. I suggest you call off the assassins, and remove all thoughts of killing her from your agenda, Dresden. For if one hair is harmed on her pretty little head, I know who to kill," Ryder growled as he let his power push through the room, raw and electrical.

"You have a lot of power for someone without a crown. The last time I felt anything close to that much power running through a Fae's veins, I was standing next to Alazander, the Horde King." Dresden said, eyeing Ryder cautiously.

"As you can see, I am not Alazander. I'm also not the Dark Heir, so I'm a free agent who can kill anyone who challenges me or tries to hurt anyone I'm protecting," Ryder growled with his lips twisting in the corners. Dresden let out a whoop of laughter that he directed at Ryder.

"No one would ever mistake *you* for the Horde King! Alazander definitely knows how to keep his people in line and respectful!" The Light King chuckled darkly and shot the Dark King a pitying look.

"As I was saying, she's mine to protect, and under contract to *me*," Ryder continued as if the Light King hadn't just mentioned the freaking Horde King.

"She will not be harmed here. This meeting was called under truce. I tend to stick to protocol even if others do not," the Light King turned his head, leveling his blue eyes on Kier.

"Synthia," Ryder said, and his men stepped away, letting me move through the now-empty space to stand beside Ryder and Kier.

The Light Fae gasped. Even the Queen stepped closer and held her hand up to her mouth to stifle a cry that would have escaped otherwise. I met the eyes of the Light King and held my ground.

"Tatiana, come here," Dresden growled from low in his chest. Anger was pushing off of him in palpable waves. I met the lilac and azure eyes of my mother and felt nothing; no connection. For all intents and purposes, she was just someone who looked a lot like me. "Is it your child?" he asked barely above a whisper.

"I feel a slight connection. Yes," she said never taking her eyes from me.

I had a feeling that she'd not been an active participant in the death of her child. She'd been given no choice in the matter. She looked as scared as I was and afraid of my reaction to her.

"The Blood Prince? Which one was it that sired this...female? I'd have his name to confirm it." Dresden barely contained the anger as he spoke to his Queen.

"No name; he was only at our palace for a week, and I asked him no name," she whispered, hiding her face in shame, but it looked practiced at best.

"You have no name for this...for this illegitimate child's sire?"

"No, Husband, you had taken to feeding from others. I only sought to sustain a meal from him. The Blood Fae are known for—"

"I know what they are known for, woman! Describe him to me," he demanded.

"He was a royal Prince. His eyes were the same as mine, and had the royal banding. His hair was midnight black. He made a feast for me, which I could not refuse."

I hated the Fae right now, more than I had before. Games! These creatures loved playing games. He'd starved his queen, so she'd taken food from where it had been available. He was messing around and mad because she was messing around as well. I had a mother and a father, and they were *nothing* like my adoptive parents.

"Was he the only Blood Fae you fucked?" he asked crudely.

"No, I took two others within the same month, Husband," she replied honestly, letting her eyes slide down my frame. They came back up with a touch of pride in them that went right through me as she didn't seem to find me lacking as many Fae did before my Transition.

"The nurse who was charged with your care disappeared when you did and never returned to us. I'd like to know which caste of Fae kept you alive, child," Dresden said with venom dripping from his lips.

"Humans," I said to more surprised looks and gasps from those who came with the King and Queen.

"Impossible!" he argued.

"No. It seems not everyone bows down to your orders. Maybe the nurse who was supposed to *kill* me gave me to the humans instead. I was hidden with ink, and taken in by the Guild. I trained as a Witch and became an Enforcer for the Guild to keep the Fae in line. Seems fate has a wicked sense of humor."

"She comes with us!" the Light King demanded.

"No. She stays with me for now," Ryder said, moving in front of me protectively.

"She's my wife's child. Therefore, I can claim her as my own. I am claiming her now."

"Then I challenge you for the right to become her guardian, Dresden. Right here, right fucking now," Ryder said with a tone that brooked no argument. The Light Fae stepped away from him as if they were afraid of him, and I blinked as I peered around his shoulder. I guess I could mark the Light Fae down as not being *complete* idiots. They were trying to set it up so I'd have to go with them. I could see the calculating gleam in the Light King's eyes as he was trying to figure out the best way to out-maneuver Ryder and Kier and get me under his control so he could kill me.

Ryder's head lowered as he met my eyes and held my gaze. He told me with those expressive eyes that he wouldn't let me go without a fight, and that he'd kill the Light King if it came down to it. I had no question in my mind which of them would win in a fight between the two Fae.

Ryder was hard, cold, and lethal. The man oozed it from his pores as much as he exuded fuck-me vibes. A warrior who fought for what he believed in with everything he had. He was bred to fight and win. In any battle, I'd choose Ryder to stand at my side. I knew with every fiber of my being that he would not let anything or anyone hurt me. The Light King was thin, and elegant; more suited for womanizing and dancing. I smiled up into Ryder's eyes with my own, showing him I trusted him to protect me.

"I will not fight you, Ryder," said the Light King. "I'll fight the Dark Prince that thinks to claim the child as his bride."

"No, Dresden, it doesn't work that way. I have claimed her pleasure already, and she is mine under contract. She is under *my* protection, Dresden. It is I who challenged you, not my *brother*."

"You fuck your brother's intended bride? And the little whore allows it, I'm sure," the Light King said. He gave a sly look at the Light Queen. "Maybe I should take her daughter, and make her my meal slave, as a warning to my wife to remain faithful."

"Oh the hell you say! You couldn't handle me in bed, ya skinny twit. I like my men to be warriors, both in bed and out of bed. Which you are not," I snapped.

"Syn," Ryder chided with a smirk lifting his lips.

"Impudent little bitch!" Dresden growled heatedly.

"Careful, Dresden, before you piss me off and I decide to kill you anyway," Ryder growled low from within his chest.

"You overstep! You are a Prince, nothing more!"

"He has been acting as my heir until his younger brother could be found, Dresden. He is used to ruling, and he has the girl locked into a contract so that she couldn't slip away until her lineage could be verified," Kier said, placing a hand on my shoulder.

I looked up at Ryder's face, taking in his sideways profile as he refused to step back from the Light King. He was standing here for me, protecting me because of the contract, and I wondered, for the first time, if he'd do so without there being a contract between us. It was dangerous territory to tread on, even if it was only inside my mind.

I stepped back into the protective wall that was Ryder and his men.

I listened to them begin to discuss the marriage contract and my future, as I walked silently to the table and sat down, accepting the drink that was handed to me. I was numb and felt completely hollow now that I'd learned from where I had come from. It was anticlimactic to say the least, and the only thing I wanted right now was to run.

Chapter
THIRTY

As soon as the Light Fae had left the club, the rest of us gathered in the bar area to go over the next steps. For the most part, we were shocked and a little amazed that the Light Fae had been in agreement with the Dark Fae about my parentage. But, something in Dresden's smug attitude, along with the terms of the contract with Kier, just left me with an uneasy feeling in the pit of my stomach. I was silent, though everyone else seemed to be chatting happily as if we'd just had some huge pissing contest with the Light Fae and won. The only other silent person was Ryder, who sat beside me.

"This couldn't have gone any better. We confirmed that Syn is who we thought she was, and they agreed to the marriage contract!" Kier said, clapping Adam on the back. "I'd have thought they would have argued more, but this is exactly what we wanted, my son."

"Yes, but something isn't adding up about them. It looked to me that they perfected that act before they showed up. They didn't seem too surprised when you told them we had found the missing heir," Adam said, running his hand through his thick hair.

"The only thing he seemed genuinely surprised

about during this entire meeting was that I was alive," I said out loud, causing Ryder to look right at me.

"He didn't quite deny or hide the fact that he wanted you dead, Synthia," Ryder growled, moving his leg so it touched mine. "That being said, we need to be careful in any future dealings we have with them."

"I saw the Blood Prince that Tatiana described several times while we suffered through round after round of their endless parties," Kier said. "He had eyes much like yours, Synthia. If I remember right, he is the Blood King's younger brother. He may have been there for only one week during *that* visit, and she didn't ask his name, because she already knew it—he often acts ·as his brother's emissary!" Kier laughed, and seemed very pleased that he'd figured out the Light Queen's turn of phrase that she had used to dodge the truth. "Everything we suspected is just being confirmed as we dig further into this."

"Explain the tattoo then," I said with a calmness I no longer felt. I was still fishing for anything that could make me not the Light Heir.

"I can't, but the theory we have put together with all of the puzzle pieces matches the rumors and stories we have all heard," Kier said calmly, soothingly.

"See? There are still too many questions. I mean, we can't just take their word, right? They're Light Fae," I said, feeling my heart kick up in tempo. Maybe there was a way out of this after all. Maybe I wasn't the Light Heir.

"Syn, even if you weren't the Light Heir, which you *are*, Ristan has seen the future," Ryder said softly as his hand that was beneath the table caressed my leg, sending heat scorching to my core. "You two will work together, and Ristan has seen the proof of it. You begin the healing of the world of Faery. We can't ignore that."

Well, there went *that* hope, right down the drain. I lowered my eyes so no one could see the pain that his words caused. His hand played softly on my thigh, teasingly. I turned to look at him, and couldn't manage a smile when he gave me reassurance. He'd made love to me, and it had broken my heart, because I wanted that softness from him. Between that, and learning that I had been right this whole time—that I wasn't supposed to be alive—I was two problems shy of a full-blown mental breakdown.

"He could have been shocked to see you alive simply due to the fact that he had you pegged for dead already. Someone did just blow up your house, with you inside of it," Adrian said, lowering his eyes to me from where he stood behind Vlad. I hadn't even noticed when they had arrived earlier to catch the tail end of the contract being negotiated.

"Hate to agree with him, but you were supposed to die in the house, Synthia," Ryder mumbled as his hand slid between my thighs.

I barely suppressed a moan as he applied pressure. His eyes held a playful sparkle in their depths. He rubbed his fingers over the soft skirt I'd glamoured on this morning. His hand lifted it until his fingers touched my tender flesh. I had to control my breathing as everyone chatted around us and *to* us.

"So, we need a firm yes or no from you, Synthia," Kier said, causing Ryder to stop his movement abruptly.

"You want me to marry Adam. I get that. What else? I know it's not as simple as just marrying him,

Kier."

"You marry him, produce an heir, and you will be groomed to become Queen of the Dark Fae. You will sign a contract agreeing to it, and agreeing to be everything Adam needs."

"I can't do that," I replied honestly, which seemed to make every conversation in the room stop. "I can't honestly sign anything that agrees for me to become everything he needs, Kier. I love Adam, but I'll never be in love with him. I'll be faithful, and I'll try to be a mother to his children. I had no mother, so I have no idea what one does for her child, but I can try. I don't want to be a queen of anything. Period. Again, I can try. That is all I can sign my name to. Anything more would be a blatant lie."

Adam let out a heavy sigh and left the table in long, angry strides that took him swiftly to the doors. I watched him go in silence.

"Love will come with time," Kier said, loud enough for it to carry to Adam, but he ignored it and left the club.

"No, it won't. Not that kind of love." *Because I'm already in love*...I shut down my mind from thinking *that* and looked carefully at Kier. "Do you love your wife?"

"With all my heart," he replied without hesitation.

"And you would so easily deprive Adam from having what you share with her?"

"Syn," Ryder said.

"No, I'd like you to answer me, Kier. Because I was raised with Adam, and, yes, I love him, with all of my heart and every fiber of my being. I'd jump in front of him and take a bullet without thinking twice about it, but I'll never be *in* love with him. I'll never play with words to make him feel otherwise, either. It will be a loveless marriage, and, as his friend, I wish for more for him."

"Synthia, I love her with all of my heart now. When I met and married her, I can't say I did. Love is a difficult concept for Fae, and it rarely happens to us. When it does, most of us don't recognize it as such. I appreciate your hopes for my son. You really are a beautiful soul, Synthia. You will make a fierce queen and a strong woman for my son and your children," he replied, bowing his head.

I closed my eyes and shook my head as nausea rolled in my stomach. "I need something before I agree to anything, Kier. It's not something you give me, or anything that will cost you."

He narrowed his eyes and nodded for me to continue.

"I have something I need to settle before I can agree to become his wife," I choked out the word wife but managed it nonetheless.

"Name it," he replied, watching me carefully.

"I want one shot at drawing out the Fae that killed my parents and blew up my house. He is one and the same. I want a chance to stop him from ever harming me or mine again. One shot, and, even if I fail to kill him, I will go willingly with you and marry your son. I have to at least try to end this before I can agree to anything."

"You're a female; you should be protected and cherished. Not out seeking vengeance," he exclaimed.

"Sir, no offense, but I've taken down plenty of Fae

in my lifetime. I'm only twenty-one, but I assure you that I can handle myself, and your son can tell you as much. I was top of my class, and I'm damn good with a blade made of iron. I want this, and, while I am sympathetic to your world's plight, I can't agree to settle down or anything else until I at least try to take out the person who murdered my parents. I owe them my very life. They saved me, Kier, and I can't just walk away without at least trying to kill the one responsible for their deaths."

His blue eyes were thoughtful, and with a nod, he agreed to discuss it with Adam. With the promise made that he would think about it, I left the room silently and with a heavy heart.

I went to the room by myself, but it didn't take long for Adam to show up. He walked in and lifted his hands as if in a helpless gesture. "Hi," he smiled uncomfortably.

"Hi," I replied, wishing I had something else to say. It was strange between us now, and it shouldn't be. I wasn't sure it would ever go back to normal again, ever. I missed my friend; I missed his jokes and wisecracks. I didn't want this to drive a wedge between us, and this awkwardness was spiraling out of control.

He exhaled on a deep sigh before he started talking. "Syn, we should talk."

"It is fine, Adam," I answered, wondering if he felt as weird as I did with this tension between us.

"We need to talk. There's a lot going on, and I know it's happening pretty fast for both of us."

I snorted and met his green eyes. "That's putting it

mildly." I rolled my eyes at him as he laughed.

"Larissa would know what to say if she was here." He hesitated, scratching his head carelessly.

"If she was here, Adam, we would be having a very *different* conversation," I muttered back at him.

He smiled sadly and nodded. "I know you don't want this, but, Syn, I've seen the infants and children they speak of, and they *are* dying, and if we can save them…"

"Adam, stop. Just stop, please. I know as well as you do that this ends with me going with you. I need to finish something, though. I need to find the one who killed my parents before I can commit to anything. Give me that much. You, of all people, know how important this is to me. I have to try. I'll become your wife, but I'm not sure where this will put us as friends. I don't love you like that."

"You want to kill the man who is currently hot for your head?" he asked, sitting on the edge of the bed with a sarcastic smile on his lips.

I scooted over and made room for him next to me and turned onto my side. He smiled and curled up beside me, reaching for my hand. It felt natural, and, yet, lying next to Adam was so different from lying down with Ryder. I felt no lust, no heat, and *zero* attraction. Adam was gorgeous; he was the stuff that many young girls' dreams were made of. He just wasn't *my* dream.

"I do. I want him gone. I want to be the one who kills him, as well as the others who killed my parents and ruined my life. If we can prove that Dresden sent him and his friends, then he will need to answer for what they did too. I don't care if that asshole is a king, either. If he is guilty of any part of it, I want him dead as well. Ryder hasn't made any progress, so it's my turn to try. Alden agreed to help me, and we have a plan."

Adam grinned knowingly. "And then you will come with us?"

"You know this won't work between us, right?" I asked, watching his face as it fell.

"We might not be *in* love, but I love you enough for this to work. I feel a connection that's hard to ignore when I'm with you. You may not love me— hell, this might not be love I'm feeling, either—but if we can save our people—the people of both worlds— I'm willing to forgo love and do it."

"You could live without what you had with Larissa?" I asked, resting my head on his shoulder and looking up at his beautiful face. "We shouldn't have to live without it. Who knows if this will even work? Ristan couldn't even see my future until this week. Now he's seeing us having kids, and, what will our kids think? This is just insane!"

"Everything we have ever done together has worked out, Syn. I know we can do this too," he whispered, nuzzling my hair as he smelled it.

He'd always done this since we'd been children. It was strangely comforting when he did it, and enticingly erotic when Ryder did it. I threaded my fingers through his and held his hand. I tried to think of a way to tell him how I felt about Ryder. I couldn't come right out and say I thought I was falling in love with him, and I couldn't lie. "Adam," I started out, and tilted my head up a little further to look at him.

I wasn't prepared for his mouth when it landed on

mine, or the door opening and Ryder's deep, angry growl as I tried to push Adam off of me. It ended up with a clumsy attempt to push him away from me. I felt nothing, and then, as he tried to deepen the kiss, he growled angrily.

"You're branded still," he half whispered, half snarled.

"Don't do that again!" I shouted, pushing at his chest, angry that he tried to force the kiss on me. I got that he was trying to show me we could do this, but it felt wrong in so many ways that it was hard to list them all.

"Wasting no time, I see. I guess I should remove the mark soon so you can *play*," Ryder growled from the threshold of the door where he'd stopped cold in his tracks.

I felt red heat rush over my face with his words. I wanted to slap them both—hard. "Get out, both of you!" I barked back, tired of dealing with everything that they expected of me.

"Syn," Adam said, unfolding himself from the bed to stand at his full height.

"I told you what I wanted first, Adam." I met his emerald and lime green eyes and showed him I wasn't giving in until I got what I wanted. I'd started this quest at five, and continued it every day after, searching every face in every crowd for those responsible for my parents' deaths.

"She wants the one who killed her parents," he said to Ryder, without turning to look at him.

Ryder hadn't moved. The only sign of his anger was the muscle in his jaw that hammered wildly, and his hands were once again clenching at his sides, as if he wanted to strangle us both. "So she does."

"You have yet to remove your mark from her."

Ryder said nothing. He just stared at me as if I'd betrayed him in some major way. He'd been pushing me toward this, and I hadn't even kissed Adam back! Anger flared inside of me as his eyes damned me. "Get out, Adam. Go talk to your father about the deal we made," I said softly, never taking my eyes from Ryder's violent, angry golden stare.

Adam walked out of the room with his shoulders squared, and his head high, unaffected by the tension stirring between myself and Ryder. He stopped and turned back to Ryder. "Remove the mark. She can draw him out by tapping a line. We can kill him, and I'll take her home—*tonight*."

Ryder continued to say nothing. His eyes were hard and angry and continued to scorch my skin. I could feel his anger pulsing from the electrical current that sizzled through the room, thick and palpable. When Adam was gone, he still stood there, just looking at me, as if he was afraid to come closer.

I watched him with pain in my heart that I was still trying to bury. He was going to let me go. I could see it in his eyes. I'd fallen for him. I was so stupid! He wasn't the enemy anymore, and it left me confused and unsure how to feel about him. My heart, on the other hand wanted Ryder to fight for me. To show me I was worth something to him. Stupid!

"You will make a good couple," he said as he exhaled a long, shuddering breath.

"No, we won't. We will end up fighting. I won't love him as he needs to be loved. You said I wouldn't belong to anyone else but you. You have to stop this from happening," I whispered, meeting his penetrating stare, pleading for him to see what was written in my eyes that I couldn't form into words.

"What would you give me if I could?" he asked as he strolled across the room, getting closer to the bed where I still sat.

"What would you want?" I asked, afraid it would be more than I could give him.

"You," he said, falling to his knees in front of me. "I'd want you, Synthia, to do with as I wished for the rest of my life. You would be mine, completely. I'd want you at my mercy, to taste, and touch when I wanted you."

"Ryder," I whispered as I brought my hands up to cradle his face between them. He looked exposed on his knees, and I wanted to kiss away my pain and his.

"You enjoy me between your legs, Pet. You enjoy it when I dominate you and control your pleasure. Your body trembles beneath mine and you cry my name when you find release. You are already mine. I wish I could keep you safe with me, for all time."

"You let them sign me away. Why didn't you stop it?" I asked as his hands parted my thighs and his long fingers played over the sensitive flesh of my inner thighs.

"Because I can't do it. I can't take away the only chance we have of healing my world, for my own pleasure. The only way for me to stop them, would be for me to steal you. Do you want me to? Would you be able to love someone who could walk away and leave an entire world to wither and die?" he asked, and, for the first time since Joseph had cut me open, I saw a sliver of fear in his eyes.

"Why can't we fix it? There has to be another way, right?"

"I've tried to find another way. There isn't one that we know of, and this is the right thing to do." he said, but he didn't give me time to think as he pushed me back onto the bed and climbed over my body, pinning my legs apart with his own. "Did Adam's kiss excite you and make you as wet as mine does?" He grabbed my hands, easily pinning them above my head. "Did the boy make you moan with pleasure from a single kiss, like I can?" His mouth lowered and claimed mine. This kiss was unlike any before it. This kiss was asserting ownership; it was staking his claim on me. "I didn't hear you moaning as you do for me—like this…"

I moaned against his mouth as his lips conquered mine. His sex pressed hard against mine, showing me he was ready for me. He broke the kiss and showered my face with soft kisses as he used his magic to remove our clothing. "I'd have to kill him. It would be the only way I know of right now to void the contract."

"No, you can't kill Adam!" I cried as he entered me in one solid move that shot him to the center of my core, creating a rush of emotion as he took control of my passion.

"I'd kill him to keep you. If my world's survival wasn't riding on the two of you, he'd already be dead. I'd kill a fucking king to claim you as mine. You feel so fucking good, so right. Your body welcomes me, caresses my cock. Fuck, it's so good."

"I don't want this to stop," I uttered between his earth-shattering thrusts.

He was gentle, and, even though he ignored my outburst, I knew he wouldn't kill my best friend. We made love for hours, and when we were done, we lay entwined together saying nothing. Both of us knew that, soon, we'd be parting ways. He would go to secure the rest of the relics, and I'd go to marry Adam and procure an heir to heal the land. It was tearing me in two knowing I'd be leaving him.

It was funny how the world worked. I'd fallen for my enemy, and now I had to leave him to cure his land. We'd been through hell and come out stronger together. Now the only way to continue was to be parted, when I'd finally surrendered to my feelings for this beautiful creature.

Chapter
THIRTY~ONE

We spent the next day sifting around checking out the locations where the three remaining relics were hidden throughout the world. Ryder had men set up at each place, watching for the Masons to move them. He figured, since we'd obtained one, they'd move the others at the first chance they got. When we returned to the club, I left the main area for the quiet of the room I still shared with Ryder.

"Syn," Ryder said, coming into the room we still shared.

"Fairy," I said, lifting my eyes to meet his.

"Are you ready for this?"

"I'm ready," I whispered.

He was not happy that he had to keep his promise to let me go after the assassin, and it was making him grumpy and growly. His time was up to find the assassin and my time in this world was running out, according to Kier, so Ryder had reluctantly agreed that I could make the attempt tonight.

He held his hand out and I accepted it. Before I could say another word, we were standing in the old cemetery. My eyes adjusted to the darkness as my Fae sight kicked in to allow me to see better in the dimly lit cemetery. I had to admit, it was better than the second sight I used as Witch; it may as well have been daylight to my eyes. I moved quickly to stand away from him and his men quickly, as they had no idea what I had planned with Alden. Alden and I made the plans while he'd been hunting relics and Mages the previous week; and it was time to put it into play. There was only so much I was going to allow Ryder and his men to become involved with, as far as confronting my assassin. If I had let him, Ryder and his men would have taken over this operation and packed me in cotton wool. The problem with that was the assassin would never show. Alden and I were very careful to let Ryder know only the absolute minimum so he could be involved. I didn't want him jeopardizing my plans. If this went down the shitter at the last minute, he was my plan B. After all, I'd been raised as a Witch, not Fae, and we believed in plan B's.

"No tricks, Syn," Ryder growled from where he stood a few feet away.

"Tricks are for kids, silly rabbit," I said, skating around my intentions. Alden was here already, and he'd brought the sixteen-inch daggers that I'd trained with for most of my life at the Guild. They were custom-made for my small hands and fighting style. They were on the long side for being daggers, yet shorter than what short swords would typically be. The Guild Armorer had handcrafted them of iron and some lighter weight metals to keep them as light as possible while still being durable and deadly to the Fae.

I carefully set my iPod down on Larissa's grey headstone and looked around, waiting, before sending enough magic out to light the torches Alden had set up. Flames shot up around us, circling the area in which the large group was standing.

The faces of those who had come to help were shadowed by the flames that leapt to life. Adam and his father had come, along with a few of their men who had come to protect them if this got too messy. Alden had also brought with him a few Guild members that he still trusted.

I stepped away from them to use the knife that would cut through my flesh and help me to raise the dead. I needed blood for the spell Alden would cast. Tonight, unlike the other times I woke the dead, I needed them to awaken with Dark Arts instead of Light, so that I would be able to borrow some of their strength. As the blood touched the hallowed ground, it sent flames shooting from the torches high into the sky. I whispered a few more words in Latin, completing the ritual, and smiled as I felt the rush of power when the dead rose from their graves.

Billy, a young child who had been here for at least fifty years and loved my iPod more than he actually liked me, was the first to greet me. He didn't have his normal cheeky grin on, as if he could sense the seriousness of why I was here and knew that this would most likely be the last visit I had with him.

Billy and I had an arrangement, as I did with the other ghosts in this cemetery. I came once a month to dance with them and allow them to feel alive for at least a little while and they blessed the earth around the graves of my friends and family. Billy normally picked the songs that we would all dance to.

"Billy, I need to know if you and the others will help me."

He tilted his cherubic face, and narrowed his

eyes with a keen sense that a child his age shouldn't have possessed. A moment passed in silence while he spoke to the others around him. The living were not meant to talk to the dead, but tonight Alden would cast an ancient spell that should allow me to hear them. Normally, I tried to interpret what they said by reading their lips or gestures.

"Alden, cast the spell," I whispered, and felt a small tingle of the rush that came from casting with a coven. I had missed it ever since I'd buried Larissa a little over a month ago. I hadn't even tried to cast with a coven since her death, not that I'd had any opportunities.

The ghosts watched in open curiosity as Alden and his fellow Witches and Warlocks stepped up with items that were needed for the spell. They formed a circle and spoke together in Latin. The wind picked up, and my hair flew into my face as the chanting grew louder. The flames from the torches shot up high into the air as leaves blew from around the trees in a circular pattern behind the coven, shielding them from the Fae in the cemetery.

I breached the circle and smiled as the hands broke from each other to touch me. I would be taking the taint of the spell into my soul tonight. I'd asked them to cast it, but I couldn't ask them to take the darkness that came from casting the spell; not when it was I who needed and had asked for this. I was no longer part of the Guild, and asking them to take darkness for me just felt wrong.

"It's done," Alden said, stepping back, as did the coven he'd brought.

I turned to look at Billy, who was watching us intensely. I waited for him to say something, and when he finally did, it wasn't to me, but someone I couldn't see.

"She's nuts. You sure you want to be stepping in now, Lady?" he spoke to someone beside him.

"Billy," I finally whispered, after years of waiting to hear him speak, I could.

"My name is not Billy, its Quinn. So stop calling me the stupid goat's name!" He balled up his fist and glared up at me.

I smiled and nodded. "Sorry about that," I replied, a little embarrassed. I was waiting for the language of the dead to take over my tongue, but it didn't come this time. "I need your help," I started to say, but he held up his hands, and shook his head.

"We know what you have come for, but it can't be done. Only *she* can help you," he replied with an accent I couldn't place.

"She?" I asked confused.

I didn't have long to wait. When she stepped out of the shadow veil that only the dead were allowed to enter and into the cemetery, I gasped and took a step back. "Oh my God," I cried and Adam made an anguished sound behind me.

Larissa stood in front of me, as beautiful as she'd been before the Mage had cut her open. "Syn," she whispered, and grabbed my hand, which made me shake to my very center.

"I can feel you!" I felt my heart rate increase as a million different thoughts erupted inside of my brain. "You're alive?" Hey, it had happened once before.

"No, Syn, I'm dead. My soul is here, and you can feel me because of the spell. Alden cast more than just a simple spell to allow you to speak to us. He cast one to allow us to rise for one night as the living."

"Larissa," Adam said as he stepped closer with a confused look on his face. His heart was on his sleeve, and tears shined in his eyes as he took her in his arms and held her close.

Larissa smiled, and I felt a hot tear flow down my cheek. I stepped back to allow them to talk alone for a minute. I hadn't realized that I was crying, or that Ryder had moved closer to me. I backed up into his solid wall of a chest, and turned when I felt the electrical current against my skin that he alone could create.

"Are you okay?" he asked for my ears alone.

"I think so, she looks…happy," I whispered back and met his eyes.

I turned to watch Adam pull Larissa against him as he kissed her deeply. I felt no jealousy at knowing I would be soon marrying him, or that he was making out with a ghost. The feel of Ryder against my back felt right; I felt safe with him.

Adam pulled away from Larissa and began to utter apologies as if the same thing had just crossed his mind, but it wasn't me he was apologizing to. It was her. "Lari, I couldn't stop the need. I tried…I couldn't stop, I was in Transition…"

"Shhh, it's okay. I understood why you did it. I feel no anger toward you or the women who took care of you during Transition. I couldn't have fed you as they did. I don't blame you for marrying Syn, either," she said, shocking us both. "Don't force yourself on her, Adam. If you do, I'll haunt your ass for eternity," she said, smiling amenably.

"You saw that," he uttered with a defeated sigh.

"I couldn't leave you. I stayed until they took you from her house. Those Fae packed my stuff with Syn's, and I was able to follow you because my essence was connected to it. I wasn't ready to be seen, nor were either of you ready to see me. The pain of loss was too raw for you both. You both needed time to heal before I allowed either of you to see me."

"I looked for you; everywhere. That fucking Demon pulled me away though. I couldn't stop it from happening, Larissa; I just couldn't stop the need I felt!"

Larissa snorted and rolled her eyes as she placed her hands on her hips. "Seriously? You were in Transition. I was there; I know you couldn't stop it."

"You *watched* me?" Adam asked, shocked.

"Of course I did. Besides, I showed you most of the moves anyway. And the guilt you felt kinda held me there. You kept me there. It wasn't as if I *wanted* to watch you with other women, but you wouldn't stop thinking of me while you did so. Which, call me petty, but even though they were absolutely gorgeous, but you wanted me, and it was one of the most wonderful feelings of my life...or death, whichever."

"Syn, now you on the other hand...bad girl! And Ryder, tsk-tsk! I underestimated your skills. I need a word with you, by the way," Larissa said as she walked over to us. I waited until she tapped her toe on the ground. "Alone, Syn. Don't worry; it's nothing bad, or about you."

"Do you blame me?" I blurted it out before she could disappear with Ryder. "For failing to save you?"

"No, and neither do your parents, Syn. You can't

fight destiny—taunt it, yes, but to fight it will only consume you and, in the end, destiny always wins." She smiled sadly and cupped my cheek. "I need a word with Ryder, and then we have some payback to dish out."

"You okay, Adam?" I asked as I stopped awkwardly beside him.

"Define okay? She watched me, and she knows about us too," he whispered, as if he was afraid Larissa would overhear him from where she stood talking to Ryder.

"Ouch," I said, unsure what else to say. He'd been planning on asking Larissa to marry him until she'd been killed right in front of me.

"Did you sleep with him again? I need to know you're being smart when you're with him." Adam's question made my head whip around to look at him. His eyes had turned bright green, and a tight strain showed around his mouth.

"Don't you think I know that?" I whispered, still watching him.

"I hope you're being careful. The entire realm of Faery is depending on us."

"I get it. I'm still on the Guild's contraceptive shot. It's stronger than the humans' birth control. I just don't know if it will wear off while I'm still in that grace period of Transition that everyone is counting on."

"You have feelings for him, and I understand it. Hell, I still love *her*. So much fucked up stuff has happened this month that I wasn't sure until now. I know that if she was alive and here to stay, I'd defy the fucking Gods to keep her. So, I get it, but we can't just allow Faery to die. The whole idea that they would come here in mass exodus is a little overwhelming."

"I know," I replied with a soft smile. "I would have given up my life for her, as I would for you. You've always been my family. I said I would go with you, and I agreed to be your wife, but I never said I would love you in that sense. I will never lie to you, even if I could."

He shook his head. "I know, baby, and if there wasn't an entire world depending on our child, I'd let you stay with him. Even if I do think he's bad for you."

"I don't think this is a conversation we should be having here. I told you I'd go. I agreed to be your wife, Adam. Let's leave it at that for now. Please?"

"Fine, but you should know my father has a huge engagement ball set up two days from now." I felt sick to my stomach hearing the news. I didn't want any of this, and yet too much depended on it happening.

"I said I didn't want a huge engagement. Besides, haven't the Dark Fae learned their lesson about engagement parties after the last one?" I said turning away to look over at Ryder who was writing something down as Larissa spoke to him.

"Ha! At least we won't have to crash this one." Adam chuckled, looking like his old self. "The Fae always have a celebration when two people are united. Although, I think I may have talked him into handfasting us, instead of marriage." He gave me a sheepish look. "I thought for a long time about this, and at least with the handfasting, it will give you a year to produce an heir, and save the world. If you decide you want someone else after that, I'll let you go, Syn. I'm trying to get you an out-clause here. When, or if, you decide to go, I'll let you." Adam smiled as if he hadn't just laid it all on me.

"Oh, I see, so I get to produce it myself..." I blushed and glared at him all at the same time. "Nice set-up," I mumbled as I rubbed the back of my neck, uncomfortable with the entire conversation.

"I've always been attracted to you. I just always kept it to myself. You ended up with Adrian, and I got lucky when Larissa caught me. Somehow, I always had a feeling it would be you and I in the end."

"Adam..."

"Adam, give her a break. We both know she's going to marry you, but I wouldn't advise pressing the issue here," Larissa said, showing her perfect white teeth as she bared them at Adam in a mocking grin.

"Larissa, are you okay with this?" he asked, barely above a whisper, and crushed her against him in a tight embrace. His eyes glowed with hunger as he looked down on her face.

"Like I have a choice? And, actually, I am. If I had to pick a woman to fill my shoes, it would be my best friend," Larissa said, winking at me as she rested her head against Adam's shoulder.

I stood beside them awkwardly until I caught sight of Ryder watching me. His eyes went from the couple back to me with surprise. I smiled and moved toward him. "What did Larissa say?"

"I will tell you later," he replied as he watched my face. "It's time to tap the leyline. I have other engagements to attend to tonight as well."

"Such as?" I asked quietly.

"I said I would tell you later," he gave me a heated look and a panty-dropping smile that was usually guaranteed to distract me. "I said it's time to tap the line. Let's see if these assholes are still waiting for you on the other end."

I shook my head, and turned back to look at Adam and Larissa. They were now smiling, and laughing at something one of them had said. Alden was watching them as well, with a sad smile on his face. He met my gaze and nodded. Everything was in place. It was time to tap the leyline.

THIRTY~TWO

"Larissa, it's time," I said, coming up behind her and Adam.

"It can wait, Syn," Adam growled as he pulled Larissa back against his body.

"Adam, you have the rest of the night with her after she and I do what we came here for." I smirked when Larissa grinned at him impishly, and wiggled her eyebrows.

"And that doesn't bother you? You know what I want to do, and it doesn't bother you at all?" Adam questioned, narrowing his eyes on me.

"That you want to get your ghost nookie on?" I smiled wider and crinkled my nose. "Nope, because I know what she means to you. I know what it felt like when you didn't get to say goodbye. Besides, I can handle sharing, at least better than you."

"Ouch," Zahruk said, coming over to us. "Ryder said it's time. He already has the veil up so they will not see us when you tap the line. So get on with it, girlie; we got shit to do after this."

"Tell him we're ready," I replied, turning to watch

as Quinn and the other ghosts closed in around us and then disappeared from sight.

The men turned at my words, and as soon as Adam had taken position next to his father, I erected the protection shield around me and Larissa. Angry growls erupted from Ryder and his men, but Adam just watched me carefully, as if he'd known the plan all along. He'd known me the longest out of everyone else here, so it stood to reason that he would have guessed my plan.

"You're sure you want to do this alone, Syn? I can only give you a boost to tap the line and hold the shield up. Anything that comes through the line will be up to you to defeat," Larissa said from beside me.

"Nope, not sure at all, but I can handle this, Larissa. I won't be responsible for him hurting anyone else."

"Fine, but you need to get whatever is bothering you off your chest now," she said with keen eyes.

"I'm not sure I can marry him. Not now, not ever."

"You're marrying Adam, we both know that," she said, and shook her head. "You need to be faithful to him, Syn. He deserves it, you both do. You are bound together by destiny. I know you don't love him yet; not as you love Ryder. I just don't think Ryder is in the stars for you. He forced his way into your life; unlike Adam, who has always been there for you when you needed him to be."

"Larissa, they're not just asking us to get married… they want us to have babies. Which means—"

"I know what it means, Syn. I'm dead, not dumb." She rolled her eyes with a small grin on her lips.

"I'm sorry. It's still a lot to take in."

"He wasn't only thinking of me when he was with those women, Syn. I lied to him, because I knew it would hurt him to hear the truth from me. He doesn't remember it all now, but he will soon enough. He felt guilt for me, and lust for you because you were nearing Transition, and your need pushed into his mind when your Transition hit. It's been messing with him pretty bad, so give him a little time. I would think it has to be a common thing when one has a bond such as the two of you do, and I guess that's why they try and marry familiars. He's always had his eye on you a little bit more than a big brother would. It's always been there, staring us in the face. Adrian and I just never wanted to admit it. I think you were meant to be together, and, in the end, it looks like you will be."

"I don't think so. I think we both deserve to be loved. Real love, Lari; the kind that makes everything else in the world seem trivial, the kind that melts your soul and melds it together with the one you truly love. I do love Adam, but I'll never be in love with him, and that's what he needs. Right now, he seems to only care about what the Fae need, and I get that too, I really do…But what happens when we have done what they need?"

"You'll have children to be happy and content with, Syn. It's more than I'll ever have."

I swallowed a twinge of regret, knowing she was right, and I shouldn't be complaining to her of all people. She'd never have anything more because her life had been cut short entirely too soon. "I just don't think I'll be a good mother. I truly never had one. She was taken before I learned anything from her."

"Being a mother will come naturally to you, Syn. Stop selling yourself short. You love unconditionally, and you never give up on a person no matter how much they deserve it sometimes," she tilted her head a little, and smiled. "And you'll kill anything that threatens those you love. You're going to be the best mother ever. You're going to make bears look timid compared to you."

"I do kill shit well," I agreed, and looked around at the angry faces watching us. "We better do this before they join forces and try to shatter my shield."

"Okay, so the plan is that I help you tap the line. I can feel the disruption in the air when they sift so I can help give you a little warning when they come through, but I can't wield a weapon or help you do the killing, as I am only a soul, even though I look like more right now. It's sort of forbidden for the dead to help the living, so let's not test the powers that be more than I already am."

"That's fine, Lari. I just need strength and a second pair of eyes."

"Then get dressed, it's time to kick some ass," Larissa said, grinning wickedly. I whispered the spell that would place the shield in darkness, making it impossible for anyone to see inside of it as we prepared for war.

I smiled, and closed my eyes, feeling my clothes change around me until the feel of leather, tight against my breasts, covered me. The tops of my breasts were pushed in by a comfortable leather vest, and leather pants hugged my frame while giving me enough room to move in. I felt Larissa's hand on my face, warm for the moment until death would claim her again, as she ran a finger over my face, leaving behind delicate Celtic markings in blue woad paint for strength, and courage.

"Holy shit, Syn, Keira Knightly has nothing on you," she whispered as I weaved my hair into leather straps that would hold it back from my face.

"Okay, dropping the darkness. Wish me luck, Lari. You might be getting company on the other side." I smiled as she frowned.

"You won't die, Syn. It's not your time to go. You have to live. Consider this: if the world of Faery dies, so too does this one. You and Adam have always been special; you can do this. You were meant for greatness, and that comes with a certain price that has to be paid."

I met her eyes and nodded. "I don't want to hate Adam, Larissa, and I don't want to resent Adam because we were forced into this. That's what scares me, and well, I'm just not attracted to him—not after having Ryder."

"You won't hate him. You know he is driven by a need to fit in. He was ripped from his family by you, and now that he has them back, he's fighting for a way to keep you in his life, because you're all he has left of this world. He's just as afraid as you are, but he's stubborn and, worse yet, he's male, so he won't say it, but he needs you in his life. His world is changing just as much as yours. He's a strong, proud man, and will not admit to being afraid of losing you, but he is."

"I know, and I feel horrible about it. But I can't change the past!"

"Exactly! That's what we keep telling you, and yet you keep holding it inside. Let it go! Quit thinking everything is your fault and just let it go. I know you thought you did when I died, but I felt your pain. You and Adam both held me here, and limbo sucks. I mean, don't get me wrong, it's not too bad, but eventually I would like to see my parents before I choose to be reborn."

"I don't know how to let go. I feel too much, and there is so much I could have changed very easily had I just done something differently. I've been holding this in and using it for strength. If I let it all go, what the hell will I have left?"

"You will be who you are destined to be. Now, tap that line, because Ryder looks like he might be able to breach the shield with that glare alone."

I turned and looked directly at him, his golden eyes piercing to my soul as he took in my garb. His eyes lowered slowly until they reached my feet, and then came up slowly as a smirk kicked up the corners of his beautiful mouth, even though he still held his lethal glare in check.

"Laugh it up, Fairy," I mouthed the words to him before turning to face Larissa as she held out her hands. I'd made the shield so I could speak to Larissa alone, so no one outside could hear us—well, at least those with Fae hearing. "On three, Lari," I said, reaching down to pick up the daggers before counting under my breath.

We touched fingers as we had done so many times as children, and combined our strength. She was giving me a good jolt of energy, considering she was a ghost. I opened my eyes and watched her chant. She was as beautiful in death as she had been in life. Her natural curls flew around her face as she chanted the words with her eyes closed. The other ghosts were chanting, and with every word the power inside of me grew in strength.

When she opened them, I released her hands and stepped back. I could hear Ryder and Adam both speaking to their men, trying to figure out how to remove the shield and get inside of it before I could tap the line. Both of those ideas would fail.

I braced my body and placed my hands at my sides as I sent out feelers for the closest leyline. I sent a silent prayer to any God who would listen, and tapped the line.

~~*~*~*  *~*~*~*~*

"Get that fucking thing open, right fucking now!" I snarl as fear tightens my chest and makes me careless. I hate that I feel this; this fucking need to protect her even from her own stupidity. Nothing I tell myself makes it go away. She's inside of me, like a drug; I crave her.

The beast wants me to drop the veil that would expose us to her enemies. I growl at him. I'd made a promise to Syn that I'd keep it up so that her Fae assassin wouldn't sift out as soon as he sifted in. The magic veil is an old Fae trick used to hide entire armies from those opposing us. Child's play, but it takes more concentration that I could be using to break through her fucking shields.

The thought of giving her to another male enrages the beast, and he's getting harder to control as time grows near. I know where the Mages are now. Larissa told me where to find them and how to kill them, but there are only a small portion of them in Washington State. They are scattered all over creation—hiding from us like worms beneath the soil. She made me give her my word that neither Adam nor Syn would be aware of what was going on until this local threat had been removed.

Syn looks fierce and beautiful with the warrior's woad, the blue simulating delicate and intricate tattooing on her face, and her hair tied up behind her head, framing her face as she lowers it into a fighting pose. The beast wants her now; he wants her to scream for him and watch as her eyes light up with desire. I growl at him, uncaring that others watch me as I do so. *This isn't the time or place for our dick to get hard, she's in real danger.*

He stiffens.

The beast inside goes wild as she taps the line and places herself in harm's way.

A male sifts in, but he's only a scout. He was there that day. He participated in that atrocity, but he is not the one she wants.

She stands perfectly still, calmly waiting for him to strike, and when his smile registers the Goddess of war in front of him, he does. She's faster. She moves with unmatched skill and speed. Her blades are almost invisible, moving in perfect harmony as they hit their mark.

She smiles and kicks the body of the Fae still standing in front of her, and it crumples as the head rolls off the body from where her blades cut through muscle, tendon, and bone as if they were no more substantial than butter to a hot knife.

My cock grows hard as she turns and prepares for more to come. *Fuck!* I hate battle wood. The beast is pacing; he wants inside the shield she has erected. He could get inside her shield, easily. He knows it; he's claimed her mentally and physically, but to do so would out us to all that were watching.

He wants to kill Adam and take his place, but fate is a fickle bitch and has plans that not even I can overcome. Not for her or for the beast that prowls inside of me. He taunts me that this will not come to pass, that he has done the ultimate stacking of the deck in our favor. For the life of me, I don't know what he means, and, stubborn beast that he is, he won't tell me more.

"Fuck, she's outnumbered!" Adam shouts as he watches four more Fae that were there that day surround Syn.

Her eyes meet mine, and I shake my head. She can allow us inside at any time she chooses, and yet she doesn't plan to. I can read it in her beautiful eyes; they say this is her battle alone. I have to give her this chance. "Z, the tall one in front of her, he's the one from her childhood memories?" I ask my second in command.

"Yes, but he's not the one who killed them. He's not Light Fae either. Assassin for hire maybe?"

"Alden, remove this fucking shield, now!" I growl, trying to contain the beast that is now rattling inside of my chest. My men sense him. They close ranks. Their inner beasts strain for release as mine demands to be allowed into the fray to protect her. She's outnumbered, and she knows it.

"I can't, Ryder. You, Adam, and I have all tried to take down her shields before. She is the only one who can do so, and she can determine who can pass through it. She will not fail; she's a born warrior. Just be ready when she drops it, because, if she does, it means she's in trouble," Alden says, watching her with fatherly pride. That fucking Warlock knew she was going to do this. *Shit!*

"And if they sift her out before she can drop the shield, and then kill her, Warlock. Could you live with yourself then?"

"She needs this. She needs the closure. As do I. If you interfere, she would never forgive you," the Warlock says, as if I'd give her a fucking choice.

"If she dies…" I warn with murder dripping from my fangs that have now filled my mouth.

"She won't. In all my time on this earth, I have never seen a fiercer fighter, or a more driven need to avenge the death of someone they loved, than her own. She's the daughter of my heart, Ryder; the only one who has given me joy in this life."

"Do you plan to tell her that you made a deal with my Demon to bring Larissa out of the shadows for one night?" I said to the Warlock, never taking my eyes away from Syn. Alden watches with me as she gets into position to face down the monsters of her past.

"She does not need to be told. It doesn't matter what I do, Ryder. I'm an old man. She has eternity now. She needed this, and I knew it was only a matter of time before she closed this chapter in her life to start a new one. She needed to say goodbye to Larissa, as did Adam. I needed to see those responsible for killing my sister dead, before I could join her in death. The Guild made a decision; I'm being replaced."

"The Guild won't let you go peacefully," I reply, knowing damn well the Mages will kill him. It's just a matter of time. *Replacing* Alden was a nice story so that they could get him out of the way without anyone catching on. I wonder if this was Marie's fate as well. They call us animals; they are the same, cut from the same fucking cloth as us.

"She doesn't need to know, as I said. I couldn't take out my sister's killers, and I raised her so she was strong enough to. I knew she and Adam were different than the others. Not just that they weren't human, which, as an elder, I should have been able to spot. Had it not been for my love for them, I might not have been so blinded to their differences from the other children. The Guild would have put them to death, had it not been for Marie and her careful planning."

"She will be pissed that you didn't tell her."

"She'll get over it. She will have you in the end."

"She's marrying Adam in two days," I snarl because I fucking hate it; hate saying it, hate thinking it.

"No, I may be just a human, Ryder, but even I have eyeballs. I have seen her look at you and just now, she wasn't looking at Adam with the thought that she might not make it—she was looking at *you*."

"That doesn't change the fact that she was brought up by you to value life. In the end, she will do what is right. It's in her code, embedded in her soul *by* you. Ristan has seen Syn and Adam with their child. I already know how this story ends." *Without me in it.*

"So you say, but even destiny can change if the will of two people is strong enough. I say fuck destiny, and let us decide what our future is. It changes every time we make a choice, and I damn sure don't think anyone can say what will happen just by seeing it. Nothing is set in stone until it's happened." The beast agrees with him wholeheartedly.

A flash of a sword catches my eye as one of the Fae decides to make the first move and strikes out at Syn. She feints with one dagger and strikes back with the other. I lose all interest in conversation, the beast unwilling to allow me to play word games with the Warlock as Syn engages in battle.

Chapter
THIRTY-THREE

I met them head on. The faces I knew from my past that haunted my dreams were here now, facing me. The blades were sure and steady in my hands as I prepared to end these assholes. The blond Fae closest to me lunged with lightning fast speed as if to grab me, and missed as I sifted just a foot to the right. Another Fae seemed to materialize in the blond one's space, swinging his sword right at my head. I jumped back, feinted with one dagger and swung with the other, blocking his attempt to separate my head from my neck. I darted after him, but moved away when he lunged at me. These were just *his* pawns, and I wanted to send a message. I picked up speed and twirled through them deftly and swiftly, light on my feet as I danced around them effortlessly, making sure the blades struck precisely where I wanted them to.

My blades carved effortlessly into one Fae's neck and sliced into the next, swirling and dancing as I did damage. I was weightless on my feet as I circled them from the outside until the last one was met and fell to the ground by my hand. I turned around, blinking rapidly past the blood that covered my face and soaked my hair. I exhaled slowly and pushed the first one I had taken my daggers to. The fight happened so fast, I don't think he realized that he was dead until his head detached from his body and tumbled to the ground.

The other two lay still on the blood-soaked ground. I moved forward and examined the bodies; their necks had been severed enough to drop them, but not enough that they wouldn't regenerate for some playtime with Ryder and his men. I looked around for the blonde fourth Fae, and he was nowhere to be seen. He must have sifted out when the other Fae sifted in for the kill.

I could feel Ryder's eyes as they drilled into my flesh. His anger was palpable, even through the shield's impenetrable surface. I could hear my own heart as it raced inside my chest. "He's not coming," I whispered, feeling disappointment that the one I wanted to kill the most wasn't going to show up to be slaughtered with his lackeys.

"Something is, I can feel it," Lari said, placing her hand on my back as she pushed more of her power inside of me.

"Lari no, if you give me everything—"

"I still have enough power to stay solid for a few more hours. I'll still be able to tell Adam goodbye."

"Talking to the dead, bitch? Hope you are getting acquainted, because I plan to send you to them very soon," a deep resonated voice said from beside me. I sifted across the shield and met my parents' murderer face to face across the distance.

He smiled coldly. His eyes took in the dead Fae on the ground. The others weren't dead, but they wouldn't be talking anytime soon. Just a little further away was the decapitated body of the first Fae who arrived here. "You did this?"

"You killed my parents," I accused, watching his

reaction carefully. "This is my eye for an eye."

Nothing—no emotion showed on his sharp features. Only a little madness was showing through his eyes.

"I was after *you*," he sneered and leapt with his sword drawn. I expected it, and dodged his blade easily.

"Why? What did I ever do to you?"

"You were born; that's enough of a reason," he shouted before he pulled magic around him, intending to use it on me.

I pulled my own magic around me, and smiled coldly as the ink Alden used pushed past the brands to light them up, and the delicate Celtic knots on my shoulders followed suit. The stars, one for each of my parents, were the last to light up. He was the cause of them, but if I allowed the anger take hold of my emotions, I could lose this, and that was just not an option.

"I watched you," I said softly, making him strain to hear me.

"Impossible!"

"You're weak; you missed me. I was there the entire time. Sloppy," I taunted as I moved closer. His eyes scanned over the beheaded Fae. "You should have searched the house better, because now I plan to kill you for what you did."

"You have yet to even tap into your powers little girl! You can't kill me, but I plan to kill you, and take everything that should have been mine! That stupid old man has no idea what he has done. And that whimpering bitch of a mother we share is a waste of fucking space!"

I stopped cold and stared at him in shock. "What?"

"Oh, that's right; you have no fucking idea what you are. Pathetic, really. They should have killed you when you were born. I should be the heir. It's supposed to be me!" He lunged, and I barely avoided being maimed by his sword, because I was trembling from his words. *Sloppy, Syn, really sloppy.*

"I'm going to cut you open, and watch you die a slow death, little sister!" He shrieked, but as he did, he noticed the crowd gathered outside the shield that had all drawn their weapons waiting for a chance to strike at him. Shit! Ryder must have dropped the veil that was hiding them so he could attack. "I'll find you, bitch, there is nowhere you can hide that I won't!"

"No!" I screamed and lunged, but he'd already sifted out.

"I'm so sorry, Syn. I tried to keep him inside the shield, but I couldn't," Larissa whispered, resting her hand on my shoulder.

"I just needed to get close to him! I should have done this alone, and then it would be over, dammit! *Dammit!*" I shouted, angry at myself for thinking he wouldn't be able to see the others this time. If I'd come by myself, he wouldn't have sifted out. He'd be dead by my blade. Finally, after all these years, my parents would have had peace.

"Z, collect the dead and transport them to Faery. If there are any that can regenerate, I want them in chains. Dristan, any brands you can read?" Ryder asked as he strode across the graveyard, every inch the leader.

"On it," Z said as he and a few other men moved

to get the bloody bodies ready to be sifted to Faery. It gave me a little satisfaction that the two that could regenerate were going to have a very miserable existence in the capable hands of Ryder's men.

"You," Ryder said, lifting his eyes to meet and hold mine.

"I failed." I felt it to my very soul. I'd failed the kill him yet again. Tears burned in my eyes as the reality of this being the last real shot that I would have at avenging my parents sank in.

"You need your ass spanked. But you did not fail; you were outnumbered, and all but two of the men from your parents slaughter are here. They have peace now; you need to get over this before it consumes you," Ryder said as Ristan came up to whisper in his ear.

"I didn't kill him, though. I had him, Ryder, he was right in front of me." I cried, frustrated with failing to do what I came here for, all because he had sent my mind into shock with his cryptic words.

"You didn't come here to kill them. You came here to show them that you could. You came here for answers. You talked to him. What did he tell you?"

"He told me he wanted me dead," I replied, chewing my lip wondering over his words.

"He said more than that, Syn," he growled as his eyes locked with mine.

"He told me how he planned to do it in graphic detail! He said he was my brother, and something about how our parents should have killed me when I was born," I shouted at him. The tears that had been threatening broke loose, and I shook with everything that was in me. Shock from my supposed brother's words, adrenaline from the fight, anger at losing my chance at him—it all had me falling apart in front of Ryder and everyone else present.

Ryder reached out and pulled me in, wrapping his arms around me, holding me tight against his body. For a few minutes, we just stood there with him holding me close and making soothing sounds against my ear. When I finally stopped shaking, he murmured in my ear. "Syn, I'll find him and bring his bloody corpse to you. I promise he won't live for much longer. We will find him." I knew Ryder would do it too. I could let this go, for now.

I took a deep breath and opened my eyes in time to see Adam and Larissa embracing yet again.

"Jealous?" Ryder whispered in my ear as one of his hands threaded through my hair at the back of my neck and kneaded my scalp soothingly.

"Of them? No, not really. My heart goes out to them. They had love, and had it ripped away from them. I just want a love that's true and earth shattering. I want that, and I want it for them again, too. I want them to have more than just one night in a cold cemetery," I said softly.

"You don't think you will end up loving Adam." He made it a statement instead of a question.

"I love him already, but not like what they had, and I want that soul-torturing love. The kind where you'd die for one last kiss, one last touch," I said letting my eyes drift to the couple. "I thought being a Fairy would suck, but it's destiny that really sucks."

He smiled hesitantly and nodded before he turned his eyes to Ristan who was talking to Alden. I watched Alden hand a piece of paper over to him and shake his head before his eyes landed on me with remorse in them. He smiled wider, his forehead wrinkling as he did so. Fear ran down my spine along with a slight tremble with what I suspected.

"What did he do?" I demanded, turning to Ryder.

"He gave his soul for you. You have that effect on men." His golden eyes said more than his lips. "He made a deal with Ristan, which is how he was able to cast the spell and bring Larissa and the other ghosts back to life tonight. He did it for you."

"Oh, the hell he did! Ristan!" I seethed, turning on the Demon who brokered the deal.

"Flower," he said genially as he strolled up, as if he hadn't just agreed to kill the only family I had left.

"Let's make a deal, Demon. My soul for his; mine is immortal," I pleaded, narrowing my eyes on Ristan.

"I don't think so. I like being alive," Ristan said looking over my head to Ryder, who stood behind me.

"Take mine," I begged. Ristan's eyes grew large with the tone of my voice; I meant it, and he knew it. "I don't need it."

"Yes, you do. You're going to be a mother, Synthia."

"No, I'm going to be a baby factory. Alden hasn't even loved yet! He doesn't deserve to die to protect me. Enough people have died trying to protect me already. I won't allow it to happen again," I cried, feeling my entire body tremble with the knowledge that he'd done this for me, and now he'd suffer because of it.

"Why would you throw your soul away, Synthia? Alden's been marked, and, if I own his soul, they can't touch him," Ristan said slowly as if I was daft. "The

Guild can't kill him if he's bound to *me*."

"Wait, you made this deal so you could save him?" I asked, unconvinced.

"You knew," Alden said, finally coming into the conversation.

"I did. I *saw* you coming before you even decided on it, Warlock. You're my wedding gift to Syn. She shouldn't have to go to a new world alone. You are going with her, after you help us with a few more things so we can bring down the Mages."

I blinked at Ristan. "You got me my uncle as my wedding present?"

"I did," Ristan said, smiling brightly, proud of his own devious deed. "Although I'm not sure you should thank me yet. If you haven't noticed, he's a bit of a pain in the arse."

I smiled through the tears forming in my eyes and threw my arms around Ristan's neck before kissing him soundly on the lips. I wasn't prepared for his tongue when it pushed through to my own, or Ryder's snarling growl, which seemed to dispel Ristan's sudden urge to kiss me. Ryder's grip around my waist tightened as he pulled me away from Ristan's reach.

"Ristan, come, we have business to attend to tonight. Syn, Savlian will see you home when you are ready," Ryder said, shaking his head at Ristan's sneak attack. "A word before I leave, Syn."

"Go ahead," I said, turning to meet his gaze.

"Alone," he whispered as his lips tugged at the corners.

We walked over to one of the many tombs that

stood above ground. I figured we had gone far enough, but he kept going until we'd rounded the corner of a mausoleum, and, before I could even gasp, he had me pressed up against the cold stone wall. His mouth clamped against mine, and he kissed me until my bones felt like they were made of mush.

When he pulled away, I was left panting and wanting more. "If you ever do anything as stupid as you did here tonight, I'll lock you up and throw away the fucking key. You're barely through fucking Transition; they could have gotten a lucky swing in, and you'd be dead right now."

I searched his face and smiled brazenly up at him. "Aw, did I scare the big, bad Fairy? Afraid I'd get hurt?" I teased softly.

"I'm serious. You could have been killed, and for what? You have nothing to fucking prove anymore. If that was for me, then I get it. You want to be seen as more than just a pretty face. Fine, I see it, but next time, do it with me, not alone. Don't make me watch without being able to do a damn thing to protect you."

I shook my head. "You're wrong. It was closure. I needed it before I could go and be what Adam needs me to be. If I went without at least trying, I'd always regret it. You told me I'd make the right choice, and I will. I needed this, and, yes, maybe I wanted to show you that I could handle myself. But that's not why I did this. I know who is trying to kill me, as do you. I brought him face to face with you, and now you can finish what I couldn't."

His eyes scanned my faced intently, and his mouth curved into a gentle smile. "Smart *and* deadly. Loving the woad...Do you have any idea how fucking hot you look right now?"

"I'm covered in blood and blue paint," I snorted, and rolled my eyes at him. Only a male would think this sexy.

"Right now? You look like a fucking warrior Goddess, and my cock is rock hard because of it," he whispered, and grabbed my hand, rubbing it over his massive erection. The rough jean material pressed against my fingers as I wrapped them around him through his pants.

My breathing hitched in my lungs as his eyes illuminated a deep, burning, amber color. I licked my lips and watched as his eyes lowered to them with hunger deep inside of his. "Be ready when I get back. I need to remove the brand from you. I want to be inside of you when it's removed. I want one more night of nothing but you. Understand?"

"You need to fuck me to remove it?" I asked breathlessly, with anticipation building inside of me.

"I need to fuck you. Period," his lips tilted up before they landed on mine again, and his hands lifted me up until I wrapped my legs around his waist. When he pulled away, his eyes changed back to their normal golden color. "I have to go." He kissed me again and ran his hands down my back before he set me back down. "Don't change. I want you just like this, my little warrior Goddess; woad and all."

Chapter
THIRTY-FOUR

I spent the next hour or so sitting on the cold ground beneath the starlit sky talking to Larissa about things I wished I could have said to her before, and the things I'd never get to tell her again. I knew that her time here was short, and Adam wanted his chance to say goodbye too. We talked a bit more about my feelings on marrying Adam and his alternative of the handfasting. We also talked a little more about my thoughts on becoming a mother. A few years ago, it had been a dream that Adrian and I had once talked about, but deep down I was always scared of becoming a mother. It had always seemed to be more his dream than mine. She squelched a few of my fears, while making a couple of them worse, even though that wasn't her intent.

"Adam's always loved you, and, yes, maybe it is this bond you share, but, in the end, if I had to pick another woman for him—it would still be you."

"He was going to ask you to marry him," I said softly, turning to watch her smile grow softly.

"I know. I always knew. I found the ring a week before Joseph came. You fought, Syn; I watched you fight for me. Thank you. I know it couldn't have been easy. You've been the only sister I've ever known, and my family. I wouldn't change it for anything. I love you. Even in death, you still feel love, and this is only temporary. I'll be reborn when the time is right. This is how I want it to be, so stop thinking I'm sad. I'm not. I get to see the other side. Yes, it totally sucked getting here, but it's not so bad. Death is only the beginning to another chapter of life. Another shot to get it right."

I smiled, but felt no peace for her. She'd died because of me, and even if she could forgive me, I couldn't forgive myself completely.

"Stop doing that! I can hear it now, ya know? When you feel it, I feel it, and I know you still blame yourself, but you shouldn't. I let him in; I thought I could hold him until you got there. *I* was cocky. I knew it was him when I let him into the apartment. Stupid of me, yes, but it was *my* mistake. Not yours. I almost got you killed too, because when he told me to call you, I did. I just wanted the pain to stop, and at that point I would have done anything to make it stop. I fucked up, and it cost me my life. Almost yours, as well. I'm to blame, not you."

"You let him in?" I asked, stupefied that she would have done something so crazy and careless with her life.

"I did, and don't look at me like that. I know now it was pretty damn stupid." She held her arms out indicating her as a whole. "Dead, remember? Next time I know not to let the boogeyman into my house."

I blanched, because, for the moment, I had almost forgotten that she was dead. I shook my head, but refrained from telling her just how stupid it had been. Adam stood up from where he'd been sitting with his father a few plots away, and walked over to us.

"My turn, Syn. She only has a few hours left," he whispered, not meeting my eyes. As if he felt guilt for wanting to be with her. I didn't feel anything except regret that he'd only have tonight with her. I wished for them to have forever, but life didn't often give us what we wanted.

I stood up and shook the dirt off the leather pants. "Larissa," I said, with tightness inside my throat that told her how hard it was for me to make words come, knowing this would be the final goodbye.

She wrapped her arms around me, and buried her head against my shoulder before whispering against my ear. "Be good to him, and when you've saved their world, find Ryder, and love him if you can't be happy with Adam. Be happy, and remember that this wasn't your fault. I never blamed you for my death. I'll see you soon, Synthia. We will meet again. Destiny has a plan for us. It's not our job to know what it is; we just have to follow it and trust that destiny will put us where we need to be."

I stepped back and smiled, even though I was puzzled over her cryptic message. The Fae didn't believe in divorce, and while they took other lovers, that wasn't something I would ever do to Adam, not even for Ryder. I wouldn't go from lover to lover. I smiled at the way Adam was trying to make this better with the proposal of the handfasting. But if the year and a day was up and I hadn't produced the child that everyone was looking for—then I'd be bound to Adam for good as we waited for me to become fertile again in ten to fifteen years. I took a deep breath, wondering if Kier would allow Adam's suggestion to come to pass. Larissa smiled and shook her head.

"Just be happy, or I'll stick around and haunt your ass. In time, even this will make sense, Synthia. You'll see. I promise."

I started to turn away, but Adam stopped me as Larissa gave us some privacy. His eyes showed a hint of worry in them. "Is this okay? Technically, we're together now, and I don't want to hurt you."

"Adam, you only have tonight with her. She will go back to being dead when the sun comes up. So, this is me, telling you to do what you need to for closure. We will be together when we enter Faery. Until then, we are just friends preparing for what has to be done. You have this night with Larissa, and I'm going to say goodbye to Ryder." I smiled as he lunged forward and wrapped his arms around me.

"Thank you," he said and stepped away. He smiled and turned to Larissa. "Most people don't get to say goodbye."

"No, they don't. I suggest you use every second of it."

~~*~*~*~*~*~*~*

Leaving them together at the cemetery was the hardest thing I'd ever done. Knowing I'd never see her again was torture. I knew they needed time; Adam had loved her, and he needed the closure as well.

I wasn't surprised to find Vlad behind the bar when Savlian brought me back to the club. It was well after last call, so I wasn't surprised that all of the human partiers had cleared the club for the night. The only remaining people were Fae that I knew to be loyal to Ryder. I walked over and sat on one of the many stools at the bar and said nothing, even as Adrian quietly walked over and sat beside me.

"I heard Alden sold his soul to raise Larissa tonight for you," he remarked softly.

"My wedding gift from Ristan," I replied. "I

get Alden and Adam gets Larissa for a night to say goodbye."

Adrian whistled. "That's…well," he choked on his words, and I laughed. Not because I thought it was funny that he couldn't get the words out, but because he had no room to talk.

"Yes, Adam is probably having sex with a ghost."

"You know what they say about the dead?" he asked.

"No, what do they say?" I asked, perking up and then deflated when he continued.

"Once you go dead, you never go back."

"That didn't even rhyme," I pointed out, smirking.

"It sounded better in my head," he offered with a grin.

"I'm sure it did." We both laughed until tears formed in our eyes.

"Did she say anything about me?" he asked as his hand played with the glass on the bar.

"She said you sucked," I smiled as he snorted and tilted his head. "No, she said to tell you to behave. And that she loved you, even though you were an ass for leaving us."

"So, you and Adam huh?" he asked, changing the subject.

"There is no way I can see to get out of it. So yes, I'll marry Adam soon and become his baby making machine. I can't let Faery die and have all of its creatures come here. She made me promise to keep this world safe."

"We could run away," he smirked and placed his hand on the top of mine.

"And what, Adrian? Wait for Faery to overrun this world and destroy everything? You wouldn't do that any more than I could."

"You'd be surprised what I'd do for you," he mumbled under his breath. We sat there silent until his eyes held my face, and his smirk turned into laughter. He shook his head, and held his glass up for Vlad to refill it.

"What's so funny?" I finally asked when he had his glass filled once more.

"You're wearing woad, leather, and *blood*; and I just noticed. I'm a crappy Vampire."

"I got some of the ones who killed my parents tonight. I failed to kill the one I wanted though," I replied.

"I know; Ryder was communicating with Vlad for some of it. He wants to know how to get inside your shield pretty damn bad. He figured I might know how."

"You can't get inside of it, unless I want you to; no one can."

"That's what I told him, but are you so sure about that? I would think anyone of stronger mind and will than the one casting it should be able to break through."

"I haven't met anyone who can get inside of it against my will."

He was about to reply when the room grew tense and everyone stopped talking, stopped moving.

Electrical current sizzled through the room thick enough to make my hair stand up on end.

I moved to stand up, but Aodhan was there pushing me back down into the chair. "Stay down. Please."

"What is it?" I asked, sending out my senses and finding nothing but raw current pulsing in the air.

Weapons were coming out, and I had a wall of Fae males building up in front of me once again. Aodhan, Zade, and Savlian were the only ones I was familiar with that I could see. I backed up until I felt hands from behind me, grabbing me, and pulling me behind the bar.

I turned and met Vlad's silver eyes. He shook his head slowly and held a single finger against his lips. I felt the pressure in the air growing thick until it literally popped. Vlad lifted his head, and it came back down slowly.

"Fuck!" he cussed in a hushed tone. "Adrian, get Syn to her room. Don't move until I tell you, and then you *sift,* boy."

I felt my skin crawl and knew something was wrong. "It's not an enemy." I whimpered, confused by their actions.

I felt no threat and heard the weapons being replaced into their holsters and scabbards. I watched Vlad look over my head to where Adrian was, and I shot up trying to see what was wrong. I'd left Adam with his father's guards, but it didn't mean that the guy I'd been trying to kill hadn't come back and hurt him.

My eyes met Zahruk's startling blue ones and flinched with shock. He was covered in blood and holding a seriously wounded Sevrin up. Blood flowed freely from multiple deep gashes on his face and arms. Other Fae were sifting in around us, all of them showing signs of battle. "Where the fuck did they go tonight?" I struggled to get the words out of my dry mouth.

"They went to shut the Mages down tonight," Adrian whispered as he pulled me against him and sifted us out of the room.

We materialized outside of Ryder's room. "Dammit, Adrian, I need to know who is hurt," I shouted, turning and heading back toward the elevator.

"Syn, stop! You can't go up there right now."

"Why not?" I shouted turning on him.

"Because, *he's* hurt. Right now, he needs to be looked over by the healer. He needs you down here for when they bring him to you."

I felt my knees go weak, and I hit the floor, hard. Adrian was there, quickly helping me to my feet, and lending his support. "No, he's fine. He's Ryder, he can't get hurt!" I felt sick to my stomach, and my hands were shaking violently. I felt as if the air was being stolen from my lungs, and the only thing I could think, was that he couldn't die. He was *mine*.

"Open the door and wait in the room. They will bring him to you if they can."

"What the fuck does that mean?"

"It means if he doesn't have to go into a healing tank, they'll bring him to you," he said, locking his eyes with mine. "You love him, don't you?" His voice was harsh, yet I could hear the pain beneath it that he was trying so hard to hide.

"What the hell is a healing tank?"

I dodged his question, and he allowed it.

"It's just what it sounds like; a healing tank is filled with water from Faery and it speeds the healing process up."

"How bad is he hurt?" I demanded.

"Bad, Syn; they all are. The smell of blood inside the club right now is very strong. And it's from many Fae, not just Ryder. He took a large force out with him tonight. Larissa told him where a large group of Mages were meeting," he replied with his finger held on his temple as if he was listening to something.

"Who's talking to you?"

"Vlad. He said to stop being stubborn, open that door, and get in the room. Ristan is coming to talk to you now."

Sure enough, Ristan materialized in front of us, covered from head to toe in blood. I couldn't tell how much of it was his. I swallowed the cry that tried to tear from my throat as his eyes met mine with worry filling them. "Ristan," I whispered brokenly as I rushed toward him.

"Syn, I need you to come with me now."

"Ryder?" I asked, shaking my head.

"It's bad, really bad. I need you to do what you did last time; save him for us. Please, I need you to help us. I don't think Eliran can do it, and, frankly, I'm not willing to wait to see if he can when I know you can do it. I need you to save him. *Fuck!* You have to do it. I'm begging you, Synthia. Please."

Chapter
THIRTY~FIVE

We sifted to the room that Ryder was being treated in; the atmosphere was one of grim apprehension. Most of Ryder's guards, including Dristan and Zahruk, had taken up positions around his bed. They refused to leave his side, even with the severity of the wounds many of them had. I couldn't see Ryder, because Eliran had a sheet drawn up around him. Healers were running in and out of the room. I flinched as someone dropped a metal container on the hard floor, the sound echoing over the sound of the machine beeping. The machinery always struck me as odd around such a mythical being, but Eliran had told me when he was treating me before that the machines humans had for monitoring patients were very useful to him.

"What happened?" I whispered as Ristan pulled me closer to Ryder, as a helper sped by to get something for Eliran who was standing on the other side of the bed from me. Ryder looked lifeless; he wasn't moving, and he wasn't breathing. I knew he was Fae, mentally, but it wasn't clicking as I stared at his ashen, motionless body.

"Iron; they shot at us with fucking iron bullets, as if they knew we were coming tonight. We got most of them, but I didn't see the bullets. I should have. *Fuck*!

I only saw that we stopped them from killing another group of Fae." His voice was hollow as he spoke. "I'm not meant to see everything, but why Danu did not want me to see this, is beyond me. I'm meant to protect him."

I reached down and held his hand; it felt as if my heart was being ripped out. Ristan was in need of comfort as much as I was, and I was in need of something to hold as I stood there staring at Ryder's inert body. A feeling of absolute wrongness stole over me—this wasn't right. Ryder *did* the damage—he wasn't supposed to be lying here like this.

Eliran shouted at the helpers rushing into the room. Everything was moving fast around us as if time stood still for Ristan and me alone. I was seeing everything in slow motion, as if it was a nightmare. My brain knew they were moving as quickly as their feet would take them, but my eyes remained glued to Ryder.

He couldn't die. Last time he'd made it through with only a few scratches. I mean, come on, he was freaking Ryder. He didn't get hurt; he did the hurting! This was something else entirely, though. Iron killed Fae, and, from the smell of the blood coming from Ryder, he'd taken the brunt of the damage.

Iron bullets. I closed my eyes and sent my senses seeking the damage; inside of him were multiple bullets, and they seemed to be everywhere, starting from his shoulders and all the way down his legs. Tissue had been damaged and cartilage was torn, unable to heal because of the iron lodged deeply within his body. I pushed with everything inside of me—everything I had—into the room, and into his body. The roar of blood rushing through my own body filled my ears as I fought to empty Ryder's body of the iron that was killing him.

Several cries erupted around me, but I ignored them and kept fighting against the iron. I felt myself waver on my feet, but Ristan was quick to hold me up against himself, which allowed me to keep fighting against the deadly metal. There were so many bullets—too many. The iron had already started fusing to his cells and was poisoning his system, making it impossible for it to begin the healing process. I started at his shoulders and began to pull the bullets with my magic and, at the same time, forced the blood-filled tissue to expel the iron and tainted tissue.

I cried out as I sent everything I had in energy, and more strength and magic than I knew I had, into his system. I was hoping it would be enough as I pushed and pulled the iron bullets to me. At first, the metal and its toxins resisted me, but I pulled harder with everything I could find in myself. Pain filled screams erupted around me as if *every* male inside the room was a part of him, or attached on a mental link. My vision wavered. I saw little grey lumps begin to reemerge through the entrance wounds as I continued to push and pull, so many of them popping up, rolling off and falling on the floor with pinging sounds as they hit the linoleum and bounced everywhere. I closed my eyes and continued my task, systematically working through his body from the shoulders to ankles; wherever I could find iron to pull.

When I couldn't do anymore, I opened my eyes and sagged wearily against the bed. I was afraid to find that the metal had won the battle. Every one of Ryder's men that had been in the room, had been taken to the floor with the pain of me pulling the iron out of Ryder's body. They all felt it, even though Ryder remained unconscious the entire time. Everyone was watching me, including Eliran, who looked from me to Ryder, and back again.

"You removed the iron," he said softly as if he

were afraid to believe it was true. He glanced at Ryder's men as they struggled to their feet. "You removed it all?"

I tried to get words out, but nothing came. Blackness was fighting for my mind, and, before I could give warning, I felt myself crumbling to the floor. Ristan caught me and hefted me back up easily.

"Eliran," he shouted.

"Get her in the room with the tanks; I'll find a cot for her. She needs to rest. I have no idea how she does that, but, right now, she needs rest before she passes out from tapping out her system," he replied.

I was fighting the darkness this time, refusing to allow it to descend and steal away my consciousness. I blinked repeatedly until the stars broke away and I could see once more. Silver and black patterned eyes looked down at me as strong arms carried me from the room. "Ryder?" I asked, worried that I had failed.

"He has to go in the tank, Syn. It will speed up the healing process so we can get him to a state where he can feed. You may have removed the iron, but he took a lot of internal damage from the bullets," Ristan replied.

Ristan held me until one of the healers pushed in a small bed that he positioned next to one of the giant tanks, and then Ristan tucked me onto it. I watched as Ryder was brought in, naked and covered in blood. He looked as if he was asleep—if you could ignore the blood, which I couldn't—but I wasn't fooling myself. He was severely injured, and in my head I knew it.

His men came in and helped remove him from the gurney. Eliran followed closely behind them, attaching cords that flowed from a beeping machine to Ryder's naked flesh. It took four of his men to hold him above the huge tank as Eliran finished the last few connections. When he was done, they released him into the water, an oxygen mask covering his nose and mouth. He sank lifelessly to the bottom of the tank. Everyone seemed to be holding their breath as they watched him until his body slowly began to rise until it stopped in the middle of the tank and floated there. Dristan closed the lid on the tank as Eliran turned a dial on the bottom, at the control panel, and millions of tiny bubbles started popping up crazily from the bottom of it. They'd stuck Ryder in a giant fish tank. I couldn't quite picture what Adrian had described earlier; this was an amazing blend of Fae magic and technology.

"I am far more optimistic about his recovery, now that you removed the iron from him," Eliran said as he came over and held out his hand. I accepted it and let my eyes move back to Ryder. His hair was moving in the water as if he was weightless.

"When will he wake up?" I asked, wanting him to do so already.

"That depends on how much damage he took trying to save his men. I couldn't open him up because—"

"Enough," Zahruk said, strolling in. "He needs to heal, Synthia. Ryder will pull through this by morning; he's very strong." He was very confident, as though he know something I didn't.

"I'm staying," I whispered, reaching out to place my hand on the tank.

"That's fine, Synthia, but nothing changes. In one more day, you go to the Dark Heir to become his wife," Zahruk said, lowering his eyes to Ryder's closed ones. The tick in his jaw was hammering, and even through his anger, I could see the pain of the unknown. They loved him, and it showed in their eyes, even if they refused to show it otherwise.

I felt drained, mentally and physically. I closed my eyes and closed out the sound of everyone around me. It was odd. For the first time, I could hear Ryder's heart beating through the brand on my hip. I fell asleep to its soothing beat. It was comforting and told me he was alive, even if he was floating in a tank of water.

I awoke, warm and snug, to the sound of snoring all around me. Ryder's men hadn't left the small room and slept in uncomfortable positions around us on the floor. Sometime in the night, Ristan had gotten into the small bed with me and was even now curled around my body like a gigantic cat. I wasn't sure if he had done it to protect me, or to push power into me like he had done before, as I felt really refreshed and strong. No matter the reason, he was going to know the moment I woke up, or moved.

I didn't move, other than to turn my head to look at Ryder. He was still sleeping, submerged in the water tank. My hand hadn't left the spot on the tank where it had been when I had fallen asleep. His hand had found mine, and was pressed against it. It was as if he could sense, even in his healing sleep, that I was there for him, waiting.

My eyes drifted slowly down his very naked body, taking in every red angry mark that had been an open wound only last night. He was healing, and it was a relief, since I would be leaving here soon, willingly or not. I flinched as my eyes landed on his leg close to his glorious cock. They'd tried to shoot him *there*. Sick bastards.

I exhaled softly, and lifted my eyes back to his face, and yelped in surprise as I found his eyes watching me. "Ryder," I whispered, sitting up to look at him better.

"Shit, he's awake. Aodhan, go get Eliran," Ristan said, unwrapping himself from me and coming off the small bed to stand and stretch. He walked around to tap on the tank with a relieved smile plastered to his face.

Ryder tapped it back three times. His golden eyes met Ristan's briefly, before coming back to land on me. Eliran was in the room within moments of being told Ryder was awake and was now barking out orders. Zahruk grabbed my arm, and was a little sharp, but his words had me off the bed and following him without hesitation.

"He's going to need to feed, Synthia. They will be bringing him to his bedroom; to you."

I didn't argue; didn't struggle to remove my arm from his hand as he sifted us to Ryder's entryway. "Strip, and be ready for him. He's going to need everything you can give—and more."

"Okay, I'll strip when you get out."

"Be under the covers when they come in, Syn, and, fair warning, he won't be gentle."

"Ryder doesn't do gentle very often," I said before I could stop the words from leaving my mouth. He'd been gentle once, and I remembered every single second of it. It wasn't an actual lie, though. Ryder was, as a rule, rough—just the way I liked him to be. I nodded as Z made a grumbling sound, but left the room.

I looked down at myself and decided I needed

to kill Ristan at the first opportunity. The demented pervert had cleaned me of all the blood and woad and had managed to dress me in a skimpy black baby-doll nightie and tiny black lacy thong. It's a good thing that Ryder said he trusted the Demon. Ristan might mess with me, but he wouldn't seriously do anything. I groaned as I realized he *had* been pushing power into me—he'd been getting Ryder's *dinner* ready. I closed my eyes, and the little baby-doll top disappeared with nothing more than a thought. It was one of the nice things about being Fae. Well, it was now that I was learning to use it. I quickly climbed beneath the covers as the door opened, and Ristan came in.

"Covered?" he asked with his eyes landing on me. I'd just barely managed to pull the covers up to my chin. "Damn," he smirked impishly, but it was short lived as the others carried a limp Ryder in, and placed him on the bed. "He's all yours. This might get a little crazy now; he might not know who he is feeding from. I'm going to be outside the door, just in case. If he gets to be too much for you, I can call another in to finish feeding him."

As if! "I can handle him," I whispered, lifting my hand to touch his cold face. The only sign that he'd been submerged in water were the small droplets still dripping from the tendrils of his inky black hair.

"Flower, I'm serious. If he hurts you, I need to know. If he gets too rough, it could be a sign that his mind has been infected by the iron. He would be livid if I allowed him to hurt you while he was unable to stop himself. Better one of the women who are here to serve the mass of Fae, than the fucking Light Heir. Understand what I'm saying?"

"Go. We'll be fine."

When the room was cleared of his men, I sat up

on my knees, letting the sheet drop to the mattress. He was deathly still. His chest wasn't rising. No air was coming out of him at all. I bent over him and kissed his lips gently as he watched me.

"You don't get to die on me. Not now; not ever," I whispered brokenly.

I stared at Ryder as he watched me from the bed. His eyes were hazy, as if it wasn't Ryder who was watching me now. He growled as he moved closer to where I sat on my knees on the soft bed. A feral growl erupted from deep in his chest, and, before I knew it, he had pinned me flat on my back to the bed, his hands firmly holding mine down to the mattress. He let out another growl and my panties dissolved as he'd intended them to.

"Mine," his voice resonated, with so much force that it constricted my throat and blocked the reply from coming out. Yes, I was his.

His legs parted my thighs roughly as his mouth lowered to my neck. Blunt teeth nipped and scraped over my skin, causing a small surprised cry to break past my lips. Ristan sifted in, as if he'd been outside the door with his ear pressed against it.

"Out, Demon!" Ryder growled, sending a chill racing down my body to my toes.

"Synthia," Ristan said as he ignored Ryder's forceful demand.

"I'm fine, Ristan, really."

"She's mine," Ryder warned the Demon in a tone so chilling, filled with such a silent threat that I closed my eyes as a bit of fear took root in the pit of my stomach. I somehow knew he wouldn't hurt me—other people were fair game—but I knew he would protect me no matter what craziness was going on around us.

"Yes, she's yours," Ristan said as he met my eyes and glanced away quickly. He didn't hesitate as I shot him what I hoped was a reassuring look as he sifted out, leaving me alone with Ryder.

"Spread your legs," he said as he went back to nipping at my neck.

I obeyed him, and felt as the head of his swollen cock entered swiftly. I cried out at the invasion of my body. His hands kept mine pressed firmly to the mattress, and I was helpless to move. His mouth growled against my neck as he continuously fucked me until he cried out with his instant release.

I held still, waiting for him to climb off. He didn't. Instead, he released my arms and flipped me over onto my stomach and entered me from behind as his hands reached for my hair, and the small of my back. One pulled and one pushed as he rode me from behind, roughly.

"So fucking good; so fucking tight. *Mine*," he snarled and lowered his mouth to nibble at my shoulder. He was rough, yet tender as he took me until we both shook from release. He hadn't fed enough, though. I could feel his hunger as surely as I could feel my own.

"Syn," he whispered after the trembling of our bodies had subsided.

I didn't reply as he pulled me over. Tears of joy erupted from my eyes as I realized Ryder was back; my Ryder was alive and sound in mind, unaffected by the iron.

"My beautiful Fairy," I whimpered with relief.

"I hate when you call me beautiful. I'm not beautiful. I'm bad. I do terrible things, and I do them very fucking well."

"I don't care," I replied vehemently. Right now, I didn't care.

"You should, since I've done some of them to you," he whispered.

"But I don't care, Ryder. You almost fucking died on me!" I snapped, finally letting out some of the pain and worry I'd felt.

"I wouldn't have died," he said, lowering his mouth to claim mine harshly. I opened for his assault and met it with a force that matched his.

He pulled away and smiled. "I'm going to fuck you," he warned.

"Good," I replied, uncaring of the soreness between my thighs he'd just created.

"Did I hurt you?" he asked as his knee once against parted my thighs.

"No, I want it harder," I replied nibbling my bottom lip as he watched.

"I don't want to hurt you."

"I want you to fuck me, hard."

"Remember, you asked for it," he replied, before nudging me with his sex between my legs as it sat poised at my entrance.

"Then I guess you better stop talking, and give me what I asked for, Ryder," I whispered through the tears building in my eyes. I was tired of being strong; tired of doing what was right. I wanted this beautiful creature that had been my enemy, but now held my heart.

"And, is that all you want, Pet?" he whispered back, kissing my forehead softly.

"You...I just want you."

He hissed as the glow ignited inside of his eyes, lighting them up with my words. He kissed small lines down my face and neck, until he hit my carotid artery where his tongue came out, and licked the wild beating pulse that his touch was creating inside of me.

"You're so fucking addictive, Synthia Raine McKenna," he growled, not letting me down as he sat us slowly to the bed as his hands cradled my head between them and his eyes searched my face.

"Good," I whispered, before crying out as he dropped me to the mattress, still standing.

"I'm going to fuck you hard and fast. I'm going to worship every inch of you with my tongue until you tremble and beg me to fuck you even harder. I'm going to make you remember me forever, right now. Then I will fuck you slow and gentle, and show you what it is like to be cherished, by me."

"Is that so? And what if I want to fuck you with my mouth, hmmm? What if I want to lick you until you come? Would you let me?"

"Saucy little Witch. What happened to my Fairy-hating death on heels Witch who wouldn't fuck me *ever*?" A small smile played on his lips.

"*You* happened to her. What happened to my Witch-hating Fairy, who didn't fuck lesser beings?" I said, running my hands over my breasts as he watched from where he hovered above me.

"I think she must have cast an enchantment spell on me. To think, all the time we wasted arguing, when we could have been busy fucking instead. Stubborn fucking Witch."

"Fucking Fairy," I shot back, smiling as I watched his cock grow in size.

"I love to watch you touch yourself. It's what made me act selfishly, and order that Adrian be removed. Your small hands stroking your wet slit, as your fingers sank inside and came out wet with a need that they couldn't cure. I wanted to cure the need; to replace yours with mine, and watch as you lit from inside with desire for me. I've never wanted to have something as much as I want you."

A single tear rolled down my face to drop into my ear. The sob that built inside of me was too much to push away and he was instantly there, pulling me against his chest. "Don't cry. Please. I can handle many things, but you crying is not one of them." He kissed the tears as they dropped, and cradled my face between his hands. His lip's drifted slowly over my flesh until they swept across mine and ignited the flame inside of me.

"I don't want to leave you, Ryder," I whispered in a cracked voice as I brought up my hands to wipe his hair away from his face.

"If it was for any other reason, I'd fight it, but you can save my world. You and Adam can do what's taken me thirty years to come to get close to doing. That's not something I can control; you're a cure to something that is killing my world and my people."

I smiled, even though the situation was serious. We'd been through hell together, and nothing had changed. "So, this is goodbye sex?" I asked, trying to lighten the situation with a soft smile.

"Let's not say goodbye. That's not us. We do the angry, snarky comments. Right now, I just need you to stop crying, so I can lick you from head to toe, and make you scream."

"Then why are you still talking, Fairy?" I asked with a soft smile as a single tear rolled down my cheek.

"You're so fucking beautiful, Synthia. You're going to make beautiful babies."

He smirked and lowered his mouth to mine, effectively stopping the argument that was bound to happen. His kiss was soft, yet scorched me inside until I felt him in my soul. His hands still cradled my head gently. He deepened the kiss, and, when he ended it, he slowly trailed his kisses down my neck.

Ryder didn't just touch. He consumed with his fingers and magic as he discovered sensitive places. His mouth left a blistering trail as it drew lower on my skin. His teeth nipped and teased as his eyes locked with mine. They were filled with lust and desire, but I could also see the pain that he was trying to hide.

He'd taken so many shots of iron to his body, and he was trying to pretend he wasn't in pain. "Ryder, you need to feed a bit more."

"I will. Trust me, Syn. I'm no fucking saint, but let me do this."

His finger slid inside of me, making my back arch up and off the bed. I moaned loudly, and he growled with approval. His eyes lit up once more with hunger. He lowered his mouth and kissed my thighs, one and then the other, trailing his way up until his breath fanned against my sensitive flesh.

"You're wet. I like you wet, knowing that it's for me."

"You're so bad," I whimpered, the storm building as his fingers hit the perfect rhythm and his tongue played over my clit.

"I'm very good at being bad, my little warrior Goddess."

"I'm far from a Goddess," I uttered in a husky voice.

"You want my cock. I can see it in your eyes. Such a greedy little Pet I've created."

"Taking credit for it? How do you know I wasn't this way before you?"

"Because I don't think that boy taught you how to fuck. He taught you the basics; I'll give him credit for that. He taught you how to make love. I don't make love, I fuck. This," he pushed another finger in, stretching me until I shuddered from the feel of it. "Didn't get played with enough by *him*. I make you wet without even touching you. Did he?"

"Flattery will get you nowhere with me, and I damn sure don't plan to be adding to that ego you got going on, Fairy."

His mouth lowered as he laughed roughly. But, the instant his mouth made contact it was back to business. His fingers came out and trailed down my leg before he pulled it back and kissed me from my thigh to calf, and back up again just as slowly.

When he had finished with one, he moved to the other. "You ready to beg yet?" He gave me a wicked grin before moving back up and spreading my thighs with his knees. His cock pressed against my opening, but only entering an inch before he pulled it back out.

"Ryder," I growled, and rolled my head back as his mouth clamped over one nipple; sucking, teasing, nipping and caressing it with his mouth.

"You want this," he whispered, entering a solid inch inside of me, before pulling out slowly.

"Yes," I whimpered, trying to make my mind work, but failing.

"That's the best begging you got?" he asked, snickering as he clamped down on the other nipple.

"Fucking Fairy! Yes I want it, right now!" I shouted, loud enough that it echoed off the walls.

The door opened. *Shit!*

"Get out or I'll fucking kill you, Ristan," Ryder said in a voice barely audible, but the tone was deadly.

"Syn?" Ristan asked from where he stood behind the door.

"Out, Demon, before I help him kill you!" I shouted. Ryder smiled as he shielded my nudity from Ristan's eyes, and met my eyes searching them with his own.

"That was sexy," he smiled boyishly, and leaned back down to continue to assault my nipple with his tongue.

"Seriously, you're driving me insane!"

"Good, I told you to beg. Now, do as I ordered."

"I'll fucking beg you, Fairy. Whatever, just do it already!"

He laughed huskily. I growled, and pushed him off of me with my feet before sitting up into a kneeling position and glared down at him. I climbed on top of him, straddling his hips. "You wanna play, baby, let's play," I whispered hoarsely as I reached down between my legs, and stroked his manhood, watching as he hissed and his head rolled back.

I lowered myself onto him and only allowed an inch inside. "Ready to beg, Fairy?" I smiled victoriously, and then groaned as he rolled my body over beneath his and drove himself deep inside of me.

"Holy fuck, you're so perfect," he growled as the tendons on his neck strained.

"Do it, Ryder, I can take it. Feed," I encouraged through a moan of pleasure at the fullness he was creating inside of me. His brands slithered and pulsed as he allowed his eyes to fully glow. He stopped and pulled out, and shook his head.

"Fucking Fairy, I can take it. You leave me to feed from another right now, and I swear to God, I will gut you," I growled.

"Blood-thirsty? I'm not sure I'll be able to stop. If it goes too far, you need to call for Ristan."

"I don't need to be saved. I need you to put your dick back in, and finish it," I ground out through clenched teeth.

He smiled, showing his teeth. "You amaze me and drive me insane, woman." He pushed in hard, and his brands grew translucent as he thrust his hips, again and again, finally giving me what I needed.

He held my legs down by placing his hands on my inner thighs. His cock pushed further inside until I felt him to my core. His thumb played gently on my clit as he watched my face, finding the perfect rhythm as he fucked me hard and relentlessly.

"You like that," he growled hoarsely as he slowed down and watched his throbbing cock as he fed it to me. "You're so tight, Syn. I can feel your pussy stretching around me. Your juices welcoming me as they invite me in further until it clenches around me. I could fuck you like this forever. Your warmth is so fucking seductive, the way it grows wet around my cock, slippery and tight."

"Ryder," I whispered as the orgasm started to build, blinding, and boiling me from the inside out. I was a pool of fire for him. His fingers played on the soft nub, sending me further into the blissful oblivion.

"That's it. Ride it, Syn. Oh God yes, you like it deep, so fucking deep."

"Yes," I purred, ignited by his words and his burning eyes as they lifted to meet mine.

"Your pussy's drenched with sleek wetness that I created. You're always soaking fucking wet, for me." He moved his hands, holding my feet as he pushed them further apart and went deeper inside of me.

"Oh God! Yes, more, give me more!" I cried as he thrust his dick further inside of me.

He was pushing inside of me slowly. Each thrust sent sparks igniting the already teetering orgasm. He had awoken the inner vixen, and she was hungry. I lifted my hips, giving him access to further depths until everything inside of me trembled and I was helpless to do more than allow him to move inside of me as the earth started to shatter.

He growled his approval as I met him with the same searing need.

I exploded as I felt him begin to feed. It was like nothing else I'd ever felt in my life. He wasn't holding back. It felt like I was soaring through the clouds and falling to earth at the same time. My blood pulsed, feeling his need. I could hear it in my ears and feel it running through my veins. Stars were exploding around me as I rode it out and he rode me. He continued to feed until I felt myself sinking. I cried out as yet another orgasm took a hold of me. It continued until he was fully sated, and then I opened my eyes.

"What's your name?" he asked with a tremor running through his voice, fear shining in his eyes for me.

"Satisfied, by a fucking Fairy."

His head dropped to my forehead, and he laughed with relief. "You are a fucking Goddess; *my* fucking Goddess. Gods, I don't want to let you go, Syn."

I met his eyes and kissed his lips gently, not wanting this to end.

Chapter
THIRTY~SIX

It was early the next morning when the knock I had been dreading came at the door, and with it my heart sank in my chest. Ryder wrapped his magic around me and cleaned the mess we'd made of each other in the hours we'd been together, then pulled me back against him when I tried to get up.

"Syn, I need to remove the mark."

I closed my eyes and exhaled. I'd hated his mark at the beginning. Losing it was only proof of what was coming; that I had no other alternatives except to go with Adam. I felt his fingers flutter over the mark before he turned me in his arms and held me close. "I thought you had to be inside me to remove it?"

"I said I *wanted* to be inside of you. I played on the words, but we don't have any more time. I know this isn't something you should have to do. Hell, I'm no good at this. You're being asked to save a world you hate, or hated. What you're doing for us, it's more than I can ever repay or thank you for."

"Wow, you do suck at this," I said, trying to make light of our goodbye even though my heart was breaking into a million pieces.

"You'll be the Dark Princess, and then Queen someday."

"Yup, and if I could get out of it I would, in a fucking heartbeat."

"Synthia," he said in a warning tone, and I snickered. I felt his fingers land solidly on the brand as pain shot through me, hot and searing as it had been when it first showed up on my skin. "The necklace?" he asked, and I exhaled.

"I'll give it to you when you say goodbye," I whispered, fighting against the slight pain in my stomach.

"I thought we agreed not to say goodbye, Pet."

"You agreed," I said, standing up to move away from him as I sent the image of jeans, and an indigo sleeveless cotton dress top to my mind. Black suede boots completed the outfit.

"Syn," he said, stopping me as I reached the door.

"Ryder," I whispered without looking back, because if I did I wouldn't be strong enough to leave him. The knock sounded again, causing me to jump slightly. I quickly opened the door and met Zahruk's sober expression.

"It's—"

"I'm ready." I cut his words short.

I felt naked without the stupid brand on my hip. I forced myself out the door and walked beside Z in miserable silence as we headed to the other room to collect the few things I had left from my house. When I had the single bag that contained my meager possessions, we headed up to the club's main floor.

I walked in shock as I took in the reality of what was happening, knowing it would most likely be the last time I was ever here. The men sat around the room, and yet no one spoke to break the deafening silence. The stillness was unnerving. Adam and his father stood by the bar, waiting. I paused in the archway just outside of the elevator, my strength caving as my legs shook. I wanted to turn around and run back to Ryder.

"Syn, you saved Ryder from spending a lot of time healing, I can't thank you enough for that, or what you are about to do for our people. You have earned the respect of the men, as well as my own," Zahruk said quietly.

"I wasn't looking for thanks. I did it because it was needed."

"You did it because you figured out that Ryder has morals and was not the evil Fae you thought he was. You are both driven by a need to fix what other people have done. You're a good person, Synthia. I hope that you find happiness with the Dark Fae, and I will keep an eye out for the Fae who showed up at the cemetery. He's made it to the top of my kill list for what he has done to you and our people."

"You think he is a part of what is happening to Faery as well?"

"No, I don't think anything. I know he's a part of it, because I've seen him on the video feed we recovered from a warehouse that was across the street from where the bodies had been dumped."

I trembled with anger over finding out that my *brother* was responsible for more senseless killing, and he was helping outsiders kill his own world. I shook my head and met Z's bright blue gaze. "He needs to die, in a very bad way."

Zahruk smirked and nodded his head in agreement. "Hence why the asshole just climbed to the top of my list," his voice was filled with tenderness.

"Syn," Adam said walking over to us, and holding out his hand for the backpack I was holding with my belongings inside of it. I allowed him to take it, so I could say my goodbyes.

"Zahruk," I smiled before wrapping myself around him as I gave him a hug he hadn't expected. "Thank you for everything. Keep Ryder from doing anything too stupid. Try not stabbing me at this engagement party." I smiled at him and moved toward Adam.

Zahruk tensed, and then relaxed as a small bubble of laughter left him. "I can't promise you that, but with him inside Faery, he is less likely to do anything too stupid. And I'll promise to try not stabbing you, *this* time."

"Syn, we need to go. My father has a few of his men holding the portal open for us."

I turned, nodding softly as I looked around the club and at the faces of Ryder's men. Ryder hadn't come up to see me off, and while I knew we'd agreed not to say goodbye, it still hurt. I'd fallen for him; he'd been a thief who stole my heart, and I'd played the part of his willing victim and allowed it to happen.

"I'm ready," I whispered, and accepted Adam's outstretched hand.

"Not going to say goodbye to me?" Adrian said, sifting in and pulling me against him.

I smiled, but his wasn't the goodbye I wanted. I felt bad that it wasn't, because saying goodbye to him at the funeral had been so much easier than what I was feeling now with Ryder. "I'd never forget to say goodbye to you," I whispered, and hugged him against me.

"Adam, if you hurt her, we *will* hunt you down," Adrian said before pulling away, and offering his hand in friendship. "It's been fun, Adam. I'd like to extend the hand of the Vampires to you. Vlad has agreed that your future wife," Adrian looked at me and shook his head in disbelief, "has already earned our respect, and loyalty."

"We accept, Adrian. Syn has that effect on people. She's going to make an amazing queen to my father's people someday."

I didn't blush; I felt nothing but denial from Adam's words. I didn't want to be a queen of anything. I wanted to scream in frustration. I wasn't ready to leave. I wanted to go back to the bed and hide in Ryder's strong arms. I felt numb, as if I was watching it happen to someone else.

I turned, scanning the faces of the friends I had made in the little time I had been here. These were my sworn enemies a little over a month ago, and now I considered them among the people I trusted. It was unreal that in such a little bit of time I had changed my opinion of these men and their leader.

I scanned the dark shadows for him, but I knew he had stayed true to his word. He wasn't coming to tell me goodbye. "I'm ready, Adam." I swallowed the lump that took hold of my throat with the words.

"Flower," Ristan said, coming up behind me. "You didn't plan on leaving without telling this Demon goodbye?" Ristan smiled and pulled me against him and whispered in my ear. "You're stronger than you think. I'll send Alden to you when it's time. Rest easy knowing he is mine. If the Guild touches him, they would be openly declaring war on the Fae. I know that they are reckless—hell, they sent us you—but they are not stupid, Synthia. I promise you that I will protect him."

"Thank you, Demon. Unfortunately, it's all I can thank you for right now. You haven't by chance seen anything changing?" I inquired, hoping he had.

"No, it's still showing me the same thing. I wish it were different, for yours and his sakes."

Adam walked me to the portal, and I refused to look back. It was time to do as I had promised. Adam deserved it from me. He'd never asked for anything but this from me. Ristan was right. I was strong enough to do this.

"You're doing the right thing here, Syn," Adam whispered as we approached the portal that his father's men held open. "We can make it work, I know we can. This is the right thing," he repeated as I gave him a sideways, slanted look.

I almost laughed; he wasn't even trying to convince me. He was trying to convince himself that what we were doing was right. I smiled inwardly and stepped through the portal, out of my world and into theirs.

Chapter
THIRTY-SEVEN

The Dark Kingdom was the opposite of what it sounded like. The outside did the name justice while the inside was bright, colorful, and beautiful. We sifted from the portal, which I ended up allowing Adam to help me with. I didn't have any idea how to sift here, since I'd never been here before and couldn't picture it.

It was exactly as the name indicated; a kingdom. I had always thought that the Fae liked to live underground—Ryder had shown that desire with Sidhe Darklands as the club had a multitude of rooms in the subterranean levels with various purposes, the main one being a retreat. Kier explained that, for the most part, the Fae do live in homes built in the side of hills and underground; however, for the royal caste, it was important that their homes...err, palaces be accessible and impressive as it was a representation of their sovereignty.

The palace was huge and put the ones built throughout history in my world to shame. It was built of dark grey stone, which created a darkness to it that did little to steal away from the beauty. The curtain wall surrounding the palace was interconnected to a series of elaborate and beautiful towers, and the barbican above the portcullis was as artistically stunning as it was defensible and deadly. In the inner bailey, there was plenty of grass, plants, and trees that I would have never expected to see leading to the keep itself. The keep was almost a mix of Romanesque and Gothic arches surrounding doors and windows, yet there were turrets and spires dotting the architecture. All of the windows had gorgeous and elaborate stained glass windows that were designed to amplify the colorful natural light they let into the place.

Inside was bright and beautiful. The stained glass windows reflected brilliant magical torches, which gave it sort of a rainbow effect inside. The ceiling seemed to soar far above our heads in the great hall with fabulous Gothic architecture that was as lovely as it was practical. It looked like a huge outpouring of the palace's inhabitants had lined up to welcome us. A woman in a Grecian cut black silk dress was among the first.

"Husband," she said as she threw herself into Adam's father's arms.

I watched them together. She was slight of build and stunningly beautiful. Her hair was dark brown with chestnut shades filtering through it. She had emerald and lime green eyes exactly like Adam's that stood out against her pale skin. She smiled and kissed Kier before looking nervously at Adam.

"I'm so glad you are home, my Cadeyrn." She smiled, and her entire face lit up showing an endless beauty.

"It is Adam now," he reminded her gently before he pulled me closer to his side. "Mother, this is Synthia, Synthia. This is my mother, Mari," Adam said as he released my hand and placed his at the small of my back.

"We've heard a lot about you. So pleased to meet you, finally," she said, but made no move to come closer and her eyes told me another story. Her words weren't a lie, but there was more to this than her words were saying.

"Pleased to meet you as well," I choked out, but didn't lower my eyes. She did not want me here—well, that made two of us.

"I'm sure it is. Adam, would you like to show Synthia to her room so that we can start the preparations for the ceremony soon? I have guests to attend to, and she can't be shown off in those rags," Mari turned up her nose at my clothes.

I almost snorted, but I *had* stolen this woman's child. She reminded me of Ryder when I'd first met him. He hadn't liked my jeans or anything else I'd worn back then, either.

"Her clothes are fine," Adam said, narrowing his eyes and turning to meet his father's shocked look. "This way, Syn. I'll show you to the rooms. My sister will meet you up there as is custom to ready the bride. My mother will be up after I have a word with her," Adam led me out of the room and up a beautifully lighted staircase.

"She doesn't like me much," I said when we were out of the earshot of curious people.

"She isn't too keen on you yet. She's a little upset still over you claiming me as your familiar. She thinks you should be mine as I am to be king." He rolled his eyes and gave me a mischievous little smile.

"Well, it's not like I planned it or anything. Honestly though, if I could undo it, I wouldn't. You made my life better for being in it," I said, turning to smile softly at him.

"I'll remind you that you said it, Syn. After we have been married for years," Adam laughed, but only in sound; his eyes were devoid of any humor.

We walked down a sterile white hall until he stopped in front of a door and opened it to reveal a room that was done in an elegant shade of blue-gray and had ornate accents of silver crown molding and trim. The bed that was positioned in the middle of the room was wide, had a golden canopy mounted to the wall behind the bed, and had darker blue curtains hanging from it that could be pulled around completely and enclose the occupants for privacy.

Tall wooden dressers made of oak sat against the far wall, while a clawfoot tub sat in the far corner, on a raised floor with steps leading up to it. Bubbles peeked from over the tub's round edge invitingly. The scent of sweet peas filled the air, and I smiled.

"Sweet peas?" I asked Adam, who was watching me.

"It's your favorite flower and the only bottle of scent I ever saw in your bedroom," he replied, making my eyebrows rise. "Syn, I was inside your apartment all the time working cases; I paid attention."

"I just didn't figure men did that kind of thing," I replied.

"I do. I need to go get my sister. Kier said it takes a few hours to prepare a female for the ceremony— even with magic," Adam said, scratching his head while he spoke. "Syn."

"Yes?" I asked quietly.

"I'm going to kiss you," he said before gently

pulling me against him and lowering his mouth to mine.

His kiss was searching, and still I felt nothing, at least nothing I should be feeling. When he pulled his lips away from me, he looked a little torn. "It will come. I promise you, Syn, it will come."

"What will?" I asked, pulling away from him.

"This internal fucking lust I feel for you, but every time I kiss you…never mind. I'll go get my sister."

He left me standing there as confused as he looked. I may be slow sometimes, but I had a sinking feeling that this bond we shared had fed him my emotions; ones that had nothing to do with him, at all. I still had yet to ask Ryder about the bond, and now I had no idea who I was supposed to learn from. Despite Ryder's assurances that Adam's mother would teach me everything I needed, she didn't seem like she was going to teach me anything except the way to the front door right now. The only one I knew here was Adam, and he was as clueless as I was.

I sat on the soft bed and waited for his sister to come. Adam had a sister; how freaking weird was that!? I hadn't even thought to ask about my family, but it didn't seem like a healthy idea to get too close to them, considering Dresden and my psychotic brother wanted me dead. Besides, they were Light Fae and snotty as all get-out from what I saw, and I wasn't interested in knowing anymore pretentious, adulteress, self-absorbed, homicidal snobs. What a screwed up family.

"I heard she was raised by humans," a voice sounded from outside the door.

"Mother says she is to be groomed to become the

Queen, and I don't see that happening. I think Cadeyrn should sire the heir and toss her back to whence she came. Could you imagine it, Astrid? Raised by humans? She must be positively horrible."

"She stole your brother; she *is* horrible, Moira. I say your father should throw her into a pit, and only allow her out to feed Cadeyrn when he is hungry; kills two birds with one stone. She can have his heir, and then we can be done with the thieving bitch."

They laughed.

"I can totally hear you," I said, glaring daggers at the cracked door.

Silence met my ears until they strolled in. The one looked like a female version of Adam—thick brown hair tumbled down her back, while lime green and emerald eyes met mine. The other was a bit taller with lustrous auburn hair, and grey and blue eyes. I was off to a smashing start with his family. Both were dressed like something out of *Pride and Prejudice*. I wanted to laugh; I may not be dressed in the most fashionable of styles, but at least it wasn't a couple of hundred years out of fashion.

"Positively rude. You will address us as is our right. I am Princess Moira, and this is my sister in-law. Princess Astrid," the shorter of the two said haughtily.

"Sorry, raised by humans. I totally have no manners," I said, watching as they looked me up and down with distaste.

Smashing fucking start.

"Girls, stop. Princesses should not act this way," Mari admonished, coming in behind them with an angry glint in her eyes.

"Look, I didn't mean to steal Adam from you, or Cadeyrn, or whatever you wanna call him," I blurted with a touch of annoyance in my tone.

"Only a selfish person would steal a child from its mother," his mother said, narrowing her eyes. So much for hoping she accepted my apology.

"*Selfish?* Didn't Kier tell you what happened? I watched my parents being raped and slaughtered in front of me. I watched Fae kill them; assassins who were hired by the Light King, to kill me. I was a child; there was no way of knowing that the pain I felt at being helpless would bring Adam to me. Hell, I didn't even know I had pulled him from your world into mine until this month! We had no idea we were even Fae. I get that it pisses you off, but it was not premeditated or done maliciously. If I could give you back the years with him, I would."

The two girls had the decency to look startled by my words. Not his mother, though, but at least she seemed to be considering my words.

"If it was your child who was stolen from his bed while you slept, how would you feel?" she asked.

"I'd be pissed, but not at the other child who didn't even know what had happened, or what she was. I didn't mean to steal him from you, and I'm sorry for my part in it. The Guild thought him just another orphaned child and raised us together. He's a good man. He's also my best friend, and I'm not sorry for that. I *am* sorry for stealing your son from you and robbing you of the right to raise him, though."

She blinked, and nodded. "I am sorry for being rude. Kier tried to tell me what happened, but I wouldn't listen," she said softly. "You can't imagine my pain to find my son missing. I grieved for him, thinking him dead by the hands of our enemies since the day he disappeared. My husband would not give up, though; he never gave up on him. He told me he would find him and bring him home to me."

"Well it's a good thing he has Ryder as his brother, or he may never have been found," I replied and watched her eyes as they grew large.

"Ryder?" Astrid asked.

"Moira's brother," Mari recovered, and said it smoothly, and yet there was something not right about her answer.

"Yes, my brother."

I turned to Mari as Moira replied. "You gave birth to him, yes?" I could play word games too if that was how they wanted to play this.

"No. He's Kier's son," she said, moving across the room and giving me her back.

"From another woman, or?" I questioned. Just how fucked up was Adam's family? They were starting to sound like mine.

"You would need to ask him. Come, we need to get you ready for your wedding," she said.

"Handfasting."

"Yes," she replied with a hint of disdain in her tone. Obviously, she wasn't happy with the handfasting.

"You didn't want us to handfast, did you?" I asked, walking to the tub she stood beside. I was hoping to sweet baby Jesus that she didn't expect me to get naked, and jump in that thing with them inside the room.

"I wanted more for my son; he has just come home. You wouldn't agree to marry him, which to me seems selfish, since he will be king someday."

"I don't love him, and this will help ensure that one day he can find the love he deserves. The handfasting was also his idea, not mine. This wasn't my choice at all. I love Adam with all of my heart as a brother. Not as my husband. I wanted to be fair to him; I want him to find real love." All three women turned and stared at me as if I'd grown another head, or horns.

"That's…well that is actually very sweet of you," Mari returned with a small smile that made her seem much younger than she was.

"But it's also a moot point. Ristan has seen us having a child who can stop this world from dying. One who can heal the land from what the Mages have done to it. So, that is why I'm here; the only reason. I came with Adam because he asked, and your husband believes we can save Faery. If you know of another way, I'm all ears, Lady." Mari sighed and shook her dark head sadly at my words.

"Come, let's get you ready."

Chapter
THIRTY-EIGHT

I stood in the room in front of a huge mirror. Only an hour had passed, in which Adam's feminine family members had done wonders. I looked like something from a fantasy movie. I was dressed in a wedding gown that was created of the softest shimmering white silk that caressed my skin lovingly. The top was a work of art. Beads created a back that held the long train of the gown. Silk wrapped around to create the Grecian-cut bodice perfectly and then floated down gracefully to an almost bell-shaped skirt. I'd never worn anything so elaborate, or beautiful, in my entire life.

Curls framed my face, and flowers and pearls had been placed through my hair to hold it up in an elegant double-braided updo. Moira painstakingly painted the thin delicate lines that symbolized unity and fertility in black ink, for the Dark Fae, along my shoulders and upper arms.

"Wow, you clean up very nicely," Moira said when she had finished the Celtic symbol for unity on my shoulder.

"Thanks," I whispered, fighting the urge to throw up. In less than twenty minutes, I would be presented to Adam as his gift. I wasn't sure why they gifted the bride, but, then again, I knew little about anything they did. The Guild had a lot of books, but there hadn't been any need for me to look into weddings of the Fae, or anything like that back then. Something scratched at the back of my mind with that thought.

"It's almost time. When you're ready, Synthia, the men would like to escort you to Adam," Mari said, looking me over quickly with the keen eye of a mother. "Do you not have anything from your parents? A sash that gives you honors among your own kind?" she asked.

"Considering the only thing they tried to give me was a painful death, I'm thinking I'm better off without anything from them," I mumbled as I stepped into the heels that I'd procrastinated putting on until the very last minute.

"I'm glad that you don't have much in the way of ties to them. They are a disingenuous people at best. They have been since Anise lost her throne. We will give you a few moments alone, since it is custom for the bride to reflect on her new life. The men will open the door when you knock on it, and then they will take you to Adam and announce your names to the gathering. My boy is fair smitten with you, Synthia, so it should run smoothly. Is there anything else you need to know before we take our places with Adam?" Mari asked, giving me another quick once over.

"I have no idea what is expected of me tonight," I replied trying to keep my hands from trembling while keeping my mind off the fact that I would like nothing better than to run right the hell out of here and back to Ryder.

"We will have dancing, and you will be expected to dance with any whom ask you if they are from a royal lineage. We also have a large gathering of women with children in attendance who would like you and my son to bless their children. Normally, they wouldn't until you are Queen, but some seem to think it will help their children live long enough for the cure to work on them as well. Word is spreading quickly that you and my son are the cure for what is ailing the land and that a seer has *seen* the fruit of your marriage. Hope is all they have right now. The contract signing will begin soon after; this is just a confirmation as to what Kier and Dresden worked out a few days ago. After this, we will progress with the handfasting. Your hands will be bound together with the multi-colored lengths of silk that represent each desirable quality of the union, and then you and Adam will speak the words of the binding of castes before Kier and Dresden. Then we will start the feast and afterward we will continue on with the bedding ceremony."

I swallowed the nerves. "Bedding ceremony?"

"Yes, it has been a custom of our people since eons ago." Mari got a twinkle in her eyes that were positively naughty. "Humans in the dark ages were such prudes about sex. One of our kind introduced it, to them as a joke to get them to loosen up a little, and I guess they liked it, as the custom spread in your world too. The bedding ceremony is the last of the night's events. The women will take you to be prepared for your new husband while the Shaman—he is Danu's Priest for the Dark Fae—blesses the bed and the union for fertility. The men will tell Adam nasty jokes and tease him unmercifully before they bring him to the marriage bed to join you."

"Well, shit," I blew out air and tried to think of something to say. "Well…shit."

"You said that," Moira pointed out.

"Shit," I replied as they laughed, until they noticed I'd turned as white as my dress.

"Oh my, are you a virgin? Your eyes look like you have been through Transition already," Astrid said.

"Oh, I went through Transition," I said as sinful images of Ryder flashed inside my mind. "I've definitely been Transitioned." *And then some.*

"Oh, then I don't understand the hesitance for the bedding ceremony," Mari said, scratching the top of her head as her son did when he was confused.

"Because I don't like the idea of the whole bedding ceremony part," I explained, hoping my point got across. I had to bite my tongue from saying there was only one bed I wanted to share, and it included my golden eyed Fairy being in it with me.

"Okay, well I will speak to Kier again on the subject and address the issue. We will leave you now."

I waited until they had left the room before turning back to the stranger who watched me in the mirror. "Run. You could do it. You could sift right the hell out of here and leave, dumbass. This isn't your fight. You don't owe them anything. So, why the hell are you still here? Hmmm? Because you think you need to fix everything! This isn't your fight."

Great…I was losing it. I was yelling at the beautiful creature in the mirror, and she was yelling the exact words back at me. I wanted to cross my arms, but it would mess up the paint that Moira had worked so hard on. I fought the angry tears that tried to fall. This wasn't my fight. Yet, I knew if I sifted out, they'd come and find me. I couldn't do that to Adam, but I was losing myself in the process.

I was giving in, and for what? To save a world

from dying and damning another as a result, that's what. I was such a sucker for people in need of help. It was my weakness. I had been taught from a young age to help if I could; to do the right thing. But, this time, it was going to destroy me.

~~*~*~*  *~*~*~*~*

She is beautiful; so fucking beautiful. Her hair is dressed in flowers and jewels that pale next to her natural beauty. They'd put make-up on her when she needs none to be the most beautiful woman in the world. She looks scared, and it is taking everything inside of me not to become visible and hold her fears at bay.

She is no longer mine; I am trespassing now, just to see how she is holding up. She looks ready to run, and I wonder if she'd run back to *me*. I hadn't been able to go one fucking day without her. She's a fucking drug that's in my system, spiking through my veins and begging me to take her again.

Her eyes scan the reflection and then she does something unexpected. She's screaming at herself to run. My hands clench in to fists as she turns around, her eyes scanning the room. Does she feel me? Does she miss me as I do her?

Fucking hell, she's addictive. I was supposed to fuck her and let her go, and that was supposed to be it. I didn't even want to claim her. What the hell has she done to me? I want to pull her against me, just to feel her skin next to mine.

I want to watch her smile as it lifts her lips and shines in her beautiful unique eyes. *You're a fucking sap.* Fuck! She's reduced me to this; pining after another man's soon-to-be wife. I fooled myself into believing I could do this; that I could see her again without needing to be close to her. I should go, because the beast is laughing at me, and that is never a good thing. Never.

Soon, she will be Adam's. She will give him and my world what it needs. Then I will come for her and make her mine. In one year and one day, she will be given the choice to choose Adam permanently, or leave him. She will choose to become mine, and I'll be here the minute their time is up to take her home and deal with the consequences then.

~~*~*~* Syn *~*~*~*~*

I'd thought I had caught a hint of his scent—the unique one that belongs only to Ryder. The raw masculine spices that were his alone. I missed him, and I wasn't sure if any amount of time would fix it.

I turned and eyed the door warily. I chewed my lip before I finally straightened my spine and walked over to knock on the door, signaling that I was ready. I'd knocked as if I were some simple-minded woman who couldn't figure out how to turn the freaking knob.

A male who looked exactly like Adam opened it and stepped back for me to exit the room. "I'm ready," I said, hating the word *ready*. I wasn't ready; not for this. No amount of time could make me ready for this. Fucking ready to run was more like it.

All of Adam's brothers filled up the hallway, barely leaving any room for air. Each of them were very similar to Adam in the gorgeous department, and, considering they were dressed in black designer-looking tuxedos, they were a devastating lot. The men parted until Ryder was revealed, but his eyes were on the floor as if he was afraid to look at me. I swallowed the urge to run and throw my arms around him. Instead, I stubbornly fisted my hands at my sides as I tried to tear my eyes from him—I couldn't. It wasn't until he lifted his that I saw his pain matched mine.

He nodded and fell in line with the rest of the group, as Adam's oldest brother stepped to the front of the group and ushered me to the middle of them. "I'm Sòlas, and I'll be your escort and presenter tonight. I find myself jealous of my newly found brother. Care to accept me instead?" His gentle jade and lime eyes searched my face.

Another of the men beside him snickered.

"I, uh," I replied, trying to think of anything to say and failing. I settled on nodding my head at him.

"Sòlas," Ryder chided from where he stood in line. "She was not raised among us. You need to tell her you are joking, or she might kick your ass when she figures it out for herself."

"As it should be," Sòlas said. "If Adam doesn't suit your need, pick me. But, all jokes aside, I'm available." He wiggled his eyebrows playfully.

"Good to know," I said with good humor. My eyes instantly sought Ryder, but he'd lowered his face again.

"I'd make a better husband to you," Sòlas said, shrugging his shoulders as he boyishly winked once again.

"I have no doubt of that," I said, letting my eyes settle on his handsome face. "It's always good to know I have backup options, Sòlas, but thank you for offering me an alternative."

He smiled and nodded. "I'm glad you think so, and relieved to know you are not immune to my charm. Adam asked me to give you a few pointers since he was not allowed back to see you. We Fae like to puff out our chests; we will taunt you just to see if you have bite. *Bite back Syn,* says Adam." He winked with a small smile. "He also said not to kill anyone tonight." Sòlas grinned wider as he recited Adam's words. "But since he says you have enough skill to pull it off, I wouldn't mind pointing you toward a few people who need it." The rest of the brothers chuckled at this little jab.

I smiled and shook my head. He held his arm out, indicating it was time, and all sane thoughts flew right out of my head as I accepted it. "How many people are down there?" I asked to try and calm my nerves.

"Few thousand—everyone wants a peek at the woman who will cure the land. They also think you must be completely disfigured because the Light Fae gave you away. Their King is now claiming you; says he made a mistake."

"Made a mistake?" I asked.

"Made a mistake in not claiming you. He's saving face basically. Your mother will not give birth to another heir while you breathe, so he is claiming you as his own," Sòlas said.

"How nice of him," I muttered. We'd reached the bottom of the steps, and the gigantic throne room was filled with people. Some of the gathering had cleared a path for us to follow. Against my better judgment, I took a step back and away from the enormous assembly of Fae.

"No fear, Syn," Sòlas gently reminded me. "Adam says you are the strongest person he has ever met. If these fuckers smell fear, they will swarm like tigers in heat."

"Got it. Let's do this," I said, stepping back up to where he stood. I put my *I'm a badass mask* back on. The one that told them I wasn't afraid; that I was the meanest one inside this room. I felt better knowing Ryder was right behind me, and having him at my back gave me a soothing calmness that I wouldn't have felt without him.

We walked through the path until we reached a raised dais where we paused. There had been several of these set up around the crowded room. The most imposing one was toward the far back, which was probably where the Dark King's throne usually rested. Adam waited for me on the dais, wearing an exquisitely tailored black tuxedo that truly showed how gorgeous he had become. I smiled and lifted my eyes to his. His smile was blinding, and yet there was sadness in his eyes. I climbed the couple of steps that led to the top of the dais and moved to Adam's side. His brothers moved behind us in a show of support. I exhaled and waited to be instructed what to do next, and I didn't have long to wait.

"My son, Cadeyrn, will make his announcement now," Kier said, coming up to stand beside Adam in a matching black tuxedo. Who the heck would have known the Fae wore tuxedos? Maybe they had a Starbucks around here as well?

"Caitlín of the Light Fae, Heir in waiting to the throne. I, Adam…Cadeyrn, Prince of the Dark Fae and acknowledged reigning Heir, choose you to become my Queen, to rule this kingdom beside me," his voice rang out as he went down to one knee.

"You sure, Adam?" I whispered, or tried to. Adam's brothers laughed from behind me.

"Very sure, Synthia," Adam said, narrowing his eyes.

Yes, I was stalling like a panicked schoolgirl, trying to buy time before losing it at prom. "Okay," I said, trying to make my arms work.

"Syn, give me your hand, please," Adam said quietly with shining eyes.

I closed my eyes and lifted my left hand until it was high enough for him to take and slip the solid gold band onto my third finger.

"Would you honor me with a dance?" he asked, releasing my hand and standing back up.

"Sure," I said and flinched as utters of disapproval went through the crowd. Shit! "Yes, Adam, I will dance with you."

He shook his head, but he had a genuine smile on his mouth as he did so. He formally took my hand and escorted me down the stairs. We stopped and he held out his hand, helping his mother up to his father's hand, where we created a circle by hands. The crowd applauded, and music started up as the Queen stood in approval beside her King.

We moved around the dance floor silently and awkwardly. I couldn't keep count of how many times Adam and I both stepped on each other's feet. We laughed, and, even knowing neither one of us wanted this, it was like old times again. We talked for several minutes in hushed tones about his encounter with Larissa. Fashions ranged from suits, like Adam and his brothers wore, to some outfits that belonged in a museum. Some of the male Fae wore what Adam called man-dresses and tights, which threatened to make me lose it laughing.

Adam apologized and told me he'd help me find a way out of this—together. When we'd danced for long enough, I kissed him softly on his cheek and excused myself.

I turned to flee to the sidelines and the safety of a wall when Ryder pulled me against him. "Dance with me, Princess. I would be humbled."

I smiled as my heart accelerated. "You are not humbled by anything, Ryder," I swallowed and allowed him to fold me gently into his arms.

Chapter
THIRTY~NINE

I inhaled his scent and closed my eyes. The feel of him against me just felt so right, but I didn't allow myself to embrace him any more than was proper for dancing, since we were at my wedding. I was about to become Adam's bride, and I owed him the respect of being faithful, even if it killed me.

"You look so beautiful this evening, Synthia. You make everyone here pale in the face of your beauty," he said softly against my ear.

"Says the man in a tuxedo. You, out of everyone else here, should be banned from wearing something that makes you look so," I stopped talking because if I finished that, I'd be begging him to sift me out of here to do inappropriate things. The man was sinful in a t-shirt, but in a Versace-styled tux, the man was dangerously seductive.

"Sexy, huh? Can't look at me?" he purred as he inhaled my scent. It made heat pool to my core for him.

"We shouldn't be dancing," I said, trying to pull away, but he kept me there.

"Why? Because you still want me or because I want you, Synthia?" He growled low against my neck as he flicked his tongue against my pulse wickedly as his head hid his actions from everyone else in the room.

"You want me to be honest? Both. I want you. Right here, right now. Is that what you wanted to hear? Are you happy now? Because the answer is yes! I'm afraid you'll make me do things I shouldn't do. I'm not the type to cheat on anyone. I refuse to become that woman to any man, and Adam deserves better from me. I can't cheat on him; not even for you, Fairy."

He smiled, and it made me blush with how sinful it looked on his beautiful mouth. Knowing that this would be the last time I allowed myself around it hurt deeply. I felt hot tears pushing against my eyes, but I managed to keep them hidden, just barely. He held me as we effortlessly continued to dance, oblivious to everyone else around us.

"Have you fed from him?" he asked quietly, and as I lifted my eyes, I flinched as I saw the pain bared in his bronze depths. "Have you fed from Adam, yet?"

"No, I was well-fed before I left your bed this morning. You are a beast when it comes to hunger, but you make sure I'm always fully sated," I replied with a small smile.

"Good," he whispered, but his smile had gone behind the clouds as surely as the sun on a rainy day.

"Are you fully healed now, from the iron?" I asked.

"Worried about me?" he asked as a smirk lit up his generous mouth.

"Always," I replied with mischief dancing in my eyes. "Someone has to worry about my fucking Fairy."

"*Your* fucking Fairy?" he asked, lifting a brow.

"Syn," Adam said from behind me. "It's time. Ryder, Eliran was looking for you a few minutes ago. He said it was urgent."

"Time for what?" I asked as he pulled me closer to his side.

"We have to sign the binding agreement with our parents," he answered. I ran my thumb over Ryder's arm before dropping my hands and stepping back and away from him. He dropped his arms at the same time, but where my face was a mask of pain, his was blank again.

I accepted Adam's arm and walked back toward the area that had been set up for this formal signing of the contracts. The signing was more than uncomfortable, considering I wanted nothing more than to wipe the ugly smirk off of the Light King's face.

We moved closer as the Kings discussed something quietly; they stopped as they noticed we were approaching. I felt the vise around me loosen with the smirk Adam shot me. He leaned over and whispered in my ear softly.

"My dad can take yours. Willing to bet on it?" he asked in a stage whisper, making me laugh outright.

"I don't like my dad, so no. I'm willing to help yours just to make sure he wins," I replied as I winked back, which caused him to beam a wide smile.

"Sign the contract," Dresden growled, not finding our little joke funny at all. I hesitated and turned to look at Adam.

"Can we have a minute?" I asked.

"No," Dresden growled.

"Of course," Kier answered.

"Which is it?" I asked, raising a brow at them both.

"You have a minute, but make it fast," Dresden said with annoyance stamped across his brow.

When we had enough privacy I turned to face Adam. "What's up, Adam?"

"Nothing. Why do you ask?" he replied, but he wouldn't look me in the eye.

"Oh, no reason; besides the fact that I have known you long enough to know when you're upset. Now spill it."

"There's nothing wrong; this is just moving fast."

"Do you want out of this? Because, if you do, I'll personally scour the earth to find another way to save Faery," I whispered.

"You know as well as I do, that there is no other way. Had there been an alternative, Ryder would have found it by now and kept you," Adam replied.

"This is me and you, Adam. We can handle this. We will make the best of it, and I do love you. We have more than most people would in our situation."

"We do, don't we?" he asked, smiling. I nodded at him, and we both took a deep breath like we were going into battle or something.

We walked over to where our parents stood with our hands entwined. I watched as Adam bent down to sign his name on the leathery vellum of the contract.

No blood was called for on this one, but it felt as if I'd signed it with much more than my own blood.

I smiled at Adam as both sets of parents shook hands warily over the table and we stood together in silence. We were doing this; we were getting married and saving Faery—together. There were more pros here than cons. I wasn't alone; I was with my best friend. It could have been a lot worse. The Demon could have seen me married to some complete stranger, and then I'd be here with him. I would marry Adam, and I'd learn to love him to the best of my ability, and, in time, it could become so much more.

Of course, I was in love with Ryder, but I wouldn't let that come between us. I could forgo what I wanted, for what was needed. We would make strong babies, and who knew? Maybe someday I would fall in love with Adam, *truly* fall in love with him.

Adam watched as I bent down to sign my life away with a grim look on his face. When our parents had done the same, something passed between us— acceptance at the cards we'd been dealt I guess. He held out his hand, and I accepted it. We made our way to the raised dais where we would be presented the children of the land. We were seated in comfortable-looking chairs, which was a blessing as the heels Mari had glamoured were already killing my feet. It was supposed to have been the first thing on the agenda from what Mari had mentioned, but everything was off-kilter here tonight. Maybe the Fae needed to hire some wedding planners or something to keep each stage of this event on track.

A long line of women with children and tiny infants lined up in front of us. I was overwhelmed as one after another pushed her child into my arms for a blessing. This went on for at least an hour, and Adam watched with a grin on his lips. Or, at least he did until

I placed one in his arms.

"What the hell, Syn? What do I do with *it*?" he exclaimed as he took the squirming bundle and held it in front of him with a look of sheer horror.

"Hey, I'm not the only one who needs practice here," I said, smiling impishly. My smile dropped as a hush stole over the entire crowded gathering. I looked across the room to find everyone staring at Adam. "Give me back the baby. I don't think you're supposed to hold it," I whispered.

He handed it back as we watched the crowd. They continued watching us closely as if Adam would have gobbled it up and digested the small being I now held against my chest. The mother quickly snatched the small child from my arms and glared down at me.

"Oops?" I offered with wide eyes, unsure of what else to say. What the hell was wrong with these people?

"Synthia, a future King does not show interest in the young. It's a woman's job, and for Adam to do so would mean he has other interests in them," Mari placed a hand gently upon my arm. A small tug at her lips and a gentle twinkle in her eyes at least told me that she didn't think I was a complete idiot.

"Oh, well I assure he has no interest in your child other than the normal prince type stuff. I'm sorry if I gave you that worry," I said a little sheepishly to the mother of the infant. Mari smiled and nodded approvingly, and gave a dismissal of the woman who was gone with the simple gesture. The woman sifted out of the room the moment she had been allowed to by the reigning queen.

"I think I'm going to need a notepad to keep up

with the dos and don'ts here," I mumbled under my breath.

"I may need to borrow it," Adam said, smiling impishly as he elbowed my shoulder.

Another infant was placed in my arms within moments of the other. I looked at it, and felt its pale, cold skin; it didn't look as healthy as many of the others had. "It's sick," I said to Adam who had also gone still at seeing the child's pale color. I looked up at the mother to find fat tears rolling down her cheeks. "She is sick already," I said and watched as the mother nodded with fear lighting in her blue and green eyes.

I felt my heartbeat accelerate, and the beat of it throbbed in my ears. I sent my power rushing through the infant and pushed with a gentle probing that made the tiny infant wail. The mother cried out, but Adam leapt from his chair to hold her back for a moment as I cleansed the infant from the sickness that was killing its small chance of survival.

When I had finished, it had a radiant glow that the other infants had. No longer was the small, pale infant sickly; its eyes had opened, and it was staring at me with the same wonder that its mother now held. "I've done what I could for the baby for now," I whispered. "We have to figure out what is wrong with the land, and why Danu isn't accepting them before it will truly be safe, though," I said softly as I handed the child back. The entire assembly sat in awe of what I had done.

"That's enough infants for now," Mari choked out. She had her hand over her mouth and looked like she was holding back tears. She took a few deep breaths and composed herself. "Time for the binding of the hands," she whispered and smiled reassuringly at the line of women.

I stood, with help from Adam; the long sweeping skirt of the dress made it impossible to do it on my own. When his mother had fixed the train and made sure I passed another quick inspection, we headed for the dais where the Dark King's throne was usually placed. Adam's father and the Light King stood at arm's length and the Light King had a calculating gleam in his eyes as he watched us make our way to them. Asshole was probably trying to figure out how to kill me after the ceremony was done without getting caught.

We climbed the stairs and stopped just in front of the two Kings. We stood with our hands entwined, and I looked through the crowd gathered around us as we held our hands out for the fathers to wrap the handfasting silk around them and complete the ceremony. I knew who I was looking for, even though I tried to keep him from my mind as I stood next to Adam.

Ryder was standing to my left with his men, close to a set of large cedar doors, as if he was planning to leave me without saying goodbye, *again*. It was probably for the best; seeing that I had fallen in love with him but was marrying Adam. I hadn't even thought it was possible for me to love a Fae, and yet, I did. His eyes were locked on our hands as Kier presented the long, multi-colored silk ribbons that would bind our wrist together.

When Adam's father began addressing the assembly, my heart increased in tempo as I felt the silk ribbons begin to wrap around our wrists. I felt a moment of panic before the calm settled over me as the warmth from Adam's hand sank into me. Or maybe it was a comfortable numbness, since I was giving up my Fairy; my enemy and one of the only men I'd truly ever loved.

I watched Ryder as he looked toward me, his eyes narrowed with cold, dangerous glint lighting in them. Eliran was telling him something with a helpless gesture of his arms and Ryder turned to him, his mouth slanted at an ugly angle as he snapped at the healer. When he turned toward us with his men at his back, I saw victory shining his eyes.

I turned to look at Adam as something tingled inside my mind with awareness. I watched in slow motion as everyone else stopped to look around, confused at what was happening. Something was off; terribly off. The air grew thick around us until it was impossible to breathe it in. Someone screamed, and it looked like Fae were trying to sift out of the room, but something was holding them trapped inside of it. I locked eyes with Ryder's, who had a look of stunned disbelief in his eyes as he comprehended what was about to happen.

I looked at Adam and tried to throw up a shield around him, as well as Kier and Dresden, a fraction of a second before there was a blinding burst of light and the dais exploded from an energy bomb that detonated somewhere underneath us.

~~*~*~* Ryder *~*~*~*~*

Watching her hold infants had been strangely amusing. She was awkward, and yet, she still accepted one after another. Watching her sign those fucking contracts had been straining my ability to hold the beast inside. I'd wanted nothing more than to sift to her and take her away from here.

"Shall we leave now? We have held up our end of this contract. It's time to go home and finish what you need to there. This is not helping you, or her. I can see the strain on your face. Let's go home, brother," Zahruk says, lowering his eyes.

"We told Kier that we would stay until the vows were spoken, and the ceremony is complete. He thinks I have some control over her," I reply, balling my hands into fists.

"You do, but not like he thinks," Z continues, and I narrow my eyes on him.

"Ryder, a word please," Eliran says, pushing his way through the crowd of onlookers.

"What is it, Eliran?" Zahruk growls, impatient to return home.

"Sire, I've been running tests on Synthia from the blood I took from her house when she was sick," he says as he steps closer.

"And," I reply coldly. As if it matters now; she hasn't been sick since I pulled her out of her house and my patience is waning.

"And I ran tests. Every one of them I could think of. She has no iron in her system, which would be the common culprit for making a newly Transitioned Fae sick, and, well, her being raised in the human world you would think her count high, but it was surprisingly low."

"This is what you came here to tell me? That her iron was low?" I growl. The beast is smiling, and he's pissing me off.

"No-no, of course not. So I continued running test after test, but everything came back negative."

"Spit it out, healer. We've no time for this right now," I snarl and have to remind myself that he is only doing his job. He isn't the one I'm upset with, I remind myself.

"So, I ran a pregnancy test on the blood, which takes longer when levels are low," he says, and I narrow my eyes on him.

"Why would you do that?" I snap. The beast is chuckling, and I feel my hackles rising. *What the fuck did you do?*

"Because it is the only test I hadn't run yet. I had also requested her files from Alden, who had been very helpful in obtaining them from the Guild," he rambles nervously and takes a small step back as I turn my full attention on him. "I ran it eight times because the hormone levels were very low," he continues, and I turn to look at the dais where their hands are about to be bound together.

"And?"

"All eight came back positive. Synthia is pregnant. She would have to have conceived within the last month. I wanted to be sure when I told you, sire. She can't be the cure to our world as Ristan has seen. Not with Adam's child anyway, because she's already pregnant," Eliran says, but I'm no longer listening to him.

Mine, she's mine; I told you...I fixed it, she's ours forever! The beast says with a victorious laugh.

I turn to head toward the dais. But as I approach them, I feel it and can see the alarm and confusion in her eyes as she looks around the room. Something is wrong. The air is thick with evil. I watch in shock as she allows her brands to glow and pulse with magic, but they don't ignite, not enough.

She looks at me as her shield goes up around Adam and the Kings, and the dais erupts into a mass of blinding light; sharp splinters and stone projecting outward from an energy bomb beneath it. The beast lets out a roar and I try to sift, but something is stopping me from doing so. *What* the *fuck*!? *Null spell.* No one is sifting, except those who cast the damn thing. I don't have time for this shit. "Find her!" I shout at them.

My men run, following me as I move as fast as my legs will take me to her. For the first fucking time in my life, I'm afraid. Fucked, that's what we are; *fucked*. Reduced to human strength, none of us can sift until the fucking spell wears off. The dais is gone now and nothing but splintered wood and stone remains. There is a choking fog of smoke and ash that tries to blind us as we dig through the wooden supports and stone. I can see and smell blood. I've tasted hers, and I can smell its crimson purity spilled within the room. She isn't immortal yet. I see Adam, Kier, and Dresden struggling to their feet from the wreckage. My men and I shift through the rubble and can't find any sign of Syn. Voices shriek in distress all around us.

"Dristan, anything?" I ask, trying to keep the panic from my voice.

"Yes, and no, Ryder. Savlian just said he saw another Fae sift out with her right as the dais exploded, but he could not prevent them from doing so. He was one of the Fae from her memory. Not the leader though; it was the one who questioned him. The one who tried to stop it from getting out of hand," Dristan says, watching me closely.

"She's pregnant, Dristan," I let out a long rumbling growl, wrestling down on everything within me so that the beast is not released. He is fighting me, and I can't allow him out yet; not even for her.

"So she is, but Ristan saw her giving birth to Adam's child. Not yours."

I close off all emotion. It's fucking useless to me. "She has no fucking idea that she is pregnant," I reply and fight the anger that radiates like a fucking oven out of my pores. She's been pregnant this entire time, since the beast took over, and now she is in the hands of the enemy with *my* child in her womb.

"We *will* find her, brother." Dristan says, but his eyes fill with doubt and it sinks beneath my skin.

"Just fucking find her, now!" I shout, knowing that wherever she is, she's alone and unguarded, unprotected and scared.

"Ryder," Ristan says, coming up beside me.

"Unless you have found Synthia…"

"No, but we will find her, brother. I'm not sure how this fits into the vision, unless there is more to the vision that Danu hasn't shown me—or, Syn miscarries your child, and still goes through with the wedding. Which, given she was just attacked," he replies with a look of guilt and hopelessness.

"I don't care if we have to scour the entire fucking earth!" My men sense the beast fighting to get out and swarm around me as my voice shakes the building. "We fucking find her! We don't sleep, and we don't feed until Synthia Raine McKenna is safe in my arms. I don't care who I have to fucking kill. I want her *found*!"

Chapter
FORTY

I landed hard on cold icy ground. I inhaled a deep breath, but it was as if this place held little to no oxygen in its air. I doubled over from a burning pain that was radiating up from my side. Strong hands wrapped around my waist, hauled me up from the cold ground and kept me firmly pinned against his body.

"Let me go! Why are you doing this? Who the hell are you? *You!*" I demanded as I was finally able to turn my head and body far enough to see his face behind me and saw that he was one of the men from my nightmares.

"We have to keep moving, Faolán and the rest of his guard are going to be here in a moment, and he wants you dead, Princess," the blonde Fae whispered harshly, his Irish accent stronger than I remembered. Before I could blink, we were in another setting. This time it was a sandy beach, and he was looking around as if he feared an attack.

"Why did you take me away from the only man who can protect me then?" I growled, trying to ignore the excruciating pain from my side, which was stealing the air from my lungs. I'd been wounded, and I was afraid to look at it. I had no idea why this man had taken me, or who he thought was after me. I knew him from my parents' house though; he'd been there on that bloody day.

"Because you are in danger, and he won't stop until you're dead," he replied as he narrowed his eyes and wrapped me into a more secure hold. Before I could try and slam my head against his nose or kick back at his knees, we sifted again; this time into a thick forest. "Stop! Who the hell are you? I know you; I want to know why you were at my parents' house that day." He let go of me, and I fell over on the thick grass on the forest floor.

"I'm the one who shielded you inside that house when you were a child, or tried to. Faolán and most of his personal guards left without me that day. I followed, as soon as I realized what he intended to do. I knew his intentions were not pure, and my king has been blinded by his love for his child. I failed your guardians, Princess. I have been part of his guard ever since, hoping to stop him if he should ever get close to you again. I will not fail you again." His voice was full of anger and pain as he ran his hands through his hair harshly, before continuing. "Enough talking; we need to move," he snapped as he tore off his shirt, revealing a well-defined muscular body. He ripped his shirt apart and tossed a piece behind a tree, but kept the bigger part in his hand as he grabbed my hand once more, and sifted us.

We landed in a dark cave, and I looked around for an exit, or any way to escape the man who was nonstop sifting us further away from Ryder, and his men. He'd find me, I knew he would. I needed to stay put long enough that he could get to me, though, and knew I was steadily losing blood.

If I was right, Ryder would be able to follow the blood trail to wherever we ended up. Or so I had thought, until I caught the Fae in front of me moving his fingers which made the small drops on the ground disappear. He looked up and glared at me before he sifted behind me and pulled me back hard against his naked chest.

Warning bells went off, and I moved to attack him, but he was faster than I was in this stupid dress, and before I could get away from him, he'd pressed me against the cave's sharp wall and chanted a quick spell. Fuck!

"Nice try, but no one must know where you are, my Princess," he gave me a sly smile. "Being able to wield a null spell is one of my few gifts. The Dark Prince and his men don't have much longer before the one I cast earlier wears off, and they can follow. For now, that will keep you from sifting so I can get you to safety," he said and grabbed my arm again, pulling me off the wall and up against him. I wanted to scream in frustration, but it wouldn't do any good. I needed to save my energy to get away from him, and the only way to do so would be to run. He said he was taking me to safety, but how the hell was I to believe him?

We sifted several more times; each place new and hauntingly beautiful. It wasn't until we landed inside a crowded room and had several weapons drawn on us that we stopped sifting. We were inside what looked to be an enormous throne room with over a hundred Fae watching us with a mixture of alarm, suspicion, and curiosity. The room was built with white stonework, and had beautiful Celtic artwork etched in gold, detailing the arches of the high vaulted ceiling as well as in the pillars that supported the cathedral like architecture. The man I was with said something to the soldiers looking at us and his next words couldn't have shocked me anymore if he'd tried.

"Tell the King to come at once. I've brought

Sorcha to him," he growled.

"Which king!?" I demanded, feeling my stomach do a somersault with his words. Here we go again!

There were only four kings, and we'd just left two of them standing in the room where he had grabbed me from. The Blood, and the Horde King were the other two, both of whom had never entered my world, to the best of my knowledge. They were the deadliest of the Fae, and I'd just been dropped into one of their laps by this idiot.

I had no weapons, and I was injured and still dressed in the bell-shaped gown from the handfasting. I looked around the huge hall, making note of each exit and finding none. The only way in was to sift, and as soon as I thought it, the Fae grabbed my arm and shook his head in warning as if reminding me that he had taken care of that little maneuver pretty well.

"I mean you no harm," he said softly, and I realized that he showed no fear in his turquoise and lime eyes. He also looked much younger than I remembered him looking when he'd been in my house when I was a child.

"Why are you doing this to me?" I asked, trying to hide the fear that was licking down my spine with the prospect of being in a strange realm, with one of the deadly kings.

He didn't have a chance to answer as a huge male, who could only be one of the Kings, came out with his eyes searching us. He had light blondish-brown hair, and eyes of the deepest violet and cobalt. I swallowed as something in my chest went off, as if something was unlocked. I felt dizzy as my eyes fastened with those of the unknown king. He looked as dazed as I felt as his hand grabbed his massive chest, as if he was feeling everything I was, at the same time.

"What is this, Cailean?" His voice grated with a heavy burr as he watched me closely. His eyes narrowed on me as I held on to the one he'd called Cailean, my legs threatening to give out from beneath me.

I felt as if the air was being knocked out of me, and everything inside of me was clicking into place like a puzzle unlocking its secrets. I turned my head as someone gasped and covered her mouth. She was almost a twin to Tatiana; only more beautiful, with golden hair and a more defined face. Tears rolled down her cheeks, from eyes that matched mine in color, and pattern.

"It cannot be, Lasair, is it true, is it her?" The woman cried, moving closer to the man who had yet to speak since asking my would-be protector the question.

"Cailean, you had better start explaining!" the King snarled.

"I bring you your daughter, my King," Cailean said as he dropped to one knee rapidly.

"We were told she was dead, so explain how this is possible," the king growled, leveling me with beautiful eyes that didn't seem to leave mine—as if I would disappear if he looked away.

"Faolán misrepresented what happened, Sire. He abused her guardians, and declared her missing, and presumed dead at their hands. He couldn't find her until a few days ago, and he has been trying to kill her ever since. I had to wait for him to strike at her again so I could bring her to you, or he would have guessed my plan."

"Impossible. Why would he lie? He is my heir. He is sworn to abide my word until he challenges me for such right!" the man shouted, and the magnificent stained glass windows shook from the anger in his tone. I remained silent as they argued, as my mind flew with what was being said, grasping onto small things as they clicked together.

"My lord, Faolán is not who you think him to be. He is not your heir; he was never blessed with Danu's true branding. He has sided with the enemy to inherit the heir's true powers. He made a deal with the Mages. They told him that if he obtained the true heir that they could drain her powers from her dead body and make him become what he wanted to be most— an heir acknowledged by Danu. In exchange for their help; he has been helping them destroy Faery."

"Be careful, Cailean: for treason upon the land is a serious crime and you speak of my son, who is not here to defend himself against your charges."

I didn't know what to do, or what to say. More people had come into the hall and were now gathering around us. I wanted to run, to sift out of the room, but, somehow, I could feel that the King was sensing my unease and was ready for anything I tried.

"Tis sorry business, Lasair, but Faolán did as I said. The Mages told him that they foresaw Sorcha as your acknowledged heir. You may ask your daughter, for she watched him kill her guardians. He tried to kill her by firebombing her house just recently, but she had the protection of the Dark King's son and men. He saved her from certain death, as she had yet to Transition fully."

"How did this happen? The brand on her neck was to prevent Transition!"

I felt my entire body shake with his words. He knew of the tattoo on my neck! I couldn't get words out, and I felt a single tear slide down my cheek. These were the people who had left me with humans to die; this man arguing before me was indeed my father.

"I sent Faolán to retrieve her! He would not have tried to kill his own sister. He knew how imperative it was to bring her back. It makes no sense at all why he would do something so horrendous."

"He wants war with the Horde King and has ensured whenever he can that the war will continue. Sorcha was hidden by her guardians when Faolán and the rest of his guard got there. When I arrived, her guardians were dying, and I barely camouflaged her in time. They tore the house apart looking for her." Cailean had so much regret in his eyes as he stated his case. "Sorcha has called him to her with the purpose of killing him, Sire. She cut down some of the warriors which were part of his guard that were also there the day her guardians were killed." Cailean turned his face to me, and the plea in is eye was unmistakable. He expected me to confirm his story.

"What he says is true," I whispered.

The king continued to look at me as if he was afraid I'd vanish.

"What were my parents' names?" I asked.

"That matters not child, for I know as well as you do, that you are my daughter, Sorcha. Our bond has once again been connected, and I feel you are of my blood."

"You sent me to humans; to die?" I asked, stepping back as the woman moved closer, as if she would touch me.

"That's a long story, and one that I will not discuss in this crowded room, child. You are dressed exceedingly well," he said, narrowing his eyes on the dress for the first time.

"I was marrying the Dark Heir," I replied.

"Marrying the Dark Heir?" he asked, looking over my wardrobe again.

"Yeah, the one they just found? I was marrying him."

"The Dark Heir wasn't missing. I would have heard about it before now."

"Uh, maybe you should get out more often?"

"So, Kier lost his boy," he said, shaking his head.

"It seems to me, that you guys seem to lose your children a lot around here."

"We didn't lose you. We hid you. It was to protect you!" the woman said, finally taking her hand away from her mouth.

I looked at the woman and felt nothing from her, but the huge male was definitely connected to me somehow. I could feel him in my bones. As if, by coming here, he'd awoken my past. We were connected. "From what?" I asked, narrowing my eyes.

"Madisyn, not here my love. In private," the king said, directing his words to the woman who still openly wept.

"I don't even know who you are," I said in exasperation, breaking up their private discussion.

"My name is Lasair, and I am the Blood King. This is my Queen, your mother," he said kindly.

I felt a rush of emotions. These people knew about the tattoo, and I felt this man before me. I mean, I really *felt* him, as if he were a part of me. The man who killed my parents said I was his sister, and the man who had taken me from Adam was the one who had tried to stop the Fae from hurting my family.

The Blood King held out his hand, and I hesitated long enough for him to look me over. His eyes went to the wound in my side. "Madisyn, call a healer, now. She's been hurt, darling."

"I'm fine," I whispered.

"Give me your hand. I'll sift you to a room where we can see how bad it is, and explain why we did what we did; to *protect* you. You have nothing to fear from us. What we did was out of love. Our only intention was to protect you," Lasair said, but something in his eyes made me hesitate.

In the end, I gave him my hand, because I was about to collapse. We sifted to a *very* pink room, and inside was a crib with a blanket that had the name Sorcha sewn into it. I looked around the room, and noticed it looked exactly like the one I had as a small child. "This room," I said, but he stopped me.

"I manifested the one they gave you. I wanted you to remember us. It was the least we could do. I need you to know something before my wife comes back. This has not been easy on her. Giving you away was the hardest thing she has ever done; she has been devastated since she gave you over to your guardians. It only became worse when Faolán announced your death. Be kind to her. I can see the hesitancy in your eyes, and we deserve it. I can also feel your need to run from us. Know this, little daughter, I *am* your father, and our blood is connected. Our bond has been re-established. If you run, I will find you. We deserve your hesitancy and the coldness you harbor for us. After we tell you why we did it, maybe then you will see it in your heart to forgive us, or at least your mother.

"She's a good woman, and, as you can tell from the state of the rocking chair, she is in this room a lot. She has never forgotten the child she had to give up. Have a seat, child. I think you should hear the full story from me, so that you understand why we did this," he finished.

"You mean the reason you gave me to humans?" I asked, eyeing the chair with longing.

"Sit down, Synthia, so I can heal your wound. I only sent your mother to find a healer so we could talk before she came back. It's deep in the tissue. No organs seem to have been harmed, or you would not be standing upright."

I sat in the lone rocking chair and eyed the pink crib. It looked as if it had been crafted with loving hands. The carpet was a plush, pale green, with a yellow color on the outskirts of the room. It was a beautiful nursery.

I felt his magic pulsing inside the room as he allowed me to feel it. Instinctively, I tensed against it and reached for the magic within me, but he stopped when he felt me pulling my own around me.

"I would never hurt you. I need you to relax and trust me for right now," he said leveling me with those expressive eyes; where mine were just as blue, his were a beautiful shade of cobalt.

I relaxed, but kept my eyes locked with his. Again, I felt the magic pushing into the torn skin and further inside of me. He was healing the wound from the inside, and I felt the blood vessels, along with the damaged skin, begin to regenerate as they started to heal. When he had finished, I pulled my first deep breath since the explosion and found the injury completely healed.

He smiled reassuringly as I nodded my head and thanked him.

"I'm going to start at the beginning. You need to know the entire story to see what we were up against." He flicked his wrist and a wide, comfortable-looking leather chair materialized, and he slowly lowered himself into it.

"Danu prefers balance between all castes. Each of the monarchs wield power, and the one who holds the most of us all is the Horde King, as he oversees the most dangerous of Faery's creatures. When Alazander ascended to his throne several millennia ago, he was a powerful king, yet peaceful with the other realms. He began taking in anyone who was casteless and his power and realm grew. Unfortunately, as his power grew, he began to abuse his powers and started to attack the other castes. A little over two hundred years ago, my father made a deal with the King of the Horde. My father agreed to not raise arms and going forward he pledged that the Blood Fae would be obedient to the Horde King. He was deceived, and when Father presented his weapon in obeisance, he fell to the treachery of the Horde. The Horde King is the only Fae who can kill another Fae outright without needing weapons. It makes him the deadliest creature in our world," he said bitterly. He held up his hand as I started to interrupt him.

"Let me tell you this, as it does pertain to why we did what we did to you, Synthia." I had no idea what the hell anything that happened two hundred years ago would have to do with me.

"I picked up my father's sword and struck against the Horde in anger, and we have been at war with the Horde ever since. Now, the Fae fight wars in a very different manner than humans. Skirmishes happen up and down our borders, but actual battle is rare, and I had no fear of my father's fate unless I faced the Horde King himself in battle. So far, our war has consisted of the Horde attacking and Blood defending—to attack his lands directly would make matters worse."

"Wait—are you saying that he has pretty much been kicking your ass for over two hundred years and all you can do is just defend?" I was outraged that the Horde King, this badass I had heard of all of my life, the one who accepts anyone, was nothing more than a bully. This idea of the Blood Fae just bending over and taking it was just too much, but if the Horde King was that powerful it made sense; it also made sense as to why the other Fae looked up to the Blood King. The man had serious balls for trying to stand up to the Horde King for over two hundred years. My father nodded grimly and continued.

"Alazander desired your mother to be one of his concubines; he requested that Anise give her as a peace offering to the Horde. He was known to ask other rulers and noble families for their daughters to keep peace between the Horde and their families; he was also not above stealing them. He took what he wanted from people, including their children. Rumors of abuse toward his wife and concubines had reached your mother's ears, and she begged Anise for an alternative. Anise was a good person and a loving great-aunt to your mother, and she arranged our union, and soon it became a love match." He shook his head sadly at the memory.

"Alazander killed Anise for her part in defying him. He hadn't forgiven her for losing the relics and this was just one more mark against her. Now that pompous little shit Dresden sits on her throne. I cut ties with the Light Fae as soon as he took the throne. Anise was ten times the ruler he is." I had to agree with him on that point; anyone was probably better than him.

"Over the years, Alazander hounded your mother and me through his emissaries. Even though your mother and I had several children together he persisted. Actually, it became worse, as all of our children were males and this seemed to be of particular interest to him. He stepped up his demands and his attacks on our borders and your mother became despondent. I would not allow her to make the sacrifice to save my people. She would have, simply because she would have sacrificed herself to save one single life. I couldn't allow her to leave our children motherless, or to allow her to be mistreated at his hands."

I nodded and digested his words. Well, that explained my own loyalty, which could be considered a fault to some.

"Then news came that the Horde was sending the daughters back to their parents in pieces, or broken of mind and body. The Horde King was sending messages to them, reminding them how he was in control of this world and the other rulers were just his puppets. When your older brother joined my army and rode at my side, I couldn't have been more proud, but we were separated in the chaos of a skirmish, and he was lost to us."

I shook my head. That didn't sound promising.

"He was captured and thrown into the Horde's prison. Tortured daily, but kept alive so that Alazander could continue punishing him and us. We had a few other boys by this time, but Liam was our first. Eventually, the Horde started sending us pieces of our son as he had done with the others of the realm. For over fifty years, he was sent back to us, piece by bloody piece. I was out on a battlefield when you were born. I should have been beside my wife, but you came too soon, and on your own time schedule."

I narrowed my eyes, but kept listening. Now, he was getting into the good stuff.

"I came home to be handed this beautiful little bundle that had the blue of my wife's eyes, and hair the color of the sands of the Fae desert. This new little being that had my blood and bond, and looked at me with so much trust. I was holding you inside the Great Hall when the missive came; one that would change our world forever." His eyes took on a distant look as his face showed lines of strain. As if the memory hurt him. "The Horde King wanted to strike a deal. He wanted my first born daughter as his concubine, in exchange for our son. Of course, we said no right away. The next day we received a pair of hands delivered to us by a messenger of the Horde. One who explained that if we made the deal, the Horde King would promise no harm to our daughter, and the torture of our beloved son would end the moment we signed."

"Me, for Liam," I said, wondering what I would have done had it been my child being cut to pieces.

"Yes," he said, shaking his tawny head. "You have to understand; Liam had been broken. From the blood bond between Fae father to child, I knew him to be alive and suffering. You, for Liam, and an end to the war; that was the agreement the Horde wanted. I had an entire caste to protect, and a son who had endured far too many years of torture. This wasn't an easy decision, and yet, it had to be made."

"But the Fae play on words, and, for some reason,

you worried that inside this was an out clause. One that would allow him to harm me," I guessed.

He smiled with pride lighting up his beautiful eyes. "You are very smart, child. Not many would guess that."

"I made myself understand as much as I could about the Fae after my par...um, my guardians were killed. I tried to find out anything I could that would help me get revenge," I replied, watching his face, but no guilt marked his bronze skin; only acceptance.

"Well, eventually we agreed to his demands. He had given us five years before we had to hand you over; a show of how magnanimous he could be I suppose. Once we signed the agreement, he gave us Liam, and, as promised, the Horde did cease hostilities to the point that many thought the war had ended already. It was a time of peace and celebration for our people, bought at our family's expense. The people rejoiced and sons stopped dying for what seemed to be a fruitless war.

"We took you to the Harvest Festival that year, and you were the most beautiful child there. You were around four months of age at that time. You had beautiful curls that framed your chubby little cheeks. The Dark King sought an engagement to his son, and it would have been the perfect union, except for the fact that you already belonged to the Horde. I couldn't bear explaining that to Kier, so I had to reject his suit outright."

"I took Cadeyrn as my familiar that day."

"I didn't know that, but you were so small, so innocent, that it would have been impossible to know until you were older that you had. When we returned home, we knew we couldn't hand you over. Not to a man who abused and killed those of the weaker sex. Your mother grew distant, and eventually I knew it was only a matter of time before she gave in and allowed Alazander to take her from us. We had just gotten Liam back, and the damage he'd endured had taken a toll on his mind. We couldn't allow the same thing to happen to you. So we worked together, to hide you. I went into the human world and met with a Warlock who owed a life debt to my brother. I explained what would happen if our war was brought to their door."

He shook his head. "I spun a tale so horrid with what could happen that they had no choice but to take you in, hiding you; not just from the Horde King, but the Guild as well. He was a good man and he and his wife were childless, so this debt became a blessing for them, or so they told me. He was very powerful in the Guild, so we knew you would be safe with them. We had you branded with the triquetra that would hide you in plain sight as a human. The triquetra was supposed to leave you with enough magic to pass as a Warlock's child, and it would prevent you from going through Transition. The only thing that would break the spell was you returning to Faery, but we'd been ensured that you would never be inside of Faery, or exposed to the Fae. I'm guessing something happened to change it." I smiled and nodded at his words. Yeah, Ryder happened. He had come in to my life like a whirlwind, and set wheels into motion that shouldn't have been.

"I painted the wards on the walls inside their house to help protect you from the Unseelie as a whole, as well as anyone seeking to harm you, and in the process broke *our* bond, we'd thought never to see you again."

I felt almost relieved to know at least half of the story. I wasn't some bastard born from a one night stand. I hadn't been rejected, and I'd actually been wanted. From a parent's point of view, I could see where they had struggled with the choice. From a child's point of view, I felt as if I'd been sacrificed. "I watched my guardians being killed by Faolán; it happened as that man Cailean said it did. After that, I put everything I had into getting revenge. My guardians gave their lives to protect me."

"Faolán would not have done what Cailean says. He was sent to retrieve you, so you would be given to the Horde to end the war that had started back up soon after we had sent you to the humans. After a few months of you being inside the human world, we reported your death to the Horde King; in essence, that was what it was like when we cut ties with you. You were, in a sense, dead to us when I cut the bond. We took a young child that had recently passed to the Harvest Feast that year, and buried her small body in a grave that was marked as your own. We'd been foolish to think it would work against the Horde, but we were desperate. Somehow, he knew you hadn't died, and he demanded we find you and bring you back, or give them Liam again, which we could never do. War started again soon after, and there's only one way to end it now. I can't let it become a full out war again. I'm sorry, my daughter."

I swallowed and prepared to say I had understood his dilemma, but before I could answer him; someone sifted in behind me, and a silver torque was placed around my neck and locked in place.

"Sorry, little sister," a rough voice whispered. "But I can't go back to *him*."

"What the hell is this?" I demanded, whipping around and off the rocking chair to look at a blonde-haired man who had scars marring his beautiful face. Piercing blue and violet eyes met and held mine.

"I'm sorry, little one, but you have to go to him.

This will prevent you from escaping until then. This war is a lost cause, and, without you, we will eventually lose to them. The Darkest Fairy still haunts my sleep, and I won't go back alive. He's induced sickness into our lands. He's promised it will stop if he is given what he asked for. *You*," the newcomer said softly. I knew that I was looking at Liam; the one I'd been traded for.

Chapter
FORTY-ONE

I was locked inside the small nursery and left alone. Only minutes had passed since they'd left me in here, but it irked me that I'd been so stupid! I'd felt sorry for the Blood King, and the sacrifices he'd made to save his son. I was such an idiot! I felt hot tears rush to my eyes, but I pushed them away angrily. Tears were useless; I needed to figure out how to escape this place. I was still glaring at the door when I felt a presence behind me. I turned and glared at the Queen of the Blood Fae.

"You look much like I had thought you would, daughter," she said and stepped closer. Her eyes scanned my face as I backed away warily. Another woman sifted in who was almost identical to the woman standing before me; she stood behind my mother. "You must hate us for what we did to you," my mother said softly as she warily tried to get a step closer to me.

"No, I could get past that. It's the whole *you're still to be gifted to the Horde* part that is pissing me off," I snapped as I took a small step back.

"Shut your mouth! You have no idea what we have been through. You will speak to my mother with respect! She is the Queen here." My mother's look alike snapped back with fire in her eyes.

"No, I don't think I will. How would you feel if you were the one being gifted to a monster? I wonder if you'd be so quick to be respectful then," I replied, never taking my eyes off the woman.

"Enough," the Queen said and shook her head. "My name is Madisyn; this is your sister Caera. She indicated the girl behind her with a small motion of her hand. Your brothers and sister in-law are waiting downstairs to meet you. I was told that you were in a marriage celebration to the Dark Heir. Was it completed?"

"No, I am not married to Adam," I said, watching pain flash through her ageless eyes. She was trying her best to hold her emotions in, as was I. At this point, I wasn't sure what to feel or think; the whole situation was rather overwhelming.

She nodded softly. "That's good. We would like to assist you in dressing, if we may, Sorcha—"

"It's Synthia," I interrupted. Sorcha was cool, but I liked my name better. She nodded and a flash of pride showed in her eyes.

"Synthia was actually the name I had hoped they would give you. Lasair and I had talked about it, but I didn't know on which name they had decided for you." She nodded with a watery smile; she looked so sad and full of regret. "Were they good to you?" she asked wistfully.

"They were very good to me. There's not a day that goes by that I don't miss them." I tried to hold the tears back. No, no matter what happened, they wanted the best for me. She nodded and it looked like she was fighting tears with the relief that this information brought. My mother abruptly cleared her throat and continued.

"Just to make you aware, the couriers have been sent in preparation of what is going to happen—we can't delay any longer, without risking more of his wrath for our actions. Tomorrow, there will be a feast held here for the celebration of your return. The Horde King will be welcomed, as will the rest of the castes, to witness the exchange for the gift of peace." I barked with laughter at her sober words.

"So, I really was the *Gift*!"

"Sorry?" She looked confused.

"When Faolán came to get me, he kept demanding to know where the *Gift* was. For over fifteen years, I have been left to wonder what he had been talking about."

"For years, that was what the family called you; it just hurt less to think of you that way." Tears began to run down her face, and my sister rushed to hug her. I felt very awkward for a moment and reached out tentatively to her, and, the next thing I knew, I was engulfed by my tearful mother who cried like her heart was breaking. After a few moments of just holding her tight, she whispered in my ear.

"I've read the Blood Oath a thousand times, Synthia. I'm afraid there is no way out of it. You must be presented to the Horde King, but that doesn't mean you have to stay his."

I felt my hands tremble. She was trying to tell me there was a way out? "Speak plainly. I don't like word games."

"Kill him, and then you can come back to us, or

go…home, to the human world. If you can escape after it is done, you will have to decide on what it is you want. He has many sons, as the Horde does not often breed female children. It's why Alazander wanted the Light Fae in his lineage. It stands to reason that his sons might allow you to live, even if you had killed the king. They need us; the Light is the one breed that usually ensures female children. Your brothers and father can't know that we plot; to do so is to go against everything the Blood Fae stand for. Your sister and I have thought long and hard on how to fix what is in the contract. This is the only solution we have found." I looked at my sister, who nodded solemnly at me, and then back at our mother. Then, I stepped away, shaking my head.

"You want *me* to *kill* the Horde King? Do you have any idea how crazy that sounds? He's the biggest, scariest thing in this world, and my own. He is the only person who can kill the Fae, and make them really dead. I was an Enforcer for the Guild; I did assassinations for a living and even I won't go down that road of crazy!"

"If you fail, you only lose your life. You will lose it anyway if he keeps you, child." Her voice was urgent and filled with more tears. She was trying hard to hide the emotion, but, like me, she was failing. "I can't live knowing that you belong to *him,* when it should have been me. How was I supposed to choose one child over another? I died the day that I handed you to your father to take away. He ordered the guards to lock me inside my room and guard me, because he knew I'd come after you, and I tried to. I never stopped looking over my shoulder, wondering if I'd see you in a crowd, or wondering if you would find your way back to us. Not knowing if you were okay—or if your family loved you enough—was worse than knowing what was happening to your brother at the hands of that monster. I replaced one hell with another."

"You tried to stop the trade. Why?" I asked with my throat closing up.

"Because you were mine. I loved you too much to just let you go, and Lasair knew it. We made the choice together, but when it came time to hide you, I just felt as if my heart was being torn from my chest. Liam knew that I loved him, but you," she stopped, and cleared her throat. "You would never know that we had loved you. You were just a baby, so sweet and innocent. I had no idea where he was taking you, or if they were good people. He thought it best that I didn't know which family he had given you to either, or which country in the human world he'd placed you in."

"They died protecting me from *your* son. They gave their lives to keep me safe. I was loved by them. I was cherished until the day they died," I said, trying to make her feel better, but unsure why I felt the need. She smiled through the tears in her eyes and nodded.

"You seek to give me comfort, while knowing that I have to hand you over to that monster. You must have had a wonderful mother indeed," she replied squeezing my hand softly.

"I did, until Faolán raped her and turned her mind to mush to do his bidding. She would have shot me, had I not been able to cast magic from an early age. He meant to kill me and would have if he had found my hiding place. He tried again right before I came out as the Light Heir, and he would have succeeded if it hadn't been for the Dark Fae warrior who saved me. From what I saw and heard, he isn't yours or your husband's biggest fan." She shook her head in confusion, trying to deny my damning words.

"Faolán tried to collect you when the war started up again. The Horde King kept demanding you and wouldn't believe you had died. Of course, we fought to buy time, but, in the end, your father had to send him," Madisyn explained.

"Well, he's lousy at following instructions. He called the king a weak idiot, and said he would finish this. He wanted war, and, even now, he is working with the Mages who destroy this world. You sent a coldblooded killer to my door; one who wanted *me* dead."

"My son wouldn't do that," she argued, but I could see the sliver of doubt in her eyes.

"When is the last time he was home? It hasn't been recently, and I'm willing to bet he reported his findings, or rather lack of finding me, without a hint of what he did to my parents in his story. Even as a child, I could tell he was kind of an evil nutcase. I don't know what his problem is, but he's definitely trying to take the Blood King and the Horde down. I Transitioned, and I can't lie—not that I would make anything like this up, because it was a pretty crappy thing to go through."

She turned pasty white as she wrung her hands in front of her. I hated telling her everything that happened, because, for some reason, I felt sorry for this beautiful woman and it made me reluctant to hurt her. "I'm sorry. I'm not saying this to upset you. You need to know what he's been up to. I won't be the only one after his head if the rest of the Fae find out he's the one helping the Mages poison this land. I already know of some Fae that have him on video in connection with an attempted mass murder of Fae in the human world."

"If what you say is true, then Faolán is lost to us.

Faery will claim him as a sacrifice to the Goddess Danu. He will pay with blood for his trespass on her children. Only she can pass judgment on her children."

My sister nodded sadly and moved to hug her again.

~~*~*~*~*~*~*~*

A little while later, I was in less clothing, and glad of it, since the other dress made moving near impossible. The shredded, bloody wedding dress was gone, and I'd changed into a more comfortable dress that was made of soft green silk that at least moved and flowed easily and covered me to my ankles. My mother—it sounded weird saying that—had done my hair. She'd smiled the entire time as she and my new sister talked happily around me, as if the Horde King wouldn't be here tomorrow, and everything was right as rain in their world.

Frankly, I felt like I had leaped from the frying pan and straight in to the fire.

I'd wondered how it would have been if I'd grown up around them. They talked about everything, including the noble my sister had been crushing on. I'd been quiet and had just listened the entire time. They were close, and it made me miss Larissa painfully.

We walked down the long, winding staircase slowly, and it seemed like they wanted to treat me as family, not an unwilling guest. My mother and sister didn't seem to want to sift while I couldn't do so. Not that I could do it well every time, but, right now, I'd take landing at Ryder's feet over the Horde King's. When our feet were firmly on the floor, the entire room hushed around us.

I felt the mask go firmly into place as I leveled the

Blood King with an unaffected look. Oh I was pissed, to be sure, but I could play the docile sheep when needed. We walked toward him, and a few blonde-haired men moved closer to him, guarding him from any unseen threat; much like Ryder's men often did.

"Wife," he said with love shining in his cobalt and violet eyes. It was a true love match that these two had together. I don't care what Kier said about the Fae having a tough time understanding love; these two had it bad for each other. It made my mind wander to Ryder. Was he even looking for me? If anyone could save me from the Horde King, it would be him.

"Where is Faolán?" Madisyn asked bluntly.

"The messenger could not find him to deliver the message. The rest of our children are home though, and it is known throughout the lands. I had Liam ring the bell of celebration."

"As it should be. Brenton, Liam, Adaryn, and Cameron, this is your sister, Synthia," Madisyn said, stepping aside for them to see me. No one said anything. We just stood there, sizing each other up. The silence was awkward and uncomfortable, and made more so as we continued in silence.

"I don't understand why we need to do this," Adaryn finally said.

"Adaryn! She's making a sacrifice for us all. For our people," Madisyn said, but no one agreed.

"Not willingly," I finally said. "If I had a choice, I'd sift the flip out of here, and not look back. I don't owe anyone here anything." I surprised myself as I said it, but the smirks from the men around us said they approved.

"She might be related yet," the one called Adaryn

said. He was a few inches taller than the others, and a little more built in the chest area.

"Look at those eyes. Do you still doubt it? Do they not look like mother's?" The one Madisyn had introduced as Cameron said as he stepped closer. I instantly stepped away from him as he continued.

"I'll not harm you," he said.

"I'd harm you. I don't trust easily, and I really don't trust the Fae," I replied carefully, letting him see the distrust in my eyes. They may be family, but I didn't trust anyone here farther than I could throw 'em.

"You *are* Fae. You're aware of this, right?" he questioned, narrowing his eyes as he regarded me as if I was slow in the head.

"So I am, but I was raised with humans. I've already met Faolán, and he's on my to-do list."

His eyes grew large and round. "What did the humans teach you?"

"They taught me to kill, and I'm damn good at it. Faolán will die by my hand. He killed the humans who protected me," I said, taking another step back as he stepped closer. He was trying to corner me against the wall; stupid move. "I wouldn't do that," I said as he pushed me further, testing just how far he could push me.

"Let's see what you got," he whispered, but it wasn't out loud. It was *inside* my head.

I lit up my brands and waited for his face to register disgust as the Light King's had, but, instead, he smiled wider.

"Glow bug; I like it," Cameron said with a smirk.

"You have my brands," my father said, lowering his eyes to my shoulders. "Someone tried to change you, though. Why?"

"I was being trained by the Guild when I got them. They enhance Dark Arts, or the magic which it is cast with. The Dark Heir has the same ones as I do."

"How did you claim the young Dark Heir? It's impossible to pull an heir to you unless you are an heir of equal powers; let alone claim him, if he is the true heir."

"And yet, I managed both. I also could glamour on clothing as early as I can remember." His eyes didn't flinch, but, inside, he was adding it up. I *was* his heir. The one he was to hand over to the Horde King.

"That can't be. Faolán is my heir; he has the markings," he said calmly, but I could hear the hesitancy in his voice. "He was just slow to use the magic."

"Or, he played it out as so. He told me he would drain me, and take what was his. I didn't know what he had meant at the time. It's getting pretty clear that he wants to be the acknowledged heir, at all costs. I've been branded with markings before. It would have been easily obtainable if he was working with the Mages."

"She's right, and he's been hard as hell to find lately," Liam agreed.

I eyed him carefully. He'd been abused, and it showed. It was hard to hate someone when their wounds were bare to see in their eyes. He was a warrior, and yet, he had a vulnerability that you could see. I was still trying to wrap my brain around the

Horde King being the monster they described. I saw that Dresden seemed to be impressed with him, but, then again, according to my father, the Horde King had handed Dresden the crown. What bothered me was Kier and Ryder were allied with the Horde. At this point, I wasn't sure what to believe and I wondered how much of a chance I had at killing the Horde King, or how long I'd live if I tried and failed. Would I be broken by his evil, as Liam now was? Probably. I was good, but I'm pretty sure I wasn't on the same level of badass as the Horde King was.

He caught the worry in my eyes and moved closer, his hands held out as if he was showing me he wouldn't hurt me. "Please, don't hate me," he said softly, his eyes pleading, which made the scar on his face stand out more. Fae normally don't scar after Transition so what had been done to him must have been beyond horrible. "You, for me. It is one hell of a trade, little sister. If he didn't also promise to end the fighting this would be going in a very different direction."

"What does he look like?" I asked curiously.

"He's a little over seven feet tall, with black wings that make him appear taller when he uses them. He's pure evil, the worst sort of creature you can imagine. He has long black hair and blackened eyes with the purest evil in their ancient depths. His power pushes from his pores until you can feel it touching you from the inside. His teeth are razor sharp when he wants them to be. The Sluagh are his warriors, and he is evil enough to rule them. He's the strongest of the Unseelie, little sister, and he gives no mercy, even when it is begged for," he said bitterly.

"Okay then, why didn't you just say he was evil incarnate?" I asked, swallowing down the nerves. They wanted me to kill him!? Seriously; I might as well slap a sticker on my ass that said *dead wench walking.*

"You must have questions for us, and we have many for you," Madisyn said and indicated a sitting area that hadn't been there a second ago. The Fae here used magic a lot more than Ryder ever had when he was around me.

I took the chair that was furthest from the family. They fell easily into them and stared at me expectantly.

"I have no questions," I quickly skipped the subject. "I didn't come here for answers. I came because I was forced to be here. I understand what you did, or some of it anyway. If you would like to ask me something, do so."

"Your mother, you said she was good to you?" Madisyn asked, wasting no time.

"From what I can remember of her, she was everything a mother should have been."

"How did the brand on your neck become inactive?" the Blood King asked next.

"I was taken into Faery for the Wild Hunt by Ryder—he's one of the Dark Princes," I said, not quite knowing if it was true or not. Nothing was as it seemed to me anymore, so I wasn't quite sure what to believe.

Hands flew to mouths on that answer. I closed my eyes and expelled a deep breath as the memory of that night heated me from the inside out.

"I've heard of Ryder. He was claimed to be the Dark Heir?" Adaryn asked.

I met his piercing eyes, and nodded. "Yeah, I guess that was the impression they gave until they found Cadeyrn, who is the Heir."

"Were you hurt? I've never heard of anyone coming out unscathed from it," Adaryn asked.

"I was not harmed. I was claimed by Ryder," I answered honestly.

"So, he took you to his bed, and you allowed this?" my father asked through narrow eyes.

"Yes," I answered, not thinking he had a right to care.

"You actually slept with one of the Dark Princes?" he growled, reminding me of Ryder.

"At the time, I was only a Witch who worked for the Guild. I had no idea what I was when I allowed it to happen, and after that—after coming back to the human world—I started to change. Adam—uh, Cadeyrn the Dark Heir, changed faster, as the brand you put on me had affected him as well. It worked so well it stopped his Transition too, but when I came back from Faery, we both began to change."

"You lived a good life?" Liam asked.

"I prefer to think I did, yes."

They'd sat listening as I told them my story. Tears fell from the women, while the men listened in silence. When I was finished, I looked around at the faces of my family; some still had tears in their eyes, while the men looked proud of what I had accomplished while I'd been assumed to be only a mere Witch.

"I would not change my life for anything. I had amazing friends, and while my life has been anything but simple, it has shaped me in to what I am today."

"You're not mad at us, then?" Lasair asked cautiously with a guarded look on his ageless face.

"I'm not mad at you. I understand now why you did it. At the same time, I'm not the only one who you should apologize to. Your actions didn't only hurt me. I had previously claimed a familiar in the Dark Prince, and when Faolán killed my parents, I stole him from this world with my pain. It was unfair to him and his family as well," I said before taking a breath.

"You are your mother's daughter. This entire time you have been talking, you have been more worried of what happened to those around you," he said, meeting and holding his wife's eyes.

We talked into the night, and, while it felt good to have closure, I missed Ryder and Adam. When I started fighting sleep, my mother smiled. "Come, child, tomorrow is a big event for the entire kingdom, and I'm sure you could use some sleep."

"If you're planning on putting me in the nursery, I think you're going to need a bigger crib," I replied.

"Of course not. I gave away a beautiful baby over twenty years ago. The beautiful woman that has returned now is much too big to fit inside the tiny crib that your father made just for you."

My mother didn't have fangs, but I'd noticed that all of her children, along with my father, did. So much for hoping they went away. I was shown to a room that was beautiful, even though it was done in white. White silk covered the bed and windows. I looked out the window, and smiled at the sheer cliff side that was the view from below the window. They didn't plan on letting me go until I was presented to the Horde King.

"You need some sleep, daughter. Tomorrow, we

will talk more of our plans," she said and stood there hesitantly.

I smiled at her. This woman had been through hell, and, even though it had been a choice, I couldn't blame her for it. I probably would have made the same stupid choices if I thought it helped those I'd loved. I stepped closer, not sure of what I had intended to do, but, in the end, I wrapped my arms around her and listened as she started to cry against my shoulder. Her arms tightened around me as she buried her face in my neck and cried. It was awkward for me, but I knew she needed this; I'd seen it in her eyes.

We were still standing like that when my father came around the door and stopped dead in his tracks. He swallowed and smiled sadly. "Madisyn," he whispered, but I shook my head.

"She's fine," I replied, tightening my own arms around her. For some reason, I didn't want her to stop hugging me. I swallowed back my own tears as my siblings sifted into the room, as if brought by their mother's tears. I wondered what it would be like to have this many people who cared about me in my life.

My sister watched with her own tears streaking down her face while my brothers looked on uncomfortably, as any male would with a crying female on hand. When Madisyn pulled away, she smiled. "Thank you. I'd thought to never hold you against me again."

I didn't say anything. I couldn't. Tears were choking down any words that tried to come up as my throat grew tight with emotion. She smiled and brought her hand up to touch my cheek. "If you need to cry, daughter, I will hold you."

"Crying will change nothing. In the end, tears can

only be used against you. You'd do well to remember it tomorrow, for if he sees a kink in our armor, he will use it."

"You sure she doesn't have balls?" Liam said, stepping closer to me.

"Liam!" my mother cried.

"Oh, I've got big balls. I beat every male in my class just to prove how big they were," I said, smirking at him.

"We need sleep, and to prepare our defenses for when the Horde King comes tomorrow," my father said with pride shining in his eyes.

Chapter
FORTY-TWO

I was dreaming. I knew it, because I felt weightless and the day's events no longer seemed as overwhelming as they really were. I was dressed in a soft, pastel-pink baby doll nightgown that showed way too much to be considered appropriate. I closed my eyes and inhaled the intoxicating scent of Ryder. I made a sound that was half need, half hunger deep in my throat, before I turned from the bed to look at the door.

He stood there in a midnight-colored cloak. His face was hidden by the shadows, until he pushed the hood off, and revealed his face. "It's about time, Pet. I was beginning to think you'd never sleep."

"I knew you would come for me," I said, slipping off of the bed and standing up. I was ready to go, but then the weightless feeling came back. "You're not here; this is a dream," I whispered and lifted my eyes to his as my smile fell.

"I need to know where you are and how badly you are hurt," he said, stepping closer to me.

"I'm with my parents, and I wasn't hurt too bad. It was easily healed."

"Funny girl," he retorted, "Tell me where you are being held, Synthia."

"I'm with the Blood King and Queen," I said and smiled as his eyes widened with shock as my words sank in.

"Why are you with the Blood King?" he asked carefully, placing his hands on my shoulders and pulling me close against his body.

"Because, he is my father," I whispered as I pressed myself against him and lifted my arms around his neck.

"Synthia, this is serious," he growled throatily as he lowered his mouth to the tender flesh behind my ear and nuzzled it with his nose softly. It sent heat pulsing to one particular spot between my thighs. "I need you to tell me why you think they are your parents, when you wouldn't believe the Light Fae was," he said.

"Ryder, they knew about the tattoo that suppressed my powers, as well as the wards on the walls of my house. They did it to hide me, so you were right, they didn't abandon me. They did it to protect me, and when I met my father something inside of me clicked into place. As if the final pieces to my life were meeting and connecting. I felt him inside of me. They said they took me to the Harvest Festival, and they also told me that they buried a child in a tomb that was marked for me. They did it all because they agreed to some sort of contract with the Horde for my father to get my brother back and stop the fighting between the Horde and the Blood Fae. Now that I'm back, they said they have to give me over to him, or this stupid war they have going will never end with him."

He pulled back from me and shook his head in wonder. "That means you really aren't the Light Heir.

Shit."

"Does this mean I don't have to marry Adam now?"

He hesitated, but when I tried to pull away from him as the pain lashed through me with his unspoken words, he pulled me back. "No, you don't have to marry Adam. The contract is void if you're not the Light Heir. This puts a new spin on things, though, and we still need to get you out of the Blood Court."

"Well, then there's also the part where I'm to be given to the Horde King tomorrow." I mumbled it, because saying it out loud just tasted dirty.

"They are planning on giving you to the Horde? Are you sure?" he asked as everything in his face, emotion wise, shut down.

"That's their plan, and, of course, I'm once again unable to sift because of a stupid necklace," I showed him the torque that Liam had magically wielded around my neck.

"At least, for now you are safe, and I know they won't harm you," he said hesitantly as he walked me with his body backward, his hard muscles pressed against mine until my legs folded as they connected with the bed.

I fell back against the soft mattress with a startled squeak, but his body pressed and held mine down, stifling any other complaints from my lips. He didn't kiss me. Instead, his lips curled in to a wicked smile as his fingers played with a soft tendril of hair that had fallen over my face.

"They plan to give me to the Horde King tomorrow in some kind of ceremony in front of the entire kingdom," I said softly, and quickly wetted my lips.

"I bet they do. It's a show to ensure the Horde does not retaliate while under truce. Do you know anything else they have planned?" he continued.

"No, they plan to go through with giving me over, and that's the end of it. Ryder, if he is like they say he is, I need you to tell me everything you know about the Horde King; weaknesses, shortcomings, anything that can help me—because I think the only way to get myself out of this mess is to kill the Horde King," I said, knowing if I could tell anyone my plan, it was Ryder.

His eyes grew large and round. "You're going to kill the Horde King? That's a joke, right?" he asked, his eyes once again narrowing as he took in my face, which was all the proof he needed to tell him I wasn't joking.

"No, it's the only way to void the contract my parents made with him. We've thought him missing this entire time and he's been here the whole time. My parents told me he makes regular demands from them, so he's got to be around. If I take him out, I'll be free, Ryder. I'll be free to go with who I want to, and I can help you find the real Light Heir and get the relics."

"You're talking about killing the Horde King; the *fucking* Horde King. Have you even thought about how disastrous that would be, not to just to your health, but to the entire caste of the Blood Fae? Or did your newly found family talk you into it?" He was mad, and it showed, resonating like a tuning fork as his entire body pressed against mine.

"It's the only way I can get away from him. I'm going to the *Horde King*! I'm supposed to be some timid female. He'll never expect it, so it's perfect."

Ryder glared down at me, "You think you're the first fucking person to try killing him? He can't be killed; your parents are sending you on a fucking suicide mission."

"My father didn't ask me to do it, and I won't let him hurt me. There's a way—there has to be a way to kill him," I argued.

He was right, it was a suicide mission, and while it sounded impossible, there had to be a way to do it. If not, how had the last Horde King managed it?

"I'm coming to get you, so get any thoughts of killing the Horde King right out of that mind of yours." He lowered his mouth and kissed my forehead gently before his hand slipped between us, and ran over the flesh of my abdomen. "Promise you will let me save you and then we can figure out what to do about the contract."

"I can't promise you that," I whispered and searched his eyes.

"Dammit, woman," he growled before claiming my lips in a bone melting kiss. "I'm coming to get you. Don't do anything stupid."

"Ryder, I need you," I moaned hungrily, but noticed he was moving away from me to stand up.

"Be a good girl for me and I'll save you from the big, bad Horde King. I'm coming to get you, Pet, so remember you just admitted that you need me. Watch for me tomorrow, and don't let these people talk you into doing anything stupid…like killing the Horde King who can't be killed by just fucking anybody."

"You gonna scale the walls and be my Prince Charming?" I asked, raising a delicate brow in question.

"No Pet, I'll be your Prince *Fucking* Charming," he smiled wickedly and disappeared.

I allowed a single sob to escape my chest, but it wasn't until someone else started to form that I really sobbed. She was beautiful with long blonde curls, and blue-green eyes. An uncontrollable sob racked my body as she looked around surprised until her eyes landed on me.

"Synthia," she whispered and ran toward me as I stood and opened my arms.

I was still dreaming, I knew, because she was dead. I'd killed her myself by deflecting the bullet she had aimed at me on that horrible day. There. I was sure I was dreaming, because, here, she had no blood from the gunshot, and no evidence of the horror that she'd endured at the hands of the Fae.

"Momma," I whispered, afraid she'd disappear on me.

"Oh, baby, you're so grown up now," she whispered and moved to close the distance between us.

"Momma," I whispered and threw myself in to her arms. God, she felt so real. "I'm so sorry!" I sobbed, finally letting it all out.

"Synthia, you were only five years old. You couldn't have saved us from the Fae. You did as I told you to, and it's the only thing I wanted you to do that night. I need you to know that we have never blamed you for what happened to us. Never has it crossed our minds, baby. You gave us what we couldn't give ourselves; a beautiful daughter who, even though she was shy, loved us in her own way. You gave us the innocent love of a child, and that itself was the greatest gift we could have ever known. We always knew that someday someone would come to try and take you away, but you were the one thing in our lives worth dying for. I wouldn't change my life. I was a mother, and you make me proud to call you mine."

"But I could have saved you both. I was strong, even then. One spell and we could have all been protected—we could have all lived," I cried, pulling away from her.

"And if you couldn't? We made a choice that night, Synthia; one that ensured that you would survive. A mother never takes a chance with her child's life. I knew what they wanted when they came to the door. I could feel their hatred even before they knocked on it, and kicked it in. I knew how evil he was then. There was no way in hell I would allow him to find you."

"I'm being given to the Horde King tomorrow, so you died for nothing," I swiped the tears away furiously.

"I know, but you won't end up unhappy, baby. You will find your love; I promise you that. Synthia Raine, listen to me carefully. Hear what I am saying. Someday someone is going to look at you with a sparkle in their eyes as if you are the most beautiful woman alive. They'll look at you like you are everything they've ever wanted, everything they've ever dreamt about. Wait for it, my daughter, for he will be the light that brings you to life, and lights your way through the darkness."

I smiled through the tears. "I want what you and daddy had," I replied softly.

"That is the key to finding what you need, Synthia; remember it always. Please remember that our sacrifice was not in vain, for you lived. You carry us with you and you will always keep us alive. In here," she touched my heart. "Never forget us. Remember, we loved you more than life, so when it became a choice, we made the right one. We have no regrets and you shouldn't either."

I woke crying this time. Screw sleep; that shit wasn't working for me. I sat up, walked to the windows, and tried to open them, but they wouldn't budge. I was freaking locked in! I paced the room angrily. I was replaying Ryder's, and then my mother's, conversation in my head. In less than twelve hours, I'd be gifted to none other than the Horde King.

I was glad to find that I wasn't walking around half-naked and that I was still in the long black nightgown I'd glamoured on before bed, not the pink baby-doll nightie from my dream. I went back to the large window and looked out again. Was Ryder out there even now, searching for me? Or was he planning to kill the Horde King outright to claim me? He'd given me to Adam, basically on a fucking platter. But that had been to save his world, and now I wasn't the Light Heir, so it had to be off the table…right? He couldn't scale the walls and save me and then hand me off to another man.

Right?

Maybe?

Dammit!

I was still pacing when Adaryn sifted into the room, wearing all black. I jumped into a fighting pose and leveled a mean glare at him, at which he laughed.

"Relax. I just came to check on you. My room is next door, and you're a loud walker."

"Is that so?" I asked.

"Come, you're not the only one still awake," he said.

I wrapped my arms around my chest and glamoured on a long black skirt and matching long sleeve knit top, since the chill of my dreams had seeped in to my bones. I walked with him down to a large room where the rest of my family were sitting and talking already.

We sat for hours with them asking me about my previous life that we didn't get to talk about yet, and me doing the same. It was sorta comforting knowing they were semi-normal. They argued like siblings and even our parents butted in with a snarky comment here and there. They had what I had pined for after my guardians had been killed.

The time came to prepare, and the palace was a flurry of activity. Spells for peace were being written in blood on the walls by artisans as weapons were being sharpened by the men at arms. They were planning for an attack, or maybe they were planning against one. It was all happening so fast.

If Ryder couldn't get me out of this, I still knew he would eventually find the cure for Faery, and, with it, our worlds would be saved. I'd escaped one life, to land in another that was way worse. One I wouldn't walk away from. I'd actually felt torn and awkward at the thought of marrying Adam, but now facing the Horde King, it seemed almost insane to have complained about it at all.

I couldn't get a break, nor could I get away from my family to see if Ryder was here to save me. I wanted to cry and scream at the unfairness of it all. But what good would it do? The McKenna's had pride, and it might be my downfall, but I'd get through this somehow. Ryder would make it; he'd promised he would get me out of this. For the first time in my life,

I felt like a damsel in distress waiting for her prince Charming.

If Prince Charming didn't come, I was probably going to kill the Horde King, or die trying...I was leaning toward the whole *die trying* part.

Chapter
FORTY-THREE

I was dressed in an elegant light blue gown that had a slit to the waist, and a crisscross bodice that sat low enough to show off the top cleavage of my breasts. My mother wept while she brushed my hair for the last time. She continued to brush it until it looked as if it was made from the same silky soft material of the dress. Silver torques of royalty had been placed on my biceps, while one with a blood-red ruby in the center was secured to my neck as the other was removed. I was asked to hold still so that the painter could paint the outlines of my brands with the small paintbrush that had crimson colored paint on the tip.

"She will paint them so he knows who you are, and of what blood you were born of," my mother explained.

It took over an hour of being prepared before my mother had me slip on the small flat sandals that tied up to my calves. No one spoke as the time grew closer. Everyone in the room was acting more like this was a mourning procession than a gifting ceremony... whatever the hell *that* was. It wasn't until a translucent veil was placed over my hair and the silver circlet was secured over the veil on my head that I allowed myself to exhale a shuddering breath.

"The room, please. I'd have a word with my daughter alone before she goes to the Horde," my mother said, while keeping her eyes to the floor. When everyone was gone, she pulled out a small silver dagger. "This was blessed by Danu, for the protection of the princesses of the realm. It is said to be the only thing that can kill the Horde…that can kill *him*," she whispered in a hushed tone as if the Horde King was lurking behind the door.

"What the hell is this supposed to do? Pick his teeth after he eats my bones?" I asked, holding the small thin-wisp of a dagger up. It was tiny! I'd seen toothpicks that were more impressive than this thing was. I raised my eyes to hers and caught her frowning.

"It's small, Synthia, but it is enchanted. You only need to pierce his heart with it."

"Do we even know if he *has* a heart?" I gave her a small smile, but it failed to help the seriousness of the situation. She helped me to tuck it away in the bodice of the dress.

"I should have gone to him when he offered for me. If I had, you wouldn't be in this situation," she said, wiping angrily at the tears that formed in her eyes.

"I'm not some weak, untrained warrior. If he tries to hurt me, I will find a way to kill him," I replied guardedly. "We can't undo the past…mother." I hesitated calling her it, but the tears that fell freely made it easier. She was my mother. This woman had worried about me and my well-being the entire time I had been gone, and she had never given up on me. "We can only move forward. If I can find a way to come back to you, I will."

She hesitated as she moved closer, but I once

again held my arms open for her. I allowed her to hug me because right now, I needed it as much as she did. When she pulled away, her hand came up to cup my cheek before she pulled the veil over my face.

"You are stronger than anything I could have wished for in a child. You are a beautiful person, Synthia. Most would have tried to escape from us. You owe us nothing, and yet you still give us this. You deserve so much more and have endured too much for someone of your tender years. I wish I had more to give you, but know this, my daughter—I never stopped loving you; even when I was told you were lost to us forever. Deep in my heart, I knew that you would find your way home to me when the time was right."

"Well, technically, I didn't find you. If it hadn't been for Cailean, Faolán probably would have killed me. Faolán might be your son, but he's not on your side anymore. I know you don't think him capable of it, but I've met him. I know it's hard to think of your child doing something like this, but I can describe everything about him. He lives inside my nightmares and haunts me. He has since I was five years old."

"I believe you, Synthia. He will be brought home to pay for his transgression."

"Mother," Caera said, coming into the room. "It's time. The Horde and his retinue will be here soon."

I chewed my bottom lip nervously. Where the hell was Ryder? He was a little late for scaling the damn walls. I turned and looked at my sister as she kept her eyes to the floor. She was afraid to look at me. I could sense it in her posture. "Caera, it was very nice to meet you."

Well, that was about the lamest thing I could have

said.

"I wish you well, I also wish you luck in what you are about to do, sister," she said, finally lifting her eyes to meet mine. Anger shone from her eyes. I smiled. Good, she hated this as much as I did.

"Don't need luck, just need him to think he's the better monster," I replied with more bravado than I was really feeling.

The door behind us opened to reveal The Blood King. He smiled, but it failed to touch his eyes. Behind him were my brothers, and they were all dressed in suits. It still sort of freaked me out how human they looked when dressed-up. "Ladies, we have to move to the hall where he will meet us." My father and brothers were all stoic and resolute with what was about to happen. I could feel the undercurrent of anger and outrage with what they were being forced into. We walked slowly down the hall. No one spoke or made a sound. Not even the children as they clung to their mothers' hands in fear of the arrival of the terrible Horde King.

I was supposed to kill the mythical Horde King, but the problem was he would be on alert for treachery while here in the Blood realm. There was no chance in hell that I'd be able to take him out here, in front of his entire retinue of his people. I'd be slaughtered along with everyone else who stood inside the hall to bear witness to the gifting ceremony.

We rounded the corner together, and I stopped abruptly. There were hundreds of Fae in the throne room, all here to catch a glimpse of the elusive King. Just like I had witnessed at the other events, the Fae were turned out with a combination of contemporary formalwear, as well as the traditional robes or more medieval types of costumes—though, they weren't really costumes for them, I guess. I turned and looked at the Blood King. He nodded, and together we walked the rest of the way to the back of the hall where the raised dais was for the Blood King's throne. A thick carpet for me to kneel upon had replaced my father's throne today.

I would be on my knees for him. Presented at his feet like some fucking animal. I stood in place as my family flanked my sides in a line of solidarity. I was pleasantly surprised and loving the looks of pride and anger that showed upon their faces. These people were doing what they had to because all other options had been taken away. But it didn't mean they would do it meekly. I looked at my father and saw why he was considered second only to the Horde King, when it came to being an alpha bad-ass. The man was, at this moment, absolutely courageous. He may have been dealt a really bad hand, but he was going to do what he had to with dignity. I felt a flash of pride for this man and the rest of my family.

It had been agreed that I would be presented to the people officially before the Horde King would claim me. I struggled to push down the butterflies of unease that were starting to kick into overdrive with what I had agreed to.

This was really happening to me. After everything I'd done to save people from the Fae, I was now to be gifted to the worst of them. It didn't seem fair or right that this was happening to me, but it looked like I just might be the next one in a very long line of abused *gifts*. No one deserved this kind of medieval crap.

Trumpets sounded from what looked like a newly reopened entrance to the hall, and with the sound of the heralding trumpets came a short red headed male who was dressed in an awful color of green. He looked more like a Leprechaun than he did Fae. He held a piece of paper in his hands as he read from it. "Yestereve, a blessed event took place. A knight of the royal Blood Fae returned something that was feared to be forever lost to us. Cailean, step forward," he paused until the knight who had brought me here stepped forward. "What say you of this?" the short red-head asked.

"I returned Princess Sorcha to her home, to her parents," Cailean answered. I could tell he was torn. He had saved me from Faolán, but turning me over to the Horde King wasn't sitting well with him. He looked like he wanted to snatch me up and save me from this too.

"Does anyone argue this charge?" Shorty asked.

Silence greeted our ears as no one disagreed with them. I looked around and almost gasped when I spotted Adam beside his father across the room from us. His eyes were wide with alarm, and he was struggling against Kier and whatever he was telling him. I was relieved to see that they were both unharmed, and so happy to see Adam's face.

I sent him reassurance through the bond. Or hoped I was doing it, since I wasn't sure how to control the bond we shared yet. He must have felt it, because he stopped struggling and looked across the room at me. Anger and fear for me were clearly written on his face.

"Are you okay?" he lipped.

I smiled to reassure him, and hoped it showed in my eyes and convinced him, even though he could probably feel my current panic through our bond.

"Lasair, do you agree that this child is of your blood?" Shorty continued in a booming voice that sounded as it had come from an ogre, not this tiny man.

"I do. The bond has been restored now that we have been united," my father said before giving me a gentle look.

"And you, state your rightful name for the people," he said to me.

"I was named Sorcha on the day of my birth, Princess to the Blood King and Queen," I replied obediently.

Adam's jaw dropped as he watched me give my name. I couldn't have said it had it been a lie, and the look on Adam's face said that he understood it as well. Pain flashed in his expressive eyes, but he quickly shielded it, which made relief filter through my soul. *"Show no weakness,"* I mouthed back at him, uncaring of who was watching us.

"You will now be presented to the royal castes, and then we shall begin the gifting ceremony," Shorty continued.

Kings and Queens, along with their heirs, moved about unhurriedly as they formed a line in front of us. I'd lost sight of Adam in the mass of people as they moved around to make a path for the royals. There was a shit load of the nobility crammed in this room.

I met about thirty or more, before Tatiana stepped forward with a murderous glare aimed right at me.

"Madisyn," she said smoothly in fake friendliness.

I raised an eyebrow at it until my mother shot one right back at her. "Tatiana, I was hoping you'd skip the celebrations."

Well shit, this was going to be entertaining.

"I guess I should have realized she wasn't mine," Tatiana drawled bitterly.

"She does look significantly like you; she and her father have confirmed the bond," Madisyn said with a sideways glance at me.

"I do so favor our mother," Tatiana continued, and reached out to touch me. I leveled her with a killing glare, and she promptly stepped back. "Such a shame you have to give her up, now that you just got her back, Madisyn."

"How is your husband, Tatiana?" my mother continued.

"He's waiting for the Horde King; you know he awarded him our throne. Dresden would like to thank him in person this time. We plan to offer him any aid he may need." Tatiana's smiled was cold, as if she thought the Horde King was a God, and, truth be told, she probably did.

I struggled to keep the laugh in, but it was hopeless, and when it came, people rubber necked to see what had made me snicker.

"I'd say she needs a few lessons in etiquette," Tatiana said, before she turned up her nose and walked away.

"Is she always like that?" I asked.

"Since the day my mother gave birth to the insufferable, two-faced, spoiled bitch," my mother replied. "Kier, this is my daughter, Synthia. Synthia, this is Kier the King of the Dark Fae," my mother said.

I wasn't paying attention to them. Instead, I was smiling at Adam, who was moving up the line to stand beside his father.

"Adam!" I squeaked with happiness and threw myself in his arms. My poor outraged mother tried to pull me back.

"Synthia, you address him as Prince Cadeyrn, for he is the heir to the throne," my mother chided.

Who gave a shit? I was about to be Horde kibble, and Adam was here!

"It's quite all right, Madisyn. Adam is Synthia's familiar. We had the pleasure of hosting her at the palace in hopes for her marriage to my son," Kier said in his usual good-natured manner.

"Ryder?" I looked hopefully at Adam who only shook his head no in reply. "He said he was coming," I whispered.

"If he is, we don't know anything about it. He left soon after you were taken and wouldn't allow me to help search for you. My father sent out warriors to help, but then word came that the Blood Heir had been found, and my father said it's like some sort of gigantic insult if we were not here for this," he finished softly.

"He said he was coming," I repeated.

"If he did, Syn, it was just hopeful thinking on his part. You haven't seen what is going on outside. It looks like the entire Horde is here, well any that could travel fast enough to make it. Let's hope he isn't stupid enough to try anything right now. My father is going to barter for you with the Horde King. He has a plan," Adam assured me, but I'd stopped listening.

Ryder had said he was coming, and out of everyone I knew that said they would do something and did it, it was Ryder. If the man said he was coming, he was, and I knew he'd die trying to protect me. Wouldn't he? I swallowed past the tightness of my throat, and looked up into Adam's eyes. "You have to find him, Adam, and make sure he doesn't try to save me. He's here somewhere; he said he would, so he's gotta be here."

"Syn…"

"Please, do this for me. *Don't* let him do something stupid to save me. We will figure out how to get me out of this later."

"Okay," he said grimly as he let me go and turned to look around the room as he stepped down from the dais with his father.

There were hundreds of people inside the room, and a vise tightened around my heart with the reality of the slim chance we had of finding Ryder and stopping him. I was presented to countless others, but I rudely ignored them as I searched the faces of the crowd for one man.

The trumpets erupted in front of us, and clapping ensued as the huge doors were opened and howls from wild animals ripped through the room. It wasn't until the first creatures of the Horde entered that my stomach dropped to my feet as they started toward us. Where was Ryder? Unless he planned on killing the Horde King…*oh shit*. Knowing Ryder, which I did, would be exactly something he would do.

I peeked from beneath my lashes, watching the spectacle the Horde made as they entered. Creatures I had only seen as drawings in Guild books poured into the grand chamber. There was a large group of the Far Darrig, as well as Phoukas, Redcaps, Bogies, Hobgoblins, Brownies, Nymphs, Satyrs, Oakmen and the Banshee along with other creatures I had never seen before took up positions in the room, and my mind raced to remember what I knew about them. It wasn't much, since these were the creatures that were kept inside of Faery for the protection of the humans. Many of the new arrivals first looked like beautiful Fae, until you caught a glimpse of the evil lingering beneath the masks they wore.

There were creatures with skin that melted against their face; sickly looking creatures with their eyes sunk into their skulls. Another that was in the front, had wicked horns, and metal pierced up his arms, and into his skin. Also, part of the Unseelie were the ancient Sluaghs. These evil creatures were haggard, walking dead with leathery looking wings and just enough flesh on their bodies to keep them from being skeletons. Still, more came in—a woman who was completely white, minus her glowing red eyes. They kept filing in as the assembled Fae who had been in the room moved away from them as if the walls would hide them. Crap, and to think I once told Ryder that I'd rather be the Horde than Light Fae.

And then *he* was there walking toward me. I wavered on my feet as I felt a blast of his power roll into the room. This wasn't happening. Not when I'd just found my family and had found love with my fucking Fairy. I may not have gotten to keep it, but I loved him. He made my heart race, and he could turn me to butter with as little as a look in my direction. I was losing it all; nothing could save me from this creature. Not even Ryder.

I was pushed to my knees by my parents. My palms were sweating, and I felt the urge to throw up pushing at my stomach, fighting to come up. I closed my eyes and pictured the golden eyes of the one thing I'd miss the most. Ryder; he was the one thing I didn't want to live without. I'd go with the Horde King, but

I'd try my damnedest to make it back to him.

I opened my eyes and watched as a pair of bare feet walked to me and stopped. Loose black silk trousers flowed just past his ankles, but stopped short from covering the top of his foot. I wasn't allowed to look up unless he said so. I was to be obedient to his every whim. As if.

"This is the true first born daughter of your blood?" The voice that came out was multi-layered and cold. The people around us gasped as I cringed.

"This is my first born daughter," my father said as he removed his hand from my shoulder.

Power vibrated through the room, unlike anything I had ever felt. My hair stood up, even though my mother had ensured it was as soft as silk. I watched as the bare feet made their way up to the dais where I was kneeling on the floor. I could just make out obsidian black wings that slightly dragged and brushed upon the floor. He was an enormous darkness, as if the entire realm could not contain him; could not contain his darkness, or his powers.

I couldn't take it anymore and risked a peek at him. He was far beyond anything I could ever imagine. The stories didn't do him any justice. It made sense now why the entire realm of Faery feared him. He was taller than I had pictured. Black velvet wings had razor sharp spikes varying in size that were fused to the bone along the top ridge of his wings and deceptively peeked out from the feathers. These spikes could tear into anything, severing and killing it instantly. His hair was long, reaching just below his shoulders, and so black and shiny it seemed like it was absorbing the light. His skin was alabaster pale and his muscular torso and arms displayed black brands that seemed to ripple with power. A silver torque threaded with obsidian that matched his brands was around his neck; it was the only thing he wore, aside from the silky trousers. Black eyes filled with the constellation of a thousand burning stars stared down at me with interest. He was breathtakingly beautiful and, yet terrifying at the same time.

It was surreal. I was sitting at the feet of the Horde King. Ryder had yet to show up, and my world was crashing down, endless waves rushing up to crush my dreams in one solid move. I could hear my siblings thinking—thinking that I was doomed. He'd take me to his bed tonight, and I was sure I wouldn't walk away from it. I could see his anticipation in his lustrous eyes.

How could I have been stupid enough to think I could do this? I couldn't kill the Horde King! He'd know it before I even tried. Hell, he'd know it before the thought crossed my mind. He was ten times more powerful than Ryder; ten times more brutal and deadly. I had to get him out of here before Ryder showed and tried to kill this creature in front of me, and we all died from it. I felt myself shaking inside and prayed that others couldn't see it.

"You belong to me now," he said as I stared, mesmerized by his brands that pulsed with power on his pale skin.

"I do," I whispered as I swallowed a lump down.

"I want your oath before this entire gathering that you belong to me," he said, watching me as I inhaled and let it out on a shuddering breath.

I held out my hand, knowing he would manifest a knife that would sever tissue easily. He probably had thousands of them. My brain whirred in panic with thoughts of how to get him out of here before Ryder showed up. I loved him! I couldn't stand here and watch him die. The hand that reached for mine was surprisingly gentle, the blade pierced my skin, but it was shallow. It wasn't the damaging slice I'd thought this monster would do.

His large hand came down to compress with mine, and I repeated the words he gave me.

"I am yours. I belong to no other. I am yours to do as you wish. Until a time of your choosing, I am given," I whispered and listened as the terrifying beautiful creature laughed wickedly. The wards on the walls lit up crimson and a multitude of other colors as the verbal contract was sealed in blood.

And just like that,

Ryder could no longer challenge him for me.

I was now the property and a concubine of the Horde King.

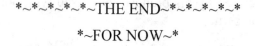

~~*~*~*~THE END~*~*~*~*~*~

~FOR NOW~

AUTHOR

Amelia Hutchins lives in the beautiful Pacific Northeast with her beautiful family. She's an avid reader and writer of anything Paranormal. She started writing at the age of nine with the help of the huge imagination her Grandmother taught her to use. When not writing a new twisting plot, she can be found on her author page, or running Erotica Book Club where she helps new Indie Authors connect with a growing fan base.

Come by and say hello!

www.facebook.com/authorameliahutchins

www.facebook.com/EroticaBookClub

www.goodreads.com/author/show/7092218.
Amelia_Hutchins